# Forever an Ex

# Victoria Christopher Murray

A TOUCHSTONE BOOK

Published by Simon & Schuster

*New York  London  Toronto  Sydney  New Delhi*

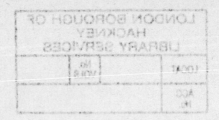

Touchstone
A Division of Simon & Schuster, Inc.
1230 Avenue of the Americas
New York, NY 10020

First Touchstone trade paperback edition June 2014

TOUCHSTONE and colophon are registered trademarks of Simon & Schuster, Inc.

For information about special discounts for bulk purchases, please contact Simon & Schuster Special Sales at 1-866-506-1949 or business@simonandschuster.com.

The Simon & Schuster Speakers Bureau can bring authors to your live event. For more information or to book an event contact the Simon & Schuster Speakers Bureau at 1-866-248-3049 or visit our website at www.simonspeakers.com.

*Interior design by Aline Pace*
*Cover photography by George Kerrington*

Manufactured in the United States of America

10 9 8 7 6 5 4 3 2 1

Library of Congress Cataloging-in-Publication Data
Murray, Victoria Christopher.
  Forever an Ex : a novel / Victoria Christopher Murray.
    pages   cm
  1. African American women—Fiction. 2. Divorced women—Fiction.
3. Women's prayer groups—Fiction. 4. Female friendship—Fiction.
5. Women—California—Los Angeles—Fiction. 6. Christian fiction. I. Title.
  PS3563.U795F67 2014
  813'.54—dc23

ISBN 978-1-4767-4885-6
ISBN 978-1-4767-4886-3 (ebook)

Asia Ingrum

# Dreams Deferred

# Chapter
## One

Whoever said that a kiss was just a kiss had never kissed Bobby Johnson.

He had kissed me again. Seven days ago. On Christmas. And, I'm telling you, I saw stars.

Now, maybe it wasn't that Bobby was all that great a kisser. Maybe it had more to do with him being the love of my life, at least until 2007 when he'd made the stupid mistake of breaking up with me and going back to his wife.

That Christmas kiss had stayed in my heart and on my mind. When I was awake, I thought about it and every time I closed my eyes, I dreamed about it.

Just like now.

My body was trying to wake up, but I was floating in unconsciousness. You know, that place where your eyes are wide shut—you're half awake, half asleep. I was holding on to the sleep part because I wanted to keep dreaming about that kiss.

My lips were right up against Bobby's and it was so deliciously good. So good that I started hearing bells—no, not bells, my ears were ringing.

But then . . . the ringing kept on and on and on, messing up my dream flow.

Dang! That was nothin' but my cell phone, and I was pissed. Who would call somebody so early on New Year's Day? Not that I knew the exact time, but if I hadn't already eaten breakfast, then it was too early for somebody to be hitting me up.

My first thought was to let my cell ring. But my eleven-year-old daughter, Angel, had spent the night with Monet, her best friend, so I had to answer . . . just in case.

So right before the call went to my voice mail, I grabbed my cell from the nightstand. Without even opening my eyes, I mumbled, "This had better be good."

"What's up, Asia?"

My eyes popped right open.

"Happy New Year!"

I pushed myself up, tugging the sheet along to cover my nakedness. "Uh . . . good morning. Happy New Year to you, too, Bobby," I said to my ex, my daughter's daddy, the Adonis of my dreams.

"I guess I woke you up."

"No." I ran my fingers through my hair, trying to look decent, though I didn't know why. It wasn't like we were Face-Timing or anything. "I'm glad you called."

"Yeah, I remembered that little superstition you had about a man calling your house first on New Year's."

He remembered that?

"So, I hope that I was the first."

"You are. And now I'll be blessed for the whole year."

He chuckled. "That's what I wish for you."

Then, a moment of silence. I needed something profound to say that would keep Bobby talking. But before I could come up with anything . . . a moan. And not just a regular moan . . .

a loud, long, masculine moan that stretched through time and my bedroom . . . and went right through my cell phone, too.

Dang! I thought, looking down at the body next to me.

"Oh," Bobby said. "You have company. I should've known. Last night being New Year's Eve . . ."

"No, I don't," I said as I kicked through the tangled sheets until I was free and away from Rocco. I had on not a stitch of clothing, but I didn't care. I jumped out of my bed and jogged straight into the hallway. "That was . . . just the TV," I said. "Yeah, it was the TV. I had it on last night and must've fallen asleep."

"I'd thought you would've been out partying the New Year in."

"Well, uh . . ." I didn't want to keep all of this attention on my lie, so I said, "I'm really happy you called." Now, that was the truth. Like I said, I hadn't stopped thinking about my ex since I'd spent Christmas Day at his house with his wife, and our daughter.

"Well, I don't want to keep you. Just wanted you to know how much I care for you and how I wish you nothing but God's best."

I sighed and smiled and tingled all over.

He finished with, "And, I wanted to wish you . . ."

"Happy New Year," we said together, then chuckled together, too.

"Thanks again for being my first, I mean, *the* first . . ."

"I know what you mean." Then, after a pause, he added, "Asia, I've been doing a lot of thinking, and in a few days I'd like to come over . . . and talk."

I inhaled.

He said, "After what happened on Christmas . . . we really need to talk."

"Okay." My smile was so wide that my cheeks hurt. I'd

been wondering how he felt about that, and now I knew. He was in the same place I was. That kiss had brought back all kinds of feelings, all kinds of memories, all kinds of wonder about why we'd ever broken up.

"I'll call you, okay?"

"Yeah." What I really wanted to say was, *Come over now*, but I'd let him lead this dance.

He clicked off and I did the same. That three-minute call was like a shot of caffeine straight into my veins. What a way to begin 2014.

"Baby, what're you doing out here?"

Before I could even face him, Rocco was on top of me, kissing my neck with his morning breath. I used the heels of my hands to push him off.

"What's up?" he said, backing away. "I want to start off the New Year right."

"We did that last night." As I marched back into my bedroom, I was mad that I'd run out without any clothes on. Because now Rocco was walking right behind my au naturel glory.

Most of the time I liked using my body to turn men on. In fact, if I had to tell the truth, that's how I made my living. My job was to maintain my size-four figure, be beautiful, and I got paid for keeping rich men company. I mean, not outright paid. It wasn't like we went out and they gave me money. But after a couple of dates, the gifts started flowing: diamonds, pearls, furs, shopping sprees at Neiman's, and vacations anywhere there was a beach and a Ritz-Carlton.

As far as Rocco was concerned, my job was done. I hoped Rocco wasn't turned on because I was so turned off. After hearing Bobby's voice, I didn't want Rocco anywhere near me. So when he wrapped his arms around my waist and pushed his full-blown nature against my butt, I wiggled away.

"What's up?" He held out his arms, beckoning me to come back. "Why you keep doing that?"

"You have to go," I said, cutting straight to the chase.

He frowned like he no longer understood English. "Go where?"

Did he really want me to answer that? I mean, it wasn't like Rocco and I had anything going on. It was just that sometime around Labor Day, I realized I didn't have a guy for the holidays.

Not that there was any kind of shortage of men in my life. I was still on the circuit and still in circulation. Plenty of athletes had my number locked in their phones. It was just that the calls were fewer. After all, no matter how much I maintained, I *was* thirty-five, which was ancient in the pro basketball/football/baseball/track groupie arena.

Now, don't get it twisted—I wasn't a groupie. I was more of a trophy girlfriend, who was working on becoming the trophy wife. No matter what you called it, though, it was my only ticket out of my ratchet life in Compton all those years ago. I needed to marry a rich athlete.

Once I set my mind to it, I'd met Bobby Johnson, the star of the Los Angeles Lakers. He wasn't my first choice 'cause he was already married. But he'd wooed me so hard that I'd believed he'd leave his wife.

Clearly, I was wrong. 'Cause six years ago, Bobby decided that he was happy with the wife he had, and didn't want a new one.

"So, what're you saying, Asia? You really want me to go?" I turned around, almost forgetting that Rocco was still here. I watched the new center for the Lakers pimp-strut toward me.

Now I had the chance to take in all of *his* naked glory, and boy, was this dude fine. Forget about being ripped in the right places, Rocco was ripped in every place. Everywhere there was a muscle, it was defined. And then, that face. He was Christopher Williams (that old R&B singer from back in the day) dipped in deep, dark chocolate.

When Rocco wrapped his arms around me, I was tempted to jump right back in bed and let this twenty-four-year-old show me what he could do. But the moment our lips touched, Bobby's lips came to mind, and again, I pushed Rocco back. "You know I would love to."

He gave me a goofy grin that said, *Of course you would, who wouldn't?*

I started to burst his oversize ego bubble, but instead I said, "But you have to go. Angel will be home soon."

Everything on that man deflated when I mentioned my daughter's name. "Oh," he said.

All the guys knew that I didn't date in front of my child. This wasn't the example I wanted to set, and not the life I wanted her to have. But I wasn't going to be one of those do-as-I-say mothers. Angel never saw me with all these men.

Plus these days I never let grown men around my daughter. No way, too many perverts out there and my eleven-year-old daughter, with her sixteen-year-old body, and a face that her agent at Ford Models called the young face of the new millennium, didn't need to be around testosterone. I did everything to protect Angel Valentine Johnson, the true love of my life.

"I thought you told me that your daughter wasn't coming home till later," Rocco said, squinting as if he was studying me to see if I was lying.

I tilted my head. "Is that what you thought? Hmm . . ." I turned around so that my back was to him. "Nope. She's coming home about"—I glanced at the clock: 7:48—"about eight. Oh, my God!" I exclaimed as if I was just noticing the time. "You've got to go. She'll be here at any moment."

"Dang!" he said, dashing to gather his clothes that he'd tossed around my bedroom. "Why she coming home so early?"

"Because . . . it's New Year's . . . and . . . we always have breakfast together on New Year's."

There was a part of me that was proud that I could come up with a good lie on the fly. But really, was that a character trait or a character flaw?

When Rocco started walking toward the bathroom, I said, "Where're you going? You've got to get outta here."

"I don't even have time to take a shower?"

I shook my head.

"Well, do I have time to take a leak? A guy's gotta take a leak first thing in the morning."

Those words made my eyes roam down his body. Damn! Maybe I could tell him that I made a mistake. That Angel wouldn't be home till nine, or ten. Or I could tell him the truth . . . that she wouldn't be home till sometime tonight.

But then . . . Bobby. I'd feel like I was cheating.

So, I let Rocco take his leak, then dress as slowly as any man ever did.

"Okay." Rocco slipped his suit jacket over shoulders that looked like he should've been playing football instead of basketball. "So," he said, straightening out his collar, "I'm gonna see you tonight?"

"We'll see." I led him down the stairs and at the door gave him one of those long, slow tongue kisses so that he wouldn't forget me. But as soon as he said, "Bye, call me," and stepped out of that door, I closed it and forgot him.

Taking the stairs two at a time, I dashed back up to my bedroom, grabbed my cell, and clicked on my best friend's name. Noon's phone rang and rang, and when her voice mail picked up, I hung up and called back. I didn't know where she was, and I didn't care whose bed she was in; I needed to talk to her.

It took four callbacks before she answered with a growl, "This had better be good."

I laughed. Hadn't I just said the same thing? We were like sisters, with a bond thicker than blood.

"This is better than good," I said.

Noon moaned.

"Wake up, I have to talk to you," I whined.

"Call me later. I'm sleep."

"Well, wake up."

"I can't."

"If you hang up, you know I'm gonna call you back."

"Ugh!" she growled again. "Hold on a second."

When she said that, that meant she was with her current man, Brett, and was getting out of bed to talk to me privately.

"Okay, what's up?" Noon asked with an attitude.

That was okay; she'd be all right after I told her this.

"Well, first, Happy New Year!" I said with glee.

There was a pause, and then, "Chiquita, if that's why you called me, I swear . . ."

I didn't even hear the rest of her sentence. Did my girl just call me by the cray-cray birth name my mama had given me? My mother, who abandoned me when I was two and left me to be raised by my grandmother, had named me after a banana. I was still pissed about it, but at least I was smart enough to have changed my name legally.

I wanted to insult Noon back, call her by her birth name. But her birth name *was* Noon . . . Noon Thursday Jones, given to her by her mama who was as cuckoo for Cocoa Puffs as mine.

So since I couldn't insult her, I got right to the point. "I'm getting back with Bobby."

"Bobby who?"

"See, you wanna play. Really, I'm getting back with Bobby."

A beat, and then, "For real?"

If Noon had been sitting in the room with me, her eyes

would be all wide, and she'd be on the edge of the chair. 'Cause if there was one thing that Noon knew, it was that I wasn't overly dramatic. I accepted whatever situation came my way.

Okay, that may be a bit of an exaggeration. But for the most part, once I did all that I could and saw that I couldn't change a situation, I accepted it.

"So, when did this happen?" Noon said, all awake now.

"Can you meet me?"

"When?"

"Now. Are you with Brett?"

"Yeah, but I can hook up with you for a few hours. Where we gonna go so early on New Year's Day?"

That was a good question, but then I said, "The malls are open, so meet me at the Beverly Center. Starbucks. In the food court."

"The Food Court?" Noon said. "Is that the name of some new restaurant, 'cause you know, I'm not pedestrian like that."

"Pedestrian?" I laughed. "Heffa, have you forgotten that we grew up on the same street in Compton?"

"Shhh . . ." She lowered her voice and chuckled at the same time. "Brett thinks I'm from Kenya."

"I'm gonna tell that white boy the truth if you don't meet me in an hour."

"I'll be there in thirty minutes," she said.

We laughed before we both clicked off our phones.

# Chapter Two

Noon had told Brett Washington (the only white person—besides the first president—that I knew with that last name) that she was from Kenya because she was convinced white men loved exotic black women.

But she didn't have to tell that lie. Noon Jones *was* exotic. She was far from the days when the mean girls at school used to follow us from the yard to the halls taunting her with chants of "Kunta Kinte's sister!"

It wasn't much better for me. They used to bully me, telling me that I thought I was cute because I looked like an Indian.

I never told Noon this, but as bad as it was for me, I really felt awful for her. I mean, it was horrible enough being outcasts—she, because they said she was ugly, and me, because they said I was cute. But the truth was, I thought those girls were right—Noon was way below average. She had this long neck that made her look like a chicken, and legs to match. And not only was she tall and skinny, but her skin was really dark, like the color of burned charcoal.

Then she did that caterpillar-butterfly thing. By the time

we were eighteen, she was top-model gorgeous, with her oval-shaped face, light brown eyes, and full African lips that people paid top dollar to get.

But it was her skin that made her so beautiful. Her black skin that looked like it had been polished to a high shine and was as smooth and soft as any piece of silk ever woven. I'm telling you, there wasn't a model alive who was as gorgeous as Noon.

That was my thought as I came to the top of the escalator and saw my friend, sitting in the center of the food court. Even from all these feet away, I could see that she didn't have on a lick of makeup beyond the mink eyelashes that we both wore every single day. And she was still the best-looking woman in the mall.

"What's up?" I stepped in front of her. "Happy New Year," I said, giving her a hug.

"Same to you, honey!"

Then Noon's eyes made a slow journey over my body. She checked out my black skinny jeans, black blazer, and red T-strap stilettos, and I checked out her sapphire-blue leather pants and matching blazer. Then, we nodded our approval.

Every time we got together, we checked each other. Whether we were partying or strolling on Venice Beach, we kept each other on point. Noon had the same career I had; in fact, she was a trophy girl because of me. So we took our first responsibility to look good seriously. I'm telling you, if I was just going out to pump gas (not that I *would ever* pump my own gas) . . . but if the world turned upside down and I had to do that, I'd have to pump and be camera-ready at the same time.

"So let's get past all the niceties. You and Bobby are getting back together?"

On the phone, Noon had sounded excited, but, with the way she twisted her lips, I could see that now, she was more skeptical than excited.

I sat up straight, placed my hands on the tabletop, ready to tell all. "Well . . ."

Before I could get another word out, Noon said, "'Cause after what went down at Christmas, I'm surprised he's even speaking to you."

"Dang," I said, pushing back in my chair. "What a way to bust someone's high."

She shrugged. "I'm just keeping it one hundred. Christmas was a wreck."

"First of all, Christmas wasn't my fault," I told Noon.

Yes, Christmas at Bobby's house had been a disaster and I'd told Noon most of what had happened: how Bobby and Angel had begged me to let them spend Christmas Day together for the first time, and how I'd only agreed because it meant so much to our daughter, and how I'd known it would be a disaster.

And I was right. Talk about an effed-up holiday. From the moment I got to Bobby's, his wife, Caroline, the Dallas-bred socialite, ignored me, embarrassed me, tortured me, and finally sat me at the kiddie table for dinner. I'd tried to keep it classy, but the bottle of Moscato I'd drunk didn't help, and I practically tore that place and Caroline up.

"And secondly," I said, continuing to set Noon straight, "there's something you don't know about Christmas." I took a deep breath. "It was bad with Caroline, but not with Bobby." A pause. "Bobby and I kissed."

She widened her eyes just a bit. "Like a *kiss* kiss?"

I nodded. "Like a real kiss! A kiss where our lips met and our tongues danced, then—"

Noon slapped her hand on the table. "Shut the front door! Where did this happen?"

"Remember, I got drunk, right?"

She nodded.

"Well, I got so drunk, I couldn't drive and I went up to Angel's room to sleep it off. Bobby came to check on me."

"And he kissed you just like that?"

"Yup. We talked a little and then he kissed me just like that. And the best part"—I paused, wanting Noon to be sitting on the edge for this one—"Caroline saw us!"

"Get the freak out of here!" Noon rose a couple of inches out of her chair. "She saw you kissing her husband and you're not dead?"

"Please, I wish she would come at me like that; you'd be reading about her beat-down in the *L.A. Times*. And anyway, it was her fault for spying. She knew she was wrong. That's why she walked away."

"Hold up," Noon said. "She just walked away?"

I nodded.

"She didn't say anything?"

I shook my head.

"Well, what did Bobby say?"

"He didn't see her and I didn't tell him. I wasn't gonna get in the middle of their drama."

Noon laughed. "You're kissing her husband and you're not in the middle?"

I waved my hand. "Whatever. These are two different relationships—Caroline and Bobby, and me and Bobby. I can't be concerned about them when I have me and Bobby to think about. And, I'm telling you, Noon, that's all I've been thinking about since Christmas. 'Cause when we kissed, it felt like we were right back where we used to be."

"Really?"

"It was a love kind of kiss," I said. "All I've been hoping for since then was that Bobby felt the same."

"But suppose it wasn't a love kiss? Suppose it was just a lust kiss? Or an I-hope-you-feel-better kiss?"

I shook my head. "Nope, it's none of the above. Because he called this morning and said he couldn't wait for us to talk about what happened at Christmas." I banged back in my chair, all smiles.

Noon stared at me like I was an oak tree. "And?"

"And what?"

"That's it?"

"What more does there need to be? I mean, how many times in the last six, going-on-seven years has he called and said he wanted to get together?" I didn't give her a chance to answer. "Nada! Not even once. Not even to talk about Angel. We do all of Angel's business on the phone. But now Bobby wants *us* to get together."

She nodded. "Okay, but suppose he just wants to talk about all that New York stuff? Suppose he just wants to talk about him and Caroline moving Angel to New York with them?"

It was a good thing that I wasn't drinking because my girl would've completely ruined my buzz. But she was right—I hadn't thought about that. New York was another fiasco at Christmas. Caroline had told me that she and Bobby were moving to New York and they were taking *my* daughter so that Angel could pursue her modeling/acting/singing career. That was what really set me off that day.

Since Christmas, I hadn't talked about New York. Not with Angel, nor with Bobby. I figured if I didn't say a word, it would go away. Now that Noon mentioned it, I wondered if that's what Bobby's call was about.

But then I shook my head. I wasn't going to let Noon talk me out of what I knew.

"No," I told Noon. "This is all about me and him. Trust that."

My confidence must've convinced her. "So let's say you're right and he wants to get back with you. Do you think it would be for anything more than what it was before? You think you'll be more than his jump-off?"

It was a good thing I didn't have a drink in front of me 'cause I would've thrown it right in Noon's face. Well, maybe not, 'cause she's my girl and all. But it was like she was on a serious mission to bring me down. Calling me Bobby's jump-off? Really?

"I was with Bobby Johnson for ten years," I snapped. "That is not a jump-off. Bobby never saw me as just his chick on the side. If he did, he would've just continued our affair and kept me hidden away. But he didn't want to do that to me."

Noon shook her head. "Uh . . . that's a nice little rewrite of history, but Bobby didn't keep you because his wife told him to get rid of you."

I blew out a long breath. I needed to carry a bottle of Moscato with me for times like these. 'Cause Noon was seriously killing my natural high. Why did she have to remind me about every little detail? "What's up with the negativity?" I asked. "You're supposed to be my girl."

"I am and that's why I'm keepin' it real. 'Cause if you really want Bobby back, you need to think this through. You can't just leave it up to him; men don't know what they want. You're gonna have to push Bobby to do what's right. And I'm here to help."

Noon had always admired my relationship with Bobby. While she'd gone from man to man, Bobby and I had ten solid years and a kid. Once Angel was born, Noon thought Bobby should've done the right thing and left his wife—since he didn't have any children with Caroline.

"Here's the question . . ." Noon paused as if something big was coming. "Even if Bobby does want to hook up with you again, would he ever leave his wife for you?"

Lord, I really needed a drink now, but how could I be mad? Because it was a good question. He hadn't left Caroline before; why would he do it now?

Noon said, "Caroline has it all; she's beautiful, she's smart, she has her own life . . . and she comes from all of that oil money."

I started slipping down in the chair. Depression was coming on fast. How had I gotten so carried away? Why *would* Bobby ever choose me over Caroline? She had everything Noon said, plus more. She was so refined, so classy; if I didn't hate her, I'd admire her.

"I'm sure I'm better in bed," I said, trying to get at least a point on the board.

"That wasn't enough to keep Bobby before."

I sighed. Forget about getting a drink when I got home; I glanced around the food court. I sure wished Baja Fresh served wine with their burritos.

"So what am I going to do?" I asked, feeling totally discouraged.

Noon leaned across the table. "Do you really want Bobby back?"

I nodded. "You don't know this, but I never stopped loving him."

At first, Noon stared at me like she was shocked, and then she busted out into a laugh that filled the entire eighth floor of the mall. And she wouldn't stop. Just laughed until she cried.

"What the hizzy?"

"Do you think I didn't know that you still loved Bobby?"

I pouted. "It was obvious?"

She nodded like she felt sorry for me. "Just the way you say," she sang, "Boooooobbbbyyy," as if his name had seven syllables.

I slapped her arm, but I had to grin. "Really? Like that?"

She nodded again. "But that's not a bad thing. Before Bobby and after him, there hasn't been one man who came close to making you as happy. Bobby Johnson is like in your bones. I'm convinced he's the love of your life."

Noon was wrong. Bobby was more than that; he was my love *for* life. No matter how many men I dated, Bobby was always in my head and always in my heart.

"But here's the thing . . . how're you gonna get Bobby? What's gonna make him leave Caroline for you?"

"I don't know," I whined.

"It has to be something that you have over Caroline."

Now I felt like crying. "I have nothing!"

"Yes, you do."

I perked up a little at Noon's words, but I had no idea what she was talking about.

She said, "Just think, Asia."

I frowned and in my head I scrolled through my assets. I could come up with a few things, but everything I had, Caroline had, too . . . in a double dose.

"Think, think," Noon said, encouraging me.

I closed my eyes as if the answer was somewhere behind my eyelids.

"Oh, my God," I said, popping my eyes open.

Noon smiled and nodded her head slowly.

Then together we said, "A baby!"

That was it. I could give Bobby a baby. Like I said, Bobby and Caroline didn't have any children, though he had never discussed that with me. I just figured his wife couldn't get pregnant.

So, if I were to get pregnant again with Bobby's child, would he leave Caroline? Hell, maybe it didn't matter. If I got pregnant, Caroline would definitely leave him. She'd forgiven him for having one child during their marriage, and had even done the right thing, accepting and loving Angel.

But there was no way she'd accept a second baby. Caroline would be up and gone and I'd win the prize.

I wasn't sure if I wanted to do it, but getting pregnant was definitely something to consider.

# Chapter
## Three

So, have you made any progress with Plan B?" Noon asked. That's what she'd called the plan she'd come up with for me to get pregnant by Bobby—Plan Bobby.

As I stood at the sink, I peeked over my shoulder at Angel scooping a spoonful of cereal from a bowl. Her eyes were on her tablet as she watched some TV show. I didn't think she even realized I was there, but still, I pressed the cell phone closer to my ear and spoke the code words to Noon. "This is one of those do-not-disturb moments."

"Oh, who's there?" Noon asked. "Angel?"

"Yup."

But then, "Mom!"

I turned around.

"I know what 'do not disturb' means," my too-smart-for-her-own-good daughter said. "But I'm grown now, so you can talk in front of me."

Grown? I had no idea who'd told her that, and as soon as I got off this phone, we were going to discuss her definition of *grown*.

"Anyway"—I turned my focus back to Noon—"nothing's happened on that front."

"He hasn't called?"

"Not yet."

"Age has really changed you. The old Asia would've had Bobby in bed five times by now."

"We just talked about this five days ago."

"Okay, so you would've had him in bed four times." Noon laughed. "So what're your plans? How're you gonna get him?"

Again I peeked at Angel. "I'm gonna let nature take its course because I'm convinced no tricks are necessary."

"I'm not saying a baby is necessary; I'm saying a baby is insurance."

I sighed. What Noon was saying was probably true, but after really thinking about it, I just didn't want to do it that way. Because there were no guarantees that he'd be happy if I got pregnant.

The last time I told Bobby I was pregnant, he was sure that I'd tricked him. I had, but that wasn't the point. I was pregnant and he needed to do the right thing.

But he was livid. He'd ranted about his wife, he'd raved about how I'd ruined his life.

That lasted for, like, a day. The idea of having a baby grew on him, and that was when we bought this condo together—with all of his money, of course. And then, once Angel was born . . . on Valentine's Day . . . he fell in love with his baby girl. I was convinced he would finally leave Caroline and marry me.

Well . . . that never happened. So, I wasn't sure it would go down better this time.

Noon broke through all of my thoughts. "I'm telling you, two children by the same woman? That's a game changer.

Bobby will either leave Caroline, or she will leave him. Either way, you win."

"If I decide to do that, I hope you're right."

"If you decide? Haven't you heard anything I've said?"

"Yeah, but suppose I don't need all of that? Suppose it's exactly the way I've told you?"

"About a little kiss on Christmas?"

"It wasn't little."

"And because of a kiss, he suddenly wants a relationship with you?"

When she said it like that, it did sound dumb. But Noon didn't see it, she didn't feel it. She didn't know that it was more than just the kiss. It was the way he'd held me, the way he'd made me feel. "Yeah," and then I lowered my voice even more: "I think he does want me."

She sighed as if I was dense. "Just consider Plan B. In case I'm right about why he really wants to talk to you."

I couldn't wait for the day when I'd say to Noon, *I was right and you were wrong.* "Let me get going. Gotta get Angel off for her first day back to school."

"Tell my niece I said hello, and call me later. I can see I'm gonna have to give you a little push."

"Okay," and then I clicked off the phone. I stared at the screen for a moment. Who was right? Me or Noon?

"Mom!"

I turned around and Angel was right up under me. "You're finished?" Before she had the chance to answer, I said, "And what's this about you being grown?"

She grinned, a wide toothy grin with braces and all. "I am. Like, I know what you and Auntie Noon were talking about."

I tried to keep the shock off my face.

She said, "You're seeing somebody new and you like him and you think that he likes you, too."

She gave me such a triumphant look that all I could do was bust out laughing. "You are so wrong and that proves that you're nowhere near grown. But you need to stop listening to my calls. That's rude."

"Sorry, Mom." But that grin stayed on her face. "But I *am* grown. Eleven is the new teenager. I might as well be nineteen."

I chuckled. "Girl, get your eleven-year-old self to school."

She grabbed her backpack, shoved her tablet inside, then swung the bag over her shoulder. When she leaned over, kissed my cheek, and said, "See ya, wouldn't want to be ya!" all I could do was shake my head. Clearly, I didn't have to worry about her being grown anytime soon.

As she walked toward the front door, I rinsed out the bowl that she'd just dumped in the sink.

I heard the two beeps indicating that the front door had been opened and then, "Daddy!"

I froze.

"What're you doing here?" Angel shrieked.

"Hey, sweetheart."

Oh, my God! Bobby? Here?

There was no way I could get to my bedroom without passing him, so I glanced at my reflection in the stainless-steel refrigerator. I had nothing on, no makeup, no gloss, my eyebrows weren't plucked. But at least my lashes were in place.

I loosened the tie that held my hair in a ponytail and combed my fingers through, letting my hair hang past my shoulders. Then, with my fingertips, I patted my cheeks, smoothed down my eyebrows, and glanced at my reflection again. This was not the way I wanted Bobby to see me. I'd dreamed of greeting him at the door, wearing some almost-nothing negligee.

But this was as good as it was gonna get. I took a deep breath and strolled out of the kitchen as if the love of my life dropped by every morning. Right as Bobby and Angel came into my view, I heard our daughter ask, "Did you come to take me to school?"

"Nope," he said, "unless you need a ride."

Angel shook her head. "No, I go in the van. So"—she frowned—"what're you doing here?"

"I came to talk to your mom," Bobby said, looking up and seeing me. His smile was immediate, but not as fast as mine.

Inside my head, I did that little *humph, humph, humph*, the way I always did when my eyes took in the full view of this man.

"Good morning," I said, bringing the words up from deep in my throat.

Bobby said his own good morning to me, but Angel frowned again.

"Mom, what's wrong with you? You sound like you have a frog in your throat or something."

I wanted to smack my *grown* daughter upside her grown head. So much for her knowing everything. "You better get downstairs."

"Okay." She hugged her dad, then turned to me. "So, you guys gonna be cool?" she asked like she really was grown. Her eyes moved from me to her father, then back to me.

"Yeah, we're fine, kiddo," Bobby assured her.

"I just want to make sure 'cause you know, you don't get along."

"That's not true," Bobby and I said together, then looked at each other and smiled.

Bobby said, "See, your mother and I are on one accord."

I chuckled and then hugged her. Not that I didn't love my daughter, but it was time for her to go. "Have a great day, sweetheart," I said, holding back my urge to shove her out the door.

When she closed the door behind her, Bobby turned to me, jammed his hands inside his jeans pockets, and shifted from one foot to the other.

It took him a few seconds to say, "I hope you don't mind me dropping by. I thought they'd call up, but the concierge on duty has seen me picking Angel up and dropping her off and I guess—"

"It's fine," I said, interrupting him. I hoped my tone and my smile put him at ease. He needed to understand, I wanted him here. "This is a good time."

He blew out a breath like he was relieved.

"Come on." I reached toward him like I was going to take his hand, but I didn't touch him. I just led him into the living room.

He paused at the arch for a moment, then took the two steps down into the massive sunken room. "Wow!"

"Oh, that's right. You haven't been here since I redecorated."

He shook his head and took in all the living room furniture that I'd bought right after he broke my heart. He and I had decorated this condo, but when he left me, I called the Salvation Army to come and get that old stuff. Once I'd thrown away Bobby's furniture the way he'd thrown me away, I brought in everything new.

"No, I haven't been here since . . ." He stopped as if that was a full sentence. "I guess I always meet Angel downstairs." Still looking around, he added, "But this is really nice," as he sat on the sofa.

"Thank you," and then just to lighten the moment I added, "and thank you for paying for it."

His eyes brightened as he laughed lightly, though he still sat on the edge as if he was ready to make a quick escape if he had to. "You know I'd do anything for you, Asia."

I'm telling you, at that moment you could've just scooped me up with a spoon.

But then he had to go mess it all up, and correct himself: "Anything for you and Angel."

That was my first clue that this conversation wouldn't be going the right way. His words felt like a reminder—that he'd always take care of me since I was the mother of his child.

But then, I reasoned, of course he would mention Angel. Because he would do anything for her, too.

I kicked off my sneakers, then tucked my feet underneath my butt. "So, what did you want to talk about?" I asked, though my eyes weren't on his. I was focused solely on his lips; those lips that I loved to kiss.

Bobby looked away and stared at his clasped hands.

Now, I knew Bobby Johnson. And these little moves, this nervousness, this was just Bobby stalling, trying to put the right words together so that he wouldn't get anything wrong.

There was only one reason for Bobby to be nervous. It was because he wanted to be with me and he didn't know how to say it.

When he finally looked up, in his eyes I saw the same love that he'd always had for me. "So, you've been good, Asia?"

"Yeah. What about you?"

It felt strange the way we sat with each other, talking as if we hadn't spoken in years, when in actuality, we talked on the regular. Of course, it was always about Angel. Before.

After Bobby nodded for a while, he said, "Yeah, I've been good. Things have been working out. I wasn't sure what life was going to be like after basketball . . ."

"You were great on ESPN," I jumped in.

That turned his smile into a grin. He pushed back from the edge of the couch and leaned against the cushions. "Being a commentator was great. I loved that gig, but six years was enough."

"Yeah, I read that you gave that up. And now you're doing the Magic Johnson." I chuckled. "Buying up all of Los Angeles."

He laughed. And my heart did that skipping thing. His laughter took me back to when Bobby and I would sit together, talk together, and laugh just like this.

"Well, it's good to be in the same category as Earvin," he said, calling Magic by the name that only those who were close to him used. Then his tone turned suddenly somber. "And, I'm following Magic in another way. I'm venturing into New York."

The mention of New York made my shoulders rise. There were two problems with those two words: First, I didn't want to talk to Bobby about New York. And second, I was starting to get this little inkling that maybe Noon had been right.

When I didn't say anything, Bobby kept on: "I want to do real estate projects in Brooklyn and Queens. I'm looking at Bed-Stuy and Jamaica."

"So"—it took everything I had in me to ask—"you're moving to New York? Is what Caroline told me true? That you *want* to take Angel with you?"

He looked at me for a moment. "No, I'm not moving to New York . . ."

I exhaled.

"At least not permanently," he added.

That made me hold my breath again.

"I'm an L.A. boy . . ."

"By way of Texas."

"Yeah." He chuckled. "But L.A.'s in my blood now."

"So, not permanently. What does that mean?"

"I'm gonna go back and forth. Be bicoastal."

I nodded slowly. "And what Caroline said? About you guys moving and *thinking* that you could take Angel with you?"

"I'm really sorry about that; she shouldn't have said anything to you."

"You apologized already . . . on Christmas." Then I paused because I wanted the next word to stand on its own. "Remember?"

He looked straight in my eyes when he said, "Yeah, I do."

So . . . he did remember our kiss.

But then he said, "I'm really sorry about the way Christmas went down. Caroline shouldn't have said anything and I told her that because nothing's been decided."

"You talked to her about what she said to me?"

He nodded.

"What did she say?" I asked for no other reason than that I wanted to know if she'd mentioned seeing our kiss. Not that I cared one bit about Caroline Fitzgerald Johnson; I just wanted to know how she was going to play this.

"She agreed. She said it just slipped out, and she's really sorry."

Yeah, right. The only thing she was sorry about was that I'd told Bobby . . . and, oh yeah; she was probably sorry that Bobby and I had kissed, though it seemed like she was going to pretend that it never happened.

Bobby said, "But that's why I wanted to talk. I wanted to talk about what Caroline said . . . about Angel going to school in New York."

Oh. My. God. Bobby didn't want to talk about us; he wanted to talk about taking my daughter away from me.

"It's not going to happen, Bobby!" I snapped. Every bit of my emotions came out in those six words. I was mad, I was hurt, I was heartbroken. He was trying to take my daughter away from me *and* he didn't want me?

"I don't want you to be upset," he said.

"Then don't mention this again."

He shook his head. "I can't do that because our daughter is so talented, she deserves for us to have this conversation. She deserves this chance."

"You think I don't want to give her the chance to pursue her dreams? We're in Los Angeles, for God's sake. She can do whatever she wants right here . . . with me, her *mother*, by her side."

"I understand what you're saying. But, we all need to sit down and talk about this. Come to some agreement."

I stood up and crossed my arms. It was time for Bobby to go.

But he didn't make a move, so I said, "There's nothing to talk about, not now, not ever."

With a sigh, he stood, too. When he reached toward me and put his hand on my shoulder, I flinched. Not that I didn't want Bobby touching me. It was just that I'd expected that the next time I'd feel his hands against my skin, he'd be my lover.

"I want the best for our daughter and I know you do, too. All I'm asking is for us to sit down . . . me, you, Angel . . . and Caroline."

Hearing his wife's name was the final stake that stopped my beating heart. For *thirteen days*, I'd been thinking that Bobby was about to get rid of her, but he just wanted to talk about getting rid of me.

"We're going to have to talk about this at some point, Asia."

He said that as if it was a threat. As if I was afraid to have this talk. Well, I wasn't afraid. There were a million ways I could say no, and I could say no a million times.

I pushed Bobby's hand off of me and stomped toward the front door, thinking that Bobby better get the hint if he wanted to walk out of here on his own two feet. 'Cause as hot as I was, I would've been able to lift him up and throw him out.

Bobby was right behind me when I opened the door. His eyes drooped with sadness and I wondered why. He didn't have a dang thang to be sad about. All of this hurt today belonged to me.

As he passed by me, I looked away, staring at the floor. I didn't even want to look at him. Not because I was so mad. I just didn't want him to look at me and see the tears welling in my eyes. Because then he would know this wasn't just about Angel. He would know he'd broken my heart once again.

"I'll give you a call," he whispered before he stepped over the threshold.

And my answer to him: I slammed the door in his face.

Then I leaned back against the door. How could I have been so dumb? How could I have thought that Bobby would ever want me?

I slid down until my butt met the carpet. "Stupid, stupid, stupid," I cried as I banged the heels of my hands against my forehead. "Just stupid."

Tears burned my eyes, but I fought hard to keep them in check. Really, there was nothing to cry about. It wasn't like Bobby was leaving me again.

But the tears came anyway. Because it was clear now, Bobby was never coming back.

# Chapter Four

"Mom, are you sleep?" Angel whispered from my doorway. With a quickness, I clicked on the nightstand light. "No, baby. What's wrong?"

She scurried across the room in her red-and-white one-piece footed pajamas and jumped into my bed the way she used to. When she tucked herself under my arm and rested her head on my chest, all kinds of memories rushed me. The best times of my life were when Angel and I would be just like this, cuddled together, watching cartoons, eating ice cream, or just having one of our girl talks about fashion.

I pulled her closer. "You couldn't sleep?"

"I kept falling asleep, but then I kept waking up." She sighed as if the world weighed heavy on her.

"What's wrong?" I asked, wondering what tween angst I had to deal with now. Were girls picking on her, bullying her the way I'd been? I understood adolescent envy, and for young girls, there was a lot to envy about Angel.

"I just have a lot on my mind," she said.

I chuckled. "Angel, you're eleven. You shouldn't have

anything more on your mind than what you're going to wear to casual Friday at school tomorrow."

"I'm not that shallow. I may not be grown, but I'm really mature for my age."

"Okay," I said, chuckling. I didn't know why my daughter was so determined to be grown. "What's on your mind?"

She released a long-drawn-out sigh. "My future."

In that instant, I knew where this conversation was going. I'd been able to avoid it with Angel for two weeks since I'd first heard this nonsense from Caroline. And I certainly hadn't said anything about the talk I had with Bobby. To me, this was a closed subject, though it felt like my daughter was about to kick it wide open.

Angel began, "Dad said that you guys talked about me going to New York. That's why he came by the other morning, right?"

I spoke slowly because everything I said had to be on point. "That's right."

She lifted her head from my chest and looked straight at me. "Mom, I really want to do it. I want to go to school in New York."

I'd said no to Bobby, but saying no to Angel wasn't going to be so easy. And clearly saying no to Bobby didn't mean much since he'd still gone behind my back and talked to Angel anyway.

"I don't want you to be mad at Dad," she said, as if she'd heard my thoughts. "It's just that today, I asked him if he had talked to you and he told me he did and that you weren't happy about it."

"He shouldn't have done that," I told her. "He shouldn't have talked to you about what he and I discussed. This is grown folks' business."

"I know, but Dad treats me differently than you do. He treats me more like an adult."

"And that would be wrong since you're a child."

"Well, maybe not like a grown, grown, grown adult, but he treats me like I'm mature, so we talk about everything."

The next time I saw Bobby . . .

Before I could plot out all the ways I was going to handle him, Angel said, "Mom, why don't you want me to go?"

"It's not necessary."

"But it is! Because my whole life I've wanted to be a singer, and a dancer, and an actress, and a model. And I know that if I want to do all of those things, I have to be really trained. And the School of Performing Arts is the best place in the world for me to get my training."

"I think 'the best place in the world' is a slight exaggeration. We're in L.A., this is the home of actors and models and dancers and singers. Look at all the classes you're taking."

Angel looked at me as if I had a "Big Dummy" tattoo on my forehead. "Okay, Mom," she said. "I know you're spending a lot of money on everything for all of my lessons and classes and I'm really grateful. But these classes right here—they're amateur hour compared to the training I'll get in New York at the School of Performing Arts."

I had to shut my mouth and look at my daughter for an extra minute before I answered. She was starting to sound—a little grown.

"What do you know about the School of Performing Arts?" I asked, trying not to sound like I was getting an attitude. And believe me, I was getting an attitude because I (with Bobby's checkbook) paid a lot of money for her dancing classes with Debbie Allen, her acting classes with Raquel Wendy Robinson, and it had cost a small fortune for Bobby to fly in one of the best photographers in the country for Angel's modeling portfolio. I was doing everything to help my daughter pursue her dreams, and everything that she wanted and needed was right here in Los Angeles.

Angel scooted away from me and crossed her legs yoga-style. Her face glowed as she said, "Mom, you should see the school. It's amazing."

"You've been there?" I asked, wondering when Bobby and Caroline had snuck Angel to New York.

"I haven't, but I know a lot about it. Mom Caroline and I used to watch this old TV show called *Fame*. It was about all these kids who wanted to grow up to be all kinds of performers, and after every show, Mom Caroline always said that I was better than all of those actors. She said that she thought that would be a good school for me."

When Angel said Caroline's name, my ears perked right up. "So, it was a TV show about the high school?" I asked, crossing my arms.

"Uh-huh. There were all these cool actors and a long, long, long time ago even Janet Jackson was on it. She was way younger then, but, Mom, so many famous people graduated from that school. Like Robert De Niro and Al Pacino and Ben Vereen and Jennifer Aniston."

How did my child know all of this?

"I did my research," she said, anticipating my question. "I've been reading everything I can. I looked on the Internet and Mom Caroline found out a lot of stuff about the school, too. She even had them mail me some information."

I was beginning to smell a rat. A refined, rich, well-dressed rat! "And where is all this information?"

"At Dad's. Mom Caroline kept it, but after we got it, we talked to Dad and told him that I really wanted to go there. And he said that it sounded like I'd thought it all out in a mature way, so that's why they're changing their whole life around. Just for me."

I wanted to ask my daughter why she'd done all of this with Caroline. Why hadn't she talked to me? But it was beginning to sound like this hadn't been Angel's idea alone.

"That's all good, but why move across the country when you're living where all the movies are made? If you need better acting lessons and dance classes, we'll find them, but—"

"No, Mom." She sighed like I didn't know anything. Then she went on to school me. "Most movies are filmed in Atlanta or even Canada now because of tax breaks."

How did Angel know this?

"L.A. used to be the film capital of the world, but not anymore," she said, shaking her head as if she were an expert.

"And really, as an actress, I think I'd like to try theater rather than film because it's live acting and you get to interact with the audience, and get immediate feedback. Being on the stage, being on Broadway, now that's real, real, real acting."

It had to be all over my face—I was in awe. My child was weeks away from being twelve, but just like Bobby said, she'd put a lot of thought into . . . her future.

Was going to New York really the best thing for my child?

No!

Especially not if it had been Caroline's idea.

"Well," I began, "you've given me a lot to think about and we still have a couple of years—"

"It's not that far away," she said, not letting me finish. "There's a lot to do. It's a public school, you have to be a resident of New York, so Dad has to pull some strings. He said I might have to do my last year of middle school in New York."

What!

She continued, "And I have to get prepared to audition."

After a moment I said, "I'll think about all of this . . ." I kept the rest of the words to myself—and my answer would still be no.

"Thanks, Mom!" She kissed my cheek. "You're the greatest."

I opened my arms expecting us to snuggle once again, but she didn't even notice. She jumped up, and then the same way she'd come into my bedroom, she scurried right back out.

She stopped suddenly, though. Right at the door, she turned around. "Mom, this is really important to me. Probably the most important thing that will ever happen in my whole life. I've been dreaming about this forever." She pressed her hands together as if she was about to pray. "So please, Mom, really think about it enough to say yes!"

I nodded 'cause I didn't want to lie out loud.

"Really, really, really. Please, please, please," she added before she dashed to her own bedroom.

I just sat there, staring at the now-empty doorway. But I still imagined her there, and heard all the words that she'd said to me. Her voice, her tone, the way she pleaded—that was a child. But the thought that she'd put behind her words—there were grown people who didn't do that much thinking and planning. She was thinking and planning for New York the way I'd schemed to hook up with a pro ballplayer. And, I had succeeded.

But I didn't want Angel to go. If she were in New York, what would that mean for us? We wouldn't be together during her high school years, and I wanted to be there for her first date, when she got her driver's license, and even when she had her first heartbreak. I wanted to spend those years cheering her on through every triumph, and wiping her tears through any trials.

But if she were in New York, my time with her would be limited to holidays and maybe part of the summer—if she wasn't too busy to come home. Angel would be spending all her time with Caroline, and I had this feeling that Caroline was doing more than just being the kind stepmother.

I clicked off the lamp on my nightstand and slid back down in the bed, but didn't close my eyes. Inside the darkness, all kinds of questions swirled around me. What if Angel really wanted to do it? What if this wasn't Caroline's idea and it was all Angel? Could I eventually find a way to say yes? If I said no, would I be holding her back?

The seconds turned to minutes, and with each new hour, new questions came to mind. I never closed my eyes because my thoughts were too loud. So, I just stayed awake and tried to make sense of the noise.

My mind never quieted, I never slept. Somewhere around four in the morning, I let insomnia have the victory. I sat up, grabbed my cell phone, and sat in the dark, waiting for more time to pass. It was way too early to make any telephone calls. I'd have to wait for a more decent hour—like seven.

But I was never one to do things decently and in order. By the time the digital numbers on my clock flipped to six, I was already pressing the phone icon on my cell.

"Sheridan," I said to the groggy voice who was one of the most important people in my life. "I really need you. Can we talk?"

# Chapter
## Five

I glanced down at my ringing phone. Dang! Was Noon really up this early? My mouth stretched into a wide yawn as I pressed ignore, exactly the way I'd done at least a hundred times over the last three days.

That's how long it'd been since I'd seen Bobby . . . and last talked to Noon.

From the time I met Noon in middle school, we'd never gone more than one day without speaking to each other, and on every voice-mail message, Noon reminded me of that.

My hope was that the blush of her new love with Brett would keep her away from my front door; and it did, but it wasn't enough to make her stop calling me.

When my cell rang again, and Noon's name popped up, I yawned and powered off my phone. My best friend's I-told-you-so's, and then her trying to convince me to do Plan B were going to have to wait. Right now I had the issue of Angel to handle.

I shoved my phone inside the pocket of my sweatshirt. This wasn't something I did often because of Angel. But it was just a little after seven; Angel was just getting up and Ms. Martinez, my nanny/housekeeper, was there to make sure she was fed and off to school.

I jumped out of my car, then scooted up on the hood. The heat of the engine warmed my butt, but that was okay. This was winter at the beach, I could use the heat. And, I could use some prayer . . . which is why, for the first time ever, I called this prayer meeting.

Me, calling a prayer meeting. With Sheridan Goodman and Kendall Stewart. Six years ago, who would've thunk it?

When my aunt hooked me up with Sheridan, Kendall, and another woman, Vanessa Martin, all those years ago, I thought that she was suffering from early-stage dementia. Really? My Aunt Beverly, who was a pastor, really wanted me to get together on the regular and pray with those old women?

But I can admit that I was wrong, she was right. Because after just a few weeks, praying with the three of them became a part of my week that I looked forward to.

But then tragedy dealt us a huge blow. Vanessa, probably one of the sweetest, gentlest, kindest women I will ever know, committed suicide. I cried so hard that day that my chest actually ached. I guess that was true heartache, and with Sheridan and Kendall going through the same thing, we really bonded after that.

Not that I would ever tell them—especially not Kendall— but the time I spent with the two of them back then really helped me through the pain of losing Vanessa . . . and Bobby. And since then, it always helped to be around grown women who made sense and who prayed.

Not that I was dissin' my girl Noon, but she was just as scandalous as I was. Sheridan and Kendall approached life with at least some semblance of God and I needed people like that around me.

So, that's what Sheridan and Kendall were—my spiritual anchors. And I guess in some way I was that for them, because no matter what time we got that call, we were always there for each other—as Sheridan and Kendall proved when I spoke to them just a little over an hour ago.

I'd called because I thought they would be able to help me find some of the answers that I couldn't. Sheridan would be kind and gentle, Kendall would be uncouth and crabby. And both would pray and help me work through this Angel–Bobby–Caroline–New York thing.

That's what I told them once Sheridan had connected Kendall to our call.

"*You* want to get together and pray?" Kendall had asked. She'd been asleep when Sheridan had called, but right then Kendall had sounded like she was awake enough to faint.

"Yes," I said, too tired to be offended. "I was hoping you guys would have some time for lunch or maybe dinner today."

"Lunch, dinner?" Kendall said. "Sheridan, what're you doing? We need to get over there and lay hands on this child right now."

Usually, I had something for Kendall when she came at me like that, but not only was I tired, I was scared, so I didn't care that Kendall was clowning me. As it turned out, though, she wasn't kidding.

"Okay, I'm getting up now," Sheridan had said. "Where do you want to meet?"

"Wait!" I said. "Now?"

"Uh, yeah, now," Kendall jumped in. "You need us! You want us to come to your place?"

"No. Let's meet at the beach, is that okay?"

"Give me an hour," Sheridan and Kendall said together as if they'd had that answer ready for a time such as this.

I was already crying when I hung up the phone. Who had

friends who would jump out of bed in the middle of the night? Well, it may not have exactly been the middle of the night, but it was to me. I hardly got out of bed before noon.

I closed my eyes and inhaled, taking in the ocean's mist. The parking lot was a couple of hundred feet from the edge of the beach, but it was like I was sitting on top of the waves. Since Bobby's latest rejection, I'd been holed up at home like a chicken in a coop. But there, I couldn't think, I could hardly breathe.

Out here in the open, I hoped to find clarity. Maybe I'd find all the solutions that would keep Angel in Los Angeles.

"Asia!"

I opened my eyes slowly, trying to maintain my calm and tranquility, even if Kendall was screaming at me.

Sheridan and Kendall stood in front of my car, both with their arms crossed as if they'd been standing there for a minute.

"Oh, yeah, we definitely need to pray for you," Kendall said. "I think you're losing your hearing."

"Leave her alone," Sheridan said as she pulled me off the car and into her arms. "Obviously, she has a lot on her mind."

"Yeah, I guess," Kendall grumbled. But then she did the same thing that Sheridan had done—she hugged me. And Kendall held me so tight, like she was trying to tell me that even though she didn't know what was going on, everything was going to be all right.

When I stepped back, Sheridan asked, "You okay?"

I didn't know what happened. Maybe it was just thinking about the talk with Angel. Maybe it was all of the fears that I had about Caroline. Maybe it was because now that Sheridan and Kendall were here, I wasn't alone.

Or maybe it was because no matter how Kendall acted, she really did love me.

"Yeah, are you okay?" Kendall repeated Sheridan's question.

That was when I lost it. I burst into tears. I could say that I just cried, but that would be a lie. I stood on the edge of that ocean and bawled like a baby; the only thing is that babies eventually stop, but I wasn't sure if I ever would.

After I got myself together, we trekked down to the edge of the beach. I took off my sneakers and let the cool ocean water wash over my feet.

Sheridan and Kendall kept their sneakers on, grumbling about it being too cold to be walking in the water. But to me, it was as refreshing as the cry fest I'd just had.

"Let us know when you're ready to talk," Sheridan said gently.

I took just a few more steps then told Sheridan and Kendall everything. From my talk with Bobby to my talk with Angel, though I did leave out the part about how I was gonna get Bobby back.

"You need to put that child on a plane tomorrow because she's brilliant," Kendall said when I'd finished.

That stopped me right in my tracks. "Are you serious? You think I should let her go?"

Kendall shrugged, then nodded. "Yeah, I don't see the big deal. Angel is smart, she's thought it out, she knows what she wants, even more than people who are triple her age, and it's not like she'll be in New York with someone she doesn't know."

Yeah, she'll be with Caroline, though I kept that thought to myself. That was another part of the story that I didn't tell Sheridan and Kendall—my suspicions about Caroline trying to steal my daughter. I didn't want them to think that this was all about some rivalry I had with Bobby's wife.

"Let her go, Asia," Kendall continued. "It'll be good for her."

I couldn't believe what Kendall was telling me and I felt like crying all over again. "Why would you say that?" Before she could answer, I said, "Oh, wait. You don't have any children. You don't know what it's like to be a mother!" Then I looked to Sheridan. And if she told me the same thing, I was going to throw myself into the ocean.

"Okay, hold on, you two," Sheridan said, being the peacemaker that she always was. "Kendall, you're right. What Angel said . . . she's clearly beyond her years. But"—she turned back to me—"I have to agree with you. It would be hard for me to let her go."

"See!" I said to Kendall as if Sheridan's words were the gospel. "I can't let her go and I don't see any reason why I have to." I held up my arms to the heavens. "This is L.A. People leave Iowa and North Dakota and Wyoming to come here."

"And people leave L.A. to go to New York," Kendall said. When I glared at her, she said, "All I'm saying is that you've got to consider what your daughter wants."

"She's eleven!"

"So what? Clearly, she's a brilliant eleven-year-old who's focused and goal-oriented."

"And every goal she wants to achieve . . . she can do it here."

Kendall shook her head.

"I can't believe you're not supporting me," I said to Kendall. She waved her hand like she was slapping my words into the ocean. "There is no way I'd be out here in this cold weather, walking on this cold beach, at seven-thirty in the morning, if I weren't supporting you."

She had a point, but I wasn't going to tell her that.

Kendall said, "I'm just telling you the truth. That's what I thought friends did. But I guess you can't handle it."

"You know what?" I said, pointing my finger in Kendall's direction. "I don't need your opinion anymore. Don't say another word to me."

"What? You think you can shut me up because you don't want to hear the truth?"

Sheridan held up her hands, stopping Kendall from saying anything else. "Of course Asia wants the truth. There's just a better way to say it." To me, she said, "Suppose Kendall is right, though. I wouldn't want Angel to ever feel like you held her back."

That was my greatest fear. If I said no, would my child end up hating me? With a sigh, I said, "Well, the good thing is we have a couple of years. Maybe by then, Angel will have changed her mind and she'll be interested in something else."

"Like what?" Kendall asked with just enough of a chuckle to let me know that she thought I was being ridiculous. Clearly my telling her to shut up didn't matter. "Your daughter was singing before she could talk and dancing before she could walk. This is in her blood, Asia. She knows what she wants."

I growled. Just because Kendall was right didn't mean I had to like it.

"The good thing is that you do have a few years," Sheridan jumped in. "And in the meantime, we'll all pray about it."

"Yeah, we can pray, but my prayer is gonna be that you come to your senses," Kendall said. "Pray over her and let that child go. And if it's that big of a deal and you can't stand to be separated, just move to New York, too."

Then the three of us stood there quietly for a moment.

Kendall seemed the most surprised at her own words. "Yeah," she said, as if she was warming to that idea. "Why don't you just move to New York with her?"

Sheridan looked at me as if she thought that was brilliant.

"I can't . . . move to New York."

"Why not?" Sheridan and Kendall asked together.

Kendall added, "You got a job that you didn't tell us about?"

I gave her the squinty eye—the look that was meant to tell her to shut up before I gave her a beat-down. The problem was, Kendall wasn't afraid of me, so she gave me the look right back.

Then Sheridan said, "That is a thought, Asia. What about you moving to New York?"

I sighed, but didn't say a word. I didn't want to move to New York. I'd been born and raised in Los Angeles and this was all I knew. "What would I do in New York?"

"The same thing that you do in L.A. . . . nothing," Kendall said.

I really wanted to take Kendall right there. Just drop her to the sand and hold her head underwater. But the thing was, even though Kendall was seven years older than me, she was in such good shape, she'd flip the script and I'd be the one drowning in the Pacific.

"I don't know anyone in New York," I said to Sheridan as if Kendall wasn't even there. "It would be scary."

"Well, what's scarier . . . having Angel in New York without you, or you and Angel doing this together?" Kendall asked, ignoring the fact that I was ignoring her.

But even though I wasn't trying to hear her, I had to pause. Kendall was right; I'd be there with Angel.

"It's something to think about," Sheridan said as she grabbed my hand and pulled me along.

For the next few minutes, we were all silent, trudging through the sand. I'm sure Sheridan and Kendall were thinking that they'd come up with a grand solution, but they were wrong. If my girls didn't want to help me the way I needed to be helped, I'd just have to figure this out myself.

Then, all of a sudden, Kendall said, "My father's surgery is today."

She might as well have been giving a weather report, that's how casual she was.

"What!" Sheridan exclaimed before I could. Both of us stopped walking, even though Kendall kept on moving.

Then Sheridan and I shouted together, "Kendall!"

Finally, she turned around and looked at us like we were the ones with a problem.

I stomped through the sand until I was in her face. "You were supposed to tell us when this was happening," I said, all thoughts of my issues totally out of my mind. Right now it was all about Kendall and her dad.

A few days before Christmas, Kendall had told me and Sheridan that her father had been diagnosed with breast cancer. I didn't believe it at first. I thought it was just a ploy by her dad to get Kendall to have Christmas dinner with him. I mean, I'd never heard of a man having that kind of cancer.

But the day before New Year's, when Sheridan, Kendall, and I had our last prayer meeting of 2013, Kendall schooled me and Sheridan, and I was shocked to find out that while it was one hundred times less common in men than women, about two thousand men were diagnosed with breast cancer each year.

Kendall's dad had stage two, so she'd told us that he was going to have a mastectomy and that was going to be followed up by chemotherapy. And we'd told Kendall then that we would be there on the day of her dad's surgery and for all of his chemotherapy treatments, too.

"So what time's his operation?" Sheridan asked.

"At noon."

Sheridan and I looked at our watches at the same time.

"Well then, we better get going," Sheridan said, turning back toward the parking lot.

I followed her. "Yeah, I just need to go home, shower, and change. And then we can all meet at Kendall's. Or should we go straight to the hospital?"

"Let's do Kendall . . ."

Sheridan stopped; we looked at each other before we turned around. We'd moved, but this time it was Kendall who was standing still.

"No," she said, holding up her hand.

"No, what?" I asked.

"I don't want you at the hospital."

"Kendall," Sheridan said, marching back to her, "we want to be there."

"I know, but the best way you can help me is to stay home and pray."

Now, here's the thing—Kendall and I fought all the time. But it was more like a sibling thing; I could beat her up, but I wasn't going to let anybody or anything bring her down.

I stomped over to Kendall. "I don't care what you say; we're going to be right there. We'll just pray in that hospital."

At first, Kendall glared at me, but then, in the next instant, she threw her arms around my neck, making me stumble backward a bit. She hugged me so tightly, and I held her, too. Over Kendall's shoulders I saw Sheridan's eyes fill up.

I was touched by this, too, 'cause the thing about Kendall is that she never showed any emotion. So, I just held her, but it only lasted a few seconds.

She backed away, wiped her eyes, and said, "Look, you know I love you both, right?"

We nodded.

"So, you've got to let me do this my way. Stay home. I promise, I'll call you." She paused when I crossed my arms. "I promise, okay?"

I was still ready to tell her no. I wanted to protest and ask Kendall why did she have to be so stubborn? Why did she always have to be the strong one? I wanted to shake her until her brain rattled and she agreed to let me and Sheridan be there with her.

But I had a feeling that no matter what bodily harm I threatened, Kendall would rather lose a limb than give in. This was her world right now, and she was making the rules.

She reached out her hands, and Sheridan took her left and I took her right. Then, with Kendall in the middle, the three of us plodded slowly through the sand, back toward the parking lot. I'd come to the beach with a heavy heart and I was leaving with one, too.

Just now my own thoughts were beyond me. My heart was heavy for my friend.

# Chapter
## Six

So, if you're not trying to get him into bed and have his baby, why're you doing this?" Noon asked.

All I could do was sigh. Two days ago, I'd finally taken Noon's call, and of course I'd had to tell her all that had gone down with Bobby. She was a better best friend than I ever thought 'cause she didn't rub it in my face that she'd been right.

But even though Bobby wasn't into me, that didn't seem to concern Noon. She still said, "So that just means that you have to go to Plan B."

"Are you kidding me? He doesn't want me."

"Of course he wants you. He just doesn't know it. Men are like children. You have to direct them, guide them, nurture them. Once you become pregnant, I'm telling you, Bobby will be all yours."

She spoke with such confidence that if I didn't know better, I would've been convinced. But she was wrong on so many levels. Level 1: She assumed that I could actually *get* Bobby in bed enough times to *get* pregnant. Level 2: That I *would* get pregnant. Level 3: That said pregnancy would be the reason why Bobby would come to his senses and come back to me.

But it wasn't going to happen. I was smart enough to just take the wonderful parting gift I'd received—our daughter—and get over it, and over him.

That's what I'd told Noon that day and that's what I told her now. "I don't even like him like that anymore."

She laughed as if I'd just done a *Def Comedy Jam* routine. "Yeah, right. So then if it's not about him, why're you meeting up with Bobby and Caroline?"

"For Angel. I want her to think that I'm really considering New York."

"But, uh . . . at some point you're gonna still tell her no."

"But, with her sitting with me and her father . . ."

"And don't forget Caroline," Noon just had to add.

I ignored my friend. "Angel'll hear all of my reasons, and after a calm discussion, she'll understand."

Noon sucked her teeth. "I wouldn't do it. If you're not trying to get him in bed, then what's the point?"

"Angel! Pure and simple, so let me go on and get in here."

"You're there already?"

"Girl, I was here when I called you," I said, looking across the street at Spago. "I just didn't want to go in."

"You should've let me come with you," Noon said.

"I wish," I said, sighing and smiling at the same time. Noon was my girl, my ride or die. If Caroline acted up, Noon would beat her down. "But what reason could I give for my best friend being part of a family meeting?"

"We could've just told them that I was your new boo."

I laughed. "I don't think Bobby will believe that since he knows you."

"True that, but then again, we don't have to give that heffa and her husband no reason. I can be there just because that's what I do," Noon said, with her Compton attitude spilling out.

Yeah, I could definitely see Noon rolling up to this five-star Beverly Hills restaurant and going straight ghetto. If Angel wasn't going to be there, I would've considered it. "Anyway, I'll call you after."

"Or call me before if you need your girl to handle anything."

I clicked off the phone, and as I made the U-turn and pulled up to the valet stand, I said a quick prayer of thanks, 'cause everybody didn't have a Noon in their life. And then I said a different prayer of gratitude for Sheridan and Kendall 'cause everybody didn't have friends like them either.

Even with what she was going through, every day, Kendall called me, asking how I was doing when all the focus should have been on her. But after she told us that her father had made it through his surgery just fine, she didn't want to talk about it anymore. She'd already told us that he had a long road of chemotherapy ahead that wasn't going to start for another four to six weeks. That's all Kendall would say.

But I knew what that meant—for the next four to six weeks, Kendall was gonna be all over me. I mean, don't get it twisted, I knew my girl thought she was doing the right thing, calling to check on me. It was just that every time she called, she was still talking that crap about me getting on a plane to New York with Angel.

I'd stopped fighting her, stopped telling her that wasn't going to happen, stopped saying anything. But I was about to shut this whole New York idea down. That's what this meeting was about.

Stepping out of my car, I sauntered toward the restaurant just in case Bobby and Caroline and Angel were sitting by a window. I felt like crap, but no one would know. I'd dressed for success. Not only was I wearing a Fendi leather pants suit, but I wore my biggest diamond-studded hoops, my diamond choker necklace, and just for good measure, I wore the four-carat diamond ring that Bobby had given me. I hadn't had this ring on my finger since the day I'd taken it off six years ago. But this morning, it was the first thing I'd decided to wear.

When I stepped into the restaurant, the hostess walked right up to me.

"How're you, Ms. Ingrum?"

"Great," I said, wishing I'd remembered the young girl's name. It had been a while since I'd been to Spago, and I'd missed it because Wolfgang Puck was one of my favorite people. Bobby had introduced us years ago.

But once we'd broken up, I wasn't interested in hanging out where Bobby might be. Wasn't interested in running into him and the woman who'd made him toss me to the side.

Following the hostess, I strolled as if my heart wasn't pounding. It was a good thing that Angel was going to be here. This had been Bobby's weekend, and so right after this dinner, Angel would be going home with me.

The hostess and I rounded a corner . . . and there was Bobby . . . and Caroline. The closer I got to the table, the deeper the lines set in my forehead.

"Hey, Asia," Bobby said, greeting me with a hug that was nothing like the last time he'd held me in his arms.

My greeting to him: "Where's Angel?"

"I called Ms. Martinez and asked her to pick her up from my house." He motioned for me to have a seat across from them. "Caroline and I thought it would be better if the three of us discussed this first."

"First?" I asked. My eyes stayed on Bobby as if his wife wasn't even there. "You've already brought Angel into this."

But then Caroline forced me to look at her. "You're right," she said. "We should've never talked to Angel before we discussed this with you."

What I wanted to know was, why was Caroline even here? But I kept that attitude to myself because the one thing I could say about Bobby's wife was that she treated my daughter well; I couldn't hate on that.

So, I gave her a half smile, half smirk.

Then she added, "And I want to apologize for even mentioning this to you on Christmas."

I didn't accept her apology because she didn't mean it. There were so many other things she needed to apologize for, and she needed to step up and acknowledge it.

But Caroline didn't say anything else. So, I just looked at her, smirked again, then lifted my hands to the table. And with my right hand, I twisted the ring on the third finger of my left hand.

Right away Caroline's gaze went to where I wanted it to be, and I could see the heat rise beneath her skin. Sure, my ring could've been given to me by anyone, but Caroline's instincts were like mine. She knew that Bobby had placed this ring on my finger.

I didn't have her man now, but I'd had him once. And not only was Angel a constant reminder of that, but today this ring would remind her, too.

"Well, now that we've apologized, let's talk," Bobby said.

"And since Angel isn't here, I can get right to my answer." I paused because I wanted Bobby and his wife to hear me clearly. "No." I looked Bobby dead in his eyes. "Angel's not moving to New York."

Right then the waiter walked up and asked if I was ready to place my drink order. I waved him away, though it was hard to do. I was dying to have a champagne cocktail as well as the filet mignon tartare. But breaking bread with Bobby and Caroline was as attractive as getting a Novocain-less root canal. I'd said what I'd come to say and it was time for me to bounce.

When the waiter walked away, Bobby said, "I think you need to hear what we're thinking before you say no."

I sat back in the chair, crossed my arms, but did it so my left hand could still be seen. I did it so that ring still glittered, still caught Caroline's eye. And, the way she kept looking at my ring, then up at me, then back at my ring made me think about calling that waiter back. Maybe I would stay awhile.

"Asia," Bobby began, "Angel has been talking about going to this school for a couple of years."

"Yes." Caroline jumped in as if I would even consider her opinion. "I think she was about eight when she first told me about it."

I narrowed my eyes at her. Really? Angel had told her about that school?

I really wanted to ask her what was she trying to do. But I knew that asking wouldn't get me an honest answer, but listening might.

Bobby said, "What we were thinking is that we would move to New York so that Angel could spend her last year of middle school there."

"And this way," Caroline piped in, "she would have no problem being accepted at the School of the Performing Arts."

Their lips were moving as if I hadn't already said no.

"We know it would be hard on you, so we would do everything we could to make sure she came home on as many weekends as possible," Bobby said.

"And we would understand if you wanted her for all the holidays," Caroline added.

What were these people talking about? This was my child. I set the rules.

"The point is, we'd work it so that it would work for everyone. For Angel with school," Bobby said.

"And for you"—Caroline paused—"as her mother." She gave me a tiny smile.

The two spoke like a tag-team, as if they'd rehearsed. But I could tell that Caroline hadn't liked her last line. Bobby had probably told her to say it.

Bobby said, "I think as parents, we have to do whatever we can to help our children reach their greatest heights. I remember how my parents let me go to basketball camp every single summer. I found out later that they'd taken out all kinds of loans so that I could do it."

"But obviously, we don't have to do that," Caroline said. "All we have to do is make it all accessible to Angel . . . and be supportive of her."

I had been listening, going from one to the other, but now I had to say, "I've always been supportive of my daughter." As I spoke, I tapped my left hand against my right arm. "And, I always will be."

My eyes were on Caroline and her eyes were on my ring. My hope was that the sunlight that shone from the outside hit my ring at the perfect angle. And maybe, just maybe, Caroline would be blinded by it. Literally.

"Of course," Bobby said. He was such a man; he was totally oblivious to what was going on between me and his wife. "You've done an amazing job raising Angel. It's because of you that she even has goals. So, I understand that this would be hard. I just want you to know that if you agree, we'll do everything we can to work it out."

I said, "Okay, let's say that I were to go along with this."

I stopped and watched smiles spread onto their faces.

"Who's going to take care of Angel?"

"What do you mean?" Now Bobby and Caroline frowned together.

"I mean, who's going to take care of *my* daughter? Who's going to help her through her life? Who's going to be there when none of the kids at school want to be her friend, or when the girls are jealous of her? Or who's gonna be there when she meets that first boy and wants to go on a date?"

Bobby said, "She'll be living with us."

"That's what I mean." Turning to Caroline, I said, "She'll be living with you when she'll need me"—I let a beat pass—". . . her mother."

Now their faces looked like I'd socked both of them in their eyes.

"If that was meant for me," Caroline said, pressing her hand to her chest, "I know that you're her mother, and I would never try to replace you."

Yeah, right.

"But you should know that I would be there for Angel for all of that. You may not know this, but Angel and I are very close. Of course, it was hard when I found out that Bobby'd had a child outside of our marriage. But once he apologized and promised me that nothing like that would ever happen again . . ." She paused as if she wanted to make sure that I'd heard her. ". . . I was able to forgive him. That meant accepting his daughter because I love him, and since she's a part of him, I love her." Then, to rub it in, she reached for Bobby's hand and held it. What was worse—he held her back.

She continued, "Over the years, Angel and I have developed a wonderful relationship." As she spoke, my eyes were on their hands. I stared, hardly hearing when she said, "When Angel's with us, she spends more time with me than she does with Bobby. And when she's with you, she calls me every day."

Those words shocked me back to my senses.

"Yeah." Bobby grinned, as if he was proud. "Angel speaks to Caroline more than she speaks to me."

Forget about what Bobby said, I couldn't get past . . . Angel called Caroline every day?

Caroline continued, "All of those things you mentioned— Angel and I have already talked about. I know that there're girls in her school who don't like her, but I've talked to her about jealousy and envy and she's learned to handle those girls. I know about the boys who come at her, especially some of the older ones, and we've talked about what it means to be chaste, why she would want to do it and what God expects. We've even talked about the kind of boys she should date when the time is right. So, while I'm not her mother . . . I've tried to be the best stepmother I could possibly be. If you were to ask Angel, she'd tell you that she'll be just fine with me in New York."

My hands dropped to my sides and I swallowed hard. I'd said what I said to hurt Caroline, but she'd turned around and cut me, slashed me straight through to my soul.

She was telling me things that I didn't even know. Angel had talked to her about things she never mentioned to me.

It wasn't like Angel and I didn't talk. But our talks were kind of limited to clothes, music, the latest gadgets, and decorating her room. Sometimes we talked about TV shows and favorite movies, but we never had deep conversations the way she and Caroline seemed to.

*I'm grown, Mom. Dad and Mom Caroline talk to me like I'm mature.*

How many times had she said something like that to me? Now, I knew what she'd been talking about. She was talking to Caroline about real issues, the types of talks a mother and daughter should have.

"Well," I began, praying that my voice stayed steady, "it's good to know that she would be taken care of."

Now Caroline smirked.

Turning to Bobby, I said, "I'm still not sure." My voice was much softer now.

He reached across the table and covered his hand with mine. "I understand. There's still plenty of time for us to talk, and to work this out."

I nodded and blinked and prayed that my emotions wouldn't betray me. I wrapped my purse's chain strap around my hand.

Bobby added, "Whatever we do, we'll all agree."

I glanced at Caroline and her smirk had turned into a smile. A smile that dismissed me. A smile that said, *Yeah, you may have that old ring, but I have Bobby* and *Angel!*

Slowly, I rose from my chair.

"Are you sure you don't want anything to eat?" Bobby asked.

I shook my head. "I'm not hungry, but thanks."

He stood, and this time, when he wrapped his arms around me, it wasn't just one of those church greetings. He held me tight, though there was no desire inside his embrace. He held me like he felt sorry for me. He held me like a father who knew that he was about to get custody of a child from her mother.

I swallowed the sob in my throat and turned away. I couldn't even give Caroline a fake good-bye; I just got out of there.

I ran out of the restaurant, holding my tears in until the valet attendant brought my car. When I jumped inside, my hands were shaking as I grabbed my cell and pressed Noon's name.

When she answered, all she said was, "You need me?"

"I do!" I shrieked. "They're trying to take Angel from me and I think they're gonna win!"

# Chapter Seven

All I could think about were Caroline's words. Whether my eyes were open or closed, Caroline was in my daydreams and my nightmares, teasing me, taunting me, tormenting me. In my dreams, she was Angel's mother . . . and I was the step, the substitute, the surrogate.

I still couldn't believe how deep Angel's relationship was with Caroline. Honestly, I'd never given any thought to the woman. I thought that when Angel went to stay with her father, she did the same thing with Bobby that she did with me—hang out in her room, talk on her phone, or play games on her iPad.

But I was wrong. Angel had a whole different life with the married Johnsons. A life with depth, where she spent quality time with Bobby . . . and Caroline.

By the time I got over my crying spell, I was ready to do better with Angel. Because there was no way Caroline was going to win this.

So on Sunday, when I left the restaurant, and after I shared all my sorrows with Noon, I got right to work. The moment I walked into my condo, I went straight up to Angel's room.

"Hey, Mom!" Angel pushed the headphones from her ears and hooked them around her neck. Then she wrapped her arms all the way around me as if she was so glad to see me. Caroline may have been trying to steal my daughter, but she hadn't stolen her heart . . . not yet.

"How was your weekend?" I'd asked her.

"It was cool." A second later, the headphones were back on her head. She closed her eyes as she bounced back onto her bed, then bobbed her head to the music. My daughter looked so content; I didn't want to disturb her.

But then I thought about Caroline, and so I poked Angel. She jumped like she'd been struck by lightning.

"Mom!"

"Take those off."

She did as she was told, but curiosity was all over her face when she looked up at me.

Now that I had her attention, I said, "Let's . . . let's . . ." I paused. As hard as I tried, I couldn't think of anything to do with my daughter. How crazy was this? Then I said, "Let's make dinner . . . together."

"What?" She frowned.

"Yeah," I said, starting to think that this was a good idea. "Let's go downstairs and make dinner. You haven't eaten yet, have you?"

"No, but Ms. Martinez cooked. She said to tell you she baked a seafood casserole and it's in the refrigerator."

"Well then, let's make a salad to go with the casserole. And you know what? We'll even eat together. Downstairs. In the dining room. No eating in our bedrooms tonight."

"Mom," Angel began, now sitting up straight. "What's wrong with you?"

If I wondered whether I had a problem before, I knew I had one now. My daughter thought me wanting to spend time with her meant that something was wrong. I shook my head. I'd taken care of my daughter, providing everything that she needed—physically. But clearly, I'd neglected a huge part of her life. The part where we were supposed to bond beyond me supplying her daily needs.

"Nothing's wrong. I'm going to change my clothes and then we're gonna go downstairs and cook together."

As I rushed out of my room, Angel yelled after me, "Making a salad is not cooking!"

We made that salad, and then ate together at the counter, since Angel thought eating in the dining room was a little too much. But the point was that we ate together and talked, and laughed. And though we didn't get as deep as I knew Angel got with Caroline, that was our beginning.

From that point on, I woke up every morning thinking of something that I could do with my daughter. On Monday, I drove her to school. But that lasted for just that day, because she told me it was so not cool to show up at school with your mother. The next day, I sat with her as she did homework, though my eyes glazed over when she began explaining the basics of calculus. Calculus? Really? In the sixth grade? But I hung in there, pretending I understood when the truth was I couldn't do anything without a calculator. And then the next day, I let Angel curl up with me in my bed while I checked my Facebook and Twitter accounts, something that I'd hope to keep away from her, at least for the next couple of years.

My plan was that this was going to be my habit, to connect with my daughter every day. My prayer was that my plan would work and Angel would never want to leave me and Los Angeles.

But to be honest, though I was working hard, I didn't expect my plan to work so well, and so quickly. It wasn't until this very moment that I knew I was doing everything right.

"Mom, why're you looking at me like that?"

"Like what?" I said, finally closing my mouth.

"Like with your mouth all wide open and your eyes all big and everything."

"I guess I'm just surprised."

" 'Cause I want to take you out to dinner?"

"Uh, yeah, you've never done that before."

"I know, but I'm only eleven, Mom. It's not like I've had money forever. So, let's go to dinner."

I jumped right off of my bed, thrilled. My efforts were being reciprocated. My daughter wanted to spend time with *me*. "Where're we going?" I asked, rushing to my closet. "Do I have to get fancy?"

Angel laughed. "No, Mom. Keep on those jeans. I only have twenty-four dollars."

"That's okay," I said. "I can give you extra money."

"If you did that, then I wouldn't be taking you out. I just want to spend my money, okay?"

"Okay." I smiled. "So where're we going?"

"Let's do the Chinese Bowl in the mall," she said, with her chest poked out like she'd just announced she was taking me to a four-star restaurant.

Now, you know, I was used to going to the best places. But the fact that I was going with Angel, and it had been her idea, made it feel like the Chinese Bowl was the best restaurant in the world. "I love the Chinese Bowl," I told her, though I hadn't eaten at one of those fast-food joints in the mall since I was a teenager.

"Great. I'll go get my stuff." As she dashed out of my bedroom, she shouted over her shoulder, "You'll have to drive, though," as if I didn't know that.

I laughed as I grabbed my purse, called down to the valet to have my car brought up from the garage, then met Angel right at the top of the staircase. Together, we bounced down the steps and chatted as we took the elevator to the lobby.

"So is this a special dinner?" I asked when I pulled out of the circular driveway of our building. "Are we celebrating anything?"

"Nope!" she said. "I just thought it's my turn to do something for you."

Right then I wondered if she'd ever done this for Caroline. But I tossed that question aside. No need to keep score; I was already ahead. I was Angel's mother, and that was the winning shot at the buzzer.

It only took us a couple of minutes to get to the Beverly Center, and after I parked, we took the elevator to the top floor. Then, with our Chinese bowls filled with fried rice, broccoli, and chicken, we sat down.

"Do you know how great this is, Angel?" I said. "To have my daughter take me out to dinner?" I shook my head. "Just so, so cool."

She nodded as she used her chopsticks to scoop up some rice. "I keep telling you, Mom. I'm really mature for my age."

I laughed. "Yes you are." I guess I had to finally admit that.

We chatted leisurely, about her upcoming dance recital, and the school play where she was auditioning for one of the lead roles. We talked about her classes and how world geography was her favorite subject.

"World geography?" I said. I didn't remember having a class like that even in high school!

"Yeah, I love learning about all the continents of the world and all the countries. Do you know how many countries are in the world?"

I didn't have a basis to guess, and thankfully, my child gave me the answer before I proved to her that I wasn't as smart as a sixth grader.

"One hundred and ninety-six," she said. "Though lots of people say that it's only one hundred and ninety-three because that's how many countries are part of the UN. But there are independent countries, too."

"Wow!" I said. Not because of the number, though I had no idea there were that many countries. The wow was for how my daughter so often blew me away.

"I have this big paper due for world geography and you should see all the pictures I've collected," she said. In a single motion, she swooped up her phone, logged in, and then in less than ten seconds had a montage of pictures on the screen.

"Look at this, Mom. The Leaning Tower of Pisa. Can you imagine being right there to take that picture?"

"Wow!" I exclaimed again. And that was all I said 'cause, though I'd heard of the Leaning Tower, I had no idea where I had to be to take the picture.

"Can you imagine being in Italy?" she asked me, and schooled me at the same time.

"No, I can't."

"And look at these."

Angel took me on a trip around the world: from the Taj Mahal in India ("Mom, did you know that this was built in the seventeenth century?") to the Great Wall of China ("Mom, the wall is something like five thousand miles long!"), I sat at that little table and received an amazing lesson from my own child.

Not only did I admire the pictures, but I admired my daughter's knowledge and zest for all of this. Her mind and life were so different from what I'd experienced at her age. When I was eleven all that impressed me were the drug dealers and their girls who always had their hair and nails done, who wore the freshest clothes and the baddest gold earrings.

But my daughter lived beyond her neighborhood. She had

grand dreams. She had aspirations at eleven that I didn't even have now.

"Have you ever wanted to go to any of these places, Mom?"

I didn't want my child to know that her dreams were far greater than mine. So, I said, "I've thought about it, but my priority has always been you. Once you were born, that's all I've been thinking about."

Her eyes got wide. "You've wanted to travel but you didn't because of me?"

Clearly, I'd said the wrong thing. "No! I'm just saying . . ." And I paused right there. Why was I lying to my child? "You know, I haven't had much of a desire to go anywhere," I said truthfully. "I love Los Angeles. This is one of the best cities in the world."

"But loving where you live doesn't mean that you won't love other places," she said. "I want to see"—she spread her arms wide—"the world! And by the time I get old, like to thirty, I'm sure they'll even have trips to outer space, like to Mars or the moon. And I'm gonna be on one of those space-ships."

In that moment I more than loved my daughter, I truly respected this child.

"Then that's my hope for you," I said. "I pray that you get to see the world every single chance you get."

She grinned. "Do you really mean that?"

"Of course." I scooped the last bit of my dinner from the bowl. "I want you to have every desire of your heart." I paused. "And you know what? Maybe we'll do that together. Maybe during the summer, we'll go somewhere."

"Really?"

"Yup, and you can even pick where you want to go."

"I want to go to Paris." She pulled one more picture up on her phone. "Look at this."

Now, this was a picture I'd seen. "Ah, the Eiffel Tower. I know where that is," I bragged. "In France."

"Yes, Paris," Angel said as if her answer were more correct than mine.

"Okay, so that's where we'll go!"

She put down her phone and lowered her eyes at the same time. "I have a chance to go to Paris now." She looked up at me. "Like right now. Like next week."

I laughed. I had no idea how Angel thought she could go to France. "Well, that's not gonna happen. You have school and you have ballet lessons, and acting lessons and—"

"Mom Caroline took care of all of that."

Those words knocked the laughter right out of me. Slowly, I pushed my empty bowl away, rested my arms on the table, and leaned toward her. My voice was low and my words were slow when I asked, "Mom Caroline took care of what?"

"Now don't be mad. Just listen to me." I squinted as she continued, "Mom Caroline has to go to Paris next week for a last-minute meeting with one of her foundations, and the lady who was supposed to go has to have surgery, and so Mom Caroline is going to speak in her place, and she's going to be there for a week, and Dad can't go because he has an important meeting here, and so Mom Caroline wants me to go with her."

My mouth was shut so tight, I started grinding my teeth. I shook my head hard. "No."

"Mom! How can you say no to a trip to Paris?"

"Because I'm the mother and I'm the only one who can say yes or no."

"But Dad has a say and Mom Caroline has a say, too."

"No, she doesn't," I said, my voice rising. "Caroline doesn't have a damn say in your life."

Now, here's the thing—once Angel was born, I decided to

live my life better. And one of those better things was to stop cursing. I wasn't perfect. I'd said that word a time or three every month. But never had I cursed my child, and her shock was as evident as mine. Her eyes widened and filled with tears.

Bringing down my voice and my tone, I touched her arm. "I'm sorry. I shouldn't have said it like that."

A single sob escaped her throat.

"Do you accept my apology?" I asked softly.

When she nodded, a tear slipped down her cheek.

My heart broke every time my child cried, but there was nothing I could do in this moment. Because her pain was about to get worse.

"But here's the thing, Angel. I'm the only one who gets to make the big decisions in your life."

"What about me? Don't I get to make any decisions about *my* life?"

I shook my head. "Not yet. You don't have enough experience to know what's best for you."

She hesitated as if she wasn't quite sure if she should speak. But then she decided to just go for it. "Do you know what's best for me?" she asked softly. "I mean, you don't even want to travel. You don't want to see the same kinds of things I want to see and learn the same kinds of things I want to learn. Mom Caroline has taught me so much, and now she's giving me the chance to go to Paris. And she spoke to the school and Ms. Downs said she thought this was an amazing opportunity, too."

My daughter had just stabbed me with the truth, but I didn't even have time to recover because now I had to deal with the fact that plans for this trip were already in motion. "Caroline went behind my back and spoke to the principal?" This time I was able to keep the volume out of my voice, but not the growl.

Angel nodded with fresh tears in her eyes. My chair scraped against the floor as I pushed it back. I grabbed my empty bowl and marched toward the trash cans.

"Mom!" Angel called after me.

I didn't turn around. At the overflowing trash bin, I stuffed that Styrofoam bowl on top, pushing it down, and imagining that the bowl was Caroline's face.

I had no doubt now. She was trying to steal my daughter. This was war!

# Chapter
## Eight

I didn't even care that Angel was sitting in the car next to me. The moment I slid inside, I clicked on my seat belt, hooked up my Bluetooth, then punched my finger so hard across Bobby's name when his number popped up that I was sure I'd cracked my phone's screen.

"What're you trying to pull, Bobby?" I screamed the moment he answered. I didn't even bother to explain what I was talking about. Bobby knew what was up. "So, I tell you Angel can't move to New York and you come up with a trip to Paris in the middle of the school year?"

"Calm down, Asia," he said. "This is a last-minute trip that Caroline has to take."

"I don't care what it is," I said. "Angel is not going."

From the passenger seat, my daughter sobbed.

"Asia," and then Bobby hesitated, "where are you? Is Angel with you?"

"Yeah, Daddy, I'm here," Angel cried even though I'd given her a wicked side-eye. I guess she felt that things couldn't get any worse so she might as well speak up.

I did hate that she was hearing all of this. I never let Angel see, hear, or be a part of any disagreement between me and Bobby. But this right here was out of control. I'd been tricked by Bobby, and ambushed with some phony dinner by my own daughter.

"Asia!" Bobby said my name as if he was about to scold me.

"Look, Bobby." I stopped him. "You were the one who brought her into this. You were the one who sent her to me when you and Caroline could have told me about this last Sunday."

"We didn't know about it then. We just found out on Wednesday, called Angel and her school on Thursday, and decided that Angel should talk to you today. But we should finish this when we can speak alone . . . and when you've calmed down."

He never raised his voice, and so to Angel I probably sounded like a raving maniac.

But I didn't care. "No, we're doing this now because I don't like the way any of this is being handled. You send Angel to talk to me, you go behind my back to the school, and you want me to calm down?"

"Caroline and I thought it would be best if Angel told you about the trip, and the only reason we went to her school was because if there was going to be any issue with her missing classes, then we wouldn't have brought it up to you at all."

"What you and your wife seem to be forgetting is that I'm Angel's mother!"

"And even if you didn't feel the need to keep telling everybody, we know that."

"Well, you need to act like you know. And you need to respect who I am. I'm the one who makes these decisions about my daughter."

"*Our* daughter. We make these decisions together. And

maybe I was wrong," he said, finally sounding a bit agitated. "Maybe I shouldn't have told Angel to talk to you, but I didn't know what was best. You make it so hard, and after last Sunday, we hoped that you'd listen to Angel. I figured you'd hear how excited she was and then you'd call me to get the details."

"Well, you were wrong and she's not going!"

I pressed the Bluetooth off, just in time to hear Bobby say, "A—" He didn't even get to the second syllable of my name.

Angel's sobs had turned into a full-fledged cry, but all I did was press the accelerator. I was smokin' mad . . .

Within five minutes, we were home . . . and from the car to the elevator, and then finally into our apartment, Angel and I didn't exchange one word. When we walked in the door, Angel ran up to her bedroom, and I would've done the same, except anger had drained all the energy out of me. So, I just stomped to mine, slammed my door, then called Sheridan.

The moment she answered the phone, I started talking, trying to tell her the whole story without hyperventilating.

"Calm down," Sheridan kept saying to me. "This sounds like we need a prayer meeting."

"Yeah . . . somebody needs prayer! Bobby and Caroline if they ever try to pull something like this again." The truth was, I didn't want a prayer meeting. I already knew what Kendall would say, but Sheridan, as a mother, would see it my way.

At least, that's what I thought until Sheridan said, "Honestly, Asia, I think this is a wonderful opportunity."

"How can you say that when this is all about them trying to take my child away from me? This is just a trick of Caroline's to get my daughter," I said, knowing that I sounded half crazy and totally paranoid. But I knew what I knew.

"I don't think so, but let's say you're right. Let's say that Caroline is using an amazing trip to take Angel from you. That would never work. Because you're her mother . . ."

"That's what I keep trying to tell everybody!"

"And you're a good mother," Sheridan continued. "There would be no basis to take her away. There's nothing for you to worry about."

What Sheridan said was true, but my worries had nothing to do with the law; my worries were about the heart. I wasn't sure Angel's heart was big enough for me and Caroline. Suppose I ended up on the losing end?

"But here's the thing," Sheridan began. "You can't keep saying no to Angel just because you don't like Caroline. Don't hold on to Angel so tightly that you choke her, because then you'll lose her for sure. Angel loves you, Asia, and that's all you need to know."

"I gotta go!" I hung up before either one of us said good-bye.

Sheridan was supposed to be ranting the way I was. Obviously, I hadn't explained the situation clearly enough. I needed to speak to someone who really understood me.

I picked up my cell and tried again. "Noon," I said, the moment she answered. "Wait until you hear this." Sheridan had sobered me up a bit, so I was way more somber as I told Noon the story.

"Girl!" Noon exclaimed when I finished. "Angel's going to Paris?" It sounded like she was over in her condo in Fox Hills doing one of those hallelujah Holy Ghost dances—and she didn't even go to church! "I've always wanted to go to Paris."

What was she talking about? Noon had never mentioned any kind of traveling to me.

"You know I speak French, right? *Oui, oui.*" She laughed.

Had everyone in my world lost their mind? "Noon, this is not funny!"

"What?"

"Didn't you hear anything I said? I don't want her to go."

"Why not?"

"Because . . . because she's gonna miss school."

"You said that's not gonna be a problem, and even if it was, tell me which is the better way for Angel to spend a week—sitting in some stuffy school reading textbooks or actually being in a foreign country and meeting people and seeing places that she's never seen before?"

I said nothing.

"Exactly," Noon said as if my silence was an answer. "She'll probably get extra credit for learning a couple of words in French."

"Well," I said, finally speaking up, "the other problem is . . . Bobby's not going. It's just going to be her and Caroline."

"So what? As much as I don't like that skank, you know she's been good to Angel and she'll take care of her. Angel's gonna have a good time, you've got to admit that."

"Well, what about me?" I pouted. Why wasn't anyone thinking about me?

"What? You wanna go to France with them?"

I hadn't said it out loud, but I was beginning to think that maybe that was going to have to happen. If Angel really wanted to go, and if I couldn't find a way to keep saying no, maybe I should get right on that plane.

But I knew that wouldn't work. Just hearing that I wanted to go with her and Caroline would probably scar Angel for life. After the way Caroline and I had fought on Christmas, almost coming to blows, it wouldn't take much for Angel to imagine all the fights Caroline and I would have in France— that is, if we ever made it off the plane.

"Look," Noon said, "just let Angel go. This ain't the New York situation. This is just a week, and all you need to do is give her plenty of money so that she can buy you something fabulous." She paused. "And make sure she brings me something wonderful, too."

As Noon went on, all I could do was shake my head. Everybody was forgetting about me.

"You just need to chill," Noon said. "Plus, if Bobby's not going with them, he'll be home alone, so here's your chance to work Plan B, ba-beeeee," she sang.

Was she freakin' kidding me? Did Noon think that after all of this I'd want to have anything to do with Bobby Johnson? Right now I just wanted Angel to get to be eighteen so that I wouldn't have to deal with Bobby . . . or his tight-ass wife.

"Forget Plan B. I'm on Plan C, which is 'see you later, Bobby!'"

"That's a good one." Noon laughed; I didn't. "Oh, come on, girl. If it were anyone else taking Angel to France, what would you say? If it were Sheridan or Kendall or even me, would you let her go? And if the answer is yes, then you have to let her go with Caroline. Because this isn't about Caroline, it's about Angel."

Just like I did with Sheridan, I hung up from Noon without saying good-bye, and this time I was feeling even worse. That was the thing about talking to Noon, she was going to come at me real. She didn't really care about my feelings, though, it seemed that nobody cared about that.

So now with her words, and Sheridan's words, and Bobby's words all mixing and mingling together in my head, how could I say no? Because what Noon said was true—if it had been anyone except Caroline, I would've already been packing Angel's bags.

In my head, I was convinced; in my heart, I'd been convicted.

Tears were rising from the very center of me as I slowly got up and took the longest walk of my life down to Angel's room.

She was in there, in the dark, sitting on the edge of the bed, with her head hanging down, staring at her hands in her lap. The way her shoulders shook, I could tell she was still crying.

I stayed silent as I walked in and sat down next to her. Neither one of us said anything, though Angel spoke through her tears. As I sat there, I thought about the week we'd just had, the times we'd shared, and how happy I'd been building something new with my daughter.

This should have been the best of times. But just like that book I'd read in high school, the best of times had somehow gotten all mixed up and now it felt like the worst time ever.

"I'm sorry," I whispered.

"You were so mad." She spoke low, too.

"Not at you."

"I thought you were, because you were yelling at me in the mall."

"Was I yelling?" I had to ask her because I didn't remember. She nodded.

"I didn't mean to do that," I said. "I lost control and I shouldn't have." I sighed. "It's just tough for me, Angel. You're getting older. You're starting to have your own life, and so much of your life seems to be around Bobby and Caroline."

"Why don't you like that?" she asked, like my words made no sense to her.

There was a part of me that wanted to direct the conversation in another direction. But all of us were so deep in this situation now that I had to be honest. "I'm afraid."

She reached for my hand, and held me as if she were the protector. "Afraid of what, Mommy?"

"I don't want to ever lose you, Angel."

She paused, needing a moment to figure that out. "How could you ever lose me? I'm your daughter. Remember, you're gonna be two hundred and five, and I'm gonna be ninety and we're still gonna be hanging out together."

I tried to chuckle through my aching heart and I wrapped my arm around her. She rested her head on my shoulder. We sat that way for a couple of minutes and then I said, "You can go to France."

Her head popped up and she hugged me. "Thank you, Mommy! Thank you so much!"

The love that I felt in that moment, in that embrace, let me know that I'd done the right thing.

"There's just one condition," I said.

She pulled away, and even in the dark, the worry was clear in her eyes. Like she had a feeling that I was about to give her an impossible mission and take this all away.

"You have to bring me back something fabulous."

For the first time in hours, my daughter laughed and she pulled me into a hug again. She was happy. And, I was not . . .

Now, eight days had passed and I had not had one happy moment since I agreed to let Angel go. I was used to her being away; she spent so much time with her father, especially during the summer. There were times when I'd looked forward to those weeks alone when I was totally free to hang out, come home when I wanted to, and bring whomever I wanted home with me.

But in those times past, I'd never felt threatened.

"Mom!" Angel screamed out.

She had no idea that I was right outside her bedroom. I'd been standing there, listening to the sounds of her packing, preparing to leave me.

"I'm ready, Mom!"

When she rolled her suitcase into the hall, I was standing right there.

"I'm so excited." She grinned.

"I am, too!" I said. Someone from the Academy needed to see me right about now, because this was an Oscar-worthy performance.

"Dad should've been here already," she said, glancing at her watch.

"I thought you and Caroline were taking a car to the airport."

"Last night Dad said he was gonna drive us."

I took the suitcase from her hand and lugged it down the stairs. At the bottom, I said, "So you have everything? Your passport?"

"Check!"

"Your money?"

"Check!"

"Well, I think there's only one thing left that you don't have."

Angel frowned.

I said, "You don't have a big hug from me."

"You're the best, Mom." She giggled as I wrapped my arms around her. "I'm gonna miss you."

"Me, too," I said just as the knock came on the door.

"That's Dad!" Stepping away from me, she swung the door open.

"Hey, sweetheart," Bobby said to Angel, and then looked up at me.

I crossed my arms.

To Angel, he said, "So, you're ready, kiddo?"

"Yup!" She turned back and hugged me again. "Thank you, Mommy. Thank you for letting me go."

I blinked as fast as I could to keep my tears away and kissed the top of her head over and over. Truly, I didn't want to let this girl out of my arms, but then I had to. "You have a wonderful time," I whispered.

The tears in my eyes made her hesitate, so I pasted the biggest, silliest, toothiest grin on my face. That was when she grinned, too. I nodded at Bobby, and he gave me a sad smile before he led our daughter away.

Right after she stepped over the threshold, Angel turned around and I gave her a finger wave. Then I closed the door.

Those last moments had literally taken my breath away, exhausting me so much that I didn't have the energy to hold back my tears anymore. So, I just let them flow.

As I cried, I kept telling myself how ridiculous this was. Angel was just going away, just for a little trip, just for a week.

So why in my heart did I feel like my daughter was gone and was never, ever coming back?

# Chapter
## Nine

The thing about drinking alone is that I feel like such an alcoholic.

But what else was I supposed to do? Noon was still hanging hard with Brett. And Sheridan and Kendall only drank on special occasions. Though if I called them, I might be able to convince them that this was certainly an occasion when something special was happening.

But since Noon was busy and I hadn't called my girls, it was just me and my colored girls' wine, as Noon liked to call my Moscato.

I raised my glass for another sip, and that was when I noticed that my glass was empty. Thank God I didn't have to go far. I just picked up the bottle from the floor and filled the flute. Once I had my wine in place, I leaned back on the couch and went back to flipping through the photo albums.

From the moment Angel was born, I'd been an old-fashioned mother. I took pictures of everything. Every moment of her life was important, so I had thousands of pictures. Most were digital, but I had hundreds printed out and stuffed into albums.

There were eleven albums in all—one for each year of Angel's life.

I'd already been through the first four books, crying over every memory. And now that I was on her first days in kindergarten, I was bawling so loud I was sure that a neighbor would soon call the police.

Each photo drew me deeper into my depression, made me feel like I was attending a memorial.

Somewhere beneath my wine, I knew that I was being a little extra. But I could blame it all on the alcohol and Caroline. That devastating combo was lethal.

Then, the knocking began. At first I thought it was in my heart, then my head, and finally, I realized that it was the door. That made me frown so hard my forehead hurt.

Since the concierge called up all visitors (well, except for Bobby), I figured one of my nosy neighbors had heard me crying and was just checking before they dialed 911.

My plan was to rush to the door, but when I stood up, the floor rocked and it took a moment for the ground to steady. Then I staggered to the front of the condo and yanked open the door.

And there stood Bobby. With his gorgeous, grinning face. "Hey, you!"

Talk about memories. That was the way Bobby used to greet me when we were in love.

But I couldn't focus on the past because I was trying to figure out the present. "What're you doing here? Is Angel all right?" I peeked over his shoulder as if I expected to see my daughter right behind him. But when I didn't see her, fear washed over me. "Oh, my God! Did something happen to Angel? Did something happen to the plane?"

"No, no, no!" he said, holding up his hands and trying to answer all of my questions at once. "There's no problem. They got off all right. Everything's good. I just came back to check on you."

"The plane took off?" I asked. Before he could even answer me, I busted out in tears. "She's gone!" I sobbed like a drunken fool.

"Awww, Asia, come on." He stepped inside, and when I turned back toward the living room, he closed the door and followed me.

I wondered what I looked like to Bobby as I stumbled across the floor that rolled like the ocean's waves. But do you think I cared? I was just relieved that I made it all the way to the sofa.

When he got to the couch, he picked up one of the empty bottles. "Seems like you're having a party."

"Yeah, a pity party." I paused for a moment. "I didn't want her to go, Bobby," I whined.

He placed the bottle on the side table, then sat down so close to me that our legs touched a little. "Why not?" he asked me softly. "For the life of me, I can't figure out why you were against this."

"'Cause she's my baby."

"She's not our baby anymore. She's growing up."

"But this is the first time she's been away from you or me for so long."

He nodded. "I thought about that. But Caroline's going to take good care of her. You know that, right?"

"Yeah, acting like she's Angel's mother," I said, speaking louder than I wanted to but having a hard time keeping my voice down. "But she's not. And somebody needs to tell her that!" Then I reached toward Bobby. "Baby, give me your phone so I can call your wife. I wanna tell her that she's not Angel's mother and she better recognize."

Bobby gently grabbed my hand as I tried to pat down his

jacket in search of his cell. "Maybe we shouldn't tell her that right now. Maybe we should let Caroline get to France, let her take care of our daughter, and then when she gets Angel back here safely, we can have that talk with her."

I squinted, then wagged my finger at him. "You got a point. 'Cause she better take care of our daughter." With a long sigh, I leaned back on the couch and rested my head on the cushions. "I don't know why I feel so sad. I've been crying ever since you and Angel left and I can't stop."

"Well," he said, glancing at the empty bottle of wine, "drinking probably doesn't help."

"What else can I do?" I cried.

"I understand you feeling sad. I mean, you've spent the last eleven years raising her into this fantastic young lady."

I sat up. "You think so?"

"Oh, my God, I am so proud of Angel. She's smart, she's talented, she loves to study, she has her priorities straight. Think about who she is. That's all because of you, Asia."

I shook my head. "You know I didn't have nothin' to do with that. That's all you . . . and Caroline. You guys treat her like she's mature." I repeated Angel's words. "You have all these sophisticated conversations with her and . . . I've done nothing."

"You've done a lot more than nothing; you've done the important work. Who recognized her talent so early, and got her into all these classes?"

"I'll give you that. But it was mostly because when I was a kid, I wanted to take ballet and I wanted to take acting lessons. But my grandmother hardly had enough money to feed me."

"Well, you don't have to worry about money anymore."

I nodded. "I don't because of you." I leaned forward and covered his hand with mine. "Thanks for that." My voice quivered. "Thank you for taking care of me." Then I sobbed more drunken tears.

He pulled me to him and held me until I was too weak to cry anymore. And then, just like Christmas, all of a sudden his lips were on mine. It was a gentle, easy kiss. Well, it started that way. But then it flipped. We went into full-fledged tongue-waltzing, hands-exploring, voice-moaning mode. For a moment I broke away and did that little thing with my tongue in his ear that used to drive him crazy.

It still did 'cause he cried out my name and shoved me back onto the couch. When he rested the full weight of his body on top of me, I spread my legs welcoming him.

After that, I can't tell you what happened. One minute, I had my clothes on, and the next, everything was off. A minute after that, he was naked, too. Then right there on that couch, we joined together the way we used to, the way we had so many times before.

I hadn't had Bobby in six years, but nothing had changed. We did this horizontal waltz as if we'd danced just yesterday. The weight of him was so familiar, his kisses were so wonderful, and the way he stroked me and made me his once again . . . I'm telling you, I jogged right up the stairway to heaven!

It was wonderful . . . until it was over.

Slowly, Bobby lifted himself off of me, still panting.

I could feel it coming; he was about to jump up and begin ranting. He was going to blame me and my colored girls' wine for what he'd just done.

But then the corners of his lips twitched and spread into a smile. And when he leaned over and pressed his lips against mine once again, I knew he was back . . . we were back.

We lay there in each other's arms until I heard Bobby's soft snore. With as much wine as I'd drunk, I would've thought that I would be asleep, too. But our making love was like a dip in cold water. I was aware, I was awake.

As Bobby slept, I gently rolled away. He stirred a little, but when I was sure that I hadn't awakened him, I tiptoed out of the living room, then sprinted up the steps.

All of my energy was back, and it was a good thing because I had to move quickly. Inside my bedroom, I rushed to my dresser and searched through every drawer for that container Noon had given me long ago.

It took a couple of minutes, but I found it, hidden between two pieces of lingerie. Moving to the other side of the room, I opened my nightstand drawer, took out the matching container with my real birth-control pills, and put the container with the fake pills in the drawer.

I wasn't sure what to do with the real pills, but finally, I tucked them inside my purse. I'd get rid of them in the morning.

With a smile on my face, I sauntered back down to the living room and stood over Bobby. He felt my presence, and when he opened his eyes, it took him a moment to remember. But when he looked up at me, every single memory came back to him.

I sucked in my stomach, put one hand on my waist, and posed, standing there in all of my naked magnificence.

And when Bobby reached for me, Noon's Plan B was in full effect.

# Chapter Ten

When I tell you it had been nothing but four days of joy, I am not lying. After that first night, Bobby didn't go home. I mean, he did go to his house to change on Sunday, and then he came back with a few things. But after that, we were always together.

Our life was just like it used to be. We'd wake up in the morning sometime between seven and eight, have sex, then jump into the shower together so that we could make love there. After that, I'd make him breakfast—if you counted toasting a couple of bagels breakfast—and we'd make love one final time before he left for his office.

By six or seven in the evening, he was back. And every day I met him at the door, wearing nothing more than my purple Prada pumps. Then, after we made love, I'd serve the dinner that I'd ordered in from one of Bobby's favorite restaurants and we'd eat, we'd talk, we'd watch movies . . . and have sex for the final time of the day.

At night, that was the best time. It was slow, it was long, it was love.

I was wearing Bobby out, but I was just trying to secure my place—double insurance. Getting pregnant, and then having Bobby so caught up he would never see our baby as a trap.

Of course, I'd always known that I had topped Caroline in the bedroom, but like Noon said, that hadn't been enough before. So this time, every time had to be special. We made love everywhere—from the kitchen to the massage chair in my beauty room. And I used everything—my hands, my mouth, and my legs in ways that made Bobby say, "Damn, girl," every single time.

We'd just finished one of those times . . . on the staircase. I'd caught Bobby by the door right as he was leaving for work. I was still wearing nothing but my nightie, and when I pushed him down on the steps and went to work, he didn't have any choice but to lean back and enjoy.

I didn't stop till he cried out my name. Then I stood up, leaving Bobby still sprawled out and panting. "Damn, girl," he said.

With the back of my hand, I wiped my mouth. "Do you think you can walk?"

"Just barely." He blew out those words.

I got a washcloth from the bathroom, cleaned him up, zipped him up, then sent him on his way.

At the door, he whined like a teenage boy. "I don't wanna go."

I laughed. "But your big meeting is today, remember? There'll be more of that when you come home."

All he did was shake his head as he walked out. It didn't even bother me that he hadn't kissed me good-bye. He . . . and his body . . . were still distracted.

Once I was alone, I strolled up to my bedroom and checked my messages. It was just barely after nine and Noon had already left six voice mails. I chuckled and punched her name into my cell; she picked up on the first ring. "You better have a good reason for not calling me back for four days."

"I do." I paused. "Plan B is in full gear." Then I pulled the phone five inches away from my ear.

It took a couple of seconds, but just like I knew she would, Noon screamed. "Are you kidding me? Are you kidding me?" she asked over and over again.

I laughed, told her to be calm, then told her how it all went down. "I'm serious, Noon, I had no intention of doing this. I didn't want Bobby, but once I had him . . ."

"Is it as good as you used to tell me?"

I lay back on my bed and kicked my feet in the air. "It's better. Oh, Noon, it doesn't even feel like we've ever been apart."

"Well, you won't have to worry about that anymore because once you get pregnant, there's no way Caroline will stay with him."

That was my prayer. "I just hope Bobby won't be mad," I said. "Though he won't be able to blame me because I make sure he sees me taking my pills every morning."

"You're still taking your birth control?"

I couldn't believe Noon asked me that. Like I was dumb or something.

"Of course not. I still have those fake pills you gave me when I was thinking about getting pregnant with Scott," I said, referring to one of the many boyfriends I'd had in the last six years.

"Girl, those things are probably stale by now."

"They are, but it's just candy."

She laughed. "Girl, aren't you glad you changed your mind about using them with Scott?"

Just the thought made me shiver. "Don't even speak that out loud. I'm using them now with the man I'm supposed to.

I'm just concerned that I might not get pregnant quickly since I've been on the pill for so long."

"Don't worry about it. Just get that man into bed as much as you can."

"I'm gonna keep him in bed till Angel and Caroline get back."

"I guess I won't see you till next week." She laughed, but then suddenly she sighed. "I'm really happy for you, Asia. This is the way it should've always been—you, Bobby, and Angel."

"Awww . . . thanks for saying that. The truth is, Bobby Johnson is the best thing that has ever happened to me, and this time I'm going to keep him."

We exchanged good-byes before I clicked off the phone. Standing there, I thought about all that I'd been through with Bobby: from the way we'd met when I was just eighteen, at an invitation-only party that welcomed the new Lakers to Los Angeles, to how we'd slipped into a comfortable relationship, to having our baby, and then finally breaking up. It had been a long journey, a hard journey, but nothing good came easy.

All that mattered was that now, finally, we were about to do that forever thing.

I gently tossed my cell onto my bed, spun around, and stared into the eyes of Bobby.

I gasped. "Oh, my goodness," I said, pressing my hand to my chest. "You scared me."

My heart was pounding, but not because I hadn't heard him come in, and sneak back into my bedroom. My fear came from not knowing how long he'd been standing there.

His expression was solemn and stern and I tried to recall every word I'd said to Noon. We'd talked about the birth-control pills, about getting pregnant, and about getting it done before Caroline came back. If Bobby had heard all of that, or any of it, it was over.

I swallowed hard as he stepped toward me. His eyes stayed on mine and I tried to come up with all kinds of good lies. The best defense was being the first with a good offense, so I opened my mouth to tell the first lie. "Bobby, I—"

Gently, he covered my lips with two fingers. "You are so sexy," he said.

"What?"

It wasn't until his eyes roamed over my body that I realized that I was standing there still in my see-through black nightie.

"So sexy," he repeated. "That's why I had to come back."

"But . . . but . . . but . . ." I couldn't get my words together because I was still recovering, just now realizing that he hadn't heard a thing. "But what about your meeting?"

He shook his head. "I kept thinking about that thing we just did on the staircase . . . I want to do it again." He wrapped his arms around me. "And again." He kissed me. "And again."

As he pushed me down onto the bed, I thought about this meeting. This meeting was the reason why he couldn't go to France. This meeting that he was now blowing off . . . because he couldn't get enough of me.


I have no idea how many times Bobby and I had watched this movie, but *The Best Man* was perfect right now. This movie was full of eye candy for women, but I hardly noticed Morris, or Taye, or Terrence, or Harold. None of them had anything on my man. He was the best of all of them, wrapped up into one.

Yes, my man! That's how it felt as we lay in the bed, wearing nothing, chomping down on popcorn, sipping soda, and laughing at the movie.

As Bobby stuffed his mouth with more kernels, I imagined that this was our life for real. All that was missing was Angel, propped in between us. And our newborn, of course.

"What're you thinking?"

I looked up and into Bobby's eyes. "What?"

He tossed a kernel of popcorn into my mouth. "You looked so far away. What were you thinking?"

"Nothing, really. It's just that it's so wonderful to be here with you."

He leaned over to kiss me, but before our lips could meet, his cell phone rang. And a millisecond later, mine did, too. We frowned at each other, then Bobby moved to the left side of the bed and I rolled to the right.

When I saw Angel's number, I grabbed my phone so fast.

"Hey, sweetheart," I said, at the same moment that Bobby said the same thing.

For a couple of seconds, I was confused. Had Angel done a three-way? And then it hit me—Caroline had called him at the same time.

"Mom!" my daughter shouted as if she thought I couldn't hear her.

"How are you, baby? Are you still having a good time?"

"Yes, yes, yes! It's even more fabulous than when I talked to you the other day. We went sightseeing and I love the architecture. All of the buildings are old and there's so much history."

"Are you taking a lot of pictures?"

"Yes, and . . ."

I loved hearing from my daughter, but I wanted to and listen to what Bobby was saying. But the way he was hunched over and whispering, I couldn't hear a thing.

"Mom . . . did you hear me?"

I tuned back in to Angel. "I'm sorry, honey, the connection is bad. What did you say?"

"I said that I really want you to come here with me. Remember you said you wanted to travel this summer?"

"Yes, baby." Right away I had new thoughts. Of me and Bobby and Angel together in Paris. That trip would be our honeymoon. "Maybe that's what we'll do." And then I couldn't help it when I asked, "Where's Caroline?"

"She's right here; she just called Dad. She wanted to know how his big meeting went today."

I wondered what Bobby was going to tell his wife.

"Well, it's really late here," Angel said. "We're getting ready to go to bed."

"Okay, I'll see you on Saturday." And then I said, "I love you," right when Bobby said the same thing to Caroline.

Damn!

I clicked off my cell, but didn't turn around. I was afraid of what I might see in Bobby's eyes. Right in the middle of our love nest, the call had come in. To remind me that there was another woman . . . his wife.

When I finally twisted around in the bed, Bobby had already turned around and was looking at me.

"Angel?" he said.

I nodded.

"Caroline?" I asked.

He nodded.

"They're having a good time," Bobby and I said together.

Then we smiled, but I pulled my glance away from his. It wasn't like I didn't know that Caroline was there. Caroline would always be there . . . until she wasn't. It was my job to get rid of her.

But now that Caroline had come into our space, what would Bobby do? How was he going to play this? How did he feel speaking to his wife when he was butt-naked in my bed?

"Asia."

He called my name softly and I forced myself to look at him. Moving on his hands and knees, he inched toward me.

Like a tiger stalking his tigress, he crept toward me, placing one limb in front of the other.

Slowly. Steadily. Seductively.

Earlier, Bobby had called me sexy, but can I tell you that nothing was sexier than this man crawling to me. And when we lay down together, it was like my mind said, *Caroline who?* 'Cause I couldn't think, I couldn't speak.

All I could do was surrender.

# Chapter
## Eleven

Bobby squeezed my hand before he jumped out of his Esca-lade. As he jogged around the front of the car, I still wasn't sure this was the brightest of ideas.

Coming to the airport together? I mean, yeah, Caroline and Angel were arriving together, but on the ride home, who would sit in the passenger seat next to Bobby?

When I told him this wasn't a good idea, all he'd said was, "Why wouldn't we hook up to pick up Caroline and Angel?"

So, I'd just shrugged and figured that any risk he was will-ing to take, I was willing, too. Because I *wanted* Caroline to find out about us; I just wasn't going to be the one to tell her. I learned last time that we were together, my telling her would never work.

Bobby shocked me when he held my hand as we walked toward the Tom Bradley International Terminal. Once we entered the building, he freed me, but as we waited by the cus-toms exit ramp, we stood so close, from far away we probably looked like we were on top of each other.

When I turned my head just a bit to sneak a peek at him, he winked, and I melted.

Then, the call of "Mom!" drew me away from my man to my daughter, and when I turned to her, my smile was as wide as hers.

Angel couldn't move very quickly; she was pushing a luggage cart with the bag that she'd taken with her plus two others.

As she guided that cart toward me, I ran to her. I guess with all the time I'd spent with Bobby, I hadn't realized how much I'd missed my child.

"Mom!" She jumped into my arms like she was five and wrapped her long legs around my waist.

I laughed, though I stumbled, but I held on to her as if she was just the forty pounds she used to be rather than the eighty pounds she was now.

"I'm so glad to see you, Mom!"

"Me, too," I said as she finally slipped down and stood on her own. Then, when she turned to her father, I had my first glimpse of Caroline. She stood, with Bobby's arms around her, but he broke their embrace to hug Angel.

When Caroline said, "Hello, Asia," I did my best to only smile and not blurt out that since she'd been gone, I'd had her husband every day, in every way.

"Thank you for taking care of my daughter," I said.

The smile that filled her face was genuine. "We had a great time."

Caroline said to Bobby, "So, did you drive?"

He nodded. "Asia and I came together."

"Together?" The frown was in her voice more than on her face.

"Yeah," Bobby said in the same tone that he'd used with me when I asked that question. "We were picking you up from the same place, so there was no need to double pay for parking."

Now, if there was one thing Bobby Johnson had no problem with in life, it was money. And paying the parking fees at

LAX? Please! He could do that with the spare change he found hidden in the SUV's seat cushions.

I wanted to tell Caroline my truth—that it made sense for me and Bobby to ride together since we'd been in bed making love until the very last moment.

"So . . . are we riding home . . . together?" Caroline asked, showing major chinks in her confidence.

"Yeah," he said with the type of sideward glance that a person gave when they'd heard a dumb question.

Then, just because, I added, "You know, Angel and I can grab a cab." I already knew what Bobby's response would be, but I wanted Caroline to hear his concern—even if she thought it was all for Angel.

"No." He shook his head. "Y'all are coming with me."

While Bobby rolled Caroline's cart out onto the street, I walked beside Angel as she chatted away. She spoke about seeing the *Mona Lisa* at the Louvre, and even though I truly wanted to hear about her adventures, at this moment I was way more interested in Caroline . . . and Bobby, together.

They walked side by side, but they didn't speak. I didn't know if this was because Angel and I were there or if it was how they always were. But I watched, and studied, and hoped to learn something that I could use for me.

At the car, Bobby piled the bags into the trunk as Angel and I slipped into the backseat. I held my smile as Caroline took her place in the front. She sat with her head high, her shoulders back as if she were a queen sitting next to her king. She just didn't have any idea that she was about to be dethroned.

Only Angel chatted as Bobby maneuvered through LAX. In the past, sitting in a car with Bobby and his wife would've had me shuddering and stuttering. But now I just sat back, kept my eyes on the back of Caroline's head, and hoped that she could feel my stare.

By the time we got to my condo, I'd figured there wasn't

much to Bobby and Caroline's relationship. The two hardly spoke, though they may have just been listening to Angel. But they could've done something, held hands . . . something. No wonder Bobby had come to me.

When he stopped the SUV, Bobby said to Caroline, "Wait here," and then he jumped out.

By the time Angel and I slid out and went to the back of the car, Bobby already had Angel's suitcases out. He was just waiting for me. "I'll take the bags up for you."

There was such lust in his eyes that I couldn't help but smile back. And I was filled with lust, too, when I told him, "No." I pointed to one of the concierges, who was pushing a luggage cart out of the building. "We'll be okay."

"Oh." His disappointment was so apparent . . . exactly the way I wanted him to be.

Of course, I wanted him to help Angel and me up to the condo. I wanted to steal every moment I could with Bobby now that his wife was back. But it was because his wife was back that I wouldn't let him. Because now my strategy was to keep Bobby wanting and waiting. I wanted to send him home with his wife, with images of me on his mind.

"Are you sure?" he asked, as if I needed a second chance to give him the right answer.

"Definitely."

"Bye, Daddy." Angel hugged her father, then she ran to the front of the car. "Bye, Mom Caroline!"

Caroline opened her door to give Angel a hug. "I'm going to miss you," she said, wrapping my daughter in her arms as if Angel belonged to her.

"I'm going to miss you, too," Angel said. "But I'll be with you next weekend."

"No, remember, we switched weekends; I won't see you for two weeks."

"Oh, that's right!" Angel exclaimed. "My birthday party."

"Yes, and it's gonna be absolutely fabulous. I'm planning the biggest birthday ever because you know, you're gonna be twelve."

As Angel giggled, Caroline kissed her cheek over and over. I frowned. Was this public display for my benefit?

That was when I wrapped my arms around Bobby and held him as if he was mine. "Thank you for taking us to the airport." Then I stepped back; my hand was still on his arm when I said, "I hope I get the chance to see you soon."

"You can count on it."

When I pivoted toward Caroline, now she was the one frowning. She needed to learn not to play games with me. I said, "Bye," to her with so much sweetness, she was sure to get a sugar high.

When Angel and I strolled into my building, I knew that both Johnsons had their eyes on us. I laughed. I was so in control.

"What're you laughing at, Mom?" Angel asked.

"I'm just glad to have you home." That was the truth, though it was just half of it. But I couldn't tell Angel that I was giddy with the thrill of victory.

I had a good portion of the win already, but complete victory was coming very, very soon.

Not even thirty minutes had passed. That was hardly enough time for Bobby and Caroline to get home and get settled.

And already I had a text.

Was he texting me in front of Caroline? Thinking that made me smile, but Bobby's text made me dance.

*I can't wait to see you . . .*

Sitting down on the bed, I texted back: *ditto!!!*

Then I jumped up and pumped my fists in the air. Bobby

wasn't in my bed right now, but I felt more confident at this moment than I'd felt all of this past week.

Falling back, I kicked my feet in the air. Twenty-fourteen was going to be the year. My new forever was starting now.

"Mom!"

I rolled back upright and looked at my grinning daughter.

"Why're you so happy?" she asked me.

"Because you're home."

For the first time in her life, my daughter gave me the side-eye. But then she sprinted over to me, jumped onto the bed, and was all over me, making us both fall back. We laughed together.

I wrapped her in a bear hug. "I really missed you."

"I missed you, too, Mom, but it was so amazing. Mom Caroline took me all over Paris, and to every museum, and we went to all of the shops. And she even took me to a jazz club."

"A jazz club?"

"Uh-huh. Don't worry, Mom. It wasn't at night and it wasn't any place that served wine or anything. It was a club for kids 'cause jazz is big in France, you know," she said in a tone that made me think she'd spent too much time with Caroline.

"Oh," I said, using the same tone that Angel had just used. "I didn't know that."

"Because of Mom Caroline, I got the chance to do everything that I wanted to do."

I was thinking that I could say the same thing.

"She even let me have ice cream for breakfast one morning 'cause the French are known for their ice cream."

"Ice cream for breakfast," I said pulling her even closer. "Well, the Americans are known for cereal. That's what we're having for breakfast tomorrow."

She giggled. "Okay, Mom. It was only because we were on vacation. When I'm over at Dad's, I hardly eat any sweets. But the ice cream was so good in Cannes. That's where we went on Thursday and spent the night."

"That's where they have the film festival."

"Yeah," Angel said, as if she was surprised that I knew. "And one day, one of the films that I'm in will be in that film festival."

I laughed. "I have no doubt about it."

"That's exactly what Mom Caroline said. She said she had no doubts about me either; she said she had no doubts about the future."

"I have no doubts about the future either."

And then I held Angel even tighter, if that was possible. The future was bright for both of us.

# Chapter
## Twelve

I was feening.

Really feening. Like back in the day when the crack addicts stood on the corner of the street where I grew up, sniffing, scratching, and shaking, I was feening like that. The only difference between those addicts and me was that my drug was Bobby Johnson.

But today, after four days, I was finally gonna get my fix.

With Caroline back, Bobby and I hadn't been able to get together, but thank God for technology, because Bobby and I had used our tablets and smartphones in ways that I'd never imagined. Tech sex was a beautiful thang, but now I was ready for the real deal.

I peeked my head into Angel's room, and like always, she was on her bed with her headphones. She was pecking away on her tablet keyboard as her head bobbed.

"Hey." I raised my voice just a little. "I thought you were doing homework."

She looked up, grinned, and hooked the headphones around her neck. "I am."

"We agreed . . . no music while you're studying."

"Oh . . . kay." She sighed. Then she looked me up and down. "You look great. You got a hot date?"

*If you only knew,* was what I wanted to tell her. I was so ready to tell Angel everything about her father and me. But though I knew she'd be thrilled, I knew it would be best to wait for Bobby and Caroline to separate.

So, all I said was, "Yup."

She tilted her head. "You really like this guy, huh?"

"Yup," I said again, because if I said anything else, I was gonna blurt it all out. So, I brought the subject back. "Finish up your homework, and then go downstairs and eat with Ms. Martinez in the kitchen. I don't want you always eating in your room."

"Okay. See ya later, alligator!" she said like a kid. Then she added, "Don't do anything I wouldn't do!"—sounding much older. But when she giggled, she was back to being a kid.

Playfully, I slapped her upside her head. In a way, though, I meant it. What did she know about what I was getting ready to do?

But the moment I stepped from her bedroom, my thoughts about Angel took flight. I thanked Ms. Martinez for staying over, and then I headed down to the lobby.

I was shivering with anticipation and it had started this morning when Bobby sent a simple text: *Tonight.*

Through the rest of the day, he'd sent messages: *dress casually. meet me downstairs at 7. follow all directions.*

Well, I had dressed casually, though if I added up the cost of my jeans, boots, and leather jacket, I could probably feed a small nation. That thought made me close my eyes for a sec and give God a quick prayer of thanks, 'cause I sure remembered where I'd come from.

The elevator doors parted and I quickened my steps, strutting pass the concierge desk. But one of the gentlemen stopped me. "Ms. Ingrum?"

"Yes," I said, hardly pausing.

Without another word, he handed me an envelope, and right away I recognized Bobby's handwriting.

Inside the envelope, a note: *Follow Tim. No questions.*

I half frowned and all the way smiled, and when I looked at the concierge, he nodded. But then, when he led me outside of the building, around to the side, and then to the back freight elevator, I was filled with all kinds of confusion.

But Bobby's note had said no questions, so I just went along, the whole time wondering what-the-what? Finally the heavy freight elevator screeched to a stop on the roof, and when the concierge opened the door, there was Bobby. With the rolling hills of Hollywood behind him.

"Oh, goodness," I said, taking in my man. He stood there, dressed as casually as I was, and looking as if he'd been waiting for me all night. My eyes wandered to the candlelit, white-tablecloth-draped table next to him and the dozens of red roses that stood as the centerpiece. "Oh, my God," I whispered. This might have been the roof, but tonight it was laid out like paradise. From the plush carpet below my feet to the oversize sofa that was pushed up against the wall. "Bobby, what is this?"

"This is dinner." He pulled me into his arms.

"How did you do all of this?"

He shrugged. "I have money."

I laughed. "I can't believe this."

"Well, believe it 'cause it's all for you." Then he sealed those words with a kiss. When he pulled back, breathless, he added, "I've really missed you."

He put his arm around my waist and gave me a tour of the rooftop heaven. "There's the Hollywood sign." He pointed and then we walked around the perimeter.

As he chatted and pointed out Palos Verdes, then downtown and Century City, I didn't say a word. I just held on to him and gave thanks for the six years that we'd been apart.

Because if this was where we were ending up, those years of separation had been worth it.

After the tour, he sat me at the table and the freight elevator opened again. It was another concierge, this time rolling a tray with two stainless-steel dome covers. When he sat the dishes on the table, I moaned with pleasure. My favorite: herb-crusted tilapia and jasmine rice.

Bobby popped a bottle of wine. "Sauvignon blanc," he said, as if he was schooling me. And he was. In the week that we'd spent together, he knew I'd developed this "personal relationship" with my Moscato.

After he filled our glasses, Bobby blessed the food, and as he said grace, I prayed that God would give me all the desires of my heart.

*Bless us, Lord,* I said inside. *Bless this relationship and all that we're meant to be.*

When I lifted my head, Bobby was smiling. "What're you thinking?"

There was so much that I wanted to tell him. But I knew when to speak and what to say. So, I just glanced around the roof again. "How perfect this night is."

He nodded. "Just like you."

We ate and chatted like we were the only two in the world. And once we pushed our plates aside, Bobby held my hand and led me to the edge of the roof, where we stood just staring at the lights twinkling from the Hollywood Hills.

"I'm so happy right now." I smiled, but at the same time I shuddered.

"You cold?"

"Just a little." I rubbed my hands up and down my arms. My leather blazer had been warm enough, but I guess not for sitting outside as the clock ticked closer to nine.

"I think I can help with that."

I was thinking that Bobby was going to take off his jacket and give it to me, but then he moved toward the sofa, picked up a huge box that I hadn't noticed before, and in just a few steps, he was back in front of me. "This is for you, baby."

My lips were stretched to my ears. Over the years, Bobby had given me jewelry, cars, even my condo. But this was special because this was the first gift, this time around.

I placed the box on the table, pulled open the cover, and gasped. "Oh, my God," I said, lifting the heavy coat. "A mink!"

"Not mink, baby . . . sable," Bobby said as if sable were one hundred times better.

I shrugged my blazer from my shoulders, then let Bobby wrap the coat around me. Can I tell you how good that coat felt? It was thick and warm and made me feel like a million dollars.

"A fur coat, Bobby?" I said. "When am I going to wear this in Los Angeles?"

"I think it works tonight." From behind, he wrapped his arms around me and held me close.

I closed my eyes, wishing I could stay right there forever. When Bobby turned me around and kissed me, I returned his kiss with all the passion within me. "These have been some of the best days of my life," I told him. "You've made me so happy."

He nodded as if he had the same sentiment. "I didn't realize how much I'd missed you until we got back together."

Back together!

"I really love being with you, Asia. It's so easy. When I'm around you, I don't feel the stress of the world. You just make me laugh and have a good time."

Those words right there . . . were great. But I couldn't get past him saying we were back together!

He pressed his lips to mine once again, and then, slowly,

led me back toward the sofa. Gently, he pushed me down onto the cushions that felt like clouds and he laid his weight on top of me as we explored each other like this was our first time. When he pulled away, I begged for mercy. "Please!" I held my arms out to him.

He smiled, then slipped my boots off. Next came my jeans, and then he took the sable off, but only for a moment. I tried to help him unbutton my blouse, but he pushed my hands away. He wanted to do it all, removing each piece and fondling me in the process. By the time I was naked, I was beyond ready.

I shivered, though I knew it wasn't just from the cool air. It was the way Bobby looked at me. As if he had never wanted a woman as much as he wanted me. After he wrapped me inside the fur once again, it didn't even take him a few seconds to be as naked as I was.

There, beneath the Los Angeles night, we made slow, long love. The kind of love that covered every inch of my body. The kind of love that, from the inside, sent chills to the outside. The kind of love that made me shudder and shiver and quiver over and over again.

It was the kind of love that, as I lay in his arms, made me say, "I love you, Bobby."

Then I froze. Because I hadn't meant to say that. I closed my eyes and waited.

Bobby held me closer. And when he said, "I love you, too, Asia," I breathed.

For the first time in six years, I took long, deep, life-filled breaths.

# *Chapter*
# Thirteen

G irl, look at you!" Noon said as I trotted down the stairs. "Bouncing off the wall and sh—"

"Don't you say that!" I held up my hand, warning Noon before she could even get the whole curse out of her mouth. "Don't bring that kind of talk in my house."

"Excuse you," she said, and folded her arms. "I guess now that you're back with Bobby, you gotta be all straight and sh—" This time Noon stopped herself as I glared at her. "Okay, okay."

I looked at Noon from the corner of my eye. "When did you start cursing so much?"

She grinned. "It's because of Brett. He loves it when I curse. You know, all part of the exotic-African-girl thing."

I shook my head, but then my smile was back when Noon said, "Girl, you are really lookin' good!"

I strutted in front of her like I was on a fashion-show runway, even though I was only wearing a jogging suit.

"Uh-huh, girl, Bobby must be laying it all on and over you." She snapped her fingers with each word.

"Shhh." I looked over my shoulder as I grabbed Noon's arm, dragging her into the living room. "Ms. Martinez is in her room," I whispered.

"She doesn't know you're back with Bobby?"

I shook my head. "No. He hasn't been here at all, except when Angel and Caroline were away."

"Why?" Then she held up her hands. "Wait," she said as she dropped onto the sofa, kicked off her sneakers, then tucked her legs underneath her. "Now start at the beginning."

The way Noon snuggled back onto the sofa, it didn't look like she was planning to move for a while. "Is this your way of getting out of jogging with me?"

She waved her hand. "No, but we can't talk while running, right? And, I won't be able to concentrate on working out if I don't know everything that's going on."

I laughed. I'd been talking to Noon every day, but there was nothing like sitting down with my girl. As I sank onto the sofa next to her, I released a long, happy sigh. "I'm telling you, Noon, being with Bobby is way better than before." Then I went into detail, telling her all the things that I'd told her before: about our rooftop rendezvous, the Rodeo Drive shopping spree that he'd taken me on the next day. Then, how we'd spent Friday going to museums, and dinner at Rendezvous on Saturday. And of course, I told her about our midnight Face-Time get-togethers.

"Wow!" Noon said when I finished. "All of that time with you? What about Caroline? I mean, the last time you guys were together, she lived in Dallas, but now she's right here. How's he getting away with it?"

"I don't think he cares. He says being with me sets him free. It's clear that I'm number one. Bobby wants to build a life with me."

She leaned back. "He said that?"

"He said something even better . . . he said that he loved me."

That may have impressed me, but it did little for Noon. She waved her hand as if the words meant nothing. "Girl, do you know how many times I made Brett say that last night?"

"And you don't believe him?" I asked.

"No, because he was naked, and when a man's naked, he'll say anything."

I thought back to when Bobby had said the words to me. On the roof. When he was naked. "Well, it's not just his words, it's his actions. We're more connected. I'm telling you, this time it's for real, it's for good, it's forever."

She clasped her hands under her chin. "Awww, that sounds so nice."

I grinned.

She said, "But you know great-sounding words ain't enough, right? What I want to know is how is Plan B going? 'Cause that's the only way you're really gonna get him."

Noon could've just picked up a bucket and tossed cold water on me.

When I didn't say anything, she asked, "You're still doing Plan B, right?," sounding like she was trying to check me.

"Yeah, I mean, I'm not taking my pills . . ."

"Look," Noon began as if she could sense my doubts. "All I know is everybody needs insurance. Ask President Obama."

She laughed and I chuckled with her. I knew Noon was trying to take a bit of the bite off of her warning. Maybe she was right. Everybody did need insurance.

Before I could tell her that, there was a knock on my door, and right away I jumped up from the couch. "That's probably Bobby," I said. Not that I was expecting him, but he was the only one the concierge let up without a call.

I really hoped it was him. Maybe if Noon saw me and

Bobby together, she would see that I didn't need to trick Bobby; I didn't need to get pregnant.

I shouted to Ms. Martinez that I would get the door right as I pulled it open.

And then I stood there. Shocked!

"Caroline!"

"May I come in?"

She'd asked the question but was already walking past me. It took me a moment to even shut the door as I tried to connect all of my thoughts and questions.

But even though her presence rattled me, once I faced her, I was cool and collected.

She said, "I hope this is a good time."

I had to take an extra breath before I said, "A good time for what?"

Her eyes moved from side to side as if she was checking out my place. "Is there somewhere we can talk?"

I shrugged and gestured toward the living room. When I walked in with Caroline, Noon's eyes got wide, but she didn't budge. My bestie had never met Bobby's wife, but we'd both seen enough pictures of the youngest child of the richest black oilman in Texas.

Facing Caroline, I crossed my arms. "What do you want to talk about?" I asked, though I was sure this had something to do with Angel. Where did she want to take my daughter now? To China? Well, I'd let this France thing happen, but Angel wasn't going anywhere else with Caroline. Trust that.

She glanced at Noon, then turned back to me. "I'd like to speak to you . . . in private."

I might have been trying to act cool, but I was so shaken by this surprise visit that it took a moment to figure out what she was talking about. It wasn't until she kept looking at Noon that I got it, but I still didn't make a move. Noon was my ride or die and I was going to end up telling her everything anyway.

But then Caroline added, "Please," and I knew she wasn't gonna talk until Noon was gone. I was too curious to tell Caroline to get out of my house, so I looked at Noon and nodded.

Now, the thing about my girl was that she couldn't just get up and walk out. No, she had to make it dramatic: she stood slowly, kept her glare on Caroline as if she was the number one enemy. (Which, I guess, she was.) Then she held her hands together and cracked her knuckles. (Really, she actually cracked her knuckles.) Then she did some kind of crazy, pimp-step-strut, the whole time still looking at Caroline.

When Noon got closer to Caroline, she said, "I'll be right upstairs . . . if you need me," in a tone that was at least three octaves lower than her normal voice.

I wanted to bust out laughing as she pimp-step-strutted out of the room.

When Noon was finally out of our sight, Caroline shook her head a little, then faced me. "May I sit down?"

At first, I was gonna tell her no. Just treat her the way she'd treated me at her house on Christmas. But then I noticed . . . she was looking at the couch. That's where she wanted to sit. And that's where Bobby and I had made love just a few weeks ago.

With a big ol' smile, I said, "Sure," and then motioned for her to sit right in the center of the sofa. When she sat down, I sat in the chair across from her so that I could look in her eyes and imagine what *would* happen if she knew what *had* happened on that couch.

She sat on the edge, crossed her ankles, cupped her hands, and rested them in her lap. The way she sat, all that was missing was her crown. Then she asked, "How's Angel?"

"She's fine; she's in school. But I'm sure you know that."

She nodded. "Angel called me this morning."

My inside voice said, *Then why are you here, heffa?* But aloud, I repeated what I'd asked her before, "What do you want?"

I guess she caught my tone, because she said, "Well, I guess this isn't going to be a friendly visit."

"Why would it be friendly when we're not friends?"

"Touché. Then I'll get right to the point." She took a second to pause and straighten her back even more. "Are you sleeping with my husband?"

At that moment, if Caroline had slipped out a feather from her Gucci purse, she could have knocked me over and knocked me out.

"What?" I said, not because I hadn't heard her, but because I needed some time to think through how I wanted to play this.

She repeated her question and I only had three seconds to react.

This was my chance. I could just break up Bobby's marriage and never look back. I mean, how could he blame me when she showed up at my door?

But as badly as I wanted to knock her off her throne, she wasn't going to hear it from me.

"Why would you ask me that?"

"I have my reasons and I would appreciate you answering the question." She remained cool and casual like she was talking to me about some charity event.

"Suppose I don't want to answer your question."

It was only the tiniest of movement; her shoulders slumped. But Caroline couldn't be broken this easily. She looked dead in my eyes when she said, "If you don't want to answer, that's an answer in itself."

I shook my head. "The only thing that would mean is that I don't want to, nor do I have to answer anything."

She tilted her head. "And why not? If you're not . . ." She stopped as if she'd said enough.

Okay, this needed to be over because the truth was rising up inside of me. Oh, my God. How I wanted to tell her. But all I did was look square in her eyes. "No. I'm not sleeping with Bobby."

She smiled just a little. And then she shocked me with, "I don't believe you."

"Then why did you even bother coming over here?"

She shrugged as she stood up. "Maybe I was hoping that you would tell me the truth."

"I did."

She chuckled, looked down at the floor, but when she looked up at me, her hazel eyes were hard and cold. "Stay away from Bobby," she said with a little extra in her tone like that was gonna scare me.

Really? Did this chick think she could step to me like this?

I laughed in her face before I walked toward the front door.

She was smart enough to follow me, but before she stepped into the hall, she said, "I don't usually repeat myself because the type of person I'm used to speaking with is intelligent enough to understand the first time. But, you . . . well, you're Chiquita from Compton."

Except for Noon and my aunt Beverly, Caroline was the only person who ever used my birth name. She'd found out my real name years ago when she'd done some "research" on me. But what did this trust-fund trick think? That she was intimidating me?

She said, "Stay away from Bobby."

"Or what?"

Her eyebrows rose just a little. "Is that an admission?"

"No," I said quickly. "I'm just saying that I'm trying to fig-ure out why you're threatening me." I crossed my arms. "And, I'm sure Bobby will want to know, too."

Now her smile reached across her whole face. "Oh, no need to say anything to Bobby."

I smirked.

She tilted her head slightly. "Just like I won't be saying anything to Angel."

My arms dropped to my side.

"You know, she'll be spending the weekend with us, since it's her birthday."

Was she threatening me with my own daughter?

"So," she began, "I'm sure you'll agree . . . no need to say anything to anyone."

If Angel hadn't been talking about this party for the last year, I would've made sure that Caroline never saw my daughter again in life. And after this weekend, I was gonna work on that.

Caroline had pissed me off, so I went for the gusto. "You think you can use *my* daughter?" I got in her face. "Well, let me tell you something about *your* husband. I may not be sleeping with Bobby right now, but I can have him whenever and wherever I want. I can have him at any time and any place."

If I was as dramatic as Noon, I would've slammed the door in her face right then. But, no; I wanted to stand there and gloat.

I'd expected tears to come to her eyes, her lips to tremble, her shoulders to shake . . . something.

She didn't do any of that. All she did was laugh. Not an all-out laugh; it was one of those demure things where she put her hand to her chest and chuckled like she was so amused. She was still kinda laughing when she said, "You may have him for a moment . . . but you'll never have him for a lifetime." She started to walk away, but then she stopped, faced me, and said, "Oh, definitely consider yourself warned."

That was when I slammed the door. I was shaking, when I turned around and heard, "Girl!"

I looked up at Noon at the top of the stairs. "Did you hear what she said to me?"

She nodded. "But that might have something to do with what you said to her. 'I can have him whenever and wherever I want?'" She quoted my words. "Girl, that was fierce. Somebody needs to put that line in a book or maybe a movie, since I don't read."

"She said I'll never have him for a lifetime!" I huffed.

Noon waved her hands as she trotted down the stairs. "Don't listen to that mess. She's running scared. I'm telling you, get pregnant, and you'll have Bobby forever."

"Yeah," I said. "Yeah. Okay, let me get my keys and we'll get out of here."

As I trotted up the steps, I tried to calm my breathing. I wasn't sure why Caroline came to see me, but she had accomplished one thing. She'd done what Noon hadn't been able to do. Caroline had just convinced me that no matter what, now I had to be all in with Plan B.

# Chapter
## Fourteen

I'm going to make this up to you." Bobby's voice came through my tablet screen.

I scooted back on the bed, leaned against the headboard, rested my iPad on my lap, then pouted. I went a little over the top so that Bobby could really see how disappointed I was.

"Awww, come on, Asia. You know there was nothing I could do."

"But this was Valentine's Day," I whined.

"Not was . . . is. It's not yet midnight, so I still have time to say 'I love you.'"

That was it! The L-word was all I needed to hear and it trumped everything else he'd done today. Even though we didn't have the chance to be with each other, Bobby had let his presence . . . and his love . . . be known.

First, he'd come by my condo this morning, under the guise of seeing Angel.

"Daddy!" Angel had exclaimed when she'd opened the door and Bobby was standing there. "What're you doing here? I thought you were picking me up from school."

"I am," he'd said just as I strolled down the stairs. He looked up at me when he said, "But today is a special day and I wanted to see you in person." Even as he hugged Angel, he was looking at me. I blew him a kiss; he licked his lips.

Then, not ten minutes after he'd left, six dozen roses arrived with a card that said: *A dozen for each of the Valentine's Days I've missed.* That would've been enough right there. But as Ms. Martinez prepared the roses, separating them and cutting the stems, she found a gift box. One of those blue boxes that every woman loves.

And inside my blue box—a diamond tennis bracelet.

"I do love you, Asia." His voice came through my tablet, taking me away from today's memories. Yes, Bobby saying those three words made up for not spending this night with him.

Really, though, I was just being a brat. I already knew that we weren't going to be together. This may have been Valentine's Day, but the bigger celebration—Angel's twelfth I'm-practically-a-teenager birthday.

And my daughter wasn't having an ordinary party. This was a weekend event, starting with a slumber party with her three closest friends tonight, then an actual party tomorrow with more than sixty guests, and then the finale, a brunch after church on Sunday to which more than twenty people were invited.

It was because of Angel's birthday that Bobby couldn't get to me. He couldn't leave Caroline at home alone with Angel and her friends.

"So, do you forgive me?" he said in a voice that was as sexy as his body.

Instead of telling him that all was forgiven, I stood, propped the tablet onto the nightstand, then stood back and began to unbutton my blouse . . . slowly.

"Ahhh, that's what I'm talking about," Bobby said. "Show it to me in HD, baby."

I tried to imagine myself on that big screen in his office and I hoped that soon I'd have a tour of his whole house—right after he kicked Caroline out. Plan B, ba-beee, was all I thought about.

As I undressed, Bobby did the same, and even though we were both trying to slow it down, we couldn't. We were too anxious to get to the good stuff.

I propped pillows up so that when I lay down, Bobby would see all of my splendor. Leaning back, I spread my legs into a split, and watched Bobby melt.

"Oh, baby," he moaned.

"You like that?" I asked as I began my show.

He groaned his approval and then we both went to work. Well, *work* may not have been the right word . . . we both walked through the doors of pleasure. I closed my eyes and imagined that my hands were Bobby's, I imagined that everywhere my hands were, his tongue had been.

I wondered if Bobby's thoughts were the same as mine. I heard his moans, I savored his groans.

And then I heard, "Mom!"

My eyes popped open at the same moment that my heart stopped beating. I'd been so gone that it took a moment for me to focus. And right on my tablet screen, there was Angel, standing with her mouth open and her eyes moving from her father to me. Standing beside her were her friends, though I wasn't sure if those girls saw me; their eyes never moved from Bobby.

"Mom!" Angel looked right at me through the camera.

Finally, my veins pumped enough blood to my brain so that I could move. I jumped off the bed, grabbed my tablet, and turned it over. Right before I turned it off, I heard Angel's cry once again: "Mom!"

Why was she calling me? Her father was right in front of her.

And then I thought about her father. "Oh, God!" I squeezed my eyes tight. Bobby was there, all alone with those girls. Lying on the sofa butt-naked.

I'd just made the coward's move, shutting off my camera, leaving Bobby to handle this. But what else was I supposed to do?

It was too late to cover up now, but still, I grabbed my robe, then paced and trembled, and wondered what was going on at Bobby's house? Bobby had told me that he was in his office, that it was in a separate wing of his house, that Caroline never came in there. So why had Angel walked in?

"Oh, God. Oh, God. Oh, God." I couldn't think of anything else to say and I couldn't figure out what to do. Should I call Bobby? Should I call Angel? Should I just wait?

No, I couldn't wait.

I picked up my cell phone and punched Bobby's name, praying the entire time as his phone rang. When the call went straight to voice mail, I hung up and then called him back because I was too afraid to call Angel.

But when Bobby didn't answer, I had to call my daughter. I had to see if she was all right or if she had been damaged for life. As her phone rang, I put myself inside Angel's shoes and walked into that room, and in my mind, I saw what she saw— the image of me on that big-screen TV. And then, her father. How long had she stood there?

I groaned right before my call went to voice mail. Not that I was surprised by that. Angel wouldn't be walking around the house with her phone. Especially since her friends were there with her . . . oh, God! Her friends!

Again I squeezed my eyes shut, but it did nothing to erase the image of Angel and those other eleven-year-olds. Standing there, staring at me, staring at Bobby, staring at what we were doing.

I took a few deep, cleansing breaths to steady my nerves. When my mind was clear enough to think, I sat down on the bed, trying to think this through. So, what were the issues? Yes, this was embarrassing; no parent wanted her child to walk in on anything sexual, but Bobby and I couldn't have been the first people this had happened to.

Really, the only issue was that now Angel knew about us, and what was so bad about that? I mean, we were going to tell her eventually, soon actually. The only thing that had happened tonight was that Angel finding us sped everything up . . . with Angel and Caroline.

The thought of Bobby's wife now finding out for sure put a little bit of a smile on my face and a whole bunch of joy in my heart. The more I thought about it, this was a very good thing. I wouldn't have to even worry anymore about getting pregnant.

Still, though, I had to make sure that Angel was all right. So, I called Bobby again. No answer. And then, Angel. No answer. Over and over I called. And each time—no answer. I could've waited, but then again, I couldn't. I was a mother who had to check on her daughter.

Quickly, I jumped back into the clothes that I'd just stripped off, and then, trying to beat the speed of light, I grabbed my wallet and keys and dashed out the door.

It had to be the frantic look on my face that made the valet bring my car up so quickly—in no more than five minutes, I was making the tires scream as I sped away.

Bobby's house was less than twenty minutes from my condo and that gave me time to think some more. By the time I rolled my car to a stop in front of his house, I was still anxious, but I had calmed myself down. I'd just explain this to Angel, and she'd be fine. And I had to remember the good part of what happened—Caroline would be gone.

When I jumped out of the car, Bobby's house was bright with lights shining from every window. It may have been close to one in the morning, but I was sure that anyone who had a beating heart inside this house was awake.

I rang the bell, then stuffed my hands into my jeans. When there wasn't a response after a few seconds, I rang the bell again, then banged on the door. I banged and banged until the door was finally opened.

"Bobby!" I exclaimed, and wrapped my arms around him.

The move must've surprised him at first, but then, instead of pulling me closer, he peeled my arms from his neck and pushed me back a bit. I took in his sober expression, drooping cheeks, and eyes that were bright and clear a half hour ago but were weary-looking now.

"Is everything okay?" I tried to push past him, but he blocked me before I could get to the door. I frowned. "I want to talk to Angel."

He stepped toward me, making me edge farther away. "This isn't a good time."

"What's wrong? Is Angel all right?"

With the tips of his fingers, he massaged his eyes and shook his head at the same time. "She's really upset."

"Then I have to see her," I said, moving once again toward the door. And again, he stopped me.

"No, Asia, really. This isn't a good time. Caroline is with her."

"Caroline?" I said her name as if it were an insult. "I don't care about her; I need to be with Angel."

He shook his head again. "She doesn't want to see you."

"What?" I screamed so loud, my voice echoed through the after-midnight air. "What do you mean? I'm her mother. I can see her whenever I want to."

Again, I pushed toward the door, but this time Bobby stopped me by planting his hands on my shoulders. "Please don't force this. She's really upset. Her and her friends . . ." He stopped, squeezed his eyes shut, then whipped his head from side to side like he was in the middle of a nightmare. When he opened his eyes, he said, "You can talk to her in the morning."

I crossed my arms. "Really, Bobby? Really? You think I'm going anywhere without seeing my daughter?" Now I had to see her, especially since she was so upset.

"Please, Asia."

I answered him with a roll of my neck.

"All right." He gave me a resigned sigh, but then just as he moved to the door, it opened and Caroline stepped out.

Before she could close the door behind her, though, I heard my child scream, "Go home, Mom! Just go home!"

The cries of my daughter made me push toward the door. I couldn't see her, but I heard her sobs.

I was blocked once again, but this time by Caroline. I glared at her smiling face. I was about to run over her like I was a linebacker when Bobby stopped me.

"Asia, it's late," he said. "Angel is tired and upset. She's embarrassed and her friends are still here. Do you really want to make this worse for her?"

What was going on? How had I become the villain?

"Please," Bobby said again. "Please."

My glance moved from Bobby's pleading eyes to Caroline's smug face, and for a moment I was confused. Wasn't I the one who should have been standing here smirking at her?

"We'll call you in the morning," Bobby said.

And then, "Mom Caroline!"

"Excuse me," Caroline said to me as if I were intruding, "I have to go take care of my . . ."

She stopped, but she might as well have said it—*my daughter.*

That was when I went from zero to sixty. My fingers curled into fists and I leaned back ready to take a swing.

But Caroline moved faster than me. She was in the house before I could do anything.

My chest was still heaving when I turned to Bobby. "What's going on?"

His eyes narrowed like he was confused. "You know what happened."

"I'm talking about all of this. Me standing out here. Angel in there."

"She's upset, Asia. All I want right now is to get her calmed down."

"So, she doesn't want to see me, but she's fine with you?"

He shook his head. "Actually, she doesn't want to talk to me at all. The only one she wants right now is Caroline."

I growled, though I didn't mean to do it out loud.

"I know you're upset, but let's be grateful that Caroline is here, and she's not taking what happened out on Angel."

I paused for a moment and imagined Caroline holding, comforting, my daughter. "I'm not leaving."

"I know you don't want to, but you heard Angel. Do you want her to be even more upset? All I'm saying is let's get her calmed down, and then you can talk to her in the morning." He paused. "She'll probably call you before you even wake up." Another pause. "Trust me on this, Asia." And then in the moment that it took me to blink, he turned and stepped into his house. Without another word, without a hug, without anything, he just walked away.

I stood there, not quite knowing what had happened. I didn't have Angel, and I didn't have Bobby.

How in the world had this happened?

# Chapter
## Fifteen

I hate you, Mom! I hate you!"

"No, Angel, no!"

When she turned and ran away from me, my eyes snapped open. Where was I? Where was Angel?

Frantically, my eyes swept the room.

*Tick . . . tick . . . tick.*

My eyes moved to the clock, and then, in the almost silence, every memory rushed back, making me moan. I jumped up, but then hardly moved. My neck was stiff, my lower back ached from sitting up on the sofa all night.

My plan had been to stay awake and then head back to Bobby's the moment the sun rose. I hadn't even taken off my clothes, but I guess that didn't matter to my exhausted body. I'd slept, though it was never restful sleep. Remnants of my nightmares remained in my mind: Angel crying. Angel screaming. Angel walking away from me forever.

As I glanced once again at the clock, the time shocked me. How had I slept till ten? And why hadn't Angel or Bobby called?

I picked up my wallet and keys, dashed to the door, then paused with my hand on the knob. I needed to take a shower . . . or at least brush my teeth and wash my face. But then I remembered my dreams and I walked right through my door. I might have been funky, but there were some things more important than washing up.

Just like last night, I was in my car within five minutes. Then another fifteen, and I was back at Bobby's. This time I didn't even think about the doorbell. I banged on the door like I was Homeland Security.

The door was opened within seconds and I recognized the woman. She was the same one who'd let me in six years ago when I'd come to Bobby's home to break up his marriage. Well, it may have taken me six years, but this time *that* mission was accomplished.

I couldn't celebrate, though. Not until I knew Angel was fine.

"May I help you?" the woman asked, peeking through the small sliver of space that she'd given herself by barely opening the door.

"I'm here to see my daughter," I said, pushing past her. Stomping through their massive foyer, I headed toward the stairs.

"Miss!"

I kept moving, but when I was halfway up the steps, Caroline appeared at the top.

"Angel's not here." Then she took steps toward me.

I stopped, though I wondered if she was lying.

When we stood on the same stair, she said, "If you don't believe me, you can check."

I *didn't* believe her, so I ran up the stairs, then turned left. I'd only been this far in Bobby's house one other time, on Christmas Day, so I knew how to get to Angel's bedroom.

My steps were really stomps as I marched across the carpet. I busted into the room at the end of the hall; it was the right room, but like Caroline said, Angel was not in it. She'd been there; the clothes and suitcases strewn across the room like a hurricane had blown through proved that.

My first mind was to search through every room, but I didn't know this house. And according to Bobby there were a couple of wings. So, I turned back and ran down to the living room, where I was sure Caroline was waiting.

Just as I thought, she was there, standing in front of the fireplace and looking down at a photo she held.

She didn't even bother to look up when she said, "This is one of my favorite pictures of me, Bobby, and Angel."

I flexed my fingers. "Where's Angel?"

She said nothing as she returned the photo to the mantel, then slowly, deliberately, lined the frame up with the others. Finally, she turned to me. "She's not here."

"Don't play games with me, Caroline."

Her left eyebrow arched. "Games? I'm not the one . . . playing games," she said. "I wasn't the one . . . playing games on that big-screen television last night."

Well, I understood what this was about. Caroline was hurt, finally realizing that she'd lost Bobby to me. But I wasn't going to go back and forth with her over that. Not right now. "If you don't want to tell me where Angel is, I'll sit right here"—I plopped onto the sofa—"and wait. She has to come back soon." I glanced at my watch. "What time does her party start?"

Caroline shook her head. "There isn't going to be a party."

I jumped up. "What do you mean?"

"Angel's party has been canceled."

"What?" Was Caroline really going to take this out on Angel like that? "You're nothing but a vindictive little—"

Before I could go straight reality-show ratchet on her, she held up her hand.

"Oh, this wasn't my fault," Caroline said. "If you want to call anyone a vindictive little . . . what were you going to call me?" She paused. "Angel canceled her party. She was humiliated last night in front of her friends and she doesn't want to face anyone right now." She shook her head as if she couldn't believe it. "So, it is you who caused Angel's pain, not I."

Caroline's words played over a couple of times in my head before I whispered, "Angel canceled her party?"

Caroline looked straight at me when she said, "I guess it's difficult for a child to feel like celebrating after finding out that her mother and her father are nothing more than . . ." She held her forefinger up and moved it in a circular motion. "What's the word I'm looking for . . . *tramps*, or *whores*, maybe."

I wanted to rip this lady apart, but before I could go in on her, I had to find out about Angel. "Whatever happened with me and Bobby we'll have to handle later. Right now my only concern is Angel."

"Oh, so now you're concerned about her?"

"Where is she?"

"She's with a friend. She didn't want to stay here."

"Then you should've called me. I would've come and taken her home."

"She's not trying to get away from me," Caroline said as if that fact were obvious. "She wanted to leave because of you; she knew you'd be back and I think her exact words were 'I never want to see my mother again.'"

My eyes became thin like slits. My daughter was twelve, and yes, she was prone to being a bit melodramatic, but this? "I'm going to ask you one more time . . . where's my daughter?"

"You know the interesting thing about young girls," Caroline began.

I frowned. I didn't know where this chick was heading, but I was going to give her ten seconds before I was all up on her.

She kept on: "Young girls are so impressionable." She kinda chuckled. "For example, take our lovely Angel. A couple of years ago, I convinced her to watch an old TV show. And while we were watching *Fame*, I made a few observations about how she was much better than any of those kids . . . and then all of sudden Angel wanted to go to school in New York."

My frown deepened.

Caroline said, "And then Angel and I took that wonderful trip to Paris . . . that just happened to pop up on my schedule."

I crossed my arms and tried to steady my breathing.

"Amid all of that shopping and sightseeing and girl talk, she's telling me that she loves me as much as she loves her own mother." Caroline held her hand to her chest like she was touched, and at that moment I knew she was touched all right. She was touched in the head. She was, like, crazy.

"And then we had that wonderful slumber party last night to set off this birthday weekend." She paused. "Did you know last night was my idea? I *wanted* Angel here with her friends."

A chill rushed through me.

"And since they were all here, I thought they should have fun exploring the house. So, I sent her and her little friends on an adventure to the other wing. The wing that has always been off-limits to her, but last night it wasn't."

I had to take in a mouthful of air. My daughter had been set up by this witch.

"You knew?" I whispered.

"Knew what, Chiquita?" She said, "Are you asking me if I knew that you were screwing my husband?" She chuckled again. "Come on. I never ask a question unless I already know the answer. I knew you were having . . ." She paused. "What is that called? Video sex?" She shuddered. "Well, anyway, I knew you were doing that TV stuff, and I knew you were once again spreading your legs for Bobby Johnson. I knew it all, and only came to your place to give you a friendly warning. But you were too dumb to accept my advice."

"So . . . what's this? You're mad about me and Bobby and so you hurt my daughter?"

"I didn't do that; you did. She's mad at you, not me."

"You really think you can turn my daughter against me?" I laughed, though I didn't feel as confident as I sounded.

"I already have," she said. She spoke with such calm, such coolness, and such certainty that all I could do was believe her.

That was when my heart started pounding, but I wasn't about to let Caroline see me weak. "So, what's your plan?" I asked, pretending to be as cool as she was. "You think you can keep her away from me? Bobby would never let you do that."

She waved her hand as if Bobby didn't matter. "He's not going to have much of a choice in this. Angel doesn't want to have anything to do with him either."

Did Caroline really think this was going to work? As if once I saw Angel, I wouldn't be able to talk to her, explain to her, get her to understand. "Look, I'm not going through this with you anymore. Just tell me, where's Angel?"

She hesitated as if she was considering my words. Then, "You want your daughter?" Another pause. "Give me back my husband."

I opened my eyes so wide, my vision would never be the same. "Are you freakin' kidding me?"

"Do I look like I'm *freakin'* kidding?"

"You're bargaining with my daughter? Holding her for ransom?"

Caroline squished her nose as if she smelled something nasty. "*Ransom* is such a dirty word."

I moved toward her. "You know, you're nothing but a low-down, dirty—"

Before I could say every curse word I'd ever heard, she said, "Uh . . . before you call me out of my name, what would you call a woman who goes around sleeping with other women's husbands?"

"I don't do that," I said. Then, with a smirk, I added, "I've only had yours."

Her face and body stiffened and I felt like I'd scored a point, except I was still losing in this game.

"You need to know, Chiquita," Caroline said with her voice so tight her lips hardly moved, "that I'm way more than these clothes and my money. Because clearly, you've been fooled by my class. But let me tell you something." Now she was the one who closed the gap between us. She came so close that I thought she was about to try to jump bad with me. Oh, I wanted her to do it. I wanted her to take one swing so that I could release all of my rage on her.

We were inches apart when she said, "You and I are so much alike. Haven't you noticed?"

I didn't say a word.

She continued, "We may have grown up differently, and I may have money and class while you have"—she paused as if she had to think about it—"nothing," she said, like she'd found the perfect word. "But I am just like you because I am still a black woman. And a black woman—with money or without money—doesn't play."

"So you're going to use my daughter?"

She answered with a shrug.

I asked, "Why do you want to be with Bobby if he doesn't want to be with you?"

She frowned and shook her head a little like she was confused. "What are you talking about? Bobby wants to be

with me . . . we've been together all these years. And so why
should I give up on my marriage? Being Mrs. Bobby Johnson
gives me a certain, shall we say, cachet. And, there are major
benefits for him having married a Fitzgerald. He doesn't want
to give that up. Bobby may have made a lot of money in his
career, but it's nothing compared to my daddy. My family's
fortune will always keep that wedding ring on Bobby's finger."

There was a part of me that believed her, but then the
other part remembered how Bobby and I were together. He
really loved me; he told me and he showed me. He had enough
money; he didn't need hers.

Caroline kept talking. "Bobby just gets a little off track
sometimes and I have to remind him." She sighed like the task
made her weary. "But I've done it so many times since we've
been married, it's just something that I have to do."

So many times? I frowned. "What?" The word escaped
from me before I could stop myself.

She stared at me for a moment, then laughter was in her
eyes when she said, "Wait, you don't think you're the only ho,
do you?"

I pressed my lips together and now she laughed out loud.

And laughed. And laughed.

And all I could do was stand there until she finished.

"Oh, Chiquita, you do amuse me." She paused to let
a few more chuckles escape through her lips. "Bobby has
had so many hos over the years it's not even funny. But you
thought"—she started to laugh again—". . . you thought you
were the only one." More laughter. "Right now he's probably
with three or four . . . not counting you."

I wanted to punch her in her face. Just knock her out so
that she would stop lying.

She continued, "Just last week I caught him in that room
doing whatever he does with some ho"—she paused and

looked me up and down—"much younger than you. But he was in his room and they were doing all kinds of nasty things on that TV."

I was crying inside, but I wasn't going to let one tear seep out of me. Not one.

It wasn't enough for her to stab me, she had to twist the knife, too. "That's why Bobby got that TV, that's why he has that room, that's why I knew what was going on last night, and since it was after midnight, I knew he'd be with you because you're his late-night ho. The one he goes to when he's just about asleep."

I was dying, dying, dying.

Caroline kept on: "So, what were we talking about before you came in here demanding to see your daughter?"

I said nothing.

She laughed. "That's what I thought." Then her face got straight serious. "So, here's what you do. You tell Bobby that you won't be seeing him anymore, ever." She looked at me as if I was standing naked right at that moment. "And then I'll work it out with Angel. Unless, of course, a man you'll never be able to trust, a man who will never commit to you, is more important to you than your own daughter."

Then, before I could say anything, before I could scratch her eyes out, before I could make her die, she shouted, "Belinda," and the woman who'd opened the door appeared. "Can you show Ms. Ingrum to the front door?" Caroline glided out of the living room without giving me another glance.

I stood there, not knowing what to do. I couldn't leave, could I?

"Miss Ingrum?"

I turned my head. "You can follow me."

All I did was nod and work hard to hold back my emotions. And, I was strong. I made it to the car.

Now, in the last few weeks, I'd been emotional. But nothing compared to what I did when I slid inside my car and closed the door. You couldn't quite call it crying. I was filled with too many emotions to cry. Instead, I howled, like I was howling at the moon.

# Chapter
## Sixteen

It was hard to see, hard to focus. Not because I was crying; I'd finally stopped. Now I could hardly move because I was in shock.

But finally, I had enough in me to swerve around the circular driveway and then drive down the long road that led to the street. Once outside the gates, I pulled over to the curb.

I squeezed the steering wheel and I lowered my head so that I could rest; I was so exhausted. And I had to find a way to stop all of this trembling. I trembled with fright, with anger, with hurt. And then there was all of that stuff going on in my head . . . thoughts that were jumbled together—where was my daughter, and how could Bobby Johnson cheat on me?

One side of my heart was so crushed by that, but I had no time to mourn the loss of that relationship. Everything in me had to be about Angel.

I grabbed my cell phone, and just before I tapped the emergency icon, I stopped myself. What would I say to the police? That my daughter was in the custody of her dad and her stepmother on the weekend that she was supposed to be there? Where was the crime in that?

And really, the only peace I had was that Angel was fine. That was the one thing I knew for sure. Caroline would make certain of that.

But while my daughter was fine physically, how was she really?

"Oh, my God," I whispered. What was I supposed to do now? That video played in my head again . . . of Angel, and her friends, walking into Bobby's office, seeing me, seeing Bobby.

And I couldn't get to Angel to explain it. I couldn't get to her to hold her and make her hurt go away.

I reached for my cell phone again, and made the call that was becoming all too familiar. But this time all I had to say was, "Sheridan," and that was it.

"Where are you, Asia!"

I sobbed.

"Are you home?"

"No."

"Can you drive?"

"Uh-huh."

"Can you get to the church?"

"Yes."

"Go there now. Kendall and I will meet you. Do you need me to stay on the phone with you?"

I sniffed back my tears. "No, I'll be okay. I'm about twenty minutes away."

"I'll be waiting for you."

When I hung up, I cried some more, but for the first time it was because I felt at least a little bit of relief. With Sheridan, with Kendall, and with prayer, maybe I'd be able to put just a little bit of my life back together.

# Chapter
## Seventeen

Kendall stomped back and forth in front of me. "Okay, come again." She paused and cocked her ear as if she needed to do that to hear me better. "Did you just say that that heffa won't tell you where your daughter is?"

Sheridan said, "Uh, Kendall, I don't think you should use that word while we're here in the church." She knelt in front of me and squeezed my hand.

"Whatever!" Kendall said, still going off. "God might even be calling Caroline that right now."

I could almost feel the steam coming out of Kendall. She was much angrier than I was. I wasn't angry anymore, I was just scared.

Kendall's rant continued. "I think it's time for us to go over there and pay this . . ." For a moment she stopped moving and stood right in front of us, then she said, ". . . this *heffa* a visit."

"Kendall! You're not helping!" Sheridan snapped.

Kendall shook her head, took a deep breath, then she knelt in front of me. She held my hand as she said, "You know Angel's all right. One thing you know is that heffa will take care of her."

If I wasn't so sad, I would've laughed. But all I could do was nod and sniff. I felt so drained, but thank God for Sheridan and Kendall. With them here now, all I had to do was keep breathing. They'd figure the rest out for me.

Sheridan added, "And Bobby, too. He'll take care of her. He always has."

"In my heart, I know Angel's okay . . . at least, physically. But mentally . . ." My eyes shut and that video played in my head again. "I still can't believe that she walked in on us like that."

Kendall moved from kneeling in front of me to sitting next to me on the front pew. "Girl, I always knew you were a freak . . ."

And there wasn't a thing that I could say because I'd told my girls everything. When I first barged into the church, I'd run right into Sheridan's arms, since she was standing by the door waiting for me. Kendall was there, too, waiting for her turn, and after a couple of seconds, I fell into her embrace.

They went back and forth, taking turns holding me, saying nothing, until I was drained of all of my emotions. Then, when Sheridan pulled me down onto the front pew and asked, "What happened?" the story poured out of me. I started with how I'd thought Bobby wanted me, when he really didn't, and then I explained how Bobby and I eventually got back together. And the grand finale: I told them how I'd put on a porn show on a sixty-inch monitor for Bobby, Angel, and her friends.

I didn't think there could possibly be anything that I could do to shock Sheridan and Kendall. Through the years they'd seen the best, but definitely the worst of me.

But this story right here had Sheridan and Kendall sitting with their mouths open in matching wide Os. It was a major achievement—I'd made Kendall speechless.

Until I told them how I'd gone to Caroline's looking for Angel. That was when Kendall's rant began. And as she paced and roared about what she wanted to do to Caroline, I was so grateful. Kendall was saying all that I wanted to say, but didn't have the energy to do right then.

"A freak," I said, finally responding to Kendall. "If that's what you're calling me, what're Angel and her friends saying?"

"Girl, please. You don't have to worry about that," Kendall said. "Angel and her friends have probably seen much worse!"

I was horrified at that thought and Sheridan must've been as shocked as I was, because Kendall looked at me, then at Sheridan, and finally Kendall asked, "What? Y'all don't really believe these kids nowadays with their iPads, and their Kindles and their Samsungs, are not watching every bit of porn that they can on YouTube?"

"No," Sheridan said. "Because you can't post porn on YouTube."

"Well, maybe not on the Tube, but trust and believe they can see whatever they want on the Internet when you're not watching."

"Oh, God!" I moaned. I didn't want to think of my little Angel seeing any of that stuff.

"Look, all I'm saying is that you're acting like Angel's ruined for life. She's not. She'll be fine."

"I want to believe you. That's why I just want to talk to her, to hear her voice and to know that she's fine and she doesn't hate me."

"Hate you because you were having tech sex with Bobby?"

"Hate me because I was having tech sex with Bobby when she loves Caroline so much."

"Girl, the only thing I'm thinking about Caroline right now is what she's going to say when we roll up there and beat her down until she tells us where Angel is."

That sounded like a good idea to me.

"So let me get this straight," Sheridan began. "You want the three of us to go busting into a house in Bel Air?"

Kendall shrugged. "I've done it before."

If my heart wasn't broken inside, I would've laughed, jumped up, and given Kendall a high five. She was my girl—even more than I thought. We always bumped heads like we didn't like each other, though I knew how much she loved me and I loved her.

But how she was talking now? After all of this was over, I was gonna invite Kendall to hang out with me and Noon!

Right now, though I wanted to go with Kendall's plan, I knew that we couldn't. "The moment we drive onto Caroline's driveway, she'll call the police," I said.

"And, she'd have a right to do that," Sheridan said, glaring at Kendall. "Especially once she found out our intentions." Turning back to me, she said, "We do have to find Angel and make sure that you at least speak to her, but we've got to do this in a calm, civilized way. So, you've called Angel, right?"

"A million times." On my drive over to the church, that's all I did. I called Angel, then I called Bobby, and then Angel again. I doubted if they were together, though; I just didn't know. All I wanted to do was speak to my child, hug her, kiss her, and tell her that we were going to be all right, together.

"Okay, so you want something calm and civilized," Kendall said more to Sheridan than to me. "Let's go to Bel Air, but we'll stop short of going through the gates. We'll have our own stakeout and wait for Angel to go back there."

Now, that was an idea! I grabbed my purse, turned to Sheridan—I was ready to roll.

Sheridan nodded. "We might be there all night, though. Angel might not go back there until tomorrow since she's not due home to you until tomorrow night, right?"

"Yeah, but at least doing this, I'd feel like I was doing something to find Angel."

Sheridan nodded again, though she wasn't as enthusiastic as Kendall, and I got that. This wasn't the way Sheridan handled things.

"You know, Sheridan, Kendall and I can do this together if you want to go back home," I said.

"Are you kidding me? If you two are there, then I'm all in, too."

I would've cried if I'd had any tears left. But since I was empty, I hugged Sheridan first, then Kendall. And as we grabbed our purses, my cell rang.

Looking down at the screen, I shrieked, "It's Angel!"

Sheridan and Kendall stood so close to me that if anyone was watching, the three of us would have looked like one person. "Angel, baby, are you okay?"

"Hi, Mom." She sounded so exhausted, like she hadn't slept all night.

"Baby, I love you. Where are you?"

"I'm back at Mom Caroline's," she said, and I did not miss the way she didn't mention her father. "She said that I had to call you and tell you that I was all right."

"Oh, thank you, Jesus. Baby, I'm so sorry, but I'll be right there—"

"Mom, no! No!"

"Please, baby."

"No, Mom. I need a little bit of time."

Angel was barely twelve. What did she know about needing time? Were those her words or was she saying what Caroline told her to say?

"I just want to see you, give you a hug."

"Mom!"

"I'm coming," I insisted.

From the corner of my eye, I could see Sheridan motioning

with her hand, trying to get me to be calm. So, I took a deep breath and spoke softer, slower. "Angel, baby, I won't come over there now."

"Thanks," she said quietly.

"But I can't wait to see you tomorrow. And then we can talk, okay?"

There was a passing moment, and then, "Okay."

I breathed. "I'll come and pick you up about—"

"No, send Ms. Martinez like you always do."

"Okay," I said, agreeing to Angel's final term in this negotiation. All that was left to say was what was most important. "I love you, Angel. I love you so much."

Seconds ticked and ticked and ticked. Then a soft "I love you, too, Mom." She hung up after that, not giving me a final good-bye. But that was okay because she'd given me something better. She'd given me hope.

My eyes were still on the cell-phone screen when I felt Sheridan's and Kendall's arms wrap around me. They stood, one on each side, holding me up, more figuratively than literally. But it was the figurative embrace that I needed the most.

"She's coming home!"

"Yes, she is," Sheridan and Kendall said together.

"She's gonna be okay," Sheridan said.

"I feel that way," I said.

Kendall just had to add, "Of course she's gonna be all right. I mean, how much damage can be done walking in on your mother with her legs spread wide open on a big-screen TV?"

Sheridan and I looked at Kendall.

"What?" she asked.

And then I busted out laughing. I laughed, and laughed and laughed. I laughed so hard I couldn't stand. I laughed until I fell back onto the front pew. Then I laughed and kicked up my feet. I laughed until I cried.

Sheridan Hart Goodman

*Bridges Burned*

# Chapter
## Eighteen

Brock rolled off of me and I felt the release of his weight, but aftershocks still rolled through my body.

How did this man do it? Six years of marriage and he still had me calling out his name . . . every single time.

We were both on our backs, huffing and puffing, our eyes focused on the ceiling. As I lay there, I just hoped that the beat of my heart would soon steady, or else I was going to have to stay in this bed forever.

Minutes had passed by the time I was able to speak. "You know what that was like?" I breathed.

"What?" Brock was as out of breath as I was.

"That was like . . . having room service . . . all night long."

He laughed and punched his fist into the air. "I'm the man!"

I propped myself up, looked down at him, and didn't say a word. All I did was stare and think that he was still the finest man I'd ever seen. And I wasn't saying that just because a part of my body was still shivering. Even absent the afterglow of a toe-curling orgasm, Brock Eugene Goodman was fine and I loved me some him. "So, you're the man, huh?"

He grinned.

"Well, good morning, Mister Man."

He lifted his head and gave me a quick peck with his soft, full lips. "Good morning and Happy Valentine's Day."

I smiled. "Valentine's Day was Friday."

"And I told you then that we were gonna rock this bed all weekend." He gave me a side glance. "You didn't believe me?"

I laughed. "It wasn't that I didn't believe you. I just didn't know that you meant it literally. All Friday night, all yesterday . . ."

He stopped me. "No, yesterday you got out of this bed for two hours, remember? You had to go meet Asia."

Yeah . . . Brock and I were in the middle of doing our thing when I got the call from Asia. All she'd said was my name, and I could tell that my girl was in trouble. I was just so grateful that Brock understood. He knew that Kendall, Asia, and I were prayer partners from way back. Our friendship was unlikely, but it was the real deal. Whenever one of them called, I went. Brock would even drive me to meet them, if he had to.

But now, being reminded about yesterday and Asia took a bit of my joy away. Thinking about my friend and what she was going through . . . I just prayed that Angel went home today.

Before I became too melancholy, my husband pulled me into his arms. "So you owe me a few more hours, woman! We're not getting out of bed today."

"We can't stay in bed . . . what about church?"

"I have a feeling that God is pleased with what I'm about to do to you."

I laughed. "This is my gift for marrying a younger man."

"And you're my gift for living my life right."

See? This man, our marriage . . . nothing but perfection. "So, we're really not going to church?"

"Not today." He lifted his head up a little and glanced down at me. "You think I'm playing? You have to make up for yesterday. And we're gonna lose a couple of hours tonight when we go out to dinner with our son and Evon . . ."

I didn't hear anything he said beyond "our son." Tingles traveled through my body once again. He'd just given me another orgasm, a mental one. All night he'd shown me how much he loved me. Now he was telling me the same thing, without even mentioning my name.

He loved me and he loved my children. Before he'd even put a ring on it, he'd taken my son, Christopher, and my daughter, Tori, into his heart. He didn't even meet Christopher until he was sixteen, and Tori when she was ten. But to Brock, Christopher was his son, Tori was his daughter.

Leaning forward, I kissed his nose. "Yes, dinner with Christopher and Evon and wedding plans. I hope they won't be insulted when we tell them that we want to help."

Brock shook his head. "Nope, they won't be. They're smart enough to take our money."

I laughed and then swung my legs over the side of the bed. Glancing over my shoulder, I said, "I'm going to get coffee. Do you want anything?"

He gave me one of those dirty-old-man sneers.

I slapped his arm. "We just finished."

"Yeah, but I already told you what's about to go down. Are you telling me that you're not up to it?" he challenged me.

"Oh, now see." I stood and grabbed my robe from the lounger across the bedroom. "You're gonna make me come back in here and hurt you."

He laughed. "Bring it on. And, oh, yeah, bring me some coffee, too."

I scampered out of the room and dashed through the cool house. Usually by now the rich aroma of brewing coffee filled

the first floor of our home. My mom, one of those six a.m. ris-
ers, always got the coffee going. But my mom had gone to San
Francisco to spend a few weeks with my brother and his family. So, coffee duty was on me.

Not having my coffee ready when I rolled out of bed was
only one of the things that I missed when my mom was away,
but I had to admit, it was wonderful having the house to ourselves this weekend. With Christopher living on his own, and
Tori back at school at Hampton University, Brock and I had
traipsed through the house naked all weekend. And I guess
we were going to spend most of today that way, too. Maybe
today we'd try to cover every single room.

I shuddered just thinking about it, but then the ringing
telephone broke through my moment. I didn't even realize I'd
left my cell in the kitchen, and I grabbed it from the counter.

"Sheridan?" the woman said right after I said hello.

Since I didn't recognize the voice, I said, "Who's speaking?" before I committed myself. Not that I was hiding from
anyone. All of our bills were paid, no one in the family was
running from the police. But if someone was calling my
house, they needed to identify themselves first.

"This is Harmony."

Her image came right to my mind. The voluptuous woman
who'd come to my home on Christmas and just about ruined
our Christmas brunch. Not that it was her fault. I didn't know
her, and she didn't know me.

But she'd shown up at Christmas with my ex-husband,
Quentin. And that had been a shocker. I couldn't get over the
fact that Quentin had come to my home with a woman that he
introduced as his fiancée. Not that I didn't want happiness for
Quentin, but with a woman?

The man was gay!

At least that's what he told me when he walked out of our

seventeen-year marriage, back in 2004, leaving me to pick up the emotional pieces.

But he'd come here on Christmas professing that he was no longer gay. Well, he didn't exactly say that. That was my guess since he was talking about marrying this much younger woman as soon as this coming June.

"Sheridan?" she called my name.

"Oh, I'm sorry, Harmony. I'm just surprised . . ."

"I'm sure you are. I'm probably the last person you expected to hear from."

"That's true," and then I paused, stopping myself from asking, *What in the world do you want?*

"I hate to bother you so early on a Sunday," Harmony said.

"That's fine, we're awake."

"Good." I heard her relief-filled exhale. "I've been thinking about calling you for the last few weeks . . . I just kept changing my mind. But today I decided to just do it."

"Okay?" That word came out like a question instead of a statement, but that was because truly, I just wanted her to get to the point.

"I'm hoping . . . I would like . . . Sheridan, can we get together for lunch? There are some things . . . I would just like for us to talk."

There was not one thing that Harmony and I had to talk about. And then I put that thought in reverse. There was something—Quentin Hart.

Yeah, we could talk about Quentin because I had some questions myself. I'd tried to get my questions answered at Christmas. All through our brunch, I'd asked Harmony if she'd known that Quentin was gay, I'd asked if Quentin had really changed, I'd asked if she really expected to have children with this man. But from my mother to my children, everyone had jumped all over me, saying that what was going on with Quentin was none of my business. And so none of my questions had been answered.

But if it was just me and Harmony, maybe I'd be able to find out the whole truth. Because my gut told me something was going on.

When I hesitated, she hurried to say, "I mean, I know you probably think it's crazy, the fiancée calling the ex-wife, and it's probably a dumb idea because we don't even know each other. You must think I'm foolish. You know what? I'm sorry to disturb you and—"

"No," I inserted, stopping her jabbering. "It's fine. I would love to get together with you."

"Oh, thank you!" she said as if she'd been holding her breath. "Thank you so much."

"When do you want to do it?"

"I was thinking the sooner the better, if that's all right with you."

I wanted to tell her to come right over now, but the problem was that my husband was here. And he'd already told me his plans for today.

"Can I call you back tonight or tomorrow? I have to find out my work schedule for the week."

"Sure," I said, and then, with a few more words, we said good-bye. I dropped the phone back into the receiver and stood there, leaning on the counter, thinking about every word she'd said. She'd given me no clue about what she wanted, but that didn't matter. I had enough questions for the both of us.

After our fiasco at Christmas, everyone asked me why did I care about Quentin? It wasn't that I cared about him. It was just that for the life of me, I couldn't understand. Even after all of these years, I couldn't wrap my mind around what had happened. When after all those years of a wonderful marriage, he'd told me that while he loved me, he'd fallen in love with Jett Jennings, one of our friends.

With one of my best uppercuts from kickboxing, I'd knocked him down, and then kicked him out that same day. Then I went to work to heal my heart and I met Brock during that time. So, I was good. My life was great and I was fine.

There was just that one nagging, lagging question that had been in my mind since the moment Quentin had looked me in the eye and told me he was gay . . . did I do anything to make my husband switch teams?

And then, just when I was beginning to finally dismiss my question as ridiculous, Quentin shows up with a woman that he wants to marry. Now I couldn't stop asking myself what part did I play in Quentin being gay?

I know, I know . . . that question was stupid, absurd, preposterous. But that question was in my heart and everyone knows that the heart isn't always smart.

So meeting Harmony . . . maybe talking to her would help me. If I could get my questions answered, I'd be able to move on. I'd never look back at Quentin or our life together.

Forget about the coffee! I scurried back into the bedroom to tell Brock.

"No!"

"What?"

"No," Brock repeated, even after I'd asked him for clarification. Then he continued, "I mean it, Sheridan, don't do it."

Okay, there were a couple of things wrong with the way this scenario was playing out. I was a grown woman. A grown black woman who made her own decisions. No one had the right to tell me what to do. And the look on my face sent that message to my husband. Or maybe it was the way I'd crossed my arms, twisted my lips, and glared down at him in the bed with a "come again?" stance.

That had to be why Brock softened his voice. "I just don't think it's a good idea. Think about it. Your ex's fiancée wants to get together with you. What good can come of this?"

Was Brock kidding? So much could come out of this. Like finally having answers.

"It's not like we're going to be planning death and destruction," I said. "Harmony said she just wanted to talk."

"About what?"

I shrugged. "Maybe she thinks I can give her some ideas about her wedding. Maybe she wants to know Quentin's favorite song for their first dance."

The long, hard stare that Brock gave me said so much, so clearly. He might as well have just called me a liar.

"Look," I said. "I don't know what she wants. But what's the harm in finding out?"

"You don't need to find out anything. You need to stay out of their business."

"She didn't say anything about discussing their business."

"Sheridan . . ."

"Okay, so let's say she does want to discuss their business. Maybe she has the same kinds of questions I had at Christmas."

"And how are you gonna help her when you have the same questions?"

I didn't say anything because that was a good point.

He said, "You'll just be two women sitting there asking each other questions. It won't even be a conversation. Just a bunch of questions going back and forth."

Imagining me and Harmony sitting at some Starbucks, asking each other questions and never getting an answer was kind of funny. And even though I was a little miffed at Brock trying to tell me what to do, I smiled. Just a little.

My smile was enough to make him toss the covers aside and push himself off the bed. "Baby, please don't do this."

My eyes roamed over the terrain of his naked body as he strolled toward me.

"We're having a fantastic Valentine's Day weekend. Let's not bring OPD into it."

OPD. Brock's acronym for Other People's Drama.

"Please," he said again.

When he wrapped his arms around me, I sighed. When he pressed soft moist lips against me, I dropped my arms to my side. And when he said, "Please," again, I agreed.

After all, how could I say no to a fine, butt-naked, begging man who had his body pressed up against mine? It was a no-brainer. And as Brock kissed me, I thought, Harmony who?

# Chapter Nineteen

Okay, Asia, I'll check on you tonight." I clicked off my cell and whispered, "Thank you, Jesus."

I was so grateful that Angel was home. Honestly, even though I'd kept telling Asia that everything was going to be all right, I couldn't say that I was sure about it. There was a part of me that had wondered on Saturday if Angel would come home on Sunday. Of course, I hadn't said that to Asia and I hadn't even mentioned it to Kendall. But I was worried that Angel would want to stay with Caroline. And I was even more worried that Caroline would be encouraging Angel to stay. After what Asia had told me and Kendall—how Caroline had set it all up, deliberately embarrassing Angel and Asia and Bobby—there wasn't a thing that I didn't think Caroline Fitzgerald Johnson would do to win.

But it seemed that Caroline had won enough. Angel was home with Asia, and Bobby was home with Caroline. I shook my head. The things some women went through . . . but then I paused. What was I talking about? I'd gone through my own marital trauma—with Quentin. Which was exactly why I was here.

I pushed open my car door, though there wasn't much room. I'd squeezed into this parking space in this small lot, right behind the Starbucks on Beverly near Cedars-Sinai Hospital.

Inside, I stood by the door and took a panoramic glance around. The coffee shop was poppin', like every other Starbucks in America at just before nine in the morning. It took a couple of seconds, but I finally spotted Harmony at a table in the corner in the back. Her head was down, her shoulders were slumped as if she were trying to make herself smaller.

I glanced at the line of patrons; I really wanted a chocolate chai, but what I wanted more than my favorite Starbucks beverage was to get to the good part, so I strolled toward Harmony.

As I walked, every single one of Brock's no's rang in my mind. He'd told me no over and over again on Sunday, and then yesterday he'd repeated it as if he wanted to make sure that I'd heard him the first hundred times. It was almost like my husband didn't trust me. As if he knew that I wouldn't be able to resist getting together with Harmony.

Well, one thing I could say about Brock Goodman was that he knew his wife.

And I knew that my husband was probably right. Meeting with Harmony was no doubt like juggling dynamite. Which was why I'd decided on Sunday that if she didn't call me, I wasn't going to call her.

But then she'd called last night, and I was all prepared to do what my husband requested, until she said, "Sheridan, you don't have any idea how much I appreciate you meeting with me. I don't have anyone else to talk to."

Being the loving, caring woman that my mother raised me to be, how in the world was I supposed to turn her away after that?

So, all I could say was "When do you want to get together?" And Harmony and I made plans to meet.

Because I didn't want Brock to know, I changed things up a little this morning. Normally, I rose when he did. But today, I'd stayed in bed until Brock was ready to leave for work.

"Are you okay?" he'd asked me when he'd sat on the edge of my side of the bed.

I felt guilty as he stroked my back, his concern for me in his touch and on his face. "Yeah, I was just so tired yesterday that I thought I'd sleep in this morning. I think I'm still recovering from our weekend."

He'd grinned. "I wore you out, huh?"

I let him believe that; at least it would assuage some of my guilt, and he wouldn't walk out of the house worrying about me. But the moment I heard the garage door close, I jumped from the bed. Harmony had said she wanted to meet as early as I could because she had to be at Cedars-Sinai, where she worked as an RN, at noon.

I'd told her nine was fine with me; three hours would give me more than enough time to get all the information I wanted.

"Harmony?"

Her eyes were filled with surprise when she looked up. As if she didn't think I'd come. "I'm glad you're here." She tried to upturn her lips into some semblance of a smile, and as I slid into the chair across from her, I smiled back.

With a quick glance, I took in the flowered top she wore. I'd seen this kind of uniform before; no longer did nurses wear just white. The modest smock made Harmony look quite different than she did on Christmas. On that day, she had on a silk wrap dress that displayed every one of her physical blessings.

"Thank you for coming," she said, looking so much younger without makeup.

And looking younger was quite a feat. Because when I met her at Christmas, I'd wondered how many years had she been out of high school? I'd been shocked when she said she was thirty-five. But today, she looked like she hadn't even graduated yet.

"No problem." And then I was silent. And she was silent, too.

I had no idea how to get us started until Harmony said, "You know, after I asked if you could meet me this morning, I wondered if this time was convenient for you. I never asked if you worked outside of your home."

"I'm self-employed," I said. This gave me the chance to bring up my ex-husband. "Actually, Quentin and I had a business together . . . a greeting-card company. Hart to Heart, which I've continued. It's pretty successful." I shrugged. "Hallmark is my largest client, though now I do a lot of digital sites, too."

"Wow."

I tilted my head to the side. "Quentin never told you?"

She shook her head, and that was when I saw all kinds of sadness in her eyes, so different from the day we met when she acted like she'd been dipped in complete joy. On that day, she radiated happiness, thrilled to be engaged to Dr. Quentin Hart. But today, she looked like she hadn't really smiled in the seven weeks that had passed since Christmas.

"Quentin never told me about your business. He hasn't told me too much of anything," she said.

*How can you be engaged to a man who hasn't told you anything?* That's what I wanted to ask. But I was trying to be way more diplomatic than I'd been on Christmas Day. So, instead of just bombarding her with everything that was on my mind, I said, "So, you didn't know he was gay?"

She bit her lip as if she had to think about what she was

going to say. "I don't know how to answer that because Quentin says he's not gay."

*The devil is a lie,* I said inside.

She continued before I could say those words out loud. "He was honest; he told me that he'd been with men and women, though he didn't tell me that right away."

If he didn't tell you right away, he *wasn't* honest. But I kept that thought to myself and let her go on.

"But when he did finally tell me, he told me everything."

Yeah, right.

"He told me that was the reason your marriage ended. He said that you couldn't handle his revelation that he was interested in men."

"You think?" came out of my mouth before I could stop myself. What kind of nonsense was that? "What woman could handle her husband being gay?" I was about to continue my rant, but I paused when Harmony lowered her eyes and wrapped her hands tighter around her coffee cup.

She said, "By the time he told me, I was all in. I loved him, and so I believed him. And he said he never cheated on you. He said that he would never cheat on anyone he loved."

I didn't hesitate for a moment. "I believe that, Harmony. At least, I believe that he didn't cheat, physically. But that didn't matter because he was already in love with Jett when he finally told me, so there was some kind of cheating going on."

She squinted her eyes, tilted her head, and studied me. "That was his name . . . Jett?"

For someone who was about to marry a man who'd been with men, Harmony knew nothing. I wanted to tell her to put on her Nikes and run, but I nodded and said, "Yes, Jett. Actually, he was a friend of ours." I paused. "But let me ask you something. Don't you think you should be having this conversation with Quentin?"

Harmony sighed and shrugged at the same time. "We've talked a lot. But recently, I've felt like there's something . . . I don't know . . . missing. Maybe I wasn't paying attention before. His being with men in the past didn't bother me because when you look at Quentin, he's such a man."

Really?

"And he loves sports . . ."

She has to be kidding.

"And fast cars . . ."

She was killing me! She was thirty-five, but she was talking like she was twelve. "Well, clearly, all of that has nothing to do with being gay or not being gay. He was doing all of that when we were married and he was gay then."

She frowned just a little. "That's the third time you've said that. Why do you keep calling him gay?"

I couldn't do a thing but give this girl a blank stare.

"I mean," she continued, "yeah, he has been with men, but why can't it be exactly the way he said—that he was curious, and just experimenting."

Okay, I got it now. Harmony wanted me to be her "yes" girl. Just say yes to everything that she hoped to be true. "Look, I'm not trying to convince you of anything and I'm not trying to get in your business with Quentin." I paused; that was a lie. I was only there to get in their business. But suddenly I didn't want to know, I didn't need any answers. All I wanted to do was leave. I said, "I only came because you said you wanted to talk and I thought . . . maybe I could help a little, but I don't think this is helping at all."

"No, no, no!" she said quickly. "I appreciate you coming, I appreciate hearing everything you have to say." She paused and slowed down her words. "Please don't misunderstand; I'm not saying that what you're telling me isn't true. It's just that this is all so overwhelming and confusing and I'm just trying to grasp this idea."

"Okay," I said, a bit calmer now, "because I don't want you to think that I'm doing anything to get between you and Quentin."

She shook her head. "I'm the one who called you. All of this has been heavy on my mind, ever since Christmas. You had so many questions; it was like you knew something that no one else did."

It was interesting that she put it that way because that's how I felt then, and really, that's what I was feeling as I sat there with Harmony. But what I felt most was that Brock had been right. I needed to get my butt home.

"I'm really sorry about what happened at Christmas. It was just that it was such a shock to meet you."

"I understand."

"But still, that was no excuse to make you feel uncomfortable in my home."

"But you asked good questions. You made me think, and after we left, I tried to talk to Quentin about everything you said, but he brushed it all aside. He said that you were still angry because of what happened between the two of you."

I narrowed my eyes. Harmony should've kept that part to herself, because now I wanted to go in. Now I wanted to tell her that Quentin *was* gay and she'd be a fool to marry him. But I pressed my lips together and moved to the edge of the chair, ready to go. "All I can say is that if you believe him—"

"I believe him!" she said a bit strongly.

"Then there's nothing more to say, is there?"

She nodded at first, but then shook her head. "I just don't want to make the wrong decision."

From the moment I'd met Harmony, I wondered what the sophisticated Dr. Quentin Hart saw in the woman that back in the day we called an around-the-way girl. But now I got it. Finally, I could see their commonality. They were two confused souls.

She said, "My friends were telling me that I shouldn't marry a man who's been with other men because once he does that, he'll always go back. But I didn't believe them. I just packed my bags and moved here so that I could be with Quentin."

"Really?" I asked, wanting to kick myself for the way I scooted back in the chair. I needed to get this checked out—my curiosity was out of control. Maybe there was some kind of medicine I could take for it, but until then, I wanted to hear about this move.

She nodded. "We did that long-distance-dating thing for a while and then a job opened up at Cedars-Sinai. Not that I was looking for anything here in L.A., I wasn't ready to move. But Quentin found the position, and it paid a lot more than I was making in Detroit. So, it seemed like the right thing to do." She paused. "But now, L.A. is so far from Detroit and I'm here alone, and I'm wondering . . ."

I told myself to get up, say good-bye, and get out. But instead I said, "Harmony, if you have any doubts, you've got to go with your gut. If your gut is telling you to marry Quentin, go with it. If your gut is telling you something else . . ." I stopped there. She had to be the one to finish that sentence.

She nodded. "My heart is telling me I'll be fine. Quentin told me that I needed to get all of these thoughts out of my head. He said that once we were married, he wouldn't be with a man or a woman. He said if God combined every man and every woman on earth, that person still wouldn't measure up to me. So why would he want to be with anyone else?"

Well, I couldn't fault her for falling for a line like that. That was Quentin Hart. When we were married, he made my knees weak with the lines he used to give me . . .

*What word can I use to describe you, Sheridan? Happiness,*

*serenity, joy? No, I've got it . . . everything. That's the perfect word because you're my everything.*

I used to swoon when he said things like that, and he used to say things like that all day long.

"Harmony, all I can tell you is that Quentin is a good man. He wasn't the right man for me, but he is a good person. He's been an incredible father to our children and my mother still loves him."

That brought a smile to Harmony's face.

"But that's really all I can say. Everything else is up to you."

"You're right."

I sat on the edge of my chair, so ready to walk out of this woman's life forever. But it was the aura of sadness that hovered over her that made me want to stay just a little bit longer. And, it made me ask, "Do you have any friends here?"

"Not yet. I've been working a couple of double shifts, and when I'm not working, I'm with Quentin. But I know I need to do something. I think that's part of my problem. I don't have anything else to occupy my mind. So when I'm not working or not with Quentin . . . I'm thinking."

That's what happened. All of these weeks, that's all Harmony had been doing. Thinking about my questions, and now she had so many doubts.

"Well, I'm sure you'll have a bunch of new friends soon. Maybe some nurses at the hospital."

She nodded. "I hope so. And the first of the month, I'm going to my sorority meeting. The Deltas will certainly keep me busy."

"You're a Delta?"

"Yes!" She grinned the type of grin that she wore at Christmas. "I'm a proud member of Delta Sigma Theta."

I sat back. "Really? I am, too!"

"Oh, my goodness! We're sorors! Well, now I understand why you came to talk to me. You just have a Delta's heart. Are you active?"

"No, but I need to be. I haven't been active in a few years, but I promised myself that after Christopher's wedding, I was going to become active again."

"That would be great. Maybe we can join the same chapter."

Inside, I screamed, *No.* Outside, I said, "Maybe." This time, when I pushed myself to the edge of my chair, I finally stood up. "I have to get going." I didn't have anyplace where I needed to be, but I didn't need to be here. "Are you walking out?" I asked when she stayed seated.

"No, I'm going to go to work from here. So maybe I'll catch up on some reading and do some thinking."

I wanted to tell her to stop thinking. That's what had her so confused. She needed to be praying . . . and for a moment I thought about asking her if she wanted to come to one of our prayer meetings. But in the next moment I remembered my prayer partners and the things they might say to Harmony. Plus, how weird would it be to be praying with my ex's next. No, the prayer group was out. What I would do was pray for her as much as I could.

Looking down at her, I said, "It'll all work out."

Harmony stood and I gave her a quick hug before I turned and walked out the door, moving faster than when I came in. But no matter how quickly I walked, I couldn't outpace my thoughts.

Harmony was looking for any reason to believe Quentin, and I didn't believe a word he said. That man was gay and I had no idea what he was trying to prove with Harmony. But whatever it was, it was going to have to stay between the two of them.

As I turned over my car's engine, I thought about what I'd say to Brock when he asked me about my day the way he did every evening when he came home. I needed to get to working on what I would say. Because I wasn't about to tell him about this.

I'd never talk about it and I'd never do it again. I was sorry, but my soror was on her own with this one.

# Chapter Twenty

M r. and Mrs. Goodman."
    I broke away from our kiss when the waiter called our names, but my eyes stayed on my husband. It was Brock who turned away and told the young man to come inside.

After he stepped through the drapes, the waiter held out a menu. "Dessert?"

When Brock glanced back at me, I slowly and seductively shook my head. "We'll have dessert at home," I whispered into his ear.

My husband's face filled with a grin. Turning back to the waiter, he said, "Check, please. Quick!"

"It's right here, sir."

I massaged Brock's thigh as he pulled out his credit card and handed it to the waiter. When the man stepped away, Brock twisted and pulled me into his arms once again.

"Thank you for this, baby," I said.

His response: he pulled me deeper into his embrace.

I couldn't count the ways I loved this man. For no reason at all, Brock had come home tonight carrying a cloth garment bag.

"This is for you," he said.

I was spoiled. This was nothing unusual. Brock always brought home gifts for me, my mom, and even Tori, when she was home. But as if this were the first time, I clapped my hands. Who could ever tire of being treated like this? "Thank you! But what's the occasion?"

"Dinner."

"Dinner?" I looked at him and at the same time scrolled through my mind trying to remember what event I'd forgotten.

Brock said, "This morning, I decided that I wanted to have a great dinner with my wife. So, I made reservations for us at Rendezvous at seven." He glanced at his watch. "You better get moving."

This was what life was like with a man who told me and showed me how much I was loved. I'd thanked him with a kiss that any other time would have led us straight to the bed. But I pulled back, leaving him breathless, and dashed into our bedroom to get ready for our Thursday-night rendezvous at one of the premier restaurants in the city.

Within a half hour, I was wearing (and really feeling) the red wrap, knee-length dress that Brock had selected for me. And another thirty minutes after that, we were snuggled on the butter-soft leather sofa at the restaurant.

Rendezvous had to be one of the most romantic places in the world. The restaurant was owned and managed by a group of ex–football players who'd really pimped it out. Designed only for parties of two, each seating area was set up like an intimate living room, with a small round table for dinner, then a cozy love seat where patrons could enjoy after-dinner drinks and dessert. And each setting was behind heavy brocade drapes, giving maximum privacy for guests to enjoy their dinners in whatever way they wished.

The ambience by itself would've been enough, but the food was world-class. Adolphe Baptiste, the chef, was a black French-man who combined the French dishes he'd grown up enjoying, with his new love . . . soul food. So the menu was filled with the kind of cuisine that could only be found at Rendezvous: barbe-cue chicken quiche, jambalaya tarts. And the desserts: pumpkin éclairs and anything you could ever imagine, chocolate.

It was always hard to leave this place, but as Brock held me now, I couldn't wait to get home to tell him, and show him, how much I loved *him*.

"Mr. Goodman?" the waiter called once again from out-side of the drapes.

"Yes."

He stepped into our space, and as Brock signed the check, I swung my legs onto the floor and slipped back into my shoes. Brock stood, then helped me up, and held my hand as we walked through the restaurant. I once again marveled at how blessed I was to call this man my husband. And like I often did, I said a silent prayer that Brock and I would be this happy all the days of our lives.

Brock stepped in front of me to push open the door just as another man was stepping inside. Both moved so fast they bumped into each other.

"Excuse me," the men said together, then looked up.

"Brock!"

"Quentin!"

My husband and my ex-husband spoke at the same time.

And, as they spoke, I did, too. "Jett!" I said, looking at the man who'd stepped into the restaurant with Quentin.

"Hello, Sheridan," Jett said to me.

Shock made me stand still for a moment as I looked this man up and down and calculated how long it'd been since I'd last seen him.

It had been almost ten years. I'd seen Jett just weeks after Quentin had told me that he'd fallen in love with this pro golfer who'd been his old friend and had become his new lover.

A few weeks after Quentin left me, Jett had done the unthinkable; he'd come to my home asking why I wouldn't let my then-ten-year-old daughter spend the weekend with him and Quentin. Jett had stepped to me boldly, with audacity, and he'd been dumb enough to come unarmed.

I'd wanted to beat him down then, and even now, just remembering, I felt my fingers curling into fists.

"How've you been?" Jett asked me, like he'd forgotten that we weren't friends.

"I'm . . . good . . ." I stuttered. I glanced from Jett to Quentin then back to Jett before I heard Brock clear his throat. "Oh . . ." Turning to him, I said, "This is my husband, Brock." Then, glancing at Brock, I said, "And this is Jett. Jett Jennings. Quentin's . . ." I left a blank at the end of my sentence and looked at my ex to finish for me.

Quentin said, "Friend." And with a smile that he passed to Jett, he added, "Jett's my friend." He spoke with no shame, no concern that he'd been seen by me and Brock.

My husband reached toward Jett, and when they shook hands, I wanted to slap Jett's hand away. Wanted to tell him to keep his hands off my man. Wanted to tell him that I didn't trust him around any man that I loved.

Then the four of us just stood there, exchanging glances, saying nothing. Seconds passed. Then more seconds of standing, more seconds of nothing.

Then, "Well . . ." all four of us said at the same time.

"We were just leaving," Brock said, saving us all. "Good to see you, Quentin, nice to meet you, Jett."

My husband spoke for me because I said nothing to either

one of them as I brushed past, relieved to be on our way outside so that I could breathe.

Brock didn't say a word as we walked to the end of the restaurant's carpeted entrance. Not until he gave his ticket to the valet attendant, then turned to me, and together we said, "Awkward."

"Who are you telling?" I asked.

"So . . . that's Jett, huh?"

I nodded. "I'm surprised you remembered his name." Of course, I'd told Brock the entire tragedy of the quick demise of my marriage. He knew everything from my shock, my hurt, and finally my deliverance from Quentin having any kind of hold on my heart.

"Well, yeah. His name isn't that common. But even if I didn't know, I would've by the way you glared at him."

"That obvious?"

"Sweetheart, if I didn't get us out of there, I was gonna have to pull you off of him." He chuckled.

"You know me well, 'cause I did think about hitting him. Just knocking him out the way I'd knocked out Quentin. The way I see it, I owe Jett one."

"That's what I love about you. You're so warm and fuzzy."

He laughed; I didn't.

"Awww, come on." He put his hand around my shoulders.

"I just don't like that man."

"Well, the good news is that you don't have to like him, and you don't have to see him again. Remember, that's Quentin's life, right?"

I nodded.

Brock's cell phone rang, and as he answered, I glanced back at the restaurant. What were those two doing here? I turned from the restaurant and glanced at Brock, still on his phone.

"Baby, I'm gonna run to the restroom," I whispered. Then I made my move before my husband could stop me, before he could give me any kind of warning.

Rushing through the restaurant's doors, I had to pause for my eyes to adjust to the dim light. And in that moment I wondered what was I doing back in here? First of all, I needed to really get delivered from this curiosity thing that I had going. And second, even if I wanted to snoop around, I couldn't. Not with the way this restaurant was set up.

The hostess greeted me with a smile. "Mrs. Goodman, is everything all right?"

"Yes," I said, giving her the same restroom story I'd given Brock.

"The restrooms are right over there," she said, pointing toward the bar.

I thanked her, then moved as slowly as I could without looking like a stalker. And again, I asked myself what did I expect to see? Even if I knew where Quentin and Jett had been seated, I wouldn't be able to see or hear a thing unless I peeked my head inside their drapes.

This really was ridiculous, but since I was already back by the restroom, I decided to use it. But the entire time, my mind was on Quentin and Jett.

They'd walked in so casually, so comfortably, like they'd always been together. They'd looked that way the first time I'd ever seen the two of them together. It had been days after Quentin had left, and they were on the golf course. They moved in concert with each other, one the melody, the other the harmony. I remember thinking that they were old friends who looked like new lovers.

Today, they just looked like old lovers.

Seriously . . . the way they'd walked in here. I knew it; Quentin hadn't changed.

And then I thought about Harmony.

Quentin's fiancée and my soror. This was why she was questioning herself. It wasn't because of me and all the questions I'd asked at Christmas. It was because she knew; Harmony knew in her heart.

But as I washed my hands, I washed away all thoughts of Quentin, Harmony, and Jett. This was their drama; and just like my husband had told me, I needed to stay out of it. I was really going to work on doing that.

Drying my hands, and then tossing away the towel, I swung open the bathroom door, rushed into the hall, and right into the chest of a man. He caught my arm as I stumbled backward.

"I'm sorry," I said, and looked up. And then I snatched my arm away from his grasp.

Jett held up his hands as if he were surrendering. "I was just trying to make sure that you didn't fall." He started to walk away and I stopped him.

"What are you doing here?" I asked him.

He turned to face me. "Here? At Rendezvous?" He paused. "I'm here with Quentin."

"I thought you moved away. Left Los Angeles."

"I did. I'm back." He grinned. "Why're you asking? Were you planning a welcome-home party for me?"

See, this was one reason why I didn't like this man. The few interactions we'd had after he'd taken my husband from me, I always felt like he was taunting me, teasing me, reminding me that he had won.

"I wouldn't even plan your funeral," I said.

He laughed. "Well, I'd love to stand here and chat, but . . ." He paused and then he came a little closer so that I could see his eyes. "Quentin's waiting for me."

Taunting, teasing . . . or maybe he was testing me. Maybe he thought that I still wanted *his* man.

I said, "Quentin's engaged. Did you know that?"

"Why're you telling me?"

"'Cause I think you need to know."

He raised a single eyebrow. "You sound like you still care about Quentin," he said.

"I care about the father of my children. I care that he's well, and that he's happy."

"Well, then," he said, with a bit of a smirk. "If that's what you care about, then be glad that I'm back in L.A. because Quentin and I are good friends. And everyone needs to have good friends around them." Then, with just a little chuckle, but without another word, he stepped into the men's room. Leaving me in that darkened hall to think about all that he'd said. Leaving me there to realize that this man was nothing but a snake. The devil, for real. For whatever reason, Jett had come back for Quentin. And Jett was going to get what he wanted. Quentin having a fiancée? That didn't matter.

I thought about waiting for Jett and telling him that he needed to back away. But that thought lasted for two seconds. He'd just laugh in my face and ask me how could I help Harmony when I hadn't been able to help myself?

So, I just walked toward the front of the restaurant, moving much faster now, my pace totally opposite from the way I'd come in. But this time, sadness and sorrow were the reasons I moved so fast. Harmony was in for the same heartbreak that had come to me.

Brock was sitting in the SUV right in front of the restaurant and the valet held the door as I stepped into the car.

When the attendant closed the door, Brock tilted his head. "You all right?"

I nodded as I clicked on my seat belt.

"Just asking 'cause you look like you've seen a ghost."

I turned to him and smiled. "I just want to get home and be with you."

"That's what I'm talking about." He smiled and for once I was grateful that my always sensitive husband wasn't having a sensitive moment right now.

I didn't want Brock to know that I'd talked to Harmony. I didn't want him to know that I'd talked to Jett. Didn't want him to know that that little talk with Jett had changed my mind.

Maybe I did need to have another talk with Harmony. Maybe Quentin and Jett's little secret needed to be exposed.

And, I was just the person to do it.

Maybe.

# Chapter Twenty-One

I'd already texted Kendall and Asia, telling them to meet me in the Learning Center right after service, and ever since I'd sent that text right in the middle of Pastor's sermon, I couldn't wait for the church service to end.

Not that I didn't enjoy my pastor's ministering. I loved to hear Pastor Ford preach. But it was her message today—"Keeping Secrets"—that had me on the edge of my seat.

"That's what I want to talk about today," she'd begun. "Keeping secrets and what part do secrets play in our lives as Christians." After a pause, she said, "Many in our faith will tell you that keeping secrets is a bad thing. That keeping secrets is hiding, holding something in the dark. And when you do something in the dark, what will a Christian tell you?" Pastor Ford held the microphone away from her mouth and pointed it toward the sanctuary.

The congregation piped in, "What's done in the dark will always come to light." We spoke in unison, as if that line had been rehearsed.

"That's right!" Pastor held up her hand and shifted her feet from side to side like she was about to break out in a little jig and testify.

The sanctuary filled with laughter.

But then she stopped suddenly, and the smile left her face. "Here's the thing. Y'all are wrong. You don't even know what you're talking about. But you know, I'm gonna set you straight, right?"

"Right!" someone yelled out as the members laughed again.

"Turn to Matthew 16:20," she told us. But before most of us could open our Bibles or click on the scripture from our tablets, Pastor Ford said, "Let me just tell you what it says, 'cause this is so good, I can't slow down. Jesus told the disciples not to tell anyone that He was the Messiah. He told them to keep it a secret." The way she shut her Bible, then stood back, she might as well have dropped the mic and walked away from the altar.

"So, if keeping people in the dark is always bad, why did Jesus tell the disciples that's what He wanted them to do?"

Usually, I took pages of notes in church because my pastor was a teacher, and even though I'd been under Pastor's leadership for more than twenty years, every single Sunday I learned something.

But today, my notebook had stayed on my lap. Because this was one of those Sundays when I felt like Pastor Ford might as well have just said, *Sheridan, this is for you.*

"So, keeping secrets, keeping people in the dark, is not necessarily bad," she said. "How do you determine when to do it? How do you determine when you should not?"

There was a bit of grumbling through the sanctuary as members gave their answers.

Pastor Ford said, "Think about motives . . . what's motivating you to keep your secret? Keep something in the dark? Because like this scripture just showed, there are good reasons to do it. Take for example the pastor who counsels his members. He keeps secrets in the name of confidentiality."

"Yes!"

"Amen!"

All kinds of agreements rang out through the sanctuary.

"But it's important to also know that keeping secrets can lead to lying. Because you can commit the sin of lying just by omission. Just by not telling what you know."

I fell back in my seat and Brock looked over at me with an "are you all right?" look.

I nodded and that's when I'd taken out my cell and texted my girls, because now I really needed to talk.

It had been a week of turmoil for me. Ever since Brock and I bumped into Quentin and Jett, I'd gone back and forth, should I say something, should I not? That question filled my mind for all of my waking moments. When I was working, I was thinking about Quentin. When I was cooking, I was thinking about Jett. When I was watching television or reading a book, or working on my iPad, I was thinking about Harmony. For hours at a time, thoughts of these people were the only thoughts in my head.

But last night, when I was making love to my husband and I was distracted by my thoughts . . . that's when I knew I had to bring this to an end.

So one moment I was having an orgasm, and in the next I made a decision. I wasn't going to say a word. Not to anyone, not about anything.

But now, this morning, this message . . . was it meant for me?

It wasn't until Brock stood that I realized the service had ended. I had drifted so far away, I had missed the end of Pastor's sermon and the altar call.

I lowered my head and held up my hand as Pastor Ford

gave the benediction, and when she said her final "Amen," I turned to my husband.

"Babe, I'm gonna meet with Kendall and Asia for a couple of minutes. Is that okay?"

He glanced at his watch. "Uh . . . yeah. But do you think one of them can give you a ride home because a couple of basketball games are coming on today that I've gotta see. Missing them would be against my religion."

I shook my head and smiled. "Of course," I said, really glad that he would be going home instead of waiting. I didn't want to have to rush. "Kendall will give me a ride," I said, thinking that I didn't want to distract Asia for too long because I was sure she wanted to spend as much time with Angel as she could. And anyway, Kendall was the one who was always free.

I kissed Brock's cheek, then hurried up the aisle toward the front door while he headed toward the side exit that led to the parking lot.

My eyes scanned the mass of people who moved slowly through the packed sanctuary. I didn't see Kendall or Asia. We all sat in different parts of the church, but I wasn't worried about them meeting me. Anytime any one of us called, the others came.

I pushed my way through the sanctuary, and kept my feet moving even if someone tried to stop me to say hello. I greeted everyone I knew; it was just that today I didn't stop to chat.

In just minutes, I was across the street in the Learning Center and I dashed into the room where we always met.

"Hey, lady," I said to Kendall, who was already inside.

She'd been pacing, and she stopped to give me a hug. "What's up?" she asked.

"This is a long story, so let's wait for Asia."

"I'm here!" Asia ran into the room just as I said her name.

More hugs and then I closed the door. "Okay, so I called this meeting, but you know I need to do a check-in and checkup on you two." I turned to Asia. "So how're things with Angel?"

She sighed. "We're making it through. She doesn't seem to be as mad at me anymore, but we'll see, 'cause this weekend, she's with Bobby and Caroline."

"Already?" Kendall and I said together.

Asia nodded. "This is their normal weekend and Angel wanted to go. You know I don't want her to, but I can't have her thinking that I'm trying to keep her away from Caroline and Bobby."

"You think Caroline is gonna be cool?" Kendall asked.

"I don't know," she said, shaking her head slightly. "But I hope so, because all she wants is Bobby, and she can have him. No man is worth me losing my daughter."

I reached for Asia and squeezed her hand. That was a tough lesson, but one that I was so glad she'd learned. There were so many other men out there who would appreciate her.

"So what about all that New York stuff? Is she moving?" Kendall asked.

"We haven't even talked about that, but if it comes up"—she paused and looked at Kendall—"I'm gonna do what you suggested. I'll move to New York, too. I've heard of plenty of parents who've done that for their kids."

"Look at you," Kendall said, leaning back a bit. "Acting all grown-up."

Kendall and I laughed, but Asia only smiled. "Don't you think it was about time?"

"Yeah, I do!" Kendall said because there was no way that she could let Asia have the last word.

All I had to do was turn to Kendall and she started talking. "My dad is hanging in there. He's only had a couple of treatments because he's having some severe side effects. Chemo is a mutha, you know."

Asia and I nodded. I said, "If you ever want someone to go with you . . ."

"Thanks, but Dad really likes to do this by himself."

"Oh, my God!" Asia gasped. "I can't believe you let him do that by himself."

"I don't! I *said* he likes to do this by himself, but I go every time." Looking at me, Kendall added, "So, I know he wouldn't want anyone else there, you know?"

"I get that. Just know that we're here." I looked over at Asia and she nodded.

"So what's up?" Kendall asked again, as if she wanted to take the focus off of her father.

I sighed. I wished that she'd let us in more. Asia and I really wanted to be there for her and her dad. But this was as close as Kendall was going to let us get. I had to just take what I could get.

When Kendall glanced at her watch, I asked, "Do you have to meet your dad?"

"No," she said. "Sabrina and Anthony are with him today. I was just asking because when I receive a text in church, it has to be serious."

"Yeah, this is. You may want to sit down."

Asia placed her purse on one of the folding chairs, then she sat down. But Kendall raised her hand and shook her head. "I'm good," she said. Then she glanced down at her Black-Berry, smiled, and typed away, sending a text. She was so distracted, I didn't have any part of her attention.

"Well, anyway, Brock and I went out to dinner last Monday at Rendezvous and—"

"Oh, my God," Asia interrupted, "Bobby and I went there."

And with just those few words, I'd taken Asia back to that sad place. I sighed. With her and Bobby, I had no idea where the emotional land mines were. Everything set her on the verge of tears.

So now I had a distracted Kendall and a solemn Asia.

"Well, anyway . . ." My voice was much softer now, as I tried to tiptoe around Asia's emotions. "We were leaving Rendezvous and we bumped into . . . Quentin and Jett."

It took a moment for the name to register, but then Kendall raised her eyes from her BlackBerry and the emotional water that was in Asia's eyes just a moment before was gone.

"Jett Jennings," Kendall said, sitting down in the chair, her focus totally on me now.

Asia said, "Jett, the guy that Quentin hooked up with when you were married?" Her tears had been replaced by shock.

I nodded slowly.

"Wait a minute . . . didn't you say Rendezvous?" Asia asked as if she was just getting the whole picture.

Kendall answered for me: "She said Rendezvous and she said Quentin and Jett." She shook her head. "Ain't this some mess?" she added.

"Yup!"

Then Distracted Kendall and Solemn Asia fired questions at me:

"Is Quentin gay again?" Asia asked. "Or, is he bi now?"

"Is Quentin back with Jett?" Kendall asked. "How long do you think they've been together?"

I held up my hands. "I have no idea. But here's why I needed to talk to you. I didn't tell you guys this, but Harmony called me a couple of weeks ago, wanting to get together."

"And you didn't tell me?" Kendall said.

"Well, I was just going to leave it alone, but then . . ." I went on to tell them the story from the beginning: about the phone call from Harmony, how Brock told me to stay away, how I'd gone anyway, and what Harmony had asked me and what I'd told her. I even told them how we were both Deltas, and I finished with, "So, I've got to say something to Harmony now, right?"

Kendall and Asia spoke at the same time.

"No!"

"Yes!

Then Kendall and Asia looked at each other. Kendall said, "No," again. "She needs to stay out of this." Then she turned to me. "You need to stay out of this because nothing good can come out of it."

"That's exactly what Brock said," I told them.

"He's right," Kendall said. "The messenger always gets shot."

"That's cynical," Asia said to Kendall. Then she turned to me. "Didn't you hear my aunt's message today?"

"That's what got me thinking. I mean, I'd be keeping Harmony in the dark if I didn't say anything, right?"

Asia nodded and Kendall shook her head.

Asia said, "Yes, and I think women should stick together, and look out for each other."

With wide eyes, Kendall continued to shake her head. "Spoken like a woman who had an affair with a married man."

"It's not the same thing," Asia snapped. "I made a mistake and I asked God to forgive me, so why can't you? Oh, that's right, I forgot . . . you're not big on forgiveness."

"Okay, maybe I shouldn't have said that." Kendall gave her a smirk with that half apology. "But my point is that Sheridan doesn't owe Harmony anything," she said before she turned to me and repeated, "Don't do it. Even if it's just to keep your husband happy because you know what'll happen if you do it and he finds out. He'll be pissed."

"How will Brock find out?" Asia asked.

"Trust and believe he will. And how will that look if he feels like she's keeping secrets from him?"

Kendall and Asia went back and forth as if I wasn't even there. That's how it always was with the two of them, and usually I jumped in and stopped it. But today, I let them go at it because I wanted to hear both sides. Kendall's point: Mind my business. Asia's point: As a woman who knew the truth, this *was* my business.

Asia said, "Plus, y'all are sorors. Shouldn't this be a sister-hood thing or something? Isn't that why women pledge those sororities?"

Before I could say a word, Kendall argued, "Yeah, but you didn't pledge together. You don't even know this woman. You've seen her twice. You don't know how she'll react, you don't know what she'll do. She's not your friend, so you're not obligated to tell her squat."

I nodded, not that I agreed. It was true, Harmony wasn't my friend, but she was my soror. And Kendall wouldn't un-derstand the sisterhood bond that went beyond any kind of friendship.

"I just feel like Harmony came to me, asked me questions, and though I didn't know the answers then, I do now."

"Okay," Kendall said. "Let's play this tape all the way through. Let's say you call Harmony. What're you gonna tell her? That Quentin is back together with Jett? Because you don't know that for sure."

"Oh, please!" Asia waved her hand in the air like she was swatting away Kendall's words. "Two men at a romantic res-taurant? What were they doing there?"

"I have no idea. Which means that whatever answer I give you is just conjecture. And conjecture means nothing. The only thing it will do is mess up someone's life," Kendall said.

"Well, it's not like I plan on saying that he's *involved* with Jett. If I were to talk to Harmony, I'd only say that I saw Quen-tin and Jett together."

Kendall shook her head as Asia nodded hers.

Kendall said, "This ain't nothin' but trouble."

Asia said, "You're doing the right thing."

Kendall huffed.

Asia said to Kendall, "Wouldn't you want someone to tell you if they saw your man all hugged up with another man?" Then she held her finger to her forehead as if she just had a thought. "Oh, wait, you don't have a man."

Asia laughed, and usually this would be the point where Kendall would jump up, ready to fight. At the very least, she'd be stomping out of here. So, it was time to stop all of this before a fight broke out in church on a Sunday.

"Okay, well," I said before Kendall could say anything, "at least I had the chance to talk it out with both of you."

"What're you going to do?" Kendall asked.

I shrugged. "I'm not sure yet." That was the truth and the safest answer because Kendall wouldn't leave until she persuaded me that she was the one who was right.

"Well, don't do anything before you pray," Kendall said.

"Yeah, God'll tell you what to do," Asia added.

"He'll tell you to mind your business." Kendall laughed and Asia rolled her eyes.

"I'm definitely going to pray," I said, though I felt as if God had already been talking to me. That's what the sermon was about. I just wasn't clear on what He was saying.

I was going to keep praying, though. Just pray that God would lead me to do the right thing . . . whatever that was.

# Chapter
## Twenty-Two

It was taking a lot for me to do this, a lot for me to make this call.

I had let time pass, hoping that the image of Quentin and Jett would fade from my memory, hoping that God would give me an answer to my prayers.

Well, time passed, but every day Quentin and Jett were as clear in my mind's eye as they'd been nine days ago. And while I didn't feel like I had an answer from God, I had a heavy heart. That had to mean something.

Glancing at the clock, I realized my time was running out. I'd procrastinated as long as I could. If I was going to do this today, it had to be now. It had to be while I was home alone, and it had to be when I thought Harmony would still be on her shift at work so that she wouldn't be able to answer.

I scrolled through my telephone, saw the 248 area code that was Harmony's number, and clicked. The words were already in my mind; I'd rehearsed them for days. And I'd practiced talking fast so that I could get it out as quickly as I could.

*Harmony, if you'd like to get together again, so would I. We can talk . . . and maybe there will be more that I can tell you. Just give me a call if you're interested.*

That was all I was going to say. The decision of what would come next was going to be made by Harmony and God.

But then, after the third ring of her phone, I heard, "Hello."

"Harmony?"

"Speaking."

"Oh, I'm sorry, this is Sheridan," I said with surprise all in my voice. "I wasn't sure that I was going to get you. I thought you'd be working and I was just going to leave a message."

"Today's my day off," she said.

There was no warmth in her tone. Not that she was rude; she just sounded like my voice was the last one she wanted to hear today, or probably even tomorrow.

"Well," I said, knowing that I sounded as hesitant as she did. But that was because my mind was a blank now. I hadn't rehearsed this scenario. I said, "I was calling to see if we could get together again."

There was a pause, a long, long pause. "You know what, Sheridan? I'm sorry I called you before. I mean, I'm not sorry that we met and we talked; I'm just sorry that I came to you with that nonsense. I don't know what I'd been thinking, but I know my fiancé, and you're right about him. Quentin's a good man. I don't have anything to worry about."

The image of Quentin and Jett walking into Rendezvous flashed through my mind. Again . . . and again. I squeezed my eyes shut, and forced my mouth to say, "Okay." Then as if I was in a speed-speaking contest, I said, "Have a good day." I hung up, not even waiting for her good-bye.

I tossed my phone onto the nightstand, then fell back against the bed. My prayers had been answered. I wouldn't have to say a word and now all I had to wait for was for God to lift this ache from my heart. Silently, I asked Him to give me peace.

And then I heard, "Now, that's the way I want my woman!"

I glanced up and Brock stood at the doorway with his arms folded. For a moment I wondered how long he'd been there. Had he heard me talking to Harmony? But the grin on his face told me that he hadn't heard a thing and was thinking only one thing.

He said, "Yup, I want my woman lying on the bed spread-eagled just like that when I come home from a hard day at work." He tilted his head, then his eyebrows came together in a frown. "Just one thing is missing." He nodded. "Yeah, just one thing."

I pushed myself up. "What?"

"Why aren't you naked, woman?"

I shook my head and he laughed as he jumped onto the bed with me. As I lay back and he kissed me, I marveled at how quickly God had answered this prayer. I'd just asked Him to take away the agony, to give me peace, and inside my husband's arms, all I felt was wonderful.

But in the middle of his kisses, my cell phone rang. It was Brock who reached for the phone. It was Brock who glanced at the screen and said, "I don't recognize the number."

He shifted the phone so that I could get a look and my smile went away. But I recovered enough to shake my head and say, "I don't know who that is." I grabbed the lapels of his jacket and pulled him and his lips back to me.

But no matter what I did, I couldn't get back into the mood. I couldn't melt at Brock's kisses the way I always did.

Because of that phone call.

I told Brock that I didn't recognize the number, but this secret I held was turning me into a liar.

I knew who was calling.

Harmony.

She was calling me back, and I knew, just knew, that meant bad news.

# Chapter
## Twenty-Three

This would've been a déjà vu moment, except this time I was the one waiting in Starbucks.

I was the one sitting in the back, in the corner, in the dark, trying my best not to be seen. I'd worn black, hoping that I would blend in with the walls, the tables, the air. If I was telling the truth, I didn't even want to be seen by Harmony.

As I wrapped my hands around the warmth of my cup, I asked myself for the one-millionth time if I was doing the right thing. And my one-millionth answer was the same. I was . . . because I understood my motives. Like Pastor Ford had said in her sermon, check your motives before you make a move.

Well, I'd checked my motives over and over again. I was doing this because to this day I wished to God that someone had told me. Plus, Harmony was the one who called me. Twice.

I hadn't even called her back. But the next morning, she reached out again, and when I answered, she said simply, "I've changed my mind. I want to get together."

She didn't even have to tell me that; I knew it was why she'd called. And so, we'd set this time to meet.

I was resolute in my decision. It was the right thing, but not easy.

Maybe I should've called Kendall. No . . . that wouldn't have worked. She would've made me cancel this meeting. Asia was the one that I should've called. She would've been right here with me. In fact, I wouldn't have had to say a word. Asia would've told Harmony everything, and then made up some stuff to make sure that Harmony got it.

"Sheridan."

I looked up. "Hi," was all I could say.

Harmony said the same as she slid into the chair across from me. Then she shifted her glance and twisted in her seat. Finally, she sat still. But she sat so straight that she looked like she was leaning against a board. Her lips were pressed together as tightly as her fingers that were curled around the straps of her purse.

I wondered how many sleepless hours she'd spent since we talked. The dark shadows beneath her eyes told me there'd been many.

Oh, God, I felt so sorry for what I was about to do.

For a moment I wondered if there was a way for me to get out of this. Harmony was going to suffer heartbreak, of that I was sure. But maybe I could postpone it. Maybe she didn't have to hear this from me. Maybe she could marry Quentin and it would be years before she found out he was seeing Jett.

But was that the right thing? Would I be culpable if something happened to her? If something happened to her sexually, mentally, or even physically?

At that moment Vanessa Martin flashed through my mind. Vanessa, my dear friend, who had been part of the Ex Files group that Pastor had put together. Vanessa, who had lost her husband, Reed, when he committed suicide. Vanessa, who had then, just months later, done the same.

Vanessa had been in such despair, and from the day that

Pastor Ford had given us the news about her death, I'd always been on the lookout for that kind of distress in any of my friends. That's why I was always so concerned about Kendall and Asia.

And that's why Harmony was now on my heart.

Harmony wasn't a friend, but she'd been put into my life for this season probably for this reason. I owed her the same concern that I gave to everyone else.

She said, "This is about Quentin, isn't it?"

I nodded. Though we'd never mentioned his name the two times we'd spoken since our last meeting, that wasn't any great revelation. What other reason would we have for getting together?

She nodded, too. "Like I told you, I'd made up my mind. I was going to get rid of all of my doubts, and just start a new life with Quentin."

I know my face was stretched with sadness when all I did was look at her.

"I know that Quentin loves me," she added, as if I needed to know that before I told her my news.

"I believe that, Harmony." I didn't tell her that I didn't think it meant anything, though. Hadn't Quentin loved me the whole time he was falling in love with Jett?

"Well, if you believe that, why are we here?" she asked.

I took a deep breath, exhaled, and reminded myself of my motive. "I think he loves you, Harmony," I said, thinking it was best to start with that good news. "Quentin's not the type of man to play with people's feelings."

She blew out such a long breath of relief that I thought she was going to collapse right there at our table.

"But . . ."

With that single word, I took all of her solace away.

I said, "I saw him the other day."

"Quentin?" She frowned as if that couldn't possibly be my big news.

I nodded.

When I said nothing more, Harmony shook her head a little. "So . . . you saw him . . . did he say something about me?"

"No, he didn't mention you at all. But, I saw him . . . with Jett."

She recognized the name right away. Still, she asked for clarification. "The man . . . who was the reason for your divorce."

I said, "Yes."

She paused and I watched her lips tremble when she said, "Well . . . okay . . . there could be lots of reasons for that, right?" She didn't give me a chance to answer, to explain. She said, "I mean, even though they're not together anymore, they could still be friends, right? You and Quentin are friends, right?"

I just let her go on.

Now there were tears in her voice when she said, "And, I guess people who are friends are bound to run into each other, right? I mean, people think L.A. is big, but it's really a small place, right? The two of them probably just had some things to talk about, right?"

The tears in her voice made their way to her eyes.

That was when I knew that there was no way that I could do this.

"You know what, Harmony," I began as I pushed my cup aside and moved to the edge of my chair so that I could stand and get out of there. "You're right. That's all it was. Two friends getting together, trying to catch up with each other." And then I smiled. But my lie was so bad, so ridiculous, that I couldn't even fool this woman who didn't know me at all.

"Where did you see them?" she asked, not letting me get away.

I leaned back in my seat, though I stayed silent.

She said, "Were they embracing?" Then her voice got a little louder. "Were they kissing?" Now even more volume. "Tell me! What was my fiancé doing with Jett?"

"Harmony!" My eyes scanned the space around us and I was grateful for the music that played through the speakers throughout the café. Thank God Luther Vandross's crooning was louder than her cries.

"What? Now you don't want to tell me?" She wept like she already knew the answer. "You tell me to meet you here and now you don't want to tell me what Quentin was doing with Jett? It had to be something; you would've never called me to tell me that you saw them chatting at the counter at Starbucks."

"You're right, but they weren't hugging or kissing or doing anything like that."

"So, what is it? I'm sitting here imagining all kinds of things. What is it, Sheridan!"

The way she spoke to me, the way she made that demand, I wanted to tell her to back up and slow her roll. But really, I understood her distress.

"I saw them at that restaurant, Rendezvous."

I wasn't sure if the name of the restaurant was going to be enough, or if I would have to tell her why it made a difference that that was the place where her fiancé was meeting his friend.

"Rendezvous." Then she started chuckling. I mean, really giggling, like what I'd told her was something funny and cute.

She kept on laughing and I wondered if I was going to have to call 911.

Then, suddenly, her laughter stopped. She placed her hands over her mouth. But while I couldn't see her trembling lips anymore, all of her emotions were right there in front of my face. Tears poured from her eyes, her hands shook with such force that I knew she couldn't control it. "That's where

Quentin took me. My first night in Los Angeles. Quentin took me to Rendezvous."

"Oh, Harmony. I'm so sorry."

She shook her head and reached into her purse, searching through the deep hobo bag. And Kendall's words came back to me . . .

*The messenger always gets shot.*

That thought made my heart pound, made me push back my chair. I was just about to duck under the table, but it was too late. Harmony's hand was already rising from her bag . . . with a tissue.

But that didn't stop my heart from beating against my chest like it was a steel drum. I kept my eyes on Harmony as she used the tissue to wipe away her tears.

"I'm really sorry, Harmony," I said again. The sadness that hovered over her was so thick, it was like I could feel her pain, her heartbreak.

She nodded. "Well, I asked you, didn't I? And, even though this hurts, it's best that I know."

I just nodded.

Then she stood. "I've got to get out of here." She moved so quickly that I didn't have a chance to say another word. But then she stopped and from a few feet away said, "Thank you."

I didn't really hear her. But, I read her still-trembling lips.

It wasn't until she ran through the door that I allowed my shoulders to drop, and I let air pass through my lungs once again.

From the moment I'd seen Quentin and Jett, somewhere deep inside of me, I knew that I was going to tell Harmony. And telling her was supposed to give me relief.

So, why did I feel worse now than I did before? Now I didn't just feel sorrow. I felt dread. And dread was always so much worse.

# Chapter
## Twenty-Four

This was the absolute best part of my life.

That was my thought as I glanced across the dining room table at Evon. What a wonderful Sunday this had been. Church, and then I spent the afternoon with my future daughter-in-law while Brock and Christopher hung out together.

Perfect peace.

Well, except for that little bit of dread that still hung over me—that dread that was all about Harmony.

It had been eleven days since I'd met with her and I was still genuinely worried. Some of it had to do with her being my soror, but most of it was because I knew the sorrow that she was probably going through. I could imagine her pain as she made her decision about what she was going to do.

All I could do was pray for her. Just about every day. I prayed that she found a place of happiness, whether that place was with Quentin or not.

"So, do you really like the design?" my future daughter-in-law asked me.

I took myself away from my thoughts and once again

studied the sketch that Evon held out for me to see. I already knew that this child was talented, but I guess I didn't know how much.

My son's fiancée was a Harvard-degreed fashion designer who'd already started her own label and sold her designs to small boutiques. She was having more than modest success, was making a name for herself throughout California, and had already received two offers from major designers to intern on their teams. But she'd optioned to stay independent, and as I stared at the dress she'd designed for me, I knew why. This jeweled one-shoulder, Empire-waisted chiffon piece was just gorgeous.

"It's beautiful," I said. "My very own LaCroix design."

She filled the room with her smile.

"I'm just a little worried, though," I said.

Evon always glowed like she was the personification of sunshine, but right then that smile faded away. "What? Is there something you don't like? I can change anything. I really want you to be happy. This is all about you and . . ." She talked so fast, she didn't give me a chance to say anything.

"Wait, hold on." I laughed. "I don't want you to change a thing. I'm just worried that this dress is so amazing that I might outshine the bride, and I don't want to do that."

"Oh." She exhaled and laughed with me. Then, more seriously, she asked, "Do you want to see my dress?"

"Have you finished it already?"

"Just about, but I have a sketch here." She reached into the portfolio that rested on the chair.

"I thought you didn't want anyone to see your dress before the wedding."

"I don't," she said as she pulled out another sketch pad. "But you and my mom aren't in that group." She smiled when she turned to me. "I want you to see it."

Now, I'd seen my share of amazing wedding dresses: Vera Wang, Carolina Herrera, and plenty of others. But this sleeveless sweetheart neckline, with the fitted jeweled corset bodice, coupled with the flowing satin skirt was by far the most beautiful wedding dress I'd ever seen.

In that moment I imagined the whole scene that was two and a half months away: Evon walking slowly down the aisle as Christopher stood at the altar. If I was crying now, I'd be a blubbering fool on that day. And I couldn't wait!

"Do you like it?"

It was only when I heard her voice that I realized I hadn't said anything. I turned to Evon and didn't care one bit that I was crying. "It's so beautiful. You're going to be a gorgeous bride."

"I hope so," she said. Even though tears made her eyes glisten, Evon still wore that smile and lit up the dining room. "I can't wait to get married."

"Every little girl's dream, right?"

I was surprised when she shook her head. "It wasn't mine. I wasn't sure that I would ever get married."

"Really?" I said. That was hard for me to imagine. I would've thought this gorgeous chocolate young lady had guys falling at her feet. Her beauty was natural—from the long locks that hug beyond her shoulder to the smooth richness of her skin. No part of her was fake; not her hair, her nails, the color of her eyes. What young man wouldn't want a beauty like her?

"I didn't date much," she said. "To be honest, I didn't date at all. I went out here and there, but the guys all saw me as super-religious since I wasn't having sex. And on top of that, I was the nerdy, smart girl who would rather study than go out anyway."

"Oh," I said, hating the fact that there had ever been any

unhappiness in her life. I knew that she'd had it tough grow-ing up in one of the roughest areas of Oakland. It was just her and her mom, who worked many minimum-wage jobs to give Evon everything that she could.

"But it was okay," Evon said as if she knew some of the sor-row I was feeling for her. "I was blessed. I was never bullied or anything. It wasn't that the kids didn't like me; it was just that I wasn't noticed all that much. Christopher is my first real boyfriend and I can't believe that we're getting married. He's made me so happy, Mrs. Goodman."

I wondered if my son knew how blessed he was. I had a feeling that he did since I'd raised him right. "You know what? We're going to have to do something about that."

Her eyebrows almost came together; she didn't have a clue as to what I was talking about.

I said, "About you calling me 'Mrs. Goodman.' I think I'd prefer 'Mom,' if that's all right with you."

A beat passed and then suddenly, Evon raised her hands and pulled me into a tight hug, and I held her, too. I already had two of the best children in the world. It was amazing to me that God felt that I deserved the blessing of a third.

When she released me, the tears that had been teetering in the corners of her eyes spilled out and rolled down her cheeks.

I laughed. "Okay, we're gonna have to get cleaned up," I said, using my thumbs to softly wipe away her tears. "Or else my husband and your future husband will come in here and wonder what in the world has us sitting here sobbing like ba-bies."

"I know." She laughed, too. "It's just that all of this is so special to me. You helping me plan the wedding, and especially you and Mr. Goodman helping us pay for it. Christopher and I were just going to go away and—"

I held up my hand, stopping her. "That was never going to happen as long as I am the mother. Brock and I are thrilled to help you and Christopher. This is our gift to you."

"Thank you." Her voice was filled with gratitude.

Glancing at my watch, I said, "Brock and Christopher should be back any minute."

"Do you think they found Mr. Goodman's tux?"

"I'm sure they did, though I had a feeling they just wanted an excuse to go out shopping. But even if they didn't find it, there's still plenty of time." I patted her hand. "Don't worry about that." Pushing back from the chair, I said, "I'm going to dash and change so I'll be ready to go when they get back. I'm starving."

"Me, too! And Crustaceans is one of my favorite restaurants."

Yup, this was the absolute best part of my life. A day with my daughter-in-law and then dinner with the four of us. What could be better?

Just as I stood, the doorbell rang.

"Brock must've forgotten his key," I said as I rushed to the door. My face had to be covered with all the joy I felt from spending this time with Evon when I pulled the door open. "What happened?" I began. But then my smile went straight away.

Quentin stood on the other side of the threshold with a scowl so deep I half expected him to start roaring. He stomped past me, pushing his way into my home.

"I cannot believe you, Sheridan!" he shouted.

"Quentin." I only said his name to give me some time to think. Because it didn't take any special kind of intelligence to figure out why Quentin was in my home on the edge of rage.

"I cannot believe you did this to me," he yelled. "Do you really hate me this much? Did our divorce affect you so much that you've turned into a vindictive . . ." He paused and the name he wanted to call me rested right on the tip of his tongue. I was sure the only thing that stopped him was that I was the mother of his children.

My heart hammered against my chest so hard I had to take a couple of quick inhales to keep breathing. "Quentin." All I could think to say was his name.

It wasn't until this moment that I realized I hadn't played this tape all the way through. I didn't know why it hadn't occurred to me that Quentin would one day come knocking on my door. I don't know, maybe I thought that Harmony wouldn't tell him where she'd heard about him and Jett. Or maybe I thought that he would never come over here, because what would he say? He couldn't be mad at the truth.

Finally, I said, "What are you talking about?" just to give me more time. To figure it out and see what he knew.

His face stretched like my words surprised him. "Is that how you're going to play this? Like you don't know what's going on? Well, let me tell you," he said, taking two steps closer to me.

The anger in his eyes made me take two steps back. But I could smell the stench of his fury. Over Quentin's shoulder, I caught a glimpse of Evon, standing in the cut between the dining room and the entryway. She was so still that it was only because she was standing that I figured she was still breathing. Her ever-present smile was gone, though her eyes were still bright. But now they shined with tears and fear.

I needed to calm Quentin down, but he moved back and forth, stomping hard, like he was digging a ditch with his feet.

He screamed, "I'm talking about you going to Harmony and telling her some nonsense about me and Jett."

Well, the jig was definitely up now. Not that I didn't already know what Quentin was talking about. But I knew now that it wasn't just some theory on his part. He had all the facts.

"Quentin, calm down," I said, trying to keep my voice steady. I leaned and glanced over his shoulder, giving him the hint that we were not alone.

He turned, saw Evon, but then turned back to me as if seeing her meant nothing. Her presence didn't do anything to calm or soothe him.

"I cannot believe this, Sheridan. I cannot believe you told Harmony to leave me!"

"Whoa!" I said, holding up my hands. "I never told Harmony that."

He stomped right up to me and pointed his finger in my face. "You're a liar. You know what you did, you b—"

"Uh, Quentin, you need to slow your roll and back up off my wife."

I don't think there'd ever been a time when I'd been so happy to hear my husband's voice. Turning around, I saw him, holding two shopping bags that he gently, slowly placed on the floor. His eyes were stuck on Quentin, and the way my husband moved, so deliberately, I knew that if my ex made one wrong move, Brock would be all over him.

Christopher stood next to Brock, frozen for a moment. Then he rushed to Evon. "Are you okay?" he asked as he pulled her into his arms.

She nodded, but didn't say a word. I wasn't surprised. She was in such a state of shock she probably would be mute for weeks.

"What's going on here?" Brock said, coming to my side.

"Ask your wife," Quentin barked.

All eyes turned to me. And I had no idea what to say.

Brock said, "Sheridan?"

I knew I had to speak then. I said, "Quentin's under the impression that I had something to do with him and Harmony breaking up. But I didn't."

"Oh, really, Sheridan?" The way he shouted, everyone faced

Quentin. "You're going to stand here and lie?" He turned from me and looked at Brock. "Just so you know that I'm not crazy, Harmony told me that your wife met with her just so she could tell Harmony that I was involved with Jett."

The eyes shifted again; every pair was back to me. If I could've, I would've clicked my heels three times and headed to Kansas.

It was Brock's stare that I felt the most. His brows framed the confusion in his eyes. "Sheridan?"

"Let me explain," I said quickly. "Harmony called *me*," I told Quentin, because Brock already knew that part. "At first, I told her no." That statement *was* meant for Brock. "But then she called again and I felt so sorry for her. She was confused, she needed someone to talk to. So we met."

"And you told her to leave me."

"No! All I told her that day was that you were a good man." I paused. "Ask her, she'll tell you that's what I said."

"So then how did you get from there to where you told her to leave me?"

"I never told her that."

"You told her that I was having an affair with Jett."

"I didn't say that either. I just told her that I saw the two of you together." When Quentin gave me a bitter chuckle, I added, "I told her that I saw you at Rendezvous."

Brock moaned, and I knew the two of us were going to have a big discussion tonight. But the thing was, everybody could be mad if they wanted to, but all I'd done was report what I'd seen. Quentin was back with Jett and he was playin' Harmony just like he'd played me.

"I just told her the truth," I added, and glared at Quentin. I was tired of standing there being the one who was wrong. "She'd been wondering if you were still gay, if you would be with a man again. And I just told her what I knew."

"You don't know anything!" Quentin said. He closed his

eyes, held his head in his hands for a moment, then released a long breath. He pointed his finger at me, but then put his hand down when Brock took a step forward. With a much softer voice, he said, "I shouldn't have to explain myself to anyone." He looked from me to Brock, then to Christopher and Evon. "But it seems that no matter what I do . . ." He paused and I swore there were tears in his eyes. He looked straight at me. "I'm not with Jett. Jett's married."

I gave him a long side-eye glance.

"He got married two years ago. To a . . . woman. Dana."

A lump popped into my throat. "Married?" I whispered. Oh, my God! Had I made a mistake? But then I shook my head. I knew what I saw, I knew what I felt in my gut. I wasn't going to buy his lies like everyone else. "But you and Jett were at Rendezvous," I said, like that was my trump card.

But then Quentin raised the stakes. "We were there to meet the chef. Adolphe Baptiste. He's . . . he's a friend of Jett's who catered his wedding. We had a meeting that night because I wanted Adolphe to cater mine. Harmony just loved the food when I took her there and I wanted him to provide the food for my wedding. My wedding that's not going to happen now."

I let his words sink in, though I still couldn't say that I believed him. "But Jett told me . . . I saw him when I went to the restroom and he made it seem . . ."

Quentin nodded. "We were sitting at the bar when you walked by, and at first, I thought that you were looking for me. I thought you were going to come right out and ask me about Jett. But you walked by, and I figured you really had to go to the restroom. Jett told me he spoke to you. Told me he said some things he shouldn't have said, but he was just messin' with you because you were being so self-righteous. And I would've cleared it up then if I had any idea you were going to go to Harmony."

I calculated it all in my head. The first meeting with

Harmony, seeing Quentin and Jett, the last meeting with Harmony. Had I been wrong about it all?

"I've lost her, Sheridan." Quentin's voice was soft and filled with sadness, now. "I lost her because of you."

"Quentin, I'm so sorry," I breathed. "I didn't mean anything . . . I thought I was doing the right thing."

"You were wrong. On so many levels, you were wrong."

"I'll speak to Harmony. I'll tell her—"

"I don't even know where she is." His words were even softer than before. Like he'd been in a losing battle and had no more energy to fight on. He said, "I hadn't been able to reach her for days, and then, this morning, she left me a voice mail and sent me an e-mail. She told me everything that you told her. I didn't even get the chance to explain," he continued. "I didn't get to tell her that you were wrong."

"Well, you've got to find her," I said. "You've got to tell her everything."

"How?" Now he shouted. "I've called and her number is no longer in service. I went to her apartment, and she's moved. I just came from the hospital and they told me that she quit." He paused. "She quit, Sheridan. Because of you. She's just gone." He lowered his head, closed his eyes, and I prayed to God that he wouldn't start crying right there in front of all of us.

The eyes had shifted from Quentin to me. But what was I supposed to say? What was I supposed to do?

An eternity of seconds passed before Quentin looked up and at me. "I never meant to hurt you, Sheridan." Now he whispered so softly that I could hardly hear him. But I wasn't about to ask him to speak up. "Really, I never did. I thought I told you that. I thought I apologized."

"You did," I said, my voice as low as his.

"But I guess my apology meant nothing." Before I could say another word, he added, "Because all these years, you wanted to get back at me. You wanted to hurt me."

"No!"

"You wanted me to feel what you felt back then."

"No!"

"All I can say is congratulations. Because in the end, you won. I've lost the only woman I've loved since you."

"Quentin, no!" I reached for him, but he jerked away from me as if my touch was poisonous. With his head bowed, Quentin moved past me and Brock, walked to the door, and then without looking back, he walked right through it.

For a couple of seconds, we all stood there, staring at the door, transfixed.

Then Christopher moved. Well, at least his eyes did—from the door to me. And he shot me a heated glare.

"Chris . . ."

Before I could step toward him, he bolted toward the door. "Dad!" he yelled. And Evon ran after him.

I lifted my hands to my mouth wondering what had I done? Looking at Brock, I pleaded with him. I begged him with my eyes. He had to be the one to understand.

But he shook his head and said, "I told you to stay out of it."

"I know. And I tried. And, I'm so sorry."

"It's a little late for sorry, don't you think?"

"Brock." For the third time, I reached toward someone who backed away. Brock stepped back, turned around, then walked toward our bedroom. Just a few seconds after that, he slammed our bedroom door shut.

I stood there in the entryway, looking from the open front door to the closed one of my bedroom. I stood there, all alone.

# Chapter
## Twenty-Five

A tornado had swept in and caused all of this chaos in my life.

The only thing was—*I* was that tornado. I'd caused the confusion.

I knew this. I could admit this. And, I was going to fix this. Now!

I looked at the bedroom door that Brock had slammed shut about ten minutes ago. But right as I took a step forward, I took three back. I wasn't ready to face my husband. Not until I could tell him that I'd apologized to Quentin and was on my way to making amends.

So I went into action. First, I grabbed my cell from the dining room table, then rushed into the family room. My hands were shaking as I scrolled through my phone to Quentin's number. Before I clicked on his name, I said a quick prayer that he would listen. That he'd be able to hear me above all the curses that I was sure he wanted to send my way.

But after just one ring, my call hit his voice mail.

I hung up and dialed again.

And this time, he answered.

"Quentin!" I breathed.

Then the click of the call ending. Without a word, Quentin had hung up on me.

I sighed and pressed his number again, but a second later I ended the call. I could've taken him hanging up on me again and again, but what good would that do? Quentin needed time, and right now that was all I could give him.

Next, Harmony.

But before I even scrolled through my phone to find her number, I stopped. Quentin said that her number was disconnected.

So without being able to talk to Harmony, I had to go to my son next.

If the timing of all of this had been just a little bit different, Christopher wouldn't even be involved. If Quentin had come yesterday, or tomorrow, or early this morning before Christopher and Evon had gotten here, or even later tonight when the four of us would've been out to dinner . . .

But Quentin had timed it so that my son and my husband heard the worst about me. Of course, Christopher was livid. I would've known that even if I hadn't seen his barefaced anger when he looked at me before he raced through the door to get to his father.

I owed my son an apology . . . I owed them all one. But Christopher also needed to hear my side. I wasn't just out there trying to ruin his father's life.

I scrolled to *Son*, clicked, and the picture of Christopher's face shining bright with his smile popped up. I held my breath, but after only one ring, the call went to voice mail. I called again. Another ring, then straight to voice mail. I hung up, called again. Same result.

I could tell that my son was pressing ignore every time he

saw my name. That was something I'd told him and Tori never to do, at least not as long as I was paying their bills.

I hadn't paid one of Christopher's bills in years.

So, without connecting with Quentin or Christopher, that only left Brock.

Just about forty minutes had passed since Brock had walked away from me. That was enough time for his anger to calm, at least a little, wasn't it?

I took short, slow steps as if I was a dead woman walking, and this time I didn't stop. When I got to our bedroom, I opened the door, stepped inside, then stood at the threshold.

My expectation was that my husband would do what he always did. Whenever I walked into any room where he was, he turned, he looked, he smiled. I wasn't exactly expecting the smile, but I thought it was a natural reflex that made him turn and face my presence.

But clearly it wasn't natural because his eyes didn't waver from the television. He stayed the way he was, sitting up with his back against the headboard, his hands clasped behind his head, and his legs stretched out in front of him.

It was as if he didn't even know I was there.

In the six years of our marriage, of course we'd had our little spats. But that's all they ever were—little and spats.

For me, that's all this was as well. After all, what I'd done with Quentin didn't have a thing to do with me and Brock. But the way Brock sat, not acknowledging me, let me know that his view was different from mine.

I let time pass . . . seconds that turned into a minute. There was nothing from my husband, so I said, "Can we talk?"

More silence. More time passing. And in those moments, I came to realize how deep my husband's anger was. Then finally, there was a slight shift of his eyes before he said, "We?" He shrugged. "Doesn't seem like we need to

talk about anything. Seems like you took care of everything already."

"I want to explain," I said, knowing that I had to be patient
in this situation. "I want you to know what I did and why I
did it."

Then, more passing time, more silence, nothing else from
my husband. Not until I said, "Please."

In the next second, Brock reached for the remote. And for
a second, it looked like he was going to point it at me. Press
exit and hope that I'd disappear. But instead, he aimed it for
the television and set the sound to mute.

He said, "Speak."

That's it. Nothing more.

Moving with more confidence than I felt, I walked to his
side of the bed, then sat on the edge. "I'm really sorry," I said,
thinking it was best to start there. "I should've listened to
you."

His left eyebrow rose, but he kept his silence.

"I didn't know what to do," I continued. "Harmony insisted that she had to talk to me because she had no one else.
And then I found out that she was my soror, and then we
saw Quentin and Jett . . ." I paused for a moment and took a
breath. "I just felt that she had to know."

"And why is that, Sheridan?" he asked with his lips so tight
it sounded like he was growling. "Why did she have to know?"

Now I raised my eyebrow. "First of all, she asked. But secondly, if something like this were happening to you, wouldn't
you want to know?" I didn't wait for him to answer. "The truth
of it, Brock, is that I wish someone had told me. Quentin is
gay and no one seems to want to talk about that." I was getting
revved up. Everyone was mad at me when, now that I thought
about it, I was the only one who'd done the right thing. "And,
I'm not even sure about this new story about Jett. I mean,
now Jett's married, and Quentin's getting married, and Jett's

moved back to Los Angeles. Doesn't this all ring strange to you?"

Brock was silent, but this time I wasn't bothered by it. The way he looked at me, the way he slowly nodded his head, he was considering what I'd said. He said, "Ring strange, huh?"

I nodded.

"Well, even if it does," he began, "the point is that you still don't get it."

I blinked.

The muscles in his jaw flexed. "You still don't get that it's none of your business. And that's the part that I don't get." He swung his legs over the side of the bed, almost hitting me with his foot. He jumped up, then stood in front of me. "Even now," he said, throwing up his hands as if he was exasperated, "you still want to be all up in Quentin's business." He paced in front of me. "What is it, Sheridan? Why is it that you won't leave your ex alone?"

"I wasn't thinking about Quentin," I said, my volume matching his. "I was thinking about Harmony."

He chuckled. "Yeah, right. Harmony's just an excuse. You're using her not to cut ties with him."

"That's ridiculous."

"Really? You need to dig deep and be honest."

"I am being honest. This was only about telling Harmony what I thought she should know."

"It has to be more than that. Because even though your ex just came here wanting to blow up this spot, and even though Christopher just called asking me to tell you to stop calling him, and even though you know that I'm really hot about this . . . even with all of that, you still sit there, curious about Quentin's life, talking about something that's strange to you."

"It's just that I'm the only one seeing clearly. I know something's not right. I know it in my gut."

"And that's what's wrong with this whole thing. You don't

need to be seeing anything in Quentin's life and you don't need to be gut-checking him. I told you before, his life is not yours. His life is not supposed to be a concern to you."

I sat there for a moment, wanting to agree with my husband, but why couldn't he agree with me? Why couldn't he see my side and understand that I was only trying to help?

But I didn't need to be right—at least not right now. I wanted to fix this with Brock. I'd convince him of all that stuff about Quentin and Harmony later.

So, I pulled back and said, "I'm not concerned about Quentin. I just didn't want Harmony to get hurt the way I'd been."

"This is a problem, Sheridan. You need to let what happened with you and Quentin go."

I nodded. "I know. And, I will from now on."

He shook his head. "You've said that before."

"I will this time. I mean, what else can happen? What more can I do? The damage is done, right?"

He frowned. "Is that what you were trying to do? Cause damage? Hurt people?"

"No, I'm just saying that everything has all played out."

"Has it?"

He paused and all kinds of emotions washed over his face. The doubt, the anger I expected to see. But it was the absolute sadness in his eyes that froze me. The sadness that let me know that he'd been hurt by what I'd done.

"Has it all played out, Sheridan?" he whispered. "I'm just not sure."

"Brock, what I did has nothing to do with you. It has nothing to do with what I feel about you."

Shaking his head, he said, "How can you say that? If you have all of these cares for Quentin, how do you have any room for me?"

"You're the only one in my heart; I love you."

Then there was silence. I mean, the type of silence where all I heard was a symphony of crickets. And here's the thing— there had never been a time when I told my husband that I loved him and he said nothing back.

Finally, he spoke. He said, "I don't want to talk about this anymore," as he slipped into his loafers.

When he grabbed his keys from the nightstand, I asked, "Where are you going?"

He shrugged. "I don't know. Maybe to get something to eat. I don't know."

"Okay," I said as I rose to go with him.

But he held up his hands. "No, I'm flyin' solo." Then he turned his back on me and marched out of our bedroom. And just for good measure, it seemed, he slammed the door closed once again.

# Chapter
## Twenty-Six

My business logo danced across the screen of my computer, but I wasn't going to press enter again. Why should I? It wasn't like I could get any work done anyway. Even though my to-do list was massive, I'd done nothing since I'd first sat behind my desk two hours ago.

But how was I supposed to do anything when it was impossible to concentrate? My head was crammed with thoughts, and the stress was piling up and weighing me down.

Three days had passed since Quentin had stormed into my house, then left with just a whimper. And in those three days, nothing had changed. Or maybe everything had changed, because life felt a whole lot worse.

Quentin wouldn't answer my calls, Christopher hadn't returned any of my messages . . . and then there was Brock.

This was the first time since we'd been married that we found ourselves in this space. That space where you mumbled your hellos, grumbled your good-byes, and said little to each other in between.

Before this, Brock and I had never let our heads hit our

pillows at night if we held any kind of anger in our hearts. We'd never given each other the silent treatment. But I guess what I'd done was a serious violation. So serious that each time I approached Brock to talk, all he did was say, "Not now, Sheridan."

How were we going to get past this if Brock wouldn't talk to me?

Pushing my chair away from my desk, I rolled it around and faced the window. From this bedroom-converted-to-my-office window, I could see the gazebo in the backyard where Brock and I had stood in front of God, Pastor Ford, and just thirty of our family and friends. Holding hands, Brock and I promised to love each other straight into eternity.

I was never naive enough to believe that between our wedding and eternity, Brock and I wouldn't have disagreements, but this didn't feel like just an argument. This was a chasm, a fissure that was filled with Brock's doubt that I loved only him.

I had to fix this, I thought as I stood. I was not going to let my ex get inside this marriage. By the time Brock and I laid our heads down tonight, we were going to be on the other side of this divide.

I could use some advice, though, and I reached for my phone, so ready to call a prayer meeting. Asia would at least listen to me, and Kendall would, of course, have some kind of smart-aleck answer that just might be my solution.

Before I even clicked on Asia's number, I remembered that she was in San Diego, with Angel, on an overnight school field trip. If I hadn't been filled with so much personal despair, I would've chuckled at that thought. Asia, on a school trip with a bunch of twelve-years-olds? This would've never happened two months ago, but since the blowup in Bel Air, Asia was a different kind of mother. She was more attentive, more involved. If Caroline thought that she was going to take Angel away in any kind of way, Asia was showing her something. I was so proud of my friend.

So, I clicked on Kendall's number. But when my call went to voice mail, I hung up without leaving a message. She was probably with her father.

But I had to talk to someone. I had to talk this out so that when Brock got home, I knew exactly what I was going to say, and exactly what I was going to do.

With a smile, I looked down at my phone. I knew exactly who to call. But before I could click on a name, it rang and a picture popped up on my screen. Startled and shocked, I answered.

"Pastor Ford, I was just about to call you," I said.

"I figured as much."

I paused. There were a couple of ways I could go with this. Either someone in my life had called Pastor to let her know what happened, or it could've been that my pastor had received a message from God. Because that's just how it was with Pastor Ford. There were times when she could look at you and know what was going on. Sometimes it was scary, but most of the time it was wonderful. Like right now. Pastor just knew that I needed her.

Pastor said, "I need to speak with you, Sheridan."

"Okay," I said, knowing that she meant for us to do this in person. Pastor didn't handle her business over the phone. She didn't do it via e-mail or texts or posts on Facebook. It was all about face-to-face relationships with her. "When do you want to see me?" I asked, hoping that she'd give me her soonest appointment, probably sometime tomorrow.

"Now," she said.

I glanced down at the sweats and T-shirt that I'd put on the moment Brock walked out the door this morning. I hadn't even showered. "Can I have an hour?"

"I'll give you forty-five minutes. See you in a bit, honey."
And then my pastor hung up.

She wouldn't have to ask me again, wouldn't have to call
me back. I dashed downstairs into my bedroom.

I wished that I'd thought about speaking with my pastor
on Sunday, right after Quentin left. Really, I should've talked
to her long before that, even before I had that first meeting
with Harmony. Because my pastor always kept it real, always
kept it right, and I wouldn't be feeling like my whole life was
a mess now.

But that was okay. In an hour, I'd know exactly what to
do. That's how it was with my pastor. She would help me to set
things right.


Just by walking into my pastor's office, I could feel the shift in
the atmosphere. It was like I was walking into a place where
God had been. I never knew what that was. Maybe it was
being surrounded by bookshelves stuffed with every kind of
Bible and all kinds of commentaries.

But really, it wasn't the books or the pictures of Pastor Ford
that hung on the wall, or the framed accolades that held everything from my pastor's degrees to her commendations and
proclamations.

It was none of that; it was the overwhelming feeling of love
that permeated all through the air in this space. Complete,
unadulterated love.

"So, how're you doing?" Pastor Ford hugged me before she
motioned for me to sit next to her on her sofa.

I shrugged. "I'm okay."

When she reached over and laid her hands on top of mine,
tears came to my eyes. I felt like crying, though not from sadness. I felt relief, like help was on the way.

She said, "It's been kinda tough, huh?"

"Who called you? Brock?"

"The first call I got was from Christopher."

I sniffed, feeling like I was really going to cry now. "I haven't even had a chance to talk to my son. He's upset at me."

"Quite," Pastor said. "He's so upset that he's canceled his wedding."

"What!" I jumped up.

Pastor nodded, then motioned for me to sit back down.

"He canceled his wedding because of this?" I asked.

My pastor nodded again.

"But why?" Now I really did cry. "What does this have to do with him marrying Evon?" Then I had another thought. "Oh, my God. It wasn't Christopher; it was Evon. She's the one who doesn't want to get married. She gave him back his ring because of me."

"You need to calm down and stop guessing so that I can tell you what's really going on."

I pressed my lips together, folded my hands in my lap, and blinked back my tears. It felt like I'd ruined everyone's life, including my own.

Then Pastor said, "They're still getting married. They're eloping."

I moaned, though that was a little bit better.

She continued, "Chris said that with what's going on between you and his father right now, he couldn't see the family gathering for any kind of celebration. He's pretty sad about it, but he and Evon are determined."

"I can't believe this." Pulling out my cell phone, I said, "I have to call him. I have to stop him from doing that. We're *going* to have this wedding."

Pastor held my hand, stopping me. "Haven't you realized yet that you can't control everything?" She shook her head.

"Christopher is grown. You need to let him do this the way he wants to."

As I tucked my phone back into my bag, all kinds of thoughts went through my mind: the months of preparation, the dresses that Evon had designed, the dreams I'd had about this day for years for both of my children.

Now I wasn't going to be part of his day all because I wanted to do what was right.

Pastor scooted over until she was close and put her arms around me. And when I sobbed, I cried for more than Christopher's wedding. I cried for this whole ordeal. How did I get here? Where my husband wasn't speaking to me, my son didn't want me to be part of his day. And his father? I doubted if Quentin would ever utter two words to me from now on.

Pastor stayed silent as I released all the anguish inside and it wasn't until my sobs turned into sniffles that she stood and reached for the tissues on her desk. After she handed me the box, she leaned back on her desk. "Now let's talk."

She didn't have to say it twice. I was so ready to tell someone my story. Someone who would listen and understand. "I really thought I was doing the right thing."

"Tell me what happened."

I looked up at her. "Christopher didn't tell you?"

"He told me his side and now I want to hear yours."

I nodded. "From the moment I met Harmony, I felt sorry for her. I don't know what it is, Pastor, but I just felt like Quentin was playing her." I paused, waiting for Pastor Ford to tell me that I was wrong, but she just nodded for me to continue. I told my pastor about the call from Harmony, and then meeting her. "Pastor, I was going to leave it right there . . . until I saw Quentin and Jett." I sniffed. "When I saw the two of them, all of those feelings I had all those years ago came right back to me. And, I thought about Harmony and how she was going to feel. I just didn't think it was right. I didn't think what Quentin was doing was right."

My pastor tilted her head a bit and nodded slowly. "Do you remember when I talked to you, Asia, and Kendall right after Christmas?"

"Yes." I'd had lots of conversations with my pastor, but the one she'd had with me and my girls after the disastrous Christmas dinners we'd all had would always stand out in my mind. My pastor always had a good word for me, but what she'd told me that day I felt was a direct word from God. It was a warning that had stayed with me, but not long enough, I guess. She'd given me words that I wished I'd heeded.

I said, "You told me that Quentin wasn't my sin and I wasn't his savior."

She said nothing.

I said, "When you told me that, I thought those words freed me. I thought that I would never be thinking about Quentin and his life again. And then Harmony called."

"Why did you decide to see her? Why didn't you listen to Brock?"

I let a couple of moments go by before I said, "Because I felt like I owed that to her. I felt that she should know." I pushed myself off the sofa and began to pace in front of Pastor Ford. "I felt like she was going to be living my life all over again and I could help her, I could stop it. Because I wish to God that someone had told me. If I'd known, I would've never married Quentin. If someone had just told me, I would've never been with him, wouldn't have had all of that pain, I wouldn't have had all that heartache."

"And, you wouldn't have had Christopher and Tori and you wouldn't have met and married Brock."

Her words startled me, stopped me right in my tracks.

"No, that's not what I was saying. I want Christopher and Tori and Brock."

"And you have them because of Quentin." Pastor Ford said, "What makes you think that you weren't supposed to marry him?" She paused as if she wanted me to answer that question, but I couldn't. I was still stuck on thoughts of not having Christopher and Tori . . . and Brock. I was so taken aback that I couldn't even pace anymore. I had to sit down and think about that.

Pastor said, "This is what people don't understand about life. All the roads you've taken have led you to this moment. You were exactly in the place God wanted you to be. All I have to do is look at the fruit that has come out of your life from your marriage with Quentin. There was a lot of fruit." She sat down next to me. "You're looking back on those days in the wrong way. You're choosing to remember the times that brought you pain. But what about all of those years of happiness? And what about the happiness that you've had after Quentin?"

Pastor stayed silent, as if she was giving me time to measure my life with Quentin. And when I added it all up, I'd really been so happy with him. Until that final day.

"Sheridan, if you had been thinking about what you received from your marriage with Quentin instead of focusing on all of your pain, you would've never gone to Harmony. You went to her out of all of the hurt and anger that you've been holding on to."

I sighed. "I never thought about it that way. And I wish I had, because it turns out that what I told Harmony wasn't true. Did Christopher tell you that?"

She nodded. "He told me what Quentin and Jett were doing together, and he told me that Harmony's gone."

"I really feel bad about that. I wasn't trying to break them up."

"I believe that. But I guess you've finally figured out that you can't get involved in that, Sheridan. Even if what you said turns out to be true."

Hold up! I replayed Pastor's last words in my mind and looked at her for a long moment. Was she saying that she, too, thought Quentin was gay? That she didn't believe this whole "I've got a fiancée" story?

But before I could ask her, she added, "Because of the circumstances, because of your marriage, you can't be involved in Quentin's life in any way."

"I get that . . . now. Now that everything's ruined." I shook my head, thinking about all the days that had passed. "And the worst of it is Brock. Brock's so angry with me and I don't know what to do about it. I've tried talking to him, but he doesn't want to talk, he doesn't want to listen. We're just passing by each other, not even speaking."

"Well, I never recommend that," Pastor said. "You two really need to talk."

"I know, but . . . what can I do?" I looked down at my hands as I folded and then unfolded them. This was the question that had brought me to the pastor's office.

"Sheridan."

I looked up. I hadn't even noticed that my pastor had stepped away, that she'd walked to the door. That's where she stood, at the opened door. And right next to her was my husband, standing with his hands stuffed into his pockets.

It was a reflex—I sprang from the sofa, ran to him, and wrapped my arms around his neck. And when Brock held me back, more sobs came from that space that I thought was empty.

"I'm so sorry," I cried. "Really, really sorry."

Brock pulled back just a little, and with the back of his hands, he wiped my tears away. "Well, what you did is not the unforgivable sin," he said softly. Then his voice stiffened just a bit. "But I called Pastor because I think we need some help."

"You called her?" Then, for the first time in minutes, I turned, remembering that Pastor Ford was someplace in this room.

She was standing behind us.

I said to her, "I thought you said Christopher called you."

"I said Christopher called me first." She chuckled and added, "Everyone was calling to tell on you. Even your mom called from San Francisco."

I moaned. I hadn't said a word to my mother, even though I'd spoken to her yesterday. Now I guessed I was going to hear her mouth, too, but you know what? I was so happy. Because my husband was standing next to me, and with him by my side, I could handle anything that came my way.

"I asked Brock if he could come here today so that I could talk to the two of you. He said that you needed help and I agree."

"Okay," I said.

Pastor said, "You know, I marry a lot of couples, but when the two of you stood in front of me, I knew, just knew, that not only was your marriage right, but that so much good was going to come out of your union." She looked straight at me when she said, "But in order to get your marriage pumping the way it's supposed to, you have to get rid of the blockage." She turned around, strolled behind her desk, and then faced us. "So let's talk." She pointed to the chairs in front of her desk and Brock and I moved toward them.

But the whole time, I never let go of my husband's hand. And if it were at all possible, my plan was to never, ever let him go again.

# Chapter
## Twenty-Seven

For the second day in a row, I received the telephone call that I really needed.

Just like yesterday, I picked up my phone—this time to call Kendall. But before I could do it, she'd called me.

"I need to see you," she'd said.

"I was just gonna call you. Is everything okay with your dad?"

"He's fine."

"Good; then I need to talk to you, too."

"Perfect," she'd said.

"Okay. Where do you want to meet? Do you want me to come to the Woman's Place?" I asked, figuring that it would be easier if I just met her at work.

"No." Then she'd given me an address in Malibu.

"What is this?" I'd asked her. "A new restaurant?"

"Just meet me there. How long will it take you?"

"Give me a couple of hours."

"I'll give you three. About eleven?"

I agreed and then I'd hung up. There was no need for me to give Kendall's call another thought. For the next couple of hours, I went to work, which was something that I hadn't done for days. But with Brock and me back on our right track, now I could focus. I answered e-mails, returned calls, and actually checked off a few items on my to-do list before I made my way to the address that Kendall had given to me.

All during the ride over, my thoughts were on me and Brock and the talk we'd had with Pastor. I thought about how Pastor once again reiterated that I had to let go of Quentin's sin.

"It doesn't belong to you," she'd said. And once again she added, "Sheridan, you've got to stop thinking that you're the world's savior. Jesus is fine doing that all by Himself."

Then her harshest words came when she said, "You're not the first woman in the world whose husband left her for a man, so stop acting that way."

I have to admit, my feelings were hurt, but I was also smart enough to know that my pastor was right. Why was I so concerned about Quentin and Harmony? I had lots of excuses, but I promised God, Pastor, Brock, and myself yesterday that I was going to work to let it go. My goal: stay out of everybody's business and just handle mine.

"Just don't say that, Sheridan," Pastor warned me. "Understand that there's something going on with you and you're going to have to take it to the altar and leave it there"—she'd paused then and looked at Brock—"if you want to save your marriage."

I was hurt, but I was smart. That's all Pastor had to say. I was putting my marriage at risk? Well then, this was going to stop.

My thoughts came back to the present when the automated voice of my GPS stated, "In a quarter of a mile turn left onto Private Road."

Private Road? Now I paid attention to the multimillion-dollar beach homes on my left that were the jewels of Los Angeles. And when the GPS led me to the left, I followed the directions, but then was pissed when I saw the sign NO OUT-LET.

Where was this dangbangit thing taking me?

The road was too narrow to make a U-turn; I was going to have to go to the end then turn around.

But at the end of the road was a little cottage . . . with the address that Kendall had given me. And then I saw Kendall's Porsche and then . . . there was Kendall.

Now I stood in the middle of the living room, doing a 360-degree slow turn, taking it all in, and hardly believing any of what I was seeing.

"So," I said as I stopped spinning and walked toward the windowed wall with the precious view of the Pacific. This was magnificent; truly, I could stretch out my hand across the private beach and touch an ocean's wave. "Explain this to me again."

Behind me, Kendall said, "This is my new place."

"You already said that part," I said, "when you opened the door. But how am I, one of your best friends—"

"Correction"—she interrupted me—"my only best friend."

"Okay, how is it that your only best friend does not know that (a) you were thinking about buying a house in Malibu and (b) that you already purchased a house in Malibu and (c) that you had already moved into said house in Malibu?"

Her grin filled half her face as she stepped over to stand next to me. "You know that I've always wanted to live in Malibu again. I've always wanted to come back to the beach." She turned and faced the ocean. "This has been my dream," she said softly.

As she stood taking in her dream, I knew in that same moment Kendall was reliving a part of her nightmare. A nightmare in which Kendall had given her first Malibu dream home to her ex in their divorce . . . her ex and his new wife, who just happened to be Kendall's sister.

As Kendall's shoulders rose and stiffened, I was sad that those memories stole any part of the joy that she had now. But then, just as quickly, the moment was gone. When she turned back to me, her cheekbones were high once again with her grin and her eyes were bright. "So, the opportunity presented itself for me to get this place, and I just took it."

"Opportunity? How? When? Who? What? And the most important question, how did you do all of this without me finding out?"

"One answer to all of those questions; I've got a good Realtor."

"Well, you're going to have to introduce me to her."

"Him," Kendall corrected me. "I have the same Realtor who helped me and Anthony get the first house." She paused a moment. "His brother." Then she walked away.

Nuh-uh. She was not going to just say that and leave it there. I followed behind her to the other side of the room and plopped down on the overstuffed sofa right next to her.

"Anthony's brother? Really?"

"Yup." And then that was it. But Kendall didn't have to say anything else. The grin on her face said so much.

I said, "Okay, you need to fess up, Fester. What's going on?"

She paused, looked down at her hands as if she needed a couple of seconds to think. When her glance returned to me, she said, "Give me some time, and then I'll tell you the whole story."

I shook my head. "Keeping secrets from your best friend." But I said that with a smile because I knew Kendall. She was a little bit different when it came to friendship. Most women ran to their best friends with their deepest secrets. But not Kendall. What had gone down between her ex and her sister had really changed her. I didn't know her back then, but what wife wouldn't be traumatized after finding her husband in bed with her sister?

I was absolutely sure that experience had turned Kendall into the woman she was today. Though she counted me as her best friend, she was a loner. She didn't share much with many; she handled her life, herself, on her own terms.

And I'd always thought that was a very lonely existence.

But maybe a shift was happening. Because for the first time since I'd known her, the burden of bitterness that hung over her like a pall, though it was still there, seemed to be lifting. I didn't know what was going on, but I knew Kendall would tell me. Eventually.

"Oh," Kendall said, "there's one other thing that I have to tell you."

It looked like eventually was going to get here sooner than I thought. I sat back and waited for the news.

She said, "Sabrina had the baby last week. My sister and my ex are now parents."

Kendall had told me and Asia that she found out her sister was pregnant at Christmas. "Oh," I said. My tone was a mix of gaiety and sorrow. I was so happy because anytime God blessed someone with a baby, I knew those parents were experiencing nothing but joy. But on the other hand, I knew this had to be a bitter moment for Kendall. "Are you okay?"

She shrugged. "Why wouldn't I be? I knew Sabrina was pregnant. The baby had to come out sometime."

I had lots of questions. Like did Anthony and Sabrina have a boy or a girl? And what was the baby's name? But I didn't ask Kendall any of those things. If she knew, she'd tell me . . . when she got ready. And if she didn't want me to know . . . well, at least she'd acknowledged that they had a child. That was a start, right?

"Your dad must be thrilled," I said.

"Yeah." She nodded. "This is a good time for him in the middle of all that he's going through."

I wanted to ask her what the doctors were saying about her father. I wanted to know how his treatments were going. But like I said, anything Kendall wanted me to know, she'd tell me.

"Now you know why I wanted you to come over," Kendall said as she leaned back on the sofa. "So, what did you want to talk to me about?"

With this house, and the news of the baby, I'd almost forgotten. "Yes! Oh, my goodness. So much has been going on. First, Christopher canceled his wedding."

She sat straight up. "What? Did they—"

I didn't even let her finish. "They didn't break up. Christopher and Evon are still together. They just decided to elope, though it's a different kind of elopement since we all know when and where they're going."

Kendall squinted. "What?"

"Yeah. My son doesn't want the wedding anymore because he doesn't think Quentin and I can be in the same room at the same time. He doesn't think his father will be able to keep his hands off my throat."

"Did Quentin threaten you?" Kendall asked like she wanted me to know that she had my back and was ready to rumble.

"No, he didn't. I need to take you back to the beginning. And I need to tell you right now, up front, that I didn't listen to you," I said, then paused. "I told Harmony about Quentin and Jett."

Kendall moaned as she kicked off her shoes and tucked her feet underneath her butt. "Okay." She motioned with her hands. "Tell me everything."

And that's what I did. I told Kendall the whole story. When I got to the part about meeting with Harmony, she shook her head. When I told her about Quentin coming over to my house, she widened her eyes. And when I relived the part about me and Brock arguing, she breathed, "Humph, humph, humph. Talk about keeping stuff from your best friend."

"Yeah, well. At least Brock and I have worked it out," I told her. "Yesterday Pastor Ford got me and him together in sort of a counseling session."

"You're doing counseling with Pastor?"

"No sessions. Just yesterday. But it was a good talk. You know Pastor, she gave it to me straight. Brock told me that he was tired of Quentin being at the center of our lives and Pastor told me that I needed to fix that if I wanted to keep my marriage."

"Whoa, it's like that?" she asked. "It'd gotten that deep?"

I nodded. "I didn't mean it to. I was just trying to help. And anyway," I said, holding up my finger like I wanted to scold somebody, "Quentin wouldn't be anywhere near us if everybody hadn't forced me to invite him for Christmas." I sighed. "But the good thing is that we're talking and I understand where Brock is coming from. And as much as I love Brock, I don't want him to ever think that I have any feelings for Quentin."

"Well, I can call Brock and tell him that," Kendall said. "Feelings, you don't have. But curiosity? I think that's why you can't leave this alone. You're trying to figure out this whole gay thing."

"That's it!" I said. "You get me. That's all I'm doing."

"I do get you, but you need to get over it. Because you're never going to figure it out. Hell, Quentin hasn't figured it out. He's with you, he's with Jett, he's with other men for all these years, and now he's engaged to Harmony. If he can't get it together, how're you gonna figure it out?"

I paused. "That's a good point."

"And, how are you gonna help him to get it together?" Before I could answer, Kendall continued. "You can't do it, Sheridan. I know it's not easy to do, but you have to just give it up and move on."

I dipped my head a little. "Listen to you, Miss Give It Up And Move On. Is that what you're doing? Is that what this is about?" I swept my hands through the air and once again looked around this living room.

"This is not about me," she said, and slapped my hands down. "This is about you still trying to be all up in Quentin's life. And it was kinda foul what you did to him and Harmony. I told you to leave it alone."

I shook my head. "You have no idea how much I wish I could make that up to Quentin. And Harmony. Because, I'm telling you, all I was doing was listening to my gut. I'm telling you, Kendall, I truly thought Quentin was playin' Harmony. When I saw him with Jett . . ." The image of the two of them together once again came to my mind. "It was intuition, and we're always told to go with our intuition."

"Yeah, when it's your life, but don't take your intuition into other people's lives. Let them use their own."

I nodded. "What makes me sad is that this is gonna all work out for me; Brock and I are fine. And even though we're not going to have the wedding that I always wished for, in a little over a week, Christopher and Evon will be married." I sighed. "The only people who are messed up are Quentin and Harmony—because of me. I really wish there was something I could do about that."

"Haven't you learned your lesson?"

"I have, but I just wish I could talk to Harmony. Take back what I said and tell her that I was wrong. She never even gave Quentin a chance to explain. She did some ol' technology breakup. He didn't stand a chance. But she might listen to me since I was the one to mess this whole thing up."

"I don't know . . ." Kendall said.

"I was just thinking that since I was the one who told her no, she might listen if I told her yes."

Now Kendall nodded, like she understood what I was saying. "Well, maybe you *should* call her."

"Her number's not in service and Quentin said that he's not even sure she's still in Los Angeles."

"Wow, she's not working at the hospital anymore?"

I shook my head. "Not according to Quentin."

"She really wanted to get away from him."

I sighed. "I know that feeling. I know how devastated she is and that's why I want to talk to her. Because there's no need to be feeling that kind of despair. Remember, that's how Vanessa felt."

Kendall and I sat as if we were giving our friend a moment of silence. And then, suddenly, Kendall said, "Stay right here." She reached for her phone. She pressed a number, then I watched her smile before she stood. "Hey, it's me," she said, turning her back so that I couldn't hear her as clearly. Then she strolled across the room; well, actually, Kendall kind of glided, because it didn't even look like her feet were touching the floor. "Can you do me a favor?" she said into her phone. A beat and then, "Can you find someone for me?" Another pause, then Kendall turned from the window and faced me. "Her name is Harmony."

Now I frowned.

Kendall asked me, "Do you know her last name?"

I shook my head. "No, it's Mac something, but I don't remember."

She nodded, then said, "No, we don't have a last name but she was a nurse at—"

"Cedars-Sinai," I piped in.

Kendall repeated that and told whoever she was talking to that Harmony was from Detroit. She nodded her head a couple of times and said, "Yeah," before she asked, "How long do you think it'll take?" A pause, and then Kendall said, "Great." Then a few seconds afterward, she turned back to the window. And though she whispered, I still heard her say, "Thank you. Thank you for everything."

I'm telling you, all I wanted to do was jump up, grab Kendall's cell phone, and demand that whoever was on the other end identify himself.

When Kendall turned back around and did that stroll-glide thing toward me, I bunched my eyebrows together. "Who was that?"

"Someone who's going to get a number so that you can talk to Harmony."

"What, you know someone who works for the CIA now?"

She grinned. "Almost." Just as she tossed her cell onto the sofa, a knock came from the front door, stopping the inquisition I was about to perform. "Right on time," Kendall said. As she danced across the living room, she spoke over her shoulder. "I ordered us lunch. We can eat on the deck."

"Great!" I said as I watched her. This whole schoolgirl-giddy was not Kendall. And what was up with that call?

Even though I was dying to know, Kendall wasn't going to give up a thing until she was ready. But I could tell that my girl had some story. And, I couldn't wait to hear it.

It couldn't have been more than a half an hour. I'm not kidding, not even thirty minutes had passed. Kendall and I were on the deck, snacking on grilled shrimp, crab cakes, and calamari and sipping iced tea. We hardly talked since neither one of us wanted to interrupt the music of the ocean. So we sat back and listened and watched a flock of seagulls stroll along the edge of the Pacific brine.

"Wait a minute," I said, sitting up in the lounge chair. "Is that Catalina?" With one hand, I pointed across the bay, and with the other, I cupped my eyes to block the sun so that I could get a clear view.

"Yup," Kendall said. "And if we stay out here long enough, we'll see a couple of dolphins out there just chillin'."

I laughed. "You know, this is the life."

She smiled.

"You deserve it," I said. And then, as if I thought I might be able to get something out of her, I added, "You deserve this and so much more."

Now a bigger smile, and just as she opened her mouth to speak, her cell phone rang.

Dang!

I watched her as she glanced down at the screen. Her joy was instant and she answered.

"You got it?" she asked. Then she nodded and handed the phone to me.

"Who is it?" I frowned.

"Harmony."

I looked at her phone as if it were some kind of foreign object because something strange had just happened here.

"Take it," Kendall said. "You want to talk to her, right?"

I reached across the table that was between our chairs and grabbed the phone. "Harmony?"

"Sheridan?" She sounded as surprised to hear my voice as I was to hear hers.

"Yes. I'm so glad to speak with you; I've been trying to reach you. How are you? Are you okay?"

"I'm fine."

"Are you still in L.A. or are you in Detroit?" I asked.

There was a pause, as if she was hesitant to tell me anything. I said, "I only asked because if you were still here, I was going to say we should get together, but it's probably best if I just come out and tell you."

"What? Has something happened to Quentin?" Her words were quick. Her concern for Quentin was so apparent.

It was clear; she still loved that man.

"No, not at all," I rushed to tell her. "At least not in the way that you're thinking. But he's just devastated, Harmony. And it's my fault."

"He told you that we broke up?"

"Yes, and I'm so sorry. That's not what I wanted to happen."

"It was the only thing I could do after you told me the truth."

"But the thing is, it wasn't the truth. I was wrong."

A beat. "What do you mean?"

"Quentin is not with Jett."

Another beat. "He told you to call me? He told you to tell me this?"

"No, he's probably going to kill me for calling you. And I probably should just stay out of this, but I can't because I caused it. The truth is, Jett is married. He's married to a woman."

"What?"

"Yes. And that's why they were at Rendezvous, because the chef is Jett's friend and Quentin wanted to hire him for your wedding because he said you loved the food there."

"Oh, my God," she whispered.

I could imagine the expression on her face, the way she weighed everything she'd just heard. "I know. I saw them and I jumped to a conclusion that was wrong. I should've never gone to you."

"No, no," she whispered. "I would've done the same thing. We're sorors."

"I feel so bad because now I know that Quentin does love you."

She sighed.

"Harmony, you have to give Quentin another chance."

She didn't say anything.

"Please, at least talk to him."

A beat, then, "I can do that. I can talk to him." Another beat. "I'll call him."

A wave of relief washed over me, but then I stiffened again. Would Quentin get mad if he found out that I talked to Harmony? Would Brock be mad, too? But I shook away those thoughts. I couldn't let anything stop me from doing the right thing.

"I really hope this works out for you, Harmony. I really do."

And that was the end of our conversation. Even after Harmony hung up, I held Kendall's phone for a moment. I'd forgotten about trying to figure out how Kendall had made this connection. My thoughts were completely on what I'd just told Harmony.

"Do you think she'll listen to you?" Kendall said, getting my attention.

"I don't know."

She took the phone from me and tilted her head. "What's wrong?"

I shook my head. "I think I did the right thing, but it doesn't feel good to me."

"Well," Kendall said, "you've done your part, now it's up to Quentin and Harmony." Then her voice turned stern, and she wagged her finger at me. "But from this point on, you stay out of it, no matter what, right?"

I nodded. "I'll stay out of it, no matter what," I said aloud. And then I repeated those words inside my head, over and over again. Repeated them until I believed them.

# Chapter
## Twenty-Eight

I couldn't stop thinking about Harmony.

On the entire ride home, my mind replayed our conversation. It was short, it was simple. I'd heard her relief, I'd heard her hope, and I'd heard her love for Quentin. I'd done what I had to do, right? So why was my stomach churning?

Maybe it was because I'd made all kinds of promises. Maybe it was because I knew Brock wouldn't be happy if he'd heard what I'd done. Maybe if I had the chance to do it all over again, I wouldn't have made that call and would've just left it alone.

But the deed was done and the bottom line was that I'd done the right thing.

I was still trying to convince myself of that when I pressed the garage remote, and once the door lifted, all thoughts of Quentin and Harmony left my mind. Brock's SUV was parked on the right side where it always was—when he was supposed to be home.

I checked the clock on the dashboard; it was only a little before three. Why was he home so early?

Grabbing my purse, I jumped out of the car with my keys in my hand. My husband never came home early. Something had to be wrong.

I rushed through the door that led to our house, then stopped.

*Lost without you . . .*

The soulful sound of Robin Thicke filled the house and the memories were instant. From the moment we were married, this was my favorite song. It was the song that we first danced to as husband and wife. Not that dance that we took in front of our wedding guests. This was the dance after everyone was gone, the dance that was for no one's eyes but ours. This was the dance we did without clothes, the dance that took me into ecstasy.

On our wedding day, we'd just said good-bye to our last guests and I was so exhausted. I had no idea how I would keep my eyes open for even another hour.

But then my new husband said, "I have a gift for you."

We were both still decked out, me in my gown and Brock in his tux. I remember I asked him, "A gift? A wedding gift?"

He nodded, then took my hand and led me into the back-yard. As we stepped outside, Robin Thicke sang through the speakers that Brock had set up in the backyard, but at that moment it wasn't the music that had my attention. It was the box that was large enough to hold a human body that sat in the center of the yard.

"What is it?" I asked.

Brock said nothing as he left me standing at the door. I watched as he opened the box and pulled out a massive mess of rope.

What in the world? That was the thought I had as I watched Brock dump the rope onto the ground, then he knelt down and began to untangle what looked like chaos.

But in only minutes, the mess became my dream. I clapped

my hands like a kid at Christmas as Brock hooked the over-size hammock between the two oak trees.

"Oh, my God. You remembered."

When we were considering which home to buy, I'd told Brock that I wanted a house with trees where I could hang a hammock and sway and sleep away the day.

But swaying and sleeping were not on my new husband's mind as he came to the door, took my hand, then led me to the hammock. Beneath those summer stars, he undressed me, slowly, planting soft kisses against every part of my skin as he disrobed me. It seemed to take too long for me, but once I was nude, I did the same to him.

Then, gently, carefully, he laid me in the hammock, and the exhaustion I'd felt a few minutes before was gone. Brock told me without singing a word how lost he'd be without me. He'd used his hands, his tongue, his legs, his . . .

*Can't help myself . . .*

Robin's voice interrupted my thoughts of that night and brought me back to the present. As I moved into the house, my steps matched the slow smile that spread onto my face. My glance swept through the living room, searching for my husband. But the room was empty.

*How does it feel . . .*

Now that I thought about it, now that I remembered our wedding night, I knew exactly where my husband was. I ran to the bedroom, and stopped at the door. My eyes searched once again, but again the room was empty. Stepping inside, I slowly walked through, peeking into the bathroom then checking inside both of our walk-in closets.

*To know that I love you, baby . . .*

Where was Brock?

As the song played through the surround-sound speakers throughout, I tiptoed through my home, expecting Brock to jump out of a corner at any moment.

I checked the family room. Nothing.

*Lost without you . . .*

I checked the bathroom. No one.

*Can't help myself . . .*

I checked the closets. Not a peep from Brock.

*How does it feel . . .*

I looked up toward the second-floor landing and placed my foot on the first step when I remembered.

Our wedding night.

My pace was slow, steady, in sync with the song as I moved toward the back of the house.

*To know that I love you . . .*

Inside the family room, the drapes were now open, as if Brock had been tracking me, and now he was ready to reveal where he'd been hiding. The sliding-glass door was open, too, and Robin Thicke's voice filled the backyard. Only Robin was not singing alone; he was singing a duet.

Brock sang, "'Baby, you're the perfect shape . . .'"

He held out his hand to me and swept me into his arms. And we danced as he serenaded me.

"'Lost without you, can't help myself, how does it feel to know that I love you, baby . . .'"

For minutes, I just swayed with him, savoring every second, locking it into my memory so that I could pull these moments from my mind when Brock was not here.

The music stopped, but Brock still held me, we still swayed, even though the song was over. But the rhythm was forever etched in our minds and we danced to our beat.

When Brock leaned over to kiss me, I was so ready to receive him. Connected, he backed me onto the hammock. And just like our wedding night, he told me once again how lost he'd be without me.

Only today, not a star twinkled overhead. Today, we made love under the bright beam of the sun.

As my husband held my hand and led me up the stairway to heaven, I thanked God that we were back. Brock and Sheridan Goodman were definitely back on track.

We'd moved our dance into our bedroom, and now as the sun finally began its descent in the western sky, Brock and I lay together, my back to the front of him, a human spoon. I snuggled deeper into his embrace, just reveling in this time that was ours.

But in the silence, my mind was clear to hear the thoughts that had never really left me. The second guesses that now haunted me about my call to Harmony.

Should I tell Brock? I didn't want him to hear that I'd interfered from anyone else. I didn't want Quentin to once again come stomping into our home without Brock knowing first.

"Brock, there's something I want to tell you." I rolled over to face him just as my cell phone vibrated from the nightstand. Twisting back around, I reached for it, then sat up straight when I saw my son's image.

"Christopher," I said. "How are you?" It had only been four days since I'd spoken to my son. But when someone is upset with you, that anger made days feel like an eternity.

"I'm good, Ma. I'm good."

There was a moment of silence and then I said, "I just want to say," just as Christopher said the exact same words.

We both stopped. We both laughed. And Brock smiled.

Then my husband motioned toward the bathroom before he jumped from the bed.

"So, Ma, you go first."

My ear was pressed to the phone, but my eyes were on my husband and his butt. His naked butt as he strutted into the bathroom. Even butt-naked my husband had so much swag. Naked swag. Nothing. But. Naked. Swag.

"Ma?"

"Oh! What? Sorry! I was distracted for a moment."

My son repeated, "I said you go first. 'Cause you raised me right, and I always know, ladies first."

That made me smile. "I just wanted to apologize for everything."

"That's what I was gonna say, too," Christopher said. "I shouldn't have gotten mad at you. I was just mad 'cause I knew Dad was hurt. But I need to leave that between the two of you. That's grown folks' business, right?"

I laughed. "Right. So . . ." I paused for a second. "Does this mean that you and Evon will reconsider and have your wedding?"

"No, Ma. And it's not because of you. All the planning, the wedding, it was just getting too big and Evon and I really want to do it this way."

"Okay."

"Don't be disappointed, Ma."

I guess he heard how I really felt.

He said, "We're just gonna go off next weekend, and when we get back, we'll take you and Brock out to dinner."

That was not enough of a consolation prize for me, but I said, "Okay," anyway.

"Think of all the money you're saving."

"That was never a problem."

"I know," Christopher said. "Then think about how much happier I am doing it this way."

"And that's all I want . . . for you and Evon to be happy."

"I am, Ma. Listen, I've got to make this run, but I'll catch you later."

"Okay, I love you."

When Christopher told me the same, I clicked off my cell, leaned back against the headboard, and smiled. I was still looking at the phone when Brock came into the bedroom.

"So, Chris is good?"

Again, my eyes took my mind away for just a moment, but I came back quickly. I did my best to look into Brock's eyes and not focus on other parts of him. I nodded. "We're back on track."

Brock nodded as if he knew that I was talking about him *and* Christopher. My husband pulled me into his arms, but then leaned away from me.

"Oh, before Chris called, you said there was something you wanted to tell me."

I looked into his eyes, thought about the call from my son, and brought my lips to his.

"Hmm . . ." he moaned.

And that was where I was going to leave it. I wasn't going to say a thing. Whatever happened with Harmony and Quentin was just going to happen. I just prayed that me and mine had been drawn into their lives for the very last time.

# Chapter
## Twenty-Nine

I had every single window rolled down as I sped up La Cienega Boulevard heading north toward Sunset. I didn't have a convertible, but it sure felt like I did as the April breeze blew through my car.

Life was so good. My home, my family, we were all lined up, once again living in perfect harmony. And then on the other "Harmony" front—it seemed like life was working out there, too.

The day after I'd spoken to Harmony, I received a text from Quentin. It was very simple. Two words: *Thank you.* And I'd sent him back a smiley face.

Then the next day, I heard from Harmony: *Soror, I can't thnk u enough 4 bringing the happiness back n2 my life. Q & I r 2gther again, in a good place & I owe it all 2 u. Let's get 2gther soon. Call me.*

My nonresponse to Harmony was my answer. I had handled this situation, and the way I'd calmed the waters, somebody needed to give me five snaps up.

But now that it was over, Harmony and I didn't need to be

friends. She was my soror, but she was my ex's next and that made her ineligible for any kind of friendship. So there was no need to pretend that we were going to be anything more than we were. I was burning that bridge. My plan was never to be in touch with Harmony or Quentin again.

All I wanted now was happier times.

That's why I was heading up toward Sunset. To prepare for happier times.

This had all been Brock's idea. He'd come up with it two days ago when I was moping over my morning coffee about the only sad spot in my life—Christopher and Evon's wedding. Even though I'd put everything back together again, I couldn't shake Christopher's resolve to go away—and not have family with them.

That was when Brock had said, "Why don't we have a celebration waiting for Christopher and Evon when they come back?"

Before the entire sentence had left his lips, I was on it. I dashed up to my office, grabbed my iPad, and ran back to the kitchen. "What a great idea," I finally said to him. Then I sat at the kitchen table ready to make notes, make calls, make plans.

And all of that made Brock hold up his hands. "Now, we don't want a big thing. You know how Chris is. Let's just do a little something. Right here. In the backyard, where we had our reception."

As if having the reception here at our home was going to stop me from making this grand. "The backyard is perfect." Then I opened up my browser. "The first thing I need is a caterer."

Brock slipped into the chair beside me. "What about trying Rendezvous?"

At first, I'd scrunched up my nose.

"What's wrong? You love that place."

"And that's where all of this stuff started. Now I have a bunch of bad memories."

"Awww, come on." Brock had laughed. "Are you telling me that you never want to go back to your favorite restaurant?"

Okay, my husband had a point there. Rendezvous was too good a place to give up because I'd messed up.

"If you don't want to do it," Brock said, "I can drop by there one day after work and speak to one of the managers."

"No, I'll call and make an appointment," I told him.

That's what I'd done and that's where I was headed now as the wind whipped through my hair.

I used my drive time to turn over all the plans in my head: my mother was coming home, and my brother and his family would be with her. Christopher would be thrilled about that. I was still searching for some kind of theme for the celebration, and I was thinking that I might have to give the wedding planner a call. At least I could get something out of the deposit that I'd lost after the cancellation.

I pushed aside those thoughts as I slowed my car and signaled to move into the left lane. I'd have to make a U-turn at the next corner and then pull around to the front of the restaurant.

As I edged to the left, I glanced across the street to the front of Rendezvous, and then I slammed on the brakes. I frowned at first—there was no way that I could be seeing what I saw. It wasn't until the car behind me blared his horn that I drove a few inches, then made that illegal U-turn. But I didn't pull up in front of the restaurant. I eased my car over and stayed a few feet back.

And then my mouth opened wide.

Once again, there was Quentin and Jett.

And this time, they were in an embrace. And not a buddy-buddy brother-man hug. This time, there was no conjecture. This embrace was real.

And so was . . . the kiss. The kiss that came next. Their pro-
longed kiss. On the lips. Not friends. Clearly lovers.

"Oh, my God!"

I slipped down just a bit in my seat and willed myself to
close my eyes. If I didn't see this, I wouldn't have to do anything.

But it was too late.

I saw everything.

Then Quentin slipped into one car, and Jett slid into the
next.

And I stayed where I was watching, not believing, stone-
cold shocked.

But then my shock began to dissipate and I was pissed.
I was mad at everyone and everything. No one had listened
to me. From Christmas straight through to this moment, I'd
been called everything except crazy.

And now it turned out that I was the only one who'd seen
the elephant in the room. I'd known it, and I'd been right.

All along, it had been in my gut.

I sat up straight and revved the engine. I'd have to re-
schedule my meeting with the Rendezvous manager.

There was something else that I had to do. Right now.

As I sped back down the boulevard, driving past everything that I'd just passed minutes before, I hit the Bluetooth
on my steering wheel.

There were some calls I had to make.

# Chapter
## Thirty

I was on my knees at the altar.

Even when I heard footsteps coming in behind me, I didn't move. I stayed with my head bowed, my eyes closed, finishing the last of my prayer to God.

I heard a creak and I knew it was one of my girls sitting in the front pew. But still I stayed right where I was because I wasn't finished, and I wasn't getting up from this altar until I was sure.

When I drove away from Rendezvous, I'd made a mad dash to my church. I mean, I drove like I was being chased, hardly stopping for red lights, slowing down only to make two calls—to Kendall, to Asia.

I needed to get to my church as fast as I could because I needed God to talk to me. Not like last time when I'd asked Him about Harmony. This time I needed Him to speak to my heart, and to make it plain.

And when I'd walked into this sanctuary, I'd felt nothing but peace. I knew I was going to get my answer today.

Behind me, I heard more footsteps, but this time the footsteps didn't stop. And after a couple of seconds, I felt the cushion beneath my knees dip a little. One of my girls had joined me on the altar.

Still, I stayed in place until I had nothing but calm, nothing but peace. Then I opened my eyes, held up my head, and looked at Kendall.

"Hey," she whispered. "Is everything okay?"

"I think so," I said, keeping my voice as soft as hers.

"Then why did you call?" I glanced over my shoulder. Asia had gotten up from the pew, and now she stood beside me.

I pushed myself up and Kendall did, too.

Asia said, "You sounded really upset."

I hoisted my purse onto my shoulder. "I was, but then I came here." I glanced to my right. "I came here and left it all on the altar."

"Well, all right, then," Kendall said.

As we started walking up the aisle toward the front doors, Asia asked, "So, I came all the way over here for nothing?"

I stopped moving, shook my head, and pointed to the front of the church. "You can always pray."

"No thanks, I'm good. I prayed this morning," Asia said as if there was a daily quota and she'd met it.

"Well, you still didn't waste your time because I'm taking the two of you to lunch."

"What's the occasion?" Kendall asked.

"We're celebrating lessons learned."

"And what lesson is that?" It was Asia's turn to question me.

"Something that your aunt told me. That I am not Quentin's savior."

"Yeah, I remember when Aunt Beverly told you that. It was deep."

"And I finally got it."

"So, that's why you called us over here? Having me driving like a maniac?" Asia asked.

"I'm sorry about that. It's just that when I got here, I

decided to go straight into prayer. And by the time you guys got here, I was already in it with God."

"Well, then it's all good to me," Asia said. "So, where are we going for lunch?"

My answer seemed to satisfy Asia, but Kendall gave me one of her long sidelong glances that let me know she knew there was more to my story.

"I'm taking you guys to Rendezvous."

The way the two of them stepped back and looked me up and down, I had to laugh.

"Don't worry. I have a meeting there. I'm having a reception for Christopher and Evon when they get back next weekend and I'm going over for a tasting meeting. I'm a little late, but I'm sure they'll fit me in. And, I didn't tell them that I was bringing friends, but y'all don't eat much, so it should be cool."

They laughed.

Kendall said, "Sounds like a good deal to me since it's free. I'll go into my office afterward."

"Is Adolphe Baptiste single?" Asia asked. When I shrugged, she said, "Well, we'll soon find out." She plopped her sunglasses onto her face, then bounced down the steps. "I'll see you over there."

Kendall and I stood there watching Asia walk to her car. "Now, that's a sight I'm glad to see. After what she's been through, I wasn't sure she was going to date anyone again," I said.

"Yeah, kids are resilient and Angel seems to be coming along, but . . ." Kendall paused and turned toward me. "You might be able to fool Asia 'cause she's so self-absorbed, but you can't fool me. What really happened?" she asked me.

If Kendall had met me before I got to the church, I probably would've told her everything. But once I bowed at the altar, I had such a strong feeling that I wasn't supposed to say a word. All I was supposed to do was pray and God would take care of it.

So all I said to Kendall was "It was something I saw, something that really bothered me, and something that I left at the altar."

She nodded her head slowly. "So, you don't want to talk about it yet?"

I shook my head.

"Well, I understand that. You know I'm here if you ever want to talk," Kendall said.

"This I know. And you know I'm here for you, right?"

"Hey!" Asia yelled out from her car window as she pulled out of the parking lot. "Are y'all gonna stand there all day or are we going to eat?"

"We're coming," I said as Kendall and I finally walked down the stairs.

"Oh, and Sheridan," Asia called out. "If I'm still hungry after this little taste testing, you can just take me over to Roscoe's. It's right down the street from Rendezvous." Then she raced off.

Kendall looked at me, shook her head, then laughed. "I'm parked around the corner. I'll meet you over there."

"Okay."

She walked to the left and I walked to the right, but then I stopped for a moment and looked back at the church. I thought of all the prayers I'd sent up. Prayers for God's direction, prayers for Harmony, and most of all prayers for Quentin. I prayed for him harder than I did for everyone else.

Because that man didn't need my judgment; Quentin just needed my prayers. He needed to be untangled from all the lies that the devil had told him, so that he could tell the truth to everyone else, especially himself.

But this time, I wasn't going to say a word. I was just going to pray and pray and pray. And leave the rest of it to the real Savior.

Kendall Stewart

# Tables Turned

# Chapter
## Thirty-One

I shot straight up in bed!

Still panting, still trying to catch my breath. My eyes focused through the darkness and then I clicked on the lamp. I took a long sweeping glance through my bedroom.

There was no one there.

But there had to be. It felt so real.

My heart was pounding as I eased out of my bed. Even though I lived at the beach, I never turned on the heat. So right away the cool March air rushed me, wrapped around my bare legs, and crept all the way up to my butt since all I wore was one of my old UCLA T-shirts.

Feeling the chill didn't stop me, though. I tiptoed through my bedroom, then peeked into the hall. I moved through the entire cottage, clicking on all the lights along the way. I even turned on the light for the deck outside, lighting up the midnight black on the beach.

Now that my house was illuminated as if it were high noon, I could see for sure, there was nothing. No one.

D'Angelo was not in my house.

I leaned against the windowed wall that faced the beach. I could've sworn that he was here. D'Angelo was right in that bed with me. Really, he was. I could still feel his hands, and his tongue and his—

"Stop it!" I scolded myself.

It had to be all of that rich food that I'd tasted at Rendezvous with Sheridan today. From the collard greens quiche to the chocolate mint éclairs, that chef, Adolphe Baptiste, was the truth, but he had not done my body good. It had to be his fault that I couldn't sleep, or rather, that I couldn't sleep without dreaming.

By the time I went into the kitchen and set my old-fashioned teapot atop the stove, I had completely convinced myself that dreaming about D'Angelo was all because of Adolphe Baptiste.

That made perfect sense to me, though it didn't quite explain all the other nights when I hadn't eaten at Rendezvous and D'Angelo still stalked my sleep. D'Angelo Stewart, the man who shared my last name since he was the brother of my ex-husband. D'Angelo Stewart, a Compton legend, who'd long ago traded the streets of Compton for militia missions on the battlefields of Iraq. D'Angelo Stewart, the bad boy who had strolled, with all of that swagger, right back into my life three months ago on Christmas Day.

It was when we'd stood in the kitchen alone, cleaning up after our dinner, that D'Angelo and I had really talked for the first time in years . . .

"See, don't you wish you got out of here a couple of hours ago?" I'd said as I passed him a dish that I'd just rinsed off.

With the dish towel I'd given him, he dried. "Nope. I'm willing to work for that dinner that you and your dad just shared with me. I haven't celebrated Christmas like this in years. So, thanks for having me."

"You don't have to keep saying that. We were glad to see you again. And anyway, I should be thanking you for helping me clean up all of this stuff. Dad's gonna have food for days."

"No doubt about that," D'Angelo said as he looked over at the containers that we'd just stacked on the counter filled with leftovers. "But what's up with washing dishes? I didn't know they made homes without dishwashers anymore."

I laughed. "When this house was built, there weren't any dishwashers."

"Yeah, but didn't a dishwasher just automatically pop up into every home back in the eighties?"

"Not for Edwin Leigh." I chuckled. "You know I would've had a dishwasher installed in here for him years ago, but he just doesn't believe that a machine can clean a glass as well as a good old dishrag."

"Your dad may have a point there." D'Angelo paused. "Are you sure he's good? I mean, he looked kind of tired."

I nodded slowly, thinking the same thing myself. My dad had just been diagnosed with breast cancer, so every time he grimaced, or sighed, or even yawned, my radar shot up. But I wasn't about to share that with D'Angelo. Anything that my father wanted anyone to know, he'd have to tell himself. "Dad's cool. Like you said, he's just tired. He'll lie down for a little while and then be back up again, probably ready for another piece of pie."

"Cool." D'Angelo nodded as I passed another plate to him. "So, it's a good thing that I stayed behind, then. Or else you would've been doing this all by yourself."

I laughed. "And, I could've handled it."

"I bet you could." His voice was softer when he said, "Seems like you can handle anything. Seems like you've had to handle a lot."

I knew where he was going with this. It was a complicated

story worthy of being on the big screen. I'd been married to D'Angelo's brother, and then one day I came home from a business trip and found his brother, my husband, in bed with my sister. It had been so traumatic and tragic and I was sure D'Angelo wanted to hear every detail.

We'd cleaned all the dishes; now it was time for us to tackle the pots and pans. But I pushed aside the dishcloth for a moment and turned to my ex brother-in-law. For a moment I had to pause. The way D'Angelo's hooded eyes looked down at me . . . I held my sigh inside. Instead, I said, "I know you're curious about what happened with me and Anthony. What do you want to know?"

He shrugged. "Whatever you want to tell me."

"Not much to tell. I found Anthony and Sabrina in bed together . . ."

"That's foul," he said.

"And Anthony and I divorced because of that."

"Just like that? No other drama? He didn't try to get back with you?"

"He tried, he lost. I said no. I filed the papers, I divorced him."

D'Angelo nodded slowly. "But you and Sabrina have worked it out. Chillin' together like nothing's happened."

"Don't let us all being in the same room without anyone getting cut fool you. Today was the first time I'd seen them in six years," I told D'Angelo.

"You're kidding? I didn't know that. Well then, I'm sorry I ran them off."

Turning back to the sink and away from his direct glance, I said, "It's not your fault that they decided not to stay." That was all I was going to say about Anthony and Sabrina walking out before our big Christmas dinner under the guise that Sabrina, who was pregnant, wasn't feeling well.

I wasn't going to tell D'Angelo that I knew the real deal. I'd overheard my ex and my sister talking as they hid away in our old bedroom. Really, I guess it was more like I was eavesdropping, but whatever, Anthony had not been happy that Sabrina had contacted D'Angelo and invited him to our dinner. Anthony hated his brother; for some reason, he blamed D'Angelo for their parents' deaths, and Anthony told Sabrina that he would never sit down and break any kind of bread with him. So, they'd left, and to be honest, that made my Christmas better—with just me, my dad, and D'Angelo.

He said, "We come from quite a dysfunctional family. My brother hates me for something I didn't do and you hate my brother and your sister for something they did do."

I shook my head. "You've got it all wrong," I said. "I don't hate them at all. In fact"—I paused and thought about what I was going to say—"I've forgiven them."

He looked at me for a long moment. "Well, then I guess you're ready to move on," he said.

"Yup, already have," I said as I scrubbed one of the pans.

"Good, then that must mean that you're free to go to the movies tonight." When I tilted my head and looked at him like I didn't understand what he was saying, he explained: "You know there are a couple of movies that opened today; we can catch any one that you want to see."

When I'd given D'Angelo that look, it wasn't because I didn't know what he meant. It was just that I could not remember the last time that someone had asked me to go anywhere. And I told him what I would've told anyone who asked me out. "Thanks, but no thanks," I said.

D'Angelo leaned back like he was shocked. I guess my answer was probably a surprise. How many women ever said no to this man who looked like Denzel, if he'd been a jock. I had no doubt women were lined up, ready and willing to do

D'Angelo's bidding. "Whoa," he said. "I guess my brother and your sister did some job on you."

Why did it have to be all that? Why couldn't it just be that I didn't want to go out with him? I guess for a man like D'Angelo, who wore his bad-boy-sexy like it was a cologne, the concept that a woman didn't want to be with him was difficult to grasp.

But I wasn't going to go there with him, so I just shook my head. "It's not Sabrina and Anthony. I told you, I've forgiven them. Plus, if the truth is told, Sabrina is much better for Anthony than I ever was."

"Ah . . . you're a progressive woman." He chuckled a bit. "But that still doesn't explain you saying no to me. You know, that doesn't happen much."

I twisted my lips trying to hold back my smile, though that didn't work. "I can imagine. But I said no because I was never meant to be a wife."

"Did I ask you to marry me?"

I laughed. "No, but . . ."

"Oh! I see what you're saying. Once a man goes out with you, he'll be so enthralled that he'll rush you to City Hall and by morning you'll be a wife."

I snatched the dish towel from his hand, swatted his arm with it, then handed it back to him. "That's not what I'm saying. I just know that a date could lead to dating could lead to something more."

"And you don't want the something more?"

"Exactly!" I said. "As much as Anthony and Sabrina were dirty for what they did, I should've never married your brother. He was in love with me, and I loved his business acumen. He wanted romantic dinners, and I wanted long planning meetings. He wanted a family and a future with me, and I wanted to open five spas and build an empire with him." I shook my head. "To be honest, he wanted it to work, and I didn't."

"Wow. It takes a grown-up to admit that."

I shrugged. "But don't get it twisted, they were still foul! They should've at least waited for me to figure all of this out."

He laughed. "So what happened to the house?"

"In Malibu? Anthony got it in the divorce, but I just heard today that they sold it."

"Man! I know how much you loved that place."

"I did. You found us the perfect home," I said, thinking back to that time. Anthony and I had just married and D'Angelo had his hand in all kinds of ventures, including real estate. The house had been a surprise after Anthony had told him in passing that my fantasy home was anywhere in Malibu.

"Well, maybe I can do that for you again," he said.

"Really?" I chuckled.

He nodded. "And if I do, will you go out with me then . . . ?"

The whistle from my teapot brought me back from Christmas, brought me back to the present and the beach cottage that D'Angelo had found for me just a few weeks ago. I jumped up, but now that the water was boiling, I didn't need any tea. I was ready to go back to bed.

This time, when I walked through my home that I loved, I turned out all the lights, and then I climbed back into my bed. It wouldn't take me long to fall asleep. Sleeping wasn't the problem. It was what went on in my subconscious after I was asleep.

But that was okay. It was only a dream. A dream that meant absolutely nothing to me.

# Chapter Thirty-Two

I stared out the window of my office, though, trust me, this wasn't the same as looking at the view when I was home. Here, there wasn't much to see except for the parking lot that served the office buildings in the business park. But I wasn't looking out for the view. I was just staring out the window. Staring because I couldn't concentrate.

This morning, I'd arrived at the Woman's Place, my spa business in Redondo Beach, even earlier than my normal seven o'clock time. Today, I walked in at just before six and did my regular workout: an hour jog around the track and thirty minutes in the weight room. I'd skipped the sauna; I was afraid that I might fall asleep in there.

But here I was, almost four hours from when I'd first arrived, and I hadn't accomplished a thing. All because my dream had followed me from the night right into this day.

Having vivid dreams and remembering every moment wasn't something that was new for me. At night, I dreamed, and in the morning, I remembered. That's just how it'd always been with me.

In the recent past, though, say the last six years, my dreams could best be defined as nightmares. A couple of times a week, I relived the horror of the final moments of my marriage. When I'd returned from a business trip early, to make up for the argument I'd had with my husband before I'd left, I was sure Anthony would be thrilled to see me, but as it turned out, he was not.

The nightmares I had were always the same, and always so true to what happened. In my dreams, I walked into the room, over to my bed, and then screamed. Then Anthony and Sabrina appeared. And they screamed. Anthony, my husband. Sabrina, my sister. The three of us screaming, though I was the only one screaming while fully clothed.

Then Anthony stopped screaming, and started shouting, "I'm sorry, it was just this one time."

Every time, I woke up at that moment. I wasn't sure why. Maybe it was because what came after didn't matter. Even though Anthony had uttered that exact apology to me, it didn't matter what he said. My marriage was over right at that moment in that bedroom.

I lived those minutes over and over in my head, and I sometimes wondered if maybe that was why I couldn't let go of that betrayal in my heart. But what could I do about it? You couldn't stop your dreams, could you?

Though it seemed like I didn't have to worry about those nightmares anymore. Because since Christmas, my old nightmares had been kicked aside for this new dream with that divine-fine D'Angelo.

I couldn't stop dreaming about him and I wasn't quite sure why. It wasn't like there was anything going on between us. I meant what I said when I told him no on Christmas, though that hadn't stopped him from trying that night . . .

I'd paused at the entrance to the living room and watched

D'Angelo as he studied the pictures on the mantel. The photos, mostly of me and Sabrina growing up, were in chronological order, and when D'Angelo picked up the frame with my high school graduation picture, I cleared my throat and stepped all the way into the living room.

He turned around with my photo still in his hand. "Your dad's okay?"

I nodded. "Yeah, he's sleeping. I woke him up for a moment, told him that we had cleaned up everything. But it was a long day, filled with lots of excitement for him, so I told him to just rest and I'd see him tomorrow."

"Cool. So where're you headed?" D'Angelo asked me.

"Home."

He paused as if he was waiting for me to say more. But I said nothing as I put on my bomber jacket and slipped my purse strap onto my shoulder.

He said, "Well, let me give you a ride."

"No thanks, I have my car."

He shrugged as if that made no difference. "I'll have your car towed to your house."

I laughed. "Now, that's funny. Why would I do that?"

"Because . . ." he began, stepping so close to me that we were almost one. But I wasn't about to let him intimidate me. So, I stood my ground and looked straight up into his eyes as he looked down into mine. He continued, "Because you don't want this night to end. You don't want to let me out of your sight, and you want to spend just a little more time with me."

Okay, this man right here . . . he was trying to take my breath away. But I guess he didn't realize that I was not the one. I was gonna keep my breath and everything else. I did take two steps back, though, before I said, "You can just walk me to my car . . ."

And that's what D'Angelo did. Just walked me the twenty

feet from my dad's front door to my car. He opened the door for me, watched as I slipped inside, made sure the doors were locked, and then he walked away.

But while I was driving home my cell phone rang. I didn't recognize the number when I answered, but I knew the voice.

"Just wanted to see if you changed you mind about going out with me," he'd said.

I laughed. "In ten minutes? I left you ten minutes ago and you think I've changed my mind?"

"It only takes a second to change your mind. Especially when you're switching to what's right."

I was still laughing, but then I frowned. "Hey, how did you get my number?"

He laughed. "You must've forgotten who you're talking to. I'm D'Angelo Stewart. Act like you know!" The next thing I heard was a click; the call had been ended.

I'd taken a deep, deep breath and released it, just like I was doing now.

I was so glad when my intercom buzzed, taking me away and bringing me back at the same time. I pressed the button on my phone, and my assistant announced, "There's someone here to see you."

I frowned and waited for Sarah to complete her sentence. She was beyond competent; it wasn't like her to just give me part of the information. But when she said nothing more, I asked, "Who is it?"

"Well . . ." She lowered her voice. "He asked me not to say . . ."

I was about to go off. Sarah worked for me, not for some stranger who showed up at my door. And, I didn't play games like this, especially not at my place of business. But then it hit me. It was D'Angelo. And that made me smile.

"Okay, go ahead and let him come in." I did my best to

wipe away my smile. I didn't want D'Angelo walking in here and seeing me grinning like a fool.

But then the door opened and I didn't have to worry about smiling at all. Because it wasn't D'Angelo. It was his brother.

"What're you doing here?" I asked my ex-husband.

Anthony said, "Wow, that's some greeting."

If he expected me to go back and amend what I'd said, he would be standing for a long time. I raised my eyebrows, like I just wanted him to answer the question.

He got the message. "I was just in the neighborhood," he said. "And I wanted to talk to you about a couple of things." He pointed to the chair. "Mind if I sit down?"

I didn't respond at first. Not that I was being totally rude, but I wanted to study Anthony for just a little while longer and it was easier to do that if he were standing.

Both of the Stewart boys were fine, there was no doubt about that. They just wore their sexiness in different ways. While D'Angelo had swag, Anthony was more refined. I always said Anthony was like a tall glass of chocolate decadence with his mocha-colored skin and his light brown eyes. The lines on his face were strong and defined—high cheeks and his square jaw. And then there were his muscles, though Anthony couldn't rival his brother. D'Angelo was a football player, straight ripped like Terrell Owens. Anthony was more of a basketball player—what LeBron James might look like in twenty years. Still in shape, but you know what I'm sayin'.

"Have a seat," I finally said.

He nodded and glanced around my office. "I didn't get a chance to walk around outside, but this place looks great," he said. "I'm really proud of what you've done with your business."

"Our business," I said. "I wouldn't have ever gotten started without you."

That made Anthony smile. I guess because he didn't expect

me to say something so kind. But I wasn't being polite; I was telling the truth and giving due credit.

"So . . ." he said.

"So," I said. That was all he was going to get out of me. I hadn't come by *his* office.

"Well, first, I wanted to thank you for the bassinet that you sent for the baby. That was really generous."

I nodded, thinking that their baby was two weeks old now. "How are Sabrina and my"—I paused and corrected myself—"the baby?"

A shadow passed over Anthony's eyes as if he was disappointed that I hadn't said "my niece." But still he nodded, and he grinned and he beamed just like a new father. "They're good. Sabrina's a little run-down, but I know that's just her being a new mom." He shook his head. "But Ciara . . . she's just gorgeous."

"Ciara." I paused and placed my hand over my heart that had just skipped a beat. I didn't know why. It wasn't the first time that I'd heard their baby's name. My father had told me the day she was born. But for some reason, it got to me today. I said, "Ciara. That's a beautiful name."

"Thanks. We're so happy that she's here. I hope you'll come by to see her."

His words were exactly the same as my sister's. Not that I'd spoken to Sabrina, but every day since Ciara was born, Sabrina called, left a message, and asked me to come by to see the baby. The truth was that's why I'd sent the gift; I thought that would be enough to stop the calls. But it wasn't.

He added, "And Sabrina would love to see you, too."

I didn't know what he expected me to say, so I just nodded. Anthony let a few more seconds pass, and then he nodded, too, as if he knew that subject was closed.

He said, "Sabrina and I know you've been doing all the heavy lifting with Dad."

"What do you mean?"

"Well, you're the one who's been with him during his chemo treatments."

"I'm cool with that. He's my dad and Sabrina was pregnant. And now, with the baby . . ." I waved my hand. "I'm fine and Dad's good, too."

"Well, thanks for saying that. But we want to start helping now, too. So, if you take him for the treatments, I'll be there when he gets home. This way, you can get back to the office, or do whatever you have to do."

"You don't have to do that."

"I know, but we really want to be more involved. We want to help out, that's all."

I nodded because there was really no way to tell them no. How could I keep them away from my father? Just because I didn't want to be around Anthony, Sabrina, and their baby didn't mean that I would ever deprive my dad. "Okay. His next treatment is a week from today, so if you want to come over after that, I usually get him home around two."

"I'll be there," Anthony said. "When we saw him the other day, he told us that the chemo was taking a lot out of him."

"Yeah, but he's good, you know. He's filled with faith, and hope, and I love that."

"I've always loved your father," my ex said. "I've learned a lot from him."

Okay, this was starting to sound like friendly chitchat, and we weren't friends and I didn't do chitchat.

"Well," I said. That was my hint that this little meeting was over.

"Well," he said. But he sat like he had more to say.

I didn't have time for this; didn't have time to sit and wait for him to come up with more words that meant nothing to me. "Is there anything else you want to talk to me about?"

"Yeah, there is."

A beat. Another beat. And I waited. I was just about to tell him to get out when he finally started talking.

He said, "My brother, D'Angelo, have you talked to him?"

"Yeah, why?" I asked, wondering if there was something wrong. Had something happened to D'Angelo? Maybe that's why I'd been dreaming about him, maybe it was some kind of prophecy. A warning. Now that I thought about it, I hadn't spoken to him in about a week.

Anthony pressed his lips together and frowned. His glance moved from me to the floor, then back to me. Then, finally, he said, "Kendall, I really don't think you should be involved with my brother."

Now my eyes narrowed. "By 'involved,' you mean?"

"I mean anything. I don't think you should go out with him, I don't think you should talk to him. Nothing."

Ain't this a blip! For a moment I saw myself jumping up, leaping over my desk, and wrapping my hands around Anthony's throat. But that would've been some mess if my assistant came into my office and saw me beating down my ex-husband.

So, I just pressed my back into the chair to stop myself from doing that. "I already told you," I began, referring to the moment when he'd said this same crap to me on Christmas. "I told you that you didn't have any right to tell me what to do. So which part of you-gave-that-up-when-you-slept-with-my-sister don't you understand?"

He blew out a long breath. "This is different."

I chuckled at his audacity.

"D'Angelo is not a good guy."

"And you are?"

"I wish you would just listen to me."

"And I wish you would just get the . . ." Now I was the one who released a long breath. "Get out of here, Anthony."

"I'm only thinking of you."

"Why start now?" And then I stood up. Because it looked like I was going to have to escort my ex out.

As I rose from my chair, Anthony did, too. As if he wondered if he was going to have to brace himself for a fight. But I just walked past him. Walked right to the closed door and opened it.

He took the hint and stepped toward me. When he paused at the door, I looked him dead in his eyes, daring him to say another word.

But he was smart enough to keep his mouth shut, and when he walked through the door, I closed it behind him.

Then I stomped to my desk. And I stomped back to the door. I was a hot-tamale kind of mad! Really? That man thought he could say anything to me? I hadn't even talked to him or my sister in the last six years. They were only in my life because of Dad's diagnosis. I only saw them for the first time in six years because Dad wanted us all there for this Christmas. Without that, I would've gone to my grave never speaking another word to either one of them bammas.

"Ugh!" I screeched.

And what was so ridiculous about this whole thing was that D'Angelo had been trying to get me to go out with him. Ever since Christmas, he'd asked me out at least a dozen times, and though I talked to him a lot by phone, I always nixed the idea. All this time I'd said no, but now I grabbed my office phone and pressed the button where I'd had his number stored.

"What's up, pretty lady," D'Angelo said the moment he answered. "You good?"

"Yeah, I'm fine," I said as I blazed a trail from my desk to the door and then back.

"So, what do you need today?" he asked. "A new house in

Malibu? Or do you need me to help you find someone else? What do you need, 'cause whatever it is, I got you, pretty lady."

I was still fighting mad, but just hearing this sweet man calmed me down a little bit. "Is it really like that?" I asked him. "Do you think I only call you when I need something?"

"I don't think it, I know it. That's just how it is. When you have a need, you call. But I don't mind. I know my purpose and I play my role. I can satisfy all of your needs, and at least I get to talk to you occasionally."

"But we talk all the time."

"Because, I call *you*." He paused. "You never noticed that? Really?"

"So you're saying I only call when I want something?"

"Yup!" I could imagine him nodding.

"Well, to keep my streak going, I'm calling because I want something."

"Shoot!"

"Will you have dinner with me?"

The pause that followed was so long that I wanted to say something like *Never mind. That was just an early April Fools' joke.* Instantly, I was embarrassed, but still I said, "Hello?"

"Oh, I'm sorry. I was just picking my jaw up from the floor."

I laughed.

"But that's what's up. I'll be there in ten minutes," he said.

"No, I said dinner, D. Not lunch." Even though when I glanced at the clock it was just barely ten thirty. It was even too early for lunch.

"I know. Dinner. But I'm gonna come over there and we're gonna spend the day together because I'm not gonna let you change your mind."

"No, I can't. Really . . ." But then I realized that D'Angelo was gone. He was on his way.

I sighed, then I smiled. I hadn't been able to get any work done anyway. I might as well hook up and hang out with D'Angelo.

Sitting back in my chair, I nodded. Anthony had done what his brother hadn't been able to do . . . he convinced me to go out on a date with D'Angelo. Even if it was just this once.

Like he said he was going to do, D'Angelo swooped into my office, and even though I tried to front like I really couldn't leave, he either didn't buy my story or didn't care.

"You have a million-dollar empire going here," he said. "You're thinking of franchising. If someone who has built all of this can't take a day off from work . . ."

His words were meant to flatter me, but what I wanted to know was how did he know all of that? A good part of it was public record—so that meant that he'd Googled me. But the part about the franchising . . . I shook my head. I guess I had to get used to hanging out with a friend who used to be a major player in the drug trade in South Central L.A. and who now ran secret missions for some militia group.

"So, are you ready?" he asked me.

He stood in front of my office door, looking like a bouncer, with his legs spread into a wide stance and his arms crossed in front of his muscular chest that couldn't even be hidden beneath his leather jacket. And, of course, he wore his dark glasses so that I could hardly see his eyes, but I knew that he was watching me.

I looked down at the jogging suit that I was wearing. "I'm not dressed to go out," I said, pointing to what was very often my office uniform. I owned a day spa and a gym; this was all I needed if I wasn't having a meeting.

"That suit cost you what? Two, three hundred? You look

fine enough." He paused. "And, I mean fine in all ways." Then he held out his large hand with his long fingers and I wondered for a moment what was I doing? Then I remembered, this was because Anthony had come stomping into my world telling me what to do.

Plus, I really did want to thank D'Angelo for all that he'd done.

So, I took his hand, and he led me from my office. I didn't even stop to respond to my gawking assistant, who'd never seen me talk to a guy, let alone leave my office in the middle of the morning holding someone's hand. I chuckled as I imagined Sarah running to the front door and pressing her face against the glass as she watched me climb into D'Angelo's Lamborghini, which he'd parked illegally right in front, blocking the entrance. Her mouth had to be wide open by now.

As we sped off to a destination unknown, at least to me, I settled into the soft leather that seemed to mold itself to my butt. And then D'Angelo pressed one of the buttons on the dashboard that looked like some kind of aircraft flight-control system and said, "Remember this."

He cranked up the speakers; first, I heard the scratching and then the voice of Dr. Dre:

*You are now about to witness the strength of street knowledge.*

And then Ice Cube:

*Straight Outta Compton . . .*

"Oh, my goodness," I said. "This was our anthem at school!"

D'Angelo nodded his head at me and to the beat. "Yup, when N.W.A. hit the streets . . ." He spoke so that I could hear his words over the bass.

And I couldn't help it. As much as I'd learned to really

dislike these songs with all of this cursing and calling women out of their names, my head bobbed to the old-school rap song that made all kinds of memories rush back to me.

I was a junior in high school, doing really well, thinking about college and how I was gonna *get outta* Compton. But every day with my friends, we jammed to this song that became our anthem, and for the next couple of years I was filled with pride for the city where I'd grown up. It hadn't always been that way for me, after I'd heard a television news anchorman call Compton "L.A.'s armpit."

"You know I don't like music like this anymore," I said, even though my head was still bobbing and my shoulders were still bouncing.

He laughed. "I hear ya! We can do better than this."

He punched another button and next came, "'Oooo, baby, baby. Baby, baby . . . get up on this!'"

Now, as we sped down the 405 Freeway, we jammed to Salt-n-Pepa. It was like D'Angelo had gone all the way to my high school life, bringing back the best of those days. By the time he slowed down the car, he and I had turned Michael Jackson's solo into a collaboration. Now a trio sang and D'Angelo and I bellowed out, "'I'm starting with the man in the mirror . . .'"

I hadn't even noticed that we'd stopped in front of Roscoe's Chicken and Waffles in Long Beach.

"It's a little late for breakfast, don't you think?" I asked D'Angelo.

"Stop playin'. It's never too early or late for Roscoe's."

Then he just got out of his car. Now, mind you, we weren't in a parking space. We were double-parked in the middle of the street.

"You're just gonna leave your car here?" I asked him as he held my hand and helped me to rise up from the low ride.

He shrugged. "Yeah, someone'll come and get it."

"But they don't have valet here."

"They do for me," he said, and opened the restaurant's door.

When we stepped inside, one of the waiters rushed over, and without a word, D'Angelo tossed him his keys. Then we were led to the room in the back that I'd understood was used only for special occasions. But clearly, there was something special about D'Angelo.

When the waitress placed our Obama Specials—three chicken wings and a waffle—in front of us, D'Angelo took hold of my hand. "Mind if I bless the food?"

"Go ahead," I said, trying not to show my surprise. As he said grace, I tried to figure out who was this man?

"All of these blessings, we ask in Your Son Jesus' name, amen."

"Amen," I said, and looked up. Clearly, there was so much more to D'Angelo Stewart than just what was obvious, and I told him that.

"Talking to God was the last thing that I expected from someone who I imagined spent more time shooting a pistol than reading a Bible."

He laughed as though I was kidding . . . I wasn't.

He said, "I've taken many roads in life, and they've all led to God for me."

"Even when you had a gun in your hand?" I asked. Not that I'd ever heard of any specific shootings that involved D'Angelo.

He said, "*Especially* when I have a gun in my hand."

I wanted him to expound on that a bit. Tell me what he was into. But the next thing that came out of his mouth was a question for me. "So, do you miss living in Compton?"

That was a hard left turn to get out of telling me more, but I was gonna play . . . for the moment. "Not at all."

"Me neither," he said, and then we chatted about our old neighborhood, our high school, and how so much had changed.

"If you ever wanna go back there to live, then you better know what I know," D'Angelo said. "You better learn some Spanish."

Less than an hour later, we were back in the sports car (that was waiting for us right outside the restaurant exactly where D'Angelo had left it), and while we sped toward downtown L.A., we jammed now to everything from Public Enemy to Teena Marie. And this time, when D'Angelo slowed the car down, he was the one singing with Keith Sweat, "'You and I together,'" D'Angelo began. He took my hand and serenaded me, "'Dream that seemed for real, if it's a dream, please don't wake me up . . .'"

I cleared my throat and looked away from him. "Where are we now?" I asked. Not that I didn't know . . . we were at LA Live; I just didn't know where we were going in this new entertainment complex that had totally revived what used to be the slums of L.A.

"Have you ever been to the Grammy Museum?"

"No!" I said, kinda excited about this.

Just like before, D'Angelo left his car in the middle of the street, and once we stepped inside, he gave his keys to someone who greeted him by name. Then D'Angelo took me by the hand and explained that the museum had four floors, so we wouldn't explore them all today.

As we waited for the elevator, he leaned into me and whispered, "But I'll bring you back here anytime you want, pretty lady." He was so close, I felt his breath.

I stepped back and inhaled. He stepped back and chuckled. And then we rode up to the Motown room, where we studied all kinds of sixties and seventies photos, put on headsets and listened to original recordings, and then sat and watched a film on the life of Berry Gordy and the history of Motown.

I couldn't imagine where D'Angelo was going to take me from there, but after another car ride, filled with more music from my teen years, we ended up at Universal City-Walk, strolling and browsing through the little shops. When D'Angelo said, "Let's go in there," and pointed to Bubba Gump's, I shook my head.

"We just ate."

"That was hours ago."

"But if I keep up with you like this, I will have reached my caloric limit for the whole week."

He looked me up and down as we stepped into the restaurant. "You're fine and everything, but I want my woman to be more than a bone."

"I'm not—"

He put his fingers over my lips before I could protest fully. "I already know what you're gonna say. You're gonna tell me that I'm not moving fast enough and you're ready to jump into bed right now. But I think we should take this slow, okay?"

I looked at him as if he'd lost his mind. Then I just busted out laughing, because what else could I do?

D'Angelo ordered the duck luck coconut shrimp, and when I ordered the pear and berry salad, he shook his head. "I thought I done told you how I like my women."

"Well then, you need to tell that to your women."

He laughed, then said, "What do you think about our day so far?"

"So far? How can there possibly be any more?"

"I can go as long as you can, pretty lady."

I wasn't sure that D'Angelo was still talking about our day, but decided to stay on subject. "It's been cool; I've had a great time. You like music as much as I do."

"Yup."

"You eat more than I do, though."

He chuckled. "I'm a growing boy."

I had so many comebacks to that because this man was so far from being a boy it wasn't even funny. "Well, I've had a good time," I said. "Thank you for taking me away for a couple of hours."

"You say that like this is gonna be over soon."

I looked at my watch. "Well, it's almost four and I've been away for the whole day."

"I thought you invited me out to dinner?"

I laughed. "I did. I guess we're just having dinner a little early."

"Okay, I'll let you get away with that this time 'cause I know you're a workaholic and it was hard to do what you did today."

"Yes, it was."

"So, tell me about your house, do you like it?"

"D, I love it. Thank you so, so much for finding that for me."

He shrugged. "No big deal. Someone called me, I thought of you, and I figured it would give me some points." He paused. "Did it work?"

As they sat our plates in front of us, I nodded. "You have so many friendship points right now, it's not even funny."

He laughed. "Love how you snuck that right in there. Friendship."

"Yup, 'cause there's nothing better than that."

"I can think of something that's a little bit better."

Then, like he'd done at Roscoe's, he lowered his head and blessed our food, as if not a morsel passed through his lips before he raised it to God. When I looked up, he was smiling at me.

"What?" I asked as I picked up my fork.

"I was just wondering . . . what made you finally decide to go out with me?"

I thought about how Anthony had barged into my office with his demands, but I wasn't going to tell D'Angelo about that. I said, "I got tired of hearing you asking me to go out."

D'Angelo didn't miss a beat. He shook his head. "That can't be it. I stopped asking you a long time ago."

I frowned. "No, you didn't. We talked a few days ago and you asked."

"That was a long time ago to me," he said. We laughed, but then he asked again, "What changed your mind?"

I put down my fork. "I decided that you're a real nice guy. And you've done so much for me. And, I thought it would be good for us to hang out and for me to say thank you."

"That's all this is?"

I nodded. "What else would it be?"

He shrugged. "Doesn't have anything to do with my brother, does it?"

My fork dropped out of my hand, and I moved quickly to recover, but I knew my body language had given it all away. How in the world did this guy know these things? I mean, I was beginning to understand that he had CIA-type connections, but how did he know my business?

My answer to him was, "What would make you think that?"

"You changed your mind so suddenly. The only thing I can think of is that you did this to get back at Anthony."

"Nope," I said, shaking my head. "I told you; I've forgiven them, so no need to get back at anyone."

"No you haven't."

"What?"

"You haven't forgiven him," he said as if he'd searched my heart and that was a fact.

"How can you say that?" I said, beginning to feel a bit annoyed. D'Angelo sounded like my father, and my pastor, and my friends. Everyone was always talking about forgiveness as if I was the one who'd done something wrong. The onus of the breakdown of our relationship seemed to fall solely on me.

"Because I can see it. You may say that you've forgiven them with your mouth. You say that over and over again. But in your heart, nothing's changed. Because when your heart changes, your actions change."

I frowned.

"Let me ask you this . . . have you been to see our niece yet?"

"Ciara?"

"Do we have another one?"

"Okay, let me explain this to you. I was married to Anthony," I said, though, of course, D'Angelo knew this already. But I was thinking that maybe a history lesson was necessary here to get him off my case. "And he cheated on me with my sister."

"Oh, don't get it twisted; I told you before that what they did was dirty to the tenth degree. I'm just sayin' that you haven't cleaned that dirt up off of you."

"And so what if I haven't?" I said, folding my arms across my chest. He had passed my annoyance threshold. I was sick of him, of my father, of Pastor Ford, of Sheridan and everyone else who preached forgiveness to the victim.

"Don't get mad at me. I'm just trying to help you out 'cause right now you have this wall up around your heart. And it's so thick that no love can get in and none can get out. You can't even find a way to love your own niece."

I glared at him.

"It's so thick, you'll never be able to feel love again. You won't even know when it's staring you right in the face."

I tightened my arms across my chest even more, but he didn't seem at all fazed by my attitude.

"Like I said, I'm just trying to help you out."

There was only one way that he could help me now. I pushed my plate aside.

D'Angelo looked over at me. "You're not hungry."

"Not anymore." I gave him a sista-girl glare. You know, the one that was meant to burn right through to his soul.

And even with that, all he did was shrug. "So, you ready to go?"

"I can't get out of here fast enough."

He nodded, then raised his hand for the waiter to return. He asked the young man to pack up our dishes and then he pulled out his cell phone. "Yo, what's up?" he said.

Now, all day long, D'Angelo had impressed me with the way he'd ignored all calls. His phone had rung all day, but he'd hardly ever glanced to see who was calling. But now I guess I didn't deserve that kind of treatment anymore.

I couldn't tell if he was talking to a male or a female, and it made me mad that I even cared. His conversation was innocuous enough, sounded more like business than personal. And when the waiter brought back our packed-up meals and the check, D'Angelo signed right away. Now he seemed like the one who was in a hurry to leave and I wondered how a day so great had flipped so quickly.

There was no music on the long ride back to Redondo Beach. And there were few words. When he pulled up in front of the Woman's Place, he slid out from his side and opened the door for me.

"Thank you," I whispered.

"No, thank you, pretty lady." He kissed my cheek softly. "I'll see you around."

Without another word, he jumped back into his car, and

two seconds later I heard the beat and then "Straight Outta Compton" . . .

I watched as his car rolled out of the parking lot and sadness draped over me like a cloak. Every time he'd been in my presence and we parted, he talked about when we would get together. I guess he'd had this one time. And one time was enough for him.

Well, it was enough for me, too. This wasn't going anywhere; I didn't even want it to. I'd done the good deed, thanked him for helping me out. Now it was over, and if he wanted, we never had to talk again. That would be cool with me.

# Chapter
## Thirty-Three

I'd been in Dr. Benjamin's office way too much.

I knew every certificate he had on the wall, I knew just about every title of the books that lined his shelf. I'd even studied the photos of his family on his desk.

Yeah, I'd been here too much and couldn't wait for the day I'd be told that my dad and I wouldn't have to ever come back.

"Okay, sweetheart," my father said into his cell phone. "I'll tell Kendall, but don't you worry about me. I'll be fine." A pause, and then, "I love you, too." Another pause and my father glanced at me. "Yeah, I'll tell her."

My father clicked off the phone, but I didn't ask him what the call was about. He was talking to Sabrina, so I wasn't interested.

But, of course, my father was going to tell me anyway. "Your sister said to tell you hello. She said she's been trying to reach you."

I wondered if my father knew that "trying to reach me" meant that she'd called every day.

He said, "She wanted me to know that Anthony won't be

able to come over this afternoon. He's stuck in a meeting in Orange County."

"That's fine," I said. "I'll stay with you."

My dad sighed. "You know you don't have to do that. I'm a grown man and I can take care of myself."

My father could flap his gums all he wanted, but I wasn't about to leave him alone after chemo. The treatments left him weak and dehydrated. I made sure that I was there, giving him plenty of water and trying to get him to eat. I never left until he went to bed for the night.

I had planned a meeting at the spa for later this afternoon since Anthony had confirmed in a message last night that he would cover me. But I had no problem canceling. This was my dad. He was and would always be priority number one.

Before I could tell my father that he had no choice in the matter, Dr. Benjamin stepped into his office.

"How're you doing, Mr. Leigh?" he asked my father, and then smiled at me.

"I'm good, Doc," my father said to the older white man who looked to be as old as my dad. I was sure the doctor was in his seventies, and at first, it had concerned me. I was thinking about all the new advances that had been made in medicine since this man had graduated from medical school.

But then I'd done my research. And Dr. Benjamin was world-renowned for some of his own studies on cancer. And when I found out that he specialized in male breast cancer because he'd survived it himself, I was sold.

"So, how are you feeling?" Dr. Benjamin asked as he tapped on a tablet that he held. "Any better with the side effects?"

"I'm feeling pretty good," my dad said.

And, I looked at him cross-eyed. "No, you're not," I said to my father, and then turned to the doctor. "My father is still very, very tired and sometimes, right after, he's too weak to stand. And besides still being nauseous even though he's not eating much, he has headaches." Then I turned back to my father and said, "Tell him."

My father hunched his shoulders. "Hell, I don't have to tell him anything now. You've told it all!" he said, sounding like he was annoyed. But then he smiled when he faced the doctor. "We almost named her Chatty Cathy because I knew she was gonna grow up to be this way. But my wife liked the name Kendall better."

Dr. Benjamin chuckled. "Well, it's a good thing that she's with you or else I wouldn't know what was going on. You've got to tell me, Mr. Leigh. I need to understand everything so that I can make any adjustments."

"I just don't want to complain . . ."

"Not complaining. It helps me."

I sighed and shook my head. Dr. Benjamin had been telling my father this since we first sat in his office before his surgery back in January. He'd told us then that the biweekly treatments were going to have side effects. He'd given us the list and then explained the entire procedure from the physical exam my dad would have each time before the chemo to how the IV would be inserted in his hand to how long the sessions would last, and finally to the effects afterward.

It was the doctor who suggested that not only should I be with my dad to drive him home after his treatments, but that I should stay for a couple of hours, since he lived alone.

"Well, let's see how you're doing after one more session and I will make adjustments then."

"That's fine with me, Doc."

"Do you have any questions for me?" Dr. Benjamin asked.

My father and I shook our heads at the same time. The only question I had he couldn't answer for me yet. All I wanted to know was if my dad was in remission. The positive answer to that question was all I wanted to hear.

I helped my father stand and then, after we said our good-byes to the doctor, I slowed my pace as we strolled from the clinic to the parking lot. After I helped my father into the passenger seat, I slid into my side and took off.

"So, what do you have a taste for?" I asked my father, already knowing his answer.

"I'm not hungry."

"Dad, you've got to eat something. What about Yee's?" That was his favorite Chinese-food place. "Even a eggroll," I said. "Something."

He was thoughtful for a moment. Then he said, "I'll make a deal with you."

I chuckled and looked at him through the corner of my eye. "I've got to negotiate with you for you to eat?"

"Yup. I'll got to Yee's if you do something for me."

"Okay, that sounds like a deal to me!" I laughed.

"I want you to go by and see Sabrina and your niece."

My smile faded straight away, and without thinking, I groaned. Not that I meant to . . . it was just that I hadn't expected that. But then again, I should have, because it was all anyone in my life wanted to talk about. Me. And Sabrina. And forgiveness. And oh, yeah, Anthony. And my niece.

Instead of lying to my dad and telling him that we had a deal, I decided to give it to him straight. "I don't know if I can do that right now, Dad. But I'm working on it. I really am. I'm working on really understanding forgiveness, and then forgiving Sabrina. And once I do that, I think I'll be able to have a relationship with Ciara, then."

I'd just told my dad the whole truth. Ever since I'd had that . . . little disagreement with D'Angelo, his words hadn't left my mind. I was trying to understand why everyone kept coming after me. I didn't get that part yet, but our conversation had left me thinking.

And after going over it in my head, I had to admit that

D'Angelo was right. I'd said it, but I hadn't forgiven Sabrina and Anthony. Not really. Not where it counted. I hadn't forgiven them in my heart. But you know why? Because they didn't deserve it. After what they'd done to me, they didn't deserve my forgiveness.

I didn't tell my father that part, though. He already knew that's how I really felt.

My dad nodded his head and paused as if he were considering my words. "Well, that's good, baby girl. That's a start."

"Thanks, but one thing, Dad. I don't want to talk about it all the time. That makes me tired, it wears me down. So, let me do this in my own way, let me forgive Sabrina and Anthony in my own time."

He nodded again, and when he was silent I thought that he finally got me. But after a couple of minutes passed, my dad said, "That's not gonna work."

"What?"

He kept on: "'Cause you see, this thing about your own time . . . you don't *own* any time. All time belongs to God. And He wants you to give forgiveness in the same time frame that He does. He gives it to you instantly when you ask for it. And He wants you to give it instantly when you have to give it.

"Now, I can understand how you couldn't forgive them instantly," my dad said. "That is way beyond human. You'd need the Holy Ghost for that. But six years . . ." He shook his head. "That worries me, baby girl. I know you think that I give you a hard time about this, but it's because I'm concerned about you, not Sabrina."

His voice was thick with sadness, and I knew what he was thinking about. He was afraid that he might pass away before Sabrina and I reconciled. I just wished there was a way for me to convince him that it wasn't going to happen and for him to be fine with that.

"I don't want you to worry. Just know that I'm really working on it."

"That's all I can ask, baby girl. Just don't take too long. 'Cause we don't know how much of . . . *God's time* . . . that we have left."

I wanted to rebuke him in the name of Jesus. I wanted to call the devil a liar if he thought he was going to take my dad away from me. "You're going to be fine, Daddy," I said as I pulled into the parking lot of Yee's. "So, stop talking like that, okay?"

"Yeah." He nodded and with a grin said, "So, I guess I gotta get something to eat, huh?"

"Yeah, you do." I kissed his cheek before I turned off the car and dashed into the restaurant.

"Give me those bags, I'll carry them inside," my father said.

"I don't know when you're gonna get that you're not running anything up in here," I kidded him. "I'm gonna help you get in the house first, and then I'll come back out and get our food."

"Or I can help your dad and you can carry the food."

I jumped at the voice behind me. "Oh, my goodness," I said, placing my hand over my heart as I looked at D'Angelo. "You scared me."

"Didn't mean to do that." Then he reached around me and helped my father out of the car. "How you doin', Mr. Leigh?"

"I'm good, D'Angelo. Great to see you, son."

"What're you doing here?" I asked him.

He and my dad were already walking away. "Sabrina called me. I'm second shift."

"Oh," my dad said. "So you got the call to pitch-hit for your brother." He shook his head. "I don't know when you kids are gonna get it. I'm just fine."

"I know you are," D'Angelo said. "So I figured I'd come over here and beat you in a couple of games of dominoes and then I'll be on my way."

My father laughed the way he used to. He always did that when D'Angelo was around and it made me smile. I grabbed the three bags of food from the backseat. There was no way my father was going to eat all of this; I wanted to stack his refrigerator so that when he was alone, all he'd have to do is put a couple of plates in the microwave.

Inside our house, my dad sat on the sofa, and clicked on the TV as I went into the kitchen. D'Angelo followed me.

"You didn't have to do this," I said. "I would've stayed with my father."

"You need to work on that. You need to find a way to accept help from family."

"It's just not necessary. I'm able to handle my father."

"I know you are; but when Sabrina told me what was going on, I wanted to help."

"Well, thanks. I appreciate it. And my dad does, too."

"No problem. Now you can go on and do what you have to do."

I paused for a moment, and then said something that two weeks ago I never would've said: "Or, I could stay anyway." Another pause. "And you could stay, too. We could stay together."

"Is this your way of saying that you still love me?"

I laughed. "No, it's my way of saying that I had a great time with you last Friday and I'm sorry the day ended the way it did."

"It was cool. I just figured if you were gonna have a heart that hard, I needed to get away from all of that. 'Cause when God teaches you the lesson finally and fully . . ." He shook his head as if he felt sorry for me.

"What do you mean?"

He shrugged. "I've just learned that hard hearts get the harshest lessons." And then he walked away, leaving me there, wondering about his words. But before I could get too deep into his words, he said, "Oh, and yeah, stay. 'Cause even with your hard heart and your hard head, I like having you around."

He grinned . . . and I did, too.

# Chapter
## Thirty-Four

This wasn't exactly a prayer meeting, though Sheridan had opened it up with prayer.

Actually, all she'd done was bless the tea, coffee, and croissants that my girls had surprised me with this morning.

I'd arrived at my office at my usual time, did my workout, and by eight thirty, I was in my office sipping tea while going through the daily sales reports of the café. I hardly looked up when I heard the knock on the door, but before I could say, "Come in," Sheridan and Asia busted through, shouting, "Surprise!"

And I was surprised. They hadn't done this before, but it was so cool to start off the day with my girls, and catch up on all that was going on.

Asia had the most exciting news. "Angel and I are going to Paris for a month this summer."

"Get out of here," Sheridan and I said at the same time.

"Yup," she said proudly. "Angel said she wants to go back there, and this time, with me. So that's what we're gonna do. I already purchased our tickets for July. Or rather, Bobby did when I called and told him what to do."

Asia beamed, and though I loved giving her a hard time, I was really proud of my girl. "See," I said. "I told you that finding out her mother was a porn princess wasn't going to ruin her for life."

Asia rolled her eyes, but her grin was still so wide. And she deserved to smile. It had been almost two months, but I knew for a fact that every single day during the last eight weeks, Asia had devoted her time to repairing her relationship with Angel.

"Does she ever say anything about walking in on you and Bobby?" I asked Asia. Then I held up my hands. "If you don't want to talk about it . . ."

"No, I don't mind. I mean, y'all know everything anyway." Asia sighed. "She didn't want to talk about it at first, but I told her that she didn't have to talk, she just had to listen. And I told her that what I did was wrong because her dad was married to Caroline. But that I had made a mistake and I was always going to try to get better. Then, a couple of days later, she told me she understood because she knew that I still loved her father."

"See," I said. "I told you that girl is smart."

"Well, I made it clear to her that I didn't love him anymore."

Asia said that with a lot of bass in her voice, like she meant it this time. Like having her daughter shout, "I hate you," had changed her whole game. Well, I was glad because she deserved someone so much better than Bobby.

"So, are you ready for the party, Sheridan?" I asked.

"Yup!" It was her turn to show off her Colgate smile. "I'm so excited; even Tori is coming home for the weekend."

"And Christopher doesn't know anything?" Asia asked.

"Nope. He has no idea about the party and he's gonna be shocked, especially when he sees his grandmother and uncle and sister there, too. I may not have been at his wedding, but this is going to be a reception that all of us will remember."

"I can't wait," Asia said. "I am so ready to get out and have a good time It's been way too long for me."

"Did you invite Quentin and Harmony?" I asked.

A cloud passed right over Sheridan's eyes. It was there for only a couple of seconds, but just like I'd been thinking for a few weeks now, something was going on. Ever since that day when Sheridan called me and Asia and told us to meet her at the church right away. She'd been so frantic on the phone, but when I rushed into that church and knelt next to her, she was completely calm. She'd said she'd left it all at the altar, and I respected that, but something had happened. And because Sheridan never went over-the-top-drama-queen on me, I suspected that whatever happened was something big.

Sheridan shook her head as she said, "I thought a lot about it and I really don't like leaving Quentin out of his children's lives in any way. But I don't want Chris and Evon to feel any kind of tension . . . so I thought it would be best if he wasn't invited." She paused. "And Brock certainly agrees with that."

I peered at Sheridan just a little longer. My friend wasn't a very good liar. Or maybe I shouldn't say she was lying. Maybe it was just that she wasn't telling the whole truth. But how could I push her? I couldn't, not when I was the master secret keeper. She'd tell me what was going on in her own time.

"Do you need any help with anything?" Asia asked.

"Nope, everything's set. Brock's gonna pick the kids up from the airport and tell them that I'm at home expecting a delivery, but that I'm dying to see them, so they have to stop by for a minute or two."

Asia clapped her hands. "So much fun." Her glee died down just a little. "The only thing is, I don't have a date." She sighed and looked over at me. "I guess it'll just be me and you, Kendall. You'll be my date."

I looked her dead in her eyes and pressed my lips together.

When I didn't say anything, Asia frowned, then slowly, her eyes widened. "Wait a minute . . ."

Still, I didn't move.

She said, "You have a date? Like with a real man?"

Sheridan laughed. "A real man? As opposed to a blow-up one?"

I let the two of them laugh, but I still didn't say a word.

"Oh. My. God! You better tell me what's going on," Asia said as if she really thought she could make that demand of me.

My face was as hard as stone when I finally spoke. "I don't know what you're talking about," I said to Asia.

But then even Sheridan moved to the edge of her seat. "Yeah, you're hiding something," she said. "And I've known it for a couple of weeks."

All I did was shake my head. But before my girls could really go in on me, there was a knock at the door.

"Come in," I said, thinking it was my assistant saving me from this inquisition.

The door opened slowly, and then I heard the soft cry of a baby, a second before my sister peeked inside. "Hi, Kendall," Sabrina said in her signature soft voice.

I rose slowly from my chair. "Wow! Sabrina." It took a moment for my brain to compute that my sister had come to my office. And then I wondered why. There was no reason for her to be here—except to bring bad news. "Is something wrong with Dad?"

"No, no," she said, now fully stepping inside. "I just wanted to see you. I wanted to talk to you. But it looks like I interrupted something."

"No," Sheridan said as she stood. She looked at me, then she looked at my sister. When I said nothing more, Sheridan did what she always did; she took over. Holding out her hand, she said, "You're Kendall's sister, Sabrina. I'm Sheridan." Then she pointed to Asia, the only one still sitting, "And this is Asia. We're good friends of Kendall's."

"It's so nice to meet you," Sabrina said.

As I took in the scene in front of me, my best friends meeting my sister, it occurred to me that my sister had no clue who these women were. They knew all about her, but she'd never heard of them. She'd been kicked off Planet Kendall so long ago that she had no idea what was going on in my world.

There were too many moments of silence, but then it was all broken by cooing.

"Oh, your baby," Sheridan said as she moved closer to Sabrina.

My sister held up the carrier that held my niece. "Yes." There was nothing but pride all on her face and in her voice when she presented her daughter for Sheridan to see.

Then Asia spoke up in the way that she always did. "Wow! You had a baby!" she exclaimed, spoiling the mood. "With Anthony . . ."

I'd filled Sheridan in but not Asia, for this very reason. I didn't want to hear her mouth. But now she'd spoken, and I wasn't sure which glare got to her more—mine or Sheridan's. But either way we did something that we weren't often able to do; we shut Asia down.

Looking down, Sheridan said, "Your daughter is beautiful. What's her name?"

"Ciara," Sabrina and I said at the same time.

And then Sabrina smiled at me. As if she was pleased and proud, but a bit surprised that I even knew her daughter's name.

That was when Asia jumped from her chair. "Let me see." A second later, "Yeah, she's really cute. She must look just like her father."

I rolled my eyes.

"I mean," Asia began. "You're cute, too, Sabrina. I was just looking at the baby's coloring. She's kinda chocolate. Like her dad."

"Asia," I said. "Just . . ."

"I know. Let me just sit right back down over here."

"Don't sit down at all," Sheridan said to Asia as she picked up her purse and motioned for Asia to do the same. "We're going to go now so that you two can talk."

"You don't have to leave," I said to my friends. Then I looked at my sister. "Is there something I can help you with, Sabrina?"

She looked from me to my friends and her eyes settled on Sheridan as if Sabrina thought that out of the three, Sheridan was her best chance to have an ally. "I did want to talk."

And Sheridan did what Sheridan does. She said, "Well, your timing is perfect because we were just finishing up." Then, when she stepped over to me, she held me close and said, "Be nice."

Then it was Asia's turn. She hugged me and whispered, "Girl, I wish I could be a fly on these walls!"

I pushed her away and chuckled before I walked my friends to the door. When I turned back, Sabrina had placed the carrier atop my desk and she was leaning over the baby.

"Is everything okay with her?" I asked.

"Yes," my sister said. "Do you want to see her?" She beckoned me with her voice.

"I can see her from here." I walked away from Sabrina and the baby to the other side of my desk.

The way her shoulders slumped and her smile faded let me know that my words had hurt. It wasn't like that'd been my objective, but I guess that's what happened when you didn't really care.

I sat in my chair, looked up at my sister, and asked, "So, what did you want?"

"May I sit down?"

For the first time, I noticed how weary my sister seemed. She always spoke softly, that's why I didn't catch it at first. But she seemed to be overly tired, which I guess was to be expected with having a newborn.

If she didn't look so tired, I would've told her to just stand. People always spoke more quickly standing, and that's what I wanted—for Sabrina to say her piece and get out.

But I nodded and Sabrina took her time sinking into the chair in front of my desk. Right away I regretted that decision. She looked so relieved the moment she took the weight off her feet; she was too comfortable already.

As she settled into the chair, I tried to remember the last time when we sat like this, face-to-face, just the two of us. My memory bank was empty; obviously, it was years back, when I still loved her as a sister. Before everything else.

Even after all these years, it was hard for me to understand how Sabrina and I were in this place. There was still a place in my mind's eye where I saw Sabrina as the little baby doll that my dad brought home when I was just seven and it was love at first hug.

And as my doll grew, she wanted to be just like me. Sabrina practiced walking like me, talking like me, we even dressed alike. And while she tried to emulate me, I adored her. We were so close, or so I thought.

"So, Sabrina, what can I do for you?"

My sister smiled, though it didn't reach her eyes. All I saw there was exhaustion. She said, "First, I just want to say this is really nice, Kendall. I walked around the spa a little before I knocked on your door." She paused as her eyes swept through my office. "I hear women talking about this place all the time. I'm really very proud of you."

"Thanks."

"You're doing such big things, such great things," she said

with the same adoration in her tone that she had when we were kids. That tugged at my heart just a little.

"Well, you've done something pretty big yourself." My eyes moved to the carrier on top of my desk.

That made Sabrina peek inside for a quick check on her daughter before she said, "I don't want to take up too much of your time." Her eyes were still on Ciara. "I have a very huge favor to ask you."

I tried my best not to shake my head, not to even blink. I didn't want to show any emotion, even though I was feeling a bunch of stuff inside. How in the world could my sister ask me to do anything for her?

She said, "I really am hoping that you'll consider this, Kendall. It will mean the world to me."

She was dragging it out, so I pushed her. "Okay, what?"

Sabrina took a deep breath. "I'd really like you to be Ciara's godmother."

Was she freakin' kidding me? She should've sent me an e-mail or a text asking this so that she wouldn't get her feelings hurt right to her face. I shook my head. "I don't think that's a good idea."

"I'm not taking this lightly—after all that's happened between us. But I think if you got to know her, you would love her. And a godmother is so important. I want Ciara to be in the hands of someone who will love her, and guide her, and teach her . . . that's what you did for me."

I shook my head. "Clearly, I didn't do a good job with that."

Sabrina looked down, and when she looked back up there were tears in her eyes. "You gave me every good part of you. The mistakes I made were me."

I reached down inside myself and I still felt . . . nothing. So I shook my head. "But thanks for the invitation."

She waited a moment and then she looked around my office as if she were waiting for someone to come and rescue her. "That's it," she said finally. And then her irritation with me and this situation rose. "This wasn't an invitation, like an invitation to a party. This was from my heart and it would mean so much to me and Anthony as we start to think about her christening."

My sister was smart. Just like me, she'd received her MBA, though she chose to go the corporate route rather than run on the entrepreneurial track like me. But she must've missed that day in statistics when the probability density function was taught. Because mentioning Anthony's name at this moment added no value to this discussion. In fact, my ex always subtracted anything that I could ever feel for my sister.

"Well," I began, "if you keep searching your heart, you'll be able to find somebody else. Somebody who really wants to do this for you."

If the tables had been turned, if I'd stolen her husband, and now I'd come to ask for a favor, and my sister treated me this way, this would've been the point where I would've stood up and stomped out of this room.

But not Sabrina. Her nature was much kinder than mine, her spirit so much more giving. She would've been the perfect woman in all ways if betrayal wasn't part of her character.

She smiled and nodded, even with tears still glistening her eyes. "Okay, I understand. I just wanted to ask you in person."

She stood and coughed a bit.

That made me frown; that couldn't be good for the baby. "Are you okay?"

"Not really, just tired." She looked down at Ciara. "I love this little girl, but I didn't know it was going to be so much."

I wanted to ask her how was it to be a mother. You know, all those things that a sister would want to know: was Ciara sleeping through the night, did Sabrina feel all the love that every woman said she experienced giving birth?

But I asked nothing.

"Well," she said, "I'm going to head over to Dad's. This is Ciara's first outing and I wanted her to visit the people most important to me." She paused and added, "The doctor said that it was fine for Dad to be around Ciara," as if she felt I really needed to know.

"That's great," I said, feeling good about being able to finally say something positive. "Dad's been taking all the precautions that the doctor told us."

Sabrina nodded. "He told me all about it, flushing the toilet twice, washing his face and hands, drinking plenty of water."

The baby gurgled and it was only reflex that made me stand and take a peek. And just like Sheridan had said, Ciara was beautiful.

As if she knew that I was looking at her, the baby blinked like she was focusing, then turned her head toward me. Her lips spread into something that looked like a smile. A smile for me.

I backed away.

Sabrina gave me her own small smile before she hooked the carrier onto her arm and then walked slowly toward the door. When she opened it, she turned back to me. "I hope you'll reconsider. And if you do, the offer will always stand. I don't care if Ciara is ten years old; I want you to be her godmother. Not for me, but for Ciara. She deserves the best that I had with you."

I smiled because that was my way of saying no way and good-bye.

After another moment Sabrina got it, and finally, she walked out the door.

# Chapter
## Thirty-Five

I didn't know why it was taking me so long to do this.

It had been on my mind all week, long before Sheridan and Asia came to my office on Tuesday.

Actually, I'd started thinking about it a week ago last Friday when I spent the afternoon with my dad and D'Angelo. When I stayed, my plan had been to have just a couple of forkfuls of shrimp fried rice and then head to my office. But I got caught up in playing games. First, dominoes and then D'Angelo actually went old school and we played Spades.

I was having such a good time that I didn't even notice the flying time. Not until my dad yawned and through the window I saw that somehow nighttime had traded places with the day.

"When did we turn on the lights?" I asked, seriously wondering since I didn't remember moving from the kitchen table.

"See," D'Angelo said, "that's what happens when you're around a man like me. You lose track of time, you lose your mind . . ."

My father had looked at D'Angelo and me, and then back at D'Angelo. The way they grinned at each other, I actually thought my dad was about to bump fists with this man like they were in a locker room somewhere.

But all my dad did was hug me, hug D'Angelo, then excuse himself, telling us that we could stay as long as we liked, but it was time for him to turn in.

I'd actually been happy about it. It was the first time that my dad had stayed up so long after chemotherapy. And he'd even gone into his bedroom with a smile on his face.

"I think you're good for my dad," I said to D'Angelo as I started cleaning up the table. "Thanks for all of this."

"I keep telling you, no problem. I got to spend time with him and with you. So what're we gonna do now?"

"I don't know about you, but I'm going home."

"Okay. Want a ride?"

I laughed. "You know my car's here."

He shrugged. "No problem. I'll have it towed."

"Do you own a tow company or something?"

"There's probably one in my portfolio. But even if I didn't, I'd still tow your car so that we could spend a little more time together."

"Well, tonight I really do have to get home."

He lowered his head, shook it a little, and chuckled.

I said, "But what're you doing tomorrow? Or Sunday? Or Monday?"

He was already grinning when he looked up. "What do you have in mind?"

And so, we'd gone out to brunch on Sunday and then to the movies on Monday. Since that time, I'd spoken to D'Angelo every day. Just casual, how-ya-doin' chats.

I had to admit, it felt good to have someone to talk to besides Sheridan and Asia. D'Angelo loved sports as much as I did (though he rooted for the wrong L.A. team; he was a Clippers fan). And he was into business as much as I was (though he was pretty secretive about what he did exactly), and then there was the fact that I could beat him in Spades.

We were a perfect match. A perfect *friendship* match.

And that was my dilemma. D'Angelo was a great distraction from my regular rigid schedule that didn't go much beyond working fourteen-hour days. I wanted to keep this on the friendship scale and D'Angelo seemed to understand that.

After his flirtations and double entendres, he was always a gentleman and always kept it on the friendship tip.

And I didn't want that to change. I didn't want D'Angelo to think that this invitation to Sheridan's party was anything beyond our friendship.

So now here I was, sitting with my phone in my hand, still turning it over in my head, asking myself the same question: should I or shouldn't I? I'd sat here for so long, asked the question so much, that I was getting on my own nerves.

"Just do it, Kendall," I said, and clicked on D'Angelo's number at the same time.

He answered on the first ring like he always did when I called. "Hey, pretty lady."

"Hey, yourself." I grinned, then tried to pull my smile back. I couldn't believe the way I got all schoolgirl-giddy when I heard his voice. It was a reflex.

"So, what's up? What do you need? Another house? Another missing person?"

"It's not that way anymore, D," I said. "Haven't I done better with that?"

"Yup, you have. So I guess you're calling 'cause you want to hang out. See, I told you that you still loved me."

I laughed. "Well, I am calling for something like that. Not the love part, though," I said, thinking I needed to correct him even if it were a joke. "But a friend of mine is having a party . . ."

"Uh-oh, this is serious."

"Why?"

"When a woman is ready to introduce you to her friends, that's serious."

I frowned. Was he kidding or was this call a serious move? It had been so long, I just didn't know.

"Well, if you don't want to go," I began.

"What're you talking about? I'd go anywhere with you."

I breathed and did that schoolgirl grin again.

"So, when am I going to have the pleasure of escorting you to said party?"

"Tomorrow; it starts at—"

"Tomorrow?" he groaned before I could even finish. "Wow, you don't give a guy much notice."

"Do you already have plans?"

"Yeah, I do. I'm really sorry."

"That's okay," I said as fast as I could, keeping my voice as light as possible, and at the same time wondering why I felt so disappointed. It was ridiculous that I'd called D'Angelo the night before the party and expected him to be free. What was I thinking?

And what was I thinking about asking him anyway? This was not who I was, this was not who we were.

"So, can I get a rain check on this?" he asked.

"Of course," I lied.

"Great, and Kendall," he said, calling me by my name for one of the first times ever, "I'm really sorry. If I could change my plans, I would."

"No biggie," I said. "I should've told you about this sooner. Listen, I really have to go. Bye-bye." I'd spoken so fast and hung up so abruptly I knew D'Angelo was probably staring at his phone. And he was probably laughing at me, too.

I tossed my phone onto my bed and walked over to my window. Why had I done that? Why didn't I just listen to my first mind? And . . . who did he have plans with and what did he plan to do?

I shook my head. I was so mad at myself. See, this is what happened when you let your guard down. I wasn't built for this. D'Angelo nor any other man on earth would ever have to worry about me making another call like this. From now on, I was going to stick to what I knew, what I did best. I was going to keep my eyes on my business and nothing or no one else.

# Chapter
## Thirty-Six

Iwas running late. On purpose. Because it took everything within me to even come to this party tonight. What I'd wanted to do was stay in my office and work. It was time for me to start thinking about a third location for my spa, maybe a Woman's Place in the Valley. That would keep me beyond busy for the next couple of years.

But in the meantime, there was no way for me to get out of this party. I had to go. I had to congratulate and be happy for Christopher and Evon, giving them blessings for however long this marriage lasted.

Now, I knew that wasn't the right attitude and it wasn't that I wished anything bad for this young couple. It's just that I knew happily-ever-after really only lasted for a couple of minutes.

I stepped up to the front door, but it swung open before I could even knock. And there I was face-to-face with Asia, the lady-in-waiting.

"You're late," she said. "Christopher and Evon are already here."

"Hello to you, too."

As I walked inside, she stepped outside and glanced to her left, then to her right. When she saw nothing, she swung around, closed the door, and with all kinds of accusations in her tone, she said, "Where is he?"

"Who?"

"The guy you were bringing to the party!"

"Is that why you were at the door waiting for me?"

She grinned. "I wanted to be the first one to greet your new man."

I shook my head. "You wanted to be nosy, but it was a waste because there is no man. I don't know where you got that idea."

She paused for a moment, then waved her hand. "You're right. What have I been drinking? You with a man?" She laughed and hooked her arm through mine. "We'll be each other's dates for tonight, but don't get it twisted and don't get used to this. I plan to get back on the playing field, so soon you'll be all by yourself."

Asia had no idea how true her words were, at least for me. I'd be fine being by myself. That's when I was at my best.

"Kendall!" Sheridan shrieked. "I was beginning to worry about you." She wrapped her arms around me.

"Sorry, I got a little caught up."

"Wait, don't tell me. At the office, right?"

But that was a rhetorical question, because before I could respond, Sheridan grabbed my hand and dragged me across the backyard, which sparkled with glittering lights that became brighter as the sun made its slow descent. A long table, flush against the back wall, was covered with a multitude of food and all along the perimeter of the back-yard about a dozen small round tables were draped with white clothes and held lavender bouquets of flowers as centerpieces.

But I didn't get a chance to admire the setting; I was too busy trying to keep up with Sheridan as my heels dug small holes into the grass with every step that I took. We stopped right at the gazebo.

"Christopher, look who's here!"

Her son and new daughter-in-law were standing under the gazebo, looking like a prince and princess awaiting their subjects. They were dressed almost alike, a bit more casually than their guests, but I figured that was because they'd just come off a plane. Evon wore skinny jeans, a white T-shirt, and a navy blazer. Christopher wore khakis, but that was the only difference between them.

"Congratulations, you two," I said, hugging Christopher.

"Thanks, Aunt Kendall," he said. Then he said, "I don't think you've met Evon." He wrapped his arms around her shoulders. "This is my wife, Evon LaCroix, and Evon, this is a good friend of my mother's."

"My name is Evon *Hart*," she said, giving her new husband a sideward glance.

"Oh, yeah!" Christopher grinned.

Turning to me, she said, "My husband keeps forgetting that." Then she held out her hand and said, "Nice to meet you."

But I playfully slapped her hand away. "We don't do hand-shakes around here, only hugs."

I wrapped her in a tight embrace. "Congratulations, and I wish you both all of God's blessings."

"Thank you," they said together, then looked lovingly into each other's eyes and beamed as if their talking at the same time, and saying those exact words, was just another sign of the destiny they were meant to share.

If this wasn't my best friend's son's reception, I would've gagged.

"I have something for the two of you." I reached into my purse and handed Evon the envelope.

"Thank you," they said together, and did that lovey-dovey-looky thing again. Then Christopher added, "And thanks for coming, Aunt Kendall."

"I wouldn't want to be anywhere else. So, were you surprised?"

"Very," they said together, then giggled.

Oh, brother! I thought, before I said, "Well, I'm going to see who else is here." I had to get away from all of that love, and I doubted if Christopher and Evon even noticed when I turned away. They were so busy gazing into each other's eyes. I was about two feet away from them when Tori, bounced over to me.

"Hey, Aunt Kendall."

I greeted Sheridan's daughter with a hug.

"I know you have one of those for me."

Right behind Tori was Mrs. Collins, Sheridan's mother, making her way toward me as she balanced herself on her cane. Just seeing her made my smile wider. "How're you?" I squeezed my arms around the woman who reminded me so much of my mother. From the moment I met her, Mrs. Collins had treated me with loving-kindness, though when she thought I was working too hard, or if I missed one too many church services, she was right on my case. A couple of times I thought she was gonna take a swing or two at me with her cane—something my mother would've done. I had really missed the weeks that this lady had been gone. "It's good to have you back."

"It's good to be home. I always have such a great time in San Francisco with my son, but they don't have anything like the Woman's Place up there. I can't wait to get there next week for one of those great massages."

I laughed. "Well, as a welcome-home gift, the first one is on me."

Mrs. Collins shook her head. "You know I pay my own way," she said, in a tone that sounded like she was scolding me.

What she said was true. I'd tried to give Mrs. Collins a couple of free treatments, but she always declined, telling me that she wanted to make sure I was making money. "Let's go get a plate of all of this fabulous food," Mrs. Collins said, leading the way.

I was happy to oblige. I hadn't eaten all day in preparation for this feast. Having been at the tasting at Rendezvous with Sheridan a few weeks back, I knew exactly what to expect.

After we filled our plates, Sheridan's mom and I sat down at one of the tables and chatted about her time in Northern California and my thoughts about opening another spa.

"That sounds exciting," she said to me. "But I hope you're taking some time to enjoy yourself. You know what they say about all work and no play?" Before I could answer, she said, "All work and no play means you'll never meet the right guy."

I was just about to tell Mrs. Collins that I wasn't one of those women who lived to have a man, when behind me, someone said, "I think the lady is right."

I was smiling before I even turned around. I jumped up and hugged D'Angelo. But then, as Sheridan's mom's eyes were on me, I pulled away. "Mrs. Collins, this is my friend D'Angelo."

He shook her hand, but neither had a chance to say a word to the other because I dragged D'Angelo away from Mrs. Collins and everyone else in the backyard and pulled him behind the gazebo.

"What're you doing here?" I whispered.

"Uh . . . I thought you invited me." He matched the volume of my voice.

"I did, but you said you had plans."

"Okay, but then when I thought about it, and I weighed my plans versus being with you . . . you won, by a landslide."

I grinned. I'm telling you . . . it was reflex with him.

"That's not a problem, is it?" He looked around, then lowered his head close to mine and whispered, "I mean, did you bring someone else?"

"No." I laughed. "I'm glad to see you, but how did you know where . . ."

He looked at me with a raised eyebrow and I didn't even bother finishing the question. If D'Angelo had proven anything to me, it was that he had no problem getting his hands on information. He seemed to have NSA-type connections and it probably took him all of two minutes to find out about my best friend and where she lived. So, instead of pursuing that line of questioning, I just thanked him again for coming and led him back around the gazebo.

"Whew! I thought you were gonna keep me hidden all night."

If I were a different woman, I would've told him he was too fine for that. But instead, I said, "Let me introduce you to my friends."

"Well, we've already met," Sheridan said. The way she came right over, I wondered how much of our conversation had she overheard. "I answered the door when D'Angelo got here," she told me.

"Well, he hasn't met me." Asia was halfway across the yard, so I had no idea how she'd zoomed in on what was going on in my lane. But she did, and she sauntered toward us, doing her normal sexy strut that I didn't find so cute today. For some reason, I wanted to punch her right in her nose.

D'Angelo's eyes did what all men's eyes did when Asia was in the vicinity—his glance took a journey up her body, then back down. He never even blinked, and neither did Asia.

She held out her hand. "I'm Asia."

D'Angelo put his arm around my shoulder before he took her hand and told her his name. But I hardly noticed the way he took her hand quickly, and then dropped it. I guess that was because all of my attention was on the way D'Angelo's arm rested on me. So comfortably, as if he belonged there.

I wasn't as comfortable as he was, though. We hadn't touched in that way; of course, he'd held my hand as he helped me out of the car or led me into a restaurant. But this arm-across-the-shoulders felt a bit intimate and I had to resist the urge to shrug him off.

Sheridan said, "D'Angelo, would you like something to eat?"

"I'll take you over there," I said, stepping away from his hold and my friends at the same time.

On the way to the buffet table, we stopped to talk to Sheridan's mother a little more, and then I introduced D'Angelo to Christopher and Evon. As we sat at a table, Brock came over, and after that, D'Angelo was taken away from me. But I didn't mind; it was good to watch him hanging with the guys. He fell right in, laughing and joking as if he'd always known those men.

As I chatted with Sheridan and Asia and the other women at the reception, D'Angelo and the guys stood off to the other side. Every few seconds I tried to peek at him. And every time I peeked, I caught him looking at me.

I did my best to keep my attention on Sheridan, Asia, and the other ladies. It was difficult, though, because all I wanted to do was sit and talk to D'Angelo. But I put in my time, and as I chatted, and laughed, and just hung out, I was amazed that I felt . . . normal. It was nice.

It was just after nine when Christopher and Evon asked for the guests' attention. And then from the center of the gazebo, they spoke.

"This was quite a surprise," Christopher said as he held Evon's hand. "And I want to thank my mother and my stepdad for putting it together. This was more special than anything we had planned and we love you." Beside him, Evon nodded, the guests cheered, Sheridan and Brock stood and gave them hugs, and D'Angelo once again wrapped his arm around my shoulders.

Christopher continued, "It's been a long day, so we're gonna get out of here, but thank you all for coming."

I stood stiffly as Christopher and Evon made their way through their guests thanking each person individually. Once they walked out the door, it seemed like everyone else wanted to follow.

"So, pretty lady," D'Angelo whispered in my ear, "can I give you a ride home?"

"I have my car and"—I held up my hand—"I don't want it towed."

We laughed together.

"So, how're you going to spend more time with me if we're not in the car together?" He sighed. "We always seem to have that problem."

I shrugged. "We'll just have to make another date." Then I spoke quickly to fix what I'd said. "I mean, not a date, a get-together." I looked up at him. "You know what I mean."

He took a step closer and nodded. "I do. Well, let me tell you what I'd like to do." He paused. "I'd like to see your place. I haven't seen what you've done to it since you moved in."

"Since I wouldn't have it without you, you can come by anytime. Just let me know."

"I'm letting you know now. I'd like to come by tonight."

"Tonight?" I said as if I didn't recognize that word.

"Yeah, tonight. Do you have other plans?"

"No." I shook my head, trying to give myself time to

come up with some excuse. "I'm just going home, going to bed."

"That's exactly what I was thinking." He chuckled like he was kidding, but I just wasn't sure.

"You know I was just kidding, right?" D'Angelo said.

"Yeah, I know that," I said, and kinda laughed.

He said, "Seriously, though, I'd like to drop by for a quick minute and take a look at your place. And if you feel like it, then we can talk. We never get a chance to do that."

"What do you call what we've been doing all night? Whenever we get together, we talk."

"I'm talking about one-on-one, face-to-face with no one else around. Just you and me. By ourselves."

"I don't see how that would make a difference."

"Are you afraid?" he asked, with a chuckle in his tone.

"Of what?"

"I don't know. Only you can answer that question, but it sure seems like you're afraid of something."

It felt like he was amused by me. And like he was challenging me, daring me to let him in my house. "You know what? Come on by. I'd love to show you what I've done to the cottage. It's really nice now."

"Great," he said, looking like he'd just won a bet. "I'll follow you. Just make sure that you drive slow enough so that I can keep up."

When he laughed, I rolled my eyes. I didn't know what he meant, but I knew that he was still teasing me, and I really didn't like it. But I was gonna be cool, show him my place, and then show him the door. In and then out, he wouldn't be there long.

I glanced around the backyard, looking for Sheridan and Asia so that I could say my good-byes and I saw them huddled by the door to the house. With the way their heads were together and whispering, I knew they were talking about me.

Asia said, "You better wrap that man up and take him home. Don't let him walk out of here by himself."

"He won't be by himself," I said.

"That's what I'm talking 'bout." Asia raised her hand to give me a high five, but I left her hanging.

I said, "He's walking me to my car and I'll get in mine and he'll get in his." I knew my friends would infer that we'd go separate ways. And that's the way I wanted it.

Sheridan held my hand. "I like him and I hope something comes out of this."

"Something has . . . a wonderful friendship."

I hugged my girls good-bye, stood as D'Angelo thanked Sheridan and then said good-bye to Asia. Then the two of us walked out together. When he held my car door open for me, he said, "Remember, I'll be right behind you."

I nodded because if I'd opened my mouth, I would've told him that I had changed my mind. That he was welcome to come to my house during any daylight hour.

But I said nothing, switched on the engine, and then sped through the streets like I was trying to lose the car behind me. As if that would've helped. D'Angelo knew where I lived.

"What are you doing, Kendall?" I whispered to myself, and glanced at the car lights that shined in my rearview mirror.

But then the other side of me asked why was I stressing? He was just coming to see the house. It was as simple as that.

And that's what I kept telling myself . . . over and over again.

# Chapter
## Thirty-Seven

I didn't see any car lights behind me when I made that left onto my private road, and for a moment I wondered if I'd lost D'Angelo. I released a long breath, but just as I was ready to inhale again, headlights beamed through my rear windshield.

D'Angelo had found me.

I waited until he got out of his car, and then I got out of mine.

"I thought you were trying to lose me back there," he said as he walked over to me.

"How can I do that when you know where I live?"

"I was getting ready to call you and tell you that!"

I chuckled and hoped that D'Angelo didn't hear any of my anxiety in that sound. My hands shook just a bit as he followed me to the door and I put the key in the lock. I stepped inside, clicked on the lights, and moved aside so that he could walk in front of me. "Here it is!"

He stood in the center of the living room, exactly the way Sheridan had done, and did a three-sixty, turning and taking in what I liked to call my Ivory Room. This was the main room of my house, which was the living room and an open kitchen.

I'd decided that with the space being so small, I'd use the same light color with everything, from the sofa to the tables, even to the floor lamps. The pots that held my plants were ivory, too, as was the entertainment center. The only things of color were the sketches that I hung on the wall of flowers and seashells.

He said, "If that spa empire doesn't work out, you have a future in interior design."

"Thanks, but it wasn't hard to decorate. This is such a great house. The challenge was that with only seventeen hundred square feet, I had to be a minimalist. Didn't want to overrun it with furniture, you know?"

"It's like a third of the size of the house that you had before, so I didn't know what you were going to do with it."

"I actually like it better. I didn't need all of that room now."

With the way D'Angelo moved around the perimeter of the house, taking everything in and nodding his approval, I was glad that I'd let him come. I'd made a big deal in my head over absolutely nothing and I loved sharing this with him.

When he opened the deck and stepped out, he said, "And this is the best part of the house."

I joined him. "This is why I wanted to come back to Malibu."

"It doesn't get better than living on the beach. Someday I might want to do this." He nodded and stuffed his hands into his pocket. "Yeah, I love my loft in downtown, but beach living . . ."

I smiled. "Thanks again."

"And again, you're welcome, pretty lady. So . . ." He turned and faced me. "Can a brotha get a drink?"

"Do you mean like water?"

He laughed. "I was thinking of something stronger."

"Well, your choices are water, tea, and I may have some hot chocolate. But that's it."

"I guess tea would be cool . . . if it's not too much trouble."

"It's not. Go ahead and have a seat," I said, pointing to one of the two loungers. "Unless you want to come back inside."

"No . . . I'll chill out here. It's worth having some cold toes to take in this view."

Inside, I set up the teapot, and as the water boiled, I breathed, surprised at how calm I was. D'Angelo didn't have any ulterior motives and neither did I.

Minutes later, I tried to hold two mugs steady as I stepped onto the deck and D'Angelo jumped up to help me.

"I would've carried this out for you." He took both cups from me and placed them on the table.

Then we sat down, with the table separating us. We leaned back, picked up our cups, and sipped as we watched the waves crash onto the sand.

The April night was much cooler than the daytime had been, especially at the beach. But even though I shivered a bit, I didn't want to go inside. There wasn't much to see in the dark of the night, though lights glittered from the island of Catalina. But it was the still of the night that I loved so much. The still of the night at the beach.

As we sat in the silence, I added another tick to the list of what I loved about D'Angelo. I loved a man who could be comfortable in the quiet; actually, I liked anyone who could appreciate moments without noise. But high-powered people who didn't have to always be movin' and groovin' were difficult to find.

Five, ten, maybe even fifteen minutes passed before D'Angelo said, "What is it that you want, Kendall?"

For a moment I said nothing, but before I could speak, he added, "And I'm not talking about your empire. Don't tell me that you want ten or fifteen more spas. Don't tell me that you want to rule the spa world. Those are things you want to achieve. I'm talking about what's right here." He bumped his fist against his chest. "What do you want for you? What do you want out of life?"

I had to roll back my thoughts because before he explained, I was set to tell him that I wanted to rule the spa world. But now my mind was a big ol' blank. Because what I wanted for myself—that was a hard question to answer. The spas were for me. Achievement was what motivated me.

"I haven't really thought about it," I said, taking another sip of what was now almost iced tea. If he didn't want to hear how I was going to open up a gazillion more spas, or if he didn't want to hear about having this home on the beach, I didn't have anything for him.

When I stayed quiet, he said, "Let me help you out . . . do you want to get married again?"

The question was barely out of his mouth when I said, "Absolutely not! I shouldn't have gotten married the first time." I paused, then added, "My mother went through something really tough when I was a kid, something that affected me more than I thought."

He nodded. "You're talking about your dad's affair . . . and Sabrina coming from that."

I looked at him. "Dang, did everybody in Compton know about that?"

"I don't know about anybody else, but I knew the story. And I always thought it was something the way your mother accepted Sabrina and raised her with love."

"She did. My mother was a saint. But I'm convinced that every bit of love she poured into my sister broke my mother's heart just a little bit more. I tell you, D'Angelo, I will always believe that my father's affair, and then him bringing home Sabrina, killed my mother. I was smart enough as a kid to recognize that it was grown folks' business. So, I stayed out of it and still loved my daddy. But my heart broke every time I heard my mother crying. And I swore that I was never going to get married; no one was ever going to get a chance to do that to me."

"But you married my brother anyway."

"He was a great business partner." When D'Angelo looked at me, I shrugged. "I'm telling you the truth."

"At least you understand yourself," he said.

"So, what about you?" I said, tossing the question over to him. "What is it that you want? Do you want to get married?"

His response was as swift as mine. "I'm not marriage material."

"Why do you say that?"

"'Cause I'm not settled. I live all over the world, and even when I'm back in L.A., I'm involved in so much. I can't see making the time for a wife."

I tilted my head, and before I could think about my words, I said, "You make time for me."

"Do you wanna be my wife?"

"No! Definitely not! I mean, you're a good catch and everything, but like I just said . . ."

He laughed. "I'm just playing with you." Then he shook his head. "I move around too much to get married."

"I was going to ask are you headed back to Iraq soon?"

"I don't know yet. If I don't go back, I won't miss it, that's for sure. Honestly, sometimes I'm ready to give up all of that. But then I think, Who will I be without it? If I were to try to settle down, what would that look like? Am I the settling-down type?"

It was interesting that D'Angelo had just as many questions about what was ahead as I did. That surprised me. He seemed to have it all together, but then, when people looked at me, that was they thought about me. Maybe it was all of us "together people" who had the most issues in life.

"Well, pretty lady. I think it's time for me to get on up out of here." He stood and stared out into the ocean for a couple of seconds, a moment of appreciation. Then he turned toward the house.

I followed him, but right before he stepped inside, he stopped, turned around, and looked down at me. "Thanks for showing me your home. I know it took a lot for you to let me in."

I shook my head. "No, it's fine." It was his look, so intense, that made me lower my eyes.

With the tips of his fingers, he lifted my chin. Tried to get me to look at him once again. "You don't have to be afraid of me," he said.

"I'm not . . ."

"But sometimes you act like . . . you're afraid. And I want you to know that you don't have to be. I really care about you, and I think you know that."

I nodded.

"I do," he said. "I really . . ." He lowered his head. "Really . . ." His lips began a slow descent toward mine. "Really do." And before I could say a word or move out of the way, our lips met.

It was a reflex . . . I closed my eyes and fell into the kiss. It was soft, it was gentle, it was natural and felt so good. And then it got better when he parted my lips. I didn't want to do this, but then again, I did.

It had been such a long time and I was just going to stay in the moment and enjoy it.

But then . . . D'Angelo touched me. And I shivered as he pulled me closer. I was just about to push him away. Until

I felt his manhood pressing against me. That was when I moaned. I wanted more.

So I used my hands. And I pulled him closer.

He lifted me up and another reflex . . . my legs wrapped around his waist. It was like my body knew what it wanted, even when my mind kept telling me to stop.

We stayed connected, groaning as we held each other. He backed up into the house, and though my mind was swirling with emotions, I captured a single thought—where was he going? But then I remembered, he knew this house. He knew where he was taking me.

D'Angelo took the few steps to the bedroom, with my legs like a vise around him. Without letting go, in moments we were on the bed—he on top of me.

My mind was still trying to control me. Still telling me not to do this. But my body sang a different song. Every fiber of my being needed this.

This felt like the first time, the way his hands caressed me, his tongue teased me; I was dizzy.

If I ever had to tell this story again, I would never be able to explain what happened next. I would never be able to tell anyone how my clothes came off or how he ended up naked. I would only be able to tell about the way I floated above the bed. And then the moment we connected and became one.

"Oh!" I cried.

I would have been embarrassed by the way I shrieked if D'Angelo hadn't called out my name at the same moment. And then our cries became a moan, a mournful melody that was a song of joy.

D'Angelo filled my body with his, but that wasn't enough for me. I wanted more. And so, as our tongues stayed connected, I rolled over, and in just a moment I was on top. As I looked down, I saw the glow of his smile. But I had no time for cheer. This was serious business.

I leaned back, closed my eyes, and let my body move with the waves. I rode like a surfer, riding up and then floating down. Each time, the waves became higher and I climbed and climbed until I reached the top.

I cried out once again and squeezed my legs as tight as I could, trying to hold on to that feeling. And when it finally slipped away from me, I collapsed on top of him.

Breathless!

I have no idea how long I lay in my bed, staring into the dark, listening to the silence that was broken every few seconds by the soft sound of the nighttime waves smashing against the beach.

I searched my heart, I searched my thoughts. And I had no regrets. Not a one.

What I had was vindication.

At least, that's the way it felt. Revenge against Anthony.

Even though Anthony might not ever find out about what happened with me and D'Angelo, this felt so good to me.

Maybe if there was a way for me to get revenge on Sabrina, maybe I'd be able to move on. But for now, this was enough.

I let more time pass and then I reached for the lamp beside my bed. The room brightened with hundred-watt lights.

"Whoa!" D'Angelo said, his voice filled with surprise. He frowned and then raised his hand to his forehead as if he was shielding his eyes from the sun. "What's with the light, pretty lady?"

"I just thought you'd want to see."

"See what?" Then he rolled over and faced me with a grin. "Oh, see you. In the light. That's what I'm talking about."

He tugged the sheet from me, but I snatched it back. "No! That's not what I meant."

With a tilt of his head, he looked at me, and then said, "Oh, it's me that you want to see in the light."

Before I could tell him that he was wrong again, he jumped up, then stood with his arms open, his stance wide, and right then I lost my mind. I'm telling you, I could not remember what I was going to say.

It actually took a couple of seconds before I was able to focus and get my thoughts back. "Oh, no. No! That's not what I meant." I looked down at my fingertips so that I could maintain my concentration. "I was thinking that you would need the light to get dressed."

"Get dressed?"

"Yeah, you know. So that you can leave."

"Leave?" he said, sounding like a parrot. "You're kicking me out?"

"Yes, I mean, no. I wouldn't put it like that. I just figured we did this, it's over, and . . ."

He shook his head. "And what? Finish your sentence."

"And, I just thought you'd want to leave."

"I don't."

Now I looked right at him when I said, "I think it's best."

He stood there for a moment, and I worked hard to keep my eyes on his. He started shaking his head, and slowly he moved toward me. This time when he tugged the sheet away that covered my chest, he didn't let me pull it back.

As he placed his hand between my breasts, he kept his eyes on mine. There was nothing sexual about this moment; it felt like D'Angelo was reaching for my heart.

"You've been so hurt, pretty lady. And I pray that somebody one day will be able to heal this for you."

I shook my head. "No, you've got this all wrong. I just figured it was over, and when something is over . . ."

"This is not business, Kendall. This wasn't one of your corporate meetings or a massage session at your spa."

Even though his voice was soft, I felt like I'd offended him in some way and I didn't want to do that. "That's not what I'm saying. I was just—"

His lips reached mine before I could get the next word out and I had to work hard to hold on to everything that I was thinking.

Suddenly he pulled away. "Let me stay."

"No," I whispered.

He kissed me again, then leaned back once again. "Let me stay, Kendall."

"No," I said, though my words were softer this time.

He kissed me again. "It's okay. Let me stay."

His lips met mine again and again. Told me to let him stay over and over.

He kissed me, until I finally kissed him back. He kissed me, until I stopped saying no.

He opened his arms, pulled me close, and just held me, caressed me, planted kisses on top of my head, and pulled me into him.

And for the rest of the night, there I stayed.

# Chapter
## Thirty-Eight

The morning light tried to squeeze its way through the miniblinds that covered my bedroom window, but it was the bright shine of the lamp that awakened me.

What was my lamp doing on? And then I felt the hands, masculine hands. My heart was already pounding when I rolled over and looked into D'Angelo's face—eyes closed, mouth open as if he was in the middle of a silent snore.

I covered my mouth with my hand.

Oh. My. God.

I thought this had been a dream. I'd had so many dreams about D'Angelo, so many dreams that had me jumping out of the bed and checking my house to see if it . . . if the dream had been real.

But this had not been a dream.

A part of me wanted to snuggle right back into his arms. But then the smart side of me knew not to do that. So, slowly, softly, I began to wiggle from D'Angelo, inching away. But just as I got to the edge of the bed, his eyes opened.

Like me, it took D'Angelo a moment to get his bearings. But then he focused on me. "Good morning, pretty lady."

"G'morning." I rushed over to the hook on the back of the bathroom door and grabbed my bathrobe.

"I liked the view much better without that terry-cloth thing." He grinned and I shook my head.

"Don't worry about covering up now," he said. "I've already seen the best of you."

I wondered what I was supposed to say at a moment like this. This felt so foreign, and I felt so disconnected, I didn't know what to say. But what I did know was that it was time for D'Angelo to go.

So, I tied my belt tightly around my waist. That was supposed to be D'Angelo's hint, but he just turned on his side, rested on his elbow, and watched me, as if he had no plans to leave, and no place to go.

"Do you know that I've been dreaming about this since high school?" he said.

"You didn't even know me in high school."

"Yes, I did. You were a freshman, I was a junior, and you had Mrs. Reid for homeroom."

I couldn't help but smile at the mention of one of my favorite teachers. "How did you know that?"

"Because I used to walk by your homeroom every morning just to get a peek at you."

"Yeah, right."

"I'm serious," he said, putting his hand across his heart like he was taking an oath. "Every morning, I told my crew that I wanted to take the long way to my homeroom. But it was just a front to see you."

I shook my head. This guy was going all the way back to his school with his lies? Major game.

"I knew all about you. I knew your name, where you lived, your classes. But you were just a kid and I couldn't mess up my rep by talking to you."

"You're really going to keep going with this story?"

"I don't know why you don't believe me. You're breaking my heart, just like you did when my brother came home with you. I couldn't believe it. I couldn't believe Anthony had stolen my girl."

Now I laughed. "If that whole militia, clandestine operative thing doesn't work out for you, you should try writing novels. And this should be your first one because it's a great story."

He shook his head. "You better believe and act like you know."

"It'll be a number one bestseller."

"I'm telling you," he kept on, still keeping a straight face. "Anthony and I were rivals and he didn't even know it. That's why it's always so funny to me now that he has this I-hate-my-brother thing going. Because I hated him first!" He chuckled.

But I didn't think that was funny and I tilted my head. "How can you make fun of that? I mean, the way Anthony talks about you, D'Angelo . . . he really does . . . hate you. At least that's how it seems to me."

He rolled over to the side of the bed, then sat up straight. I sat next to him, and the moment I did, I wanted to get up, run into the bathroom, and give this man a towel to place across his lap.

But I didn't want to be so obvious. So, I pretended that he wasn't sitting next to me in the magnificence of his nakedness. And I kept my eyes on his light brown ones. But honestly, that wasn't much better. All I could do was pray that I didn't drown in his gaze.

He didn't seem to notice that just his presence was a distraction. He said, "There's no basis for Anthony to feel the way he does. I had nothing to do with our parents' deaths, but that's not to say that I take Anthony's feelings lightly. I know he hurts, and I know he believes what he thinks, but there's nothing that I can do about it. I can't control grown folks and their feelings, and their thoughts, and their emotions."

"But doesn't it bother you?"

He shrugged. "No, 'cause it's not coming from me. I don't have any beef with my brother, and I know deep down, he doesn't really think I had anything to do with our mom and dad and that car accident."

"I don't know. I mean, he's been talking about that for years. And the way he treats you . . ."

"He just needs someone to blame. That's the only way he can handle losing Mom and Dad. For some reason, it's easier for him to blame somebody. So when they died, and Anthony heard those rumors on the street, he knew about the life that I'd led back in the day, so it was easy for him to believe that. Easier to believe that than losing the two people he loved the most to something like that freak accident."

"You always sound so casual, like you're not at all upset about it."

"Let me tell you what I know. Anthony is my brother and I'll always love him. And one day, he's gonna come around. And when he does, I'll be right here for him as if none of this ever happened."

"You're a forgiving soul, huh?"

"I don't know what you call it. I don't know if it needs a name. Anthony's family. And to me, family is more important than revenge. Even family who've effed up are worth it. I fig- ure that God brought us together as brothers, and so, I'm not gonna do anything to mess that up no matter what Anthony's done. God put us here for a purpose, so I'm gonna play my part and keep it movin'."

I'd told him that he could be a novelist, but along with being a top-selling author, D'Angelo might need to think about a stint in the pulpit. Yeah, he could be the gangsta preacha.

"Plus," he kept on, "everybody comes around at some point or another. God makes sure of that. So, I'm not worried about Anthony. He'll come around and we'll be fine."

I wondered if D'Angelo really believed that or if that was a message for me. Folks needed to accept that I had come around and I'd gone as far as I was gonna go. I mean, the fact that I spoke to Sabrina, the fact that she could be in the same room with me and not get cut—that was coming around to me.

"Yup," he said. "God will do it. He'll sure bring you to your knees."

Okay, I'd had enough of all of this talk about God. It was already bad that I wasn't going to be able to go to church this morning. Not after the way I'd spent the night.

"Well," I said, wanting to change the subject, "I think I'm going to go into my office."

D'Angelo blinked, like it was taking him a moment to get back on track with me. "Work? On a Sunday?"

I was just about to ask him if going to church would be better when the phone rang. I frowned. It wasn't even seven yet and I couldn't imagine who would call me this early. Even after glancing at the number on my screen, I had no idea. I didn't recognize the number, but I picked up anyway.

"May I speak with Kendall Stewart?" the woman said after I said hello.

"Speaking."

"This is Harmony McCray, I'm a nurse at Cedars-Sinai. Your father was just admitted—"

"What?" I trembled. "Is he okay?"

"Yes, but you may want to get over here if you can."

"He's at Cedars?"

"Yes, this is his doctor's main hospital and Dr. Benjamin is here today. He's on the fourth floor. In oncology."

"Thank you." I looked down at the screen to click off the call, but my hands shook so much that I couldn't do it.

D'Angelo grabbed the phone from my hand. "What's wrong?"

"It's my dad," I said, looking from one end of the room to the next as if the answer to what I should do next was hidden somewhere in there. "He's been taken to the hospital."

"Okay, stay calm. Did the person say why he's there?"

"No, she just said that I had to get there."

"Okay. I'll drive you."

"No." I shook my head. "You don't have to do that. You can just go—"

"Kendall!" He shouted my name and grabbed my shoulders. "Stop it," he said, slightly shaking me. "I want to be here for you. I'm going to be here for you. Let me be here."

"But—"

"Stop it and get dressed. Now!"

I nodded and turned away, but before I could move, my knees buckled and I crumbled. Right before I hit the floor, D'Angelo caught me and he dropped to the floor with me.

And right there in his arms, I did something that I hardly ever did. I cried. I held on to D'Angelo and sobbed into his chest. And I prayed. I prayed like I never did before. "Please, God, please, God, please, God. Please don't let anything happen to my daddy!"

If there was anybody that I ever wanted to have my back, it was D'Angelo Stewart.

Once I'd dried my eyes and he was sure that I was okay, he went into superhero action mode.

I'd rushed into the bathroom, brushed my teeth, washed my face, and then jumped into a sweatsuit. I'm sure that not more than five minutes passed, but when I was ready, D'Angelo was already standing by the door.

In two seconds flat, we were in his car, and I swear, when he turned the corner onto PCH, he was on two wheels.

The car was silent, and I was glad that D'Angelo was leaving me to my thoughts. My head filled with memories of my dad and my early years—how he read to me at night, how he taught me to ride a bike, and even the day when he came into the house with a baby that I thought at the time was just for me.

And in between every memory, I prayed. I prayed for God to save my father and to spare me. Because I'd lived so much of my life without my mother, I didn't want to live a day without my father.

In the middle of what might have been my one-hundredth prayer, D'Angelo reached over and touched my hand. I opened my eyes and appreciated his comfort. Until he said, "You should call Sabrina and Anthony."

I pulled away from him.

"Kendall, the bottom line—this is family. If something's happening with your dad, Sabrina needs to know."

"Just let me get to the hospital and check it all out. I don't want to raise a false alarm."

"It's not false if the hospital called you," he said. When I said nothing, he added, "Okay, we'll get to the hospital, but if I think she needs to be called, I'm calling Anthony."

I shook my head because I could see it coming. Not only was I going to have to deal with whatever was going on with my father, but everyone was going to use this situation to "fix" me and Sabrina. I just didn't want to deal with all of that right now. My focus had to be, would always be, my dad.

We didn't say another word until D'Angelo screeched into

the hospital parking lot. This time, he didn't leave his car in the middle of the street. He pulled into the handicapped slot, and before he'd even really stopped the car, I was out of there. He caught up to me right as we walked through the sliding-glass doors.

And the first person I saw walking toward us was Anthony. His eyes were swollen and weary and fear struck me like a bolt of lightning.

"How's Dad?" I asked. I was a little surprised that Anthony and Sabrina had been called. And even more surprised that they'd beaten me to the hospital. "Where is he?" I asked my ex.

"Who?" he asked as if he were disoriented.

"Whoa, bruh, what's wrong?" D'Angelo asked.

"Did something happen to my father?" Kendall shouted. "Anthony, tell me!"

Anthony stood, shaking his head, looking confused.

My tears came instantly. Something had happened to my father; I hadn't made it in time.

"Where's my father?" I asked, two seconds away from grabbing Anthony and shaking him until he told me what I needed to know.

"I don't know," Anthony said. "I came out here to call him. I needed air. I was wondering if I left the keys in the car."

I frowned.

"Slow down, bruh," D'Angelo said. "Just tell us."

Anthony inhaled as if he needed air to start all over. "I've been trying to reach Dad, but he won't answer his phone. I have to tell him about Sabrina."

"What about Sabrina?" D'Angelo and I said together.

"She's here . . . in intensive care," and then he looked at me and D'Angelo as if he just noticed we were there. Next, his body shook, his shoulders quaked, and sobs raked through his body. He bent over as if he were in pain. D'Angelo reached for his brother, helped him to stand up straight.

"Sabrina's here? In this hospital?" I asked. "Is she with my father?" I was so confused.

"No." He shook his head. "She had a fever and she was breathing fast. So, I drove her here, but maybe I should've called an ambulance. And now they're thinking that there may be poison in her blood. She's . . . she's . . . it's not good."

"So, she was brought here?" I asked.

He nodded. "She's been here for a couple of hours. I've been calling Dad, but he won't answer his cell."

"Oh, my God," I whispered. All kinds of thoughts were colliding in my mind, all moving too fast for me to figure out what to do. Where was I supposed to go? What was I supposed to do now? I wanted to know more about my sister, but I had to find my father.

D'Angelo took over. "Go to your dad, I'll go with Anthony, find out what's going on, and I'll call you."

"Okay." And then, after a brief moment of hesitation, I reached up and hugged Anthony. He sobbed as I held him for a moment, but then I had to let go and I dashed toward the elevators.

My heartbeat was fast and furious. How could this be happening? My father, my sister?

Inside the elevator, I mustered up the only words I could think of: "God, please. God, please."

On the fourth floor, I ran as if I were in a race and the nurses' station was the finish line. "I'm here for Edwin Leigh."

"Yes," one of the nurses said to me. "Are you his daughter?"

I nodded because I didn't have any more words in me.

"I'm Harmony McCray. I called you."

"What's wrong with my dad? Is he okay?"

"He'll be fine," she said calmly. But then she frowned at me. "Are you okay?"

My lips trembled. "I was just so worried."

She came from behind the counter and held my arm

gently. "He's going to be fine. He was just severely dehydrated. His heart rate had sped up and he was weak, but he was able to make the call to 911 and we got him here."

I followed her to a room right across the hall, and in the bed next to the window, there was my father. His head turned toward me.

"Hey, baby girl."

"Daddy," I said, rushing to his side. "Are you okay?"

"I feel much better now, though they got this needle in me and you know how I hate that."

On the other side of the bed, the nurse checked the bag that was connected to the intravenous needle in his hand. "We just want to make sure you're feeling better, Mr. Leigh," she said.

Looking at me, my father said, "I did what you told me, baby girl. I called the ambulance instead of calling you."

I nodded with a smile. That was something that my dad and I had agreed upon when I first found out that he was ill. Knowing my dad, he would've called me first, wasting moments that may matter.

"That's good, Dad. But were you drinking the water from the pitcher that I left by your bed?"

"No." He waved his free hand. "You know I hate getting up in the middle of the night to go to the bathroom."

I glared down at him as if I was annoyed. "You're going to have to find a way to be a better patient. You have to follow Dr. Benjamin's orders."

"So what? I'm lying here in this hospital bed and you're lecturing me?" He shook his head and turned to the nurse. "Can you believe how my daughter is treating me?" he kidded.

I asked the nurse, "So he's going to be okay, right?"

She nodded. "We'll get him hydrated. He'll be here for a few hours and then Dr. Benjamin will want to check him out to see if he should stay overnight." Then she turned to my dad.

"But your daughter's right. You're going to have to make sure you're drinking your water at home."

"Okay, okay." He shook his head. "Now I got two women on my case. And you shouldn't be fussing at all. With a name like Harmony, I thought you'd be singing to me."

She laughed, and for the first time, it clicked. Harmony. A nurse. At Cedars-Sinai. This would be too much of a coincidence. This had to be Quentin's Harmony.

But my dad brought my thoughts right back to him when he said, "I don't want you calling your sister. She has too much to be concerned about with that granddaughter of mine and I don't want her to be worried."

Sabrina.

I nodded. "Okay. Listen, I'm going to step out for just a few minutes, Daddy, and I'll be right back."

"Go 'head. Handle your business. I'm not going anywhere."

I kissed his forehead, then walked into the hallway. There was a sign right across from my father's room: NO CELL PHONES PLEASE.

I looked to my left, then my right, and tried to decide between the restroom and the stairwell. I chose the restroom. As I stepped into one of the stalls, my mind was on Sabrina, though I wasn't as concerned as I'd been before. God had certainly answered the prayer with my father and he'd answer my prayer for Sabrina, too.

Thankfully, I had two signal bars on my cell and I pressed D'Angelo's number. The first time, the call went to voice mail, and I hung up and called again.

"Hey," he whispered.

"What's going on with Sabrina?"

"How's your dad?"

"He's fine. He was really dehydrated and they may have to keep him overnight, but he's good. How's Sabrina?" I repeated.

"Where are you?" he asked. "I want to come to you."

"I'm on the fourth floor. Room four twenty-eight."

"I'll be right there." He hung up before I could ask him again what was wrong with my sister. I stared at the phone for a couple of extra moments before I stepped out of the stall. As I stood at the sink, I replayed D'Angelo's words in my head. He had not mentioned my sister's name. Why couldn't he tell me what was wrong? That as a new mom, she was just severely tired, was run-down, just needed a place to get some rest for a moment.

But he had said none of that. And I knew why.

Because the truth was, something was very, very wrong. Something was wrong with my sister.

# Chapter
## Thirty-Nine

I paced back and forth in front of my father's room, thinking that it was better to wait for D'Angelo out here rather than inside. I didn't want my father to see my concern. When he found out about Sabrina, I wanted to tell him everything, and most importantly, I wanted to tell him that she was going to be all right.

The nurse came out of the room and held the door slightly open for me. "You can go back in there, you know."

I nodded. "I will. I'm just waiting for a friend."

She patted my arm gently. "Your father is going to be fine," she said like she thought I really needed the assurance. "We're just going to have to tell him again about the importance of fluids."

"Thanks," I said, then watched her as she walked away.

For a moment I was taken back to who this nurse was and I studied her. Harmony. The woman who Sheridan had told me about. The woman who was engaged to Quentin.

It was interesting how life was, how paths crossed. She had no idea that I was the reason she'd been found. The reason why she'd come back to the hospital and was once again planning to marry Quentin Hart.

But before I could get too deep into thoughts about Harmony, my attention was brought back to my own business when I saw D'Angelo strutting toward me. But I couldn't appreciate this scene because of the look on his face and the sadness that shrouded his eyes.

"What's wrong with Sabrina?" I asked.

It was just a slight move the way he shook his head. "Where's your dad?"

"He's in there," I said, pointing to the door, "but I don't want to say anything to him until I know first."

He nodded, then held my arm as he said to one of the nurses at the station, "Is there a room where we can talk privately?"

"What?" I said. "No, D'Angelo. I don't want to go anywhere. Just tell me. What's wrong with Sabrina. Is it serious?"

"Kendall . . ."

"Just tell me!" I shouted.

He nodded. He breathed. And then he said, "She didn't make it."

There were only four words that he'd spoken, but I couldn't get those words to make any sense. I tried scrambling them, changing the order, dividing them into syllables, turning the words upside down.

But no matter what I did, nothing made sense.

"What?" I asked.

He shook his head and then wrapped his arms around me. But I pulled away. "You have to tell me. You have to tell me what you just said. And you have to say it slowly. Because . . . because . . . because . . ."

"She didn't make it, Kendall. Sabrina passed away."

"No." I shook my head.

"I'm so sorry."

"Please take that back."

Now D'Angelo teared up. He reached for me, but here's the thing. I knew that if I let him hold me, then what he said would be true. So, I backed away from D'Angelo, and his outstretched arms, and his words. I backed away and told him no. I was never going to accept what he'd said.

But as I shook my head no, he nodded yes. As I moved back, he moved forward.

Until I was stopped by the wall. And I could move no farther. And D'Angelo was right on top of me.

"No," I cried as he wrapped me in his arms.

"I'm sorry."

"No."

"I'm sorry."

"Noooooooooooooo!"

# Chapter
## Forty

Sorrow hurt.

My head pounded like never before. Not even the aspirin that Harmony had given to me helped. But as much as my head ached, it didn't come close to what was going on with my heart. Because of what I had to do.

But why did I have to do this? How had this happened? And so suddenly?

Probably an infection that had raged out of control. At least that's what Harmony said—off the record—after D'Angelo told her what he knew.

"I have to go now," I said to D'Angelo, who knelt beside me. Then I looked up and said the same thing to Harmony, who stood at the edge of the room against the door.

We were in an empty hospital room, three doors down from my father's. A room that Harmony had led D'Angelo to, when he literally lifted me into his arms and brought me in here. I guess it was better for me to wail in private—and not disturb the patients, especially my father.

There was no way I could let my father find out about Sabrina's death by me passing out in the hallway.

Sabrina's death.

Just putting those two words together made everything that was in me hurt. And brought brand-new tears to my eyes.

"I've got to go talk to my father."

"Are you sure you're ready?" Harmony asked. "You can stay in here as long as you need to." She had told us that my father was strong enough to hear this news. "If you want, I'll be in there with you. For your father."

"That would be great," I said. I had a feeling that she wanted to be there not just for my father. She knew that I needed her. And, I needed D'Angelo, too.

D'Angelo pushed himself from the floor beside me, then held my hand as he helped me to stand. Without a word, he pulled me into his arms as if he wished to give me strength. And, I held him because I needed courage.

He kissed my forehead, then squeezed my hand as he led me from the room. It was the longest journey ever, that walk to the third door. I paused and lowered my eyes, going over in my head what I was going to say.

"I'm ready," I whispered, and D'Angelo pushed the door open for me.

My father was still leaning back in the bed, but he was propped up a bit now, watching television.

"And the Lord is always there," the televangelist's voice boomed from the television.

"Amen!" my father said. "Hallelujah!"

Was it still Sunday?

"Hey, Daddy," I whispered.

He turned his head. "Hey, baby girl," my father said with cheer. "What's up, D'Angelo?"

"How ya doin', Mr. Leigh?"

"I'm hanging in there." Then my father turned to me and said, "You were gone so long, I thought you forgot about me."

"I would never do that, Daddy," I whispered.

He peered at me for a moment and then his eyebrows came together in a deep frown. "What's wrong?" he asked.

I had the words all ready for him, everything was prepared in my mind. But seeing him, and thinking about my sister . . . I couldn't look at him, and there was no way that I could say the words that I'd prepared. All I could do was lower my head to my chest and sob.

"Baby girl!" When my father tried to move out of his bed and come to me, the nurse stopped him. "Mr. Leigh, you have to stay in the bed."

"Well, somebody up in here better tell me what's going on." He paused. "D'Angelo?"

"Sir," he said, and then looked at me.

I shook my head. I had to be the one who gave my father this news.

I moved toward the bed where my father lay, and as I got closer, I saw the confusion in his eyes. He said nothing, as if he was giving me a chance to get myself together.

When I stood by his side, I inhaled oxygen and wished that it came with a shot of grit. Then I took his hand that wasn't hooked up to the machine. "Daddy," I began, and then stopped.

He nodded.

"It's Sabrina."

He twisted his head as if my sister's name was the last thing he expected to hear in this moment.

"Daddy, your golden girl . . ." Tears came into my throat. "She's gone." I sobbed. "She's gone, Daddy."

"Sabrina," he whispered. "She's gone?"

I nodded and cried some more. But through my tears, I told him, "She wasn't feeling well, and Anthony brought her here."

"She's here?"

I nodded. "But she passed away. I don't know a lot of the details," I said, and looked up at D'Angelo.

He stepped closer. "Mr. Leigh, I'm so sorry."

"Lord, Jesus!" my father cried. "What happened?"

D'Angelo shook his head like he couldn't believe any of this either. "Sabrina hadn't been feeling well."

"I know. She told me last night that she was so tired," my dad said. "I told her to get some rest and I was gonna see her today."

"Well, apparently, she got worse through the night and Anthony brought her here a few hours ago. But it was too late. They weren't able to save her."

"What happened?" he shouted, and the nurse moved closer to the bed.

"I don't know everything. The doctors said something about septic shock. But Anthony . . . he'll be able to tell you."

"Lord, Jesus!" my father said again. He bounced back in the bed and closed his eyes.

I would've given anything to take back those words. Anything to take away the agony that contorted his face.

It was the longest minute before my father opened his eyes. And just to be sure, he asked, "So, Sabrina's gone? She died?"

"Yes, Daddy," I sobbed. "I'm so sorry. I'm so, so sorry."

"Oh, baby girl." My father opened his arms and I laid my head on his chest.

Right there in his hospital room, as fluids dripped slowly into his veins, tears spilled from his eyes.

My father and I lay in his bed and we wept together.


There was so much sadness in that room and I just had to step away. So, I left my father with D'Angelo and Pastor Ford and I hid out in the restroom. Just for a little while.

I stepped into a stall, sat on the commode, and held my face in my hands. I was trying everything in my power to get my thoughts under control. But I couldn't capture any—except for one.

Sabrina was dead. My sister had died.

Time passed, though I had no idea how much. All I knew was that not enough time had passed to change the facts. So, I went to the sink, rinsed my face, but when I glanced up and into the mirror, I had to turn away. I didn't want to look into my eyes. My own unforgiving eyes

At the restroom door, I heard Asia before I even opened it, and when I stepped into the hallway, Sheridan and Asia stood at the nurses' station with Harmony.

"There she is." Harmony pointed.

Before I could take another step, Asia sprinted to me and swung her arms around my neck. "Oh, Kendall."

I held my friend and tried to comfort her as she sobbed and said, "I'm so sorry, I'm so sorry."

"It's going to be fine; we're going to be fine," I told her.

It took a couple of moments for Asia to get herself together enough so that I could turn to Sheridan and accept her embrace.

Tears were still rolling from Asia's eyes. "I can't believe this happened to your sister after all you guys have been through. And you didn't even have a chance to forgive her! Oh, god! That must be horrible for her and for you!"

Sheridan glared at Asia, trying to get her to shut her mouth, but Asia didn't even notice. And the truth was, what she said didn't bother me. Asia was just being herself, saying the most inappropriate things at the most inopportune times.

"How're you?" Sheridan asked.

"I'm good," I said, wanting to assure both of them. "I'm just concerned about my father, you know?"

"Well, there are a bunch of people in his room, so he's getting a lot of love."

"Really?" I said. "I just needed to get out of there for a couple of minutes."

"Well, let's get you back in there," Sheridan said.

Sheridan was right. The news had spread and just about everybody that my father knew was in his room. There were far too many folks than any hospital allowed. But I guess tragedy allowed for the breaking of rules.

My eyes did a quick scan and what I noticed first was that D'Angelo was gone. That saddened me, but then I thought that maybe it was because Anthony was in here now. Maybe he didn't want to cause his brother any more grief.

I spoke to no one, at least not at first. I walked straight toward my father's bed. As I moved, sorrowful glances bore into me like a laser, but my focus was on my dad.

I held him as if I hadn't seen him in days. "Hey, Daddy."

"You good, baby girl?"

I hoped my father didn't feel me flinch as he called me that. Baby girl. It hit me then that he'd never get to call Sabrina his golden girl again.

"Yeah," I said.

Turning next to Anthony, I reached out my arms to my brother-in-law. And I had another moment. I was sure that this was the first time I thought of Anthony this way. Not as my ex, not as the man who betrayed me, not as my sister's boo-in-crime, but as my brother-in-law.

It was amazing how grief trumped it all. It was like grief made me forget. Or maybe it was that grief made me remember. Made me remember that all that other stuff was just stuff. None of it was as important in this moment as it was before. And maybe it had never been important.

All I knew was that as I held Anthony and laid my head against his chest, there was only one emotion in my heart—love. That was all I felt for Anthony. A sisterly love.

"How're you?"

Anthony shook his head and I understood that response completely. There was only one answer to that question—he was still standing, he was still breathing. That was as good as it was going to get for now.

Then he said, "I've got to get going . . . in a little while. I've got to get back . . ." He stopped, and I knew what he was going to say. He had to get home to his baby. Sabrina's baby.

I hugged him again. "I know," I whispered.

From Anthony, I moved through the room, hugging my pastor, and her daughter, Gail, and Sister Henderson, my father's friend from our church who cooked occasionally for my father, and others from our church whose names there was no way for me to recall right now.

But I hugged everyone and accepted all the condolences. I had just moved away from the last person when Dr. Benjamin stepped into the room, but then he stopped when he looked at me. The shock showed in his eyes, but he recovered like any good professional.

I guess he'd been told that Edwin Leigh's daughter had died. I guess he'd just figured out that Edwin Leigh had more than one.

"Well, we have quite a crowd," the doctor said. He nodded as he came inside and then over to my father. "The nurses told me about your daughter. I'm so sorry." And again, he was the good doctor because there was not a drip of emotion in his tone.

But my father accepted the sentiment, and even gave the doctor a small smile.

"I know this is a tough time, but would you mind if I talked to you for a moment?" the doctor asked as he glanced quickly through the room.

Pastor Ford waved her hand in the air. "Just give me ten seconds, Doctor, and I'll have everyone out of here," she said as she started herding the group from the room.

Sheridan whispered, "We'll be right outside."

I nodded and moved to the other side of my father's bed. I held his hand and Dr. Benjamin stayed silent until it was only the three of us in the room.

He said, "So, you had a little bit of a scare, I heard."

"I felt really dizzy and weak," my father said. "I wasn't even sure I was gonna be able to dial 911."

"Well, you already know that you were dehydrated. But I want to keep you overnight, just for observation."

"Oh, no," my father said. "I have to get home. We have things we have to take care of."

"Daddy, there's nothing that we have to do tonight." To tell the truth, I was glad that my father would stay in the hospital. Not that I knew a thing about cancer and treatments and recovery, but I was concerned. This kind of stress couldn't be good in any way for my father, and there was no way that I was going to let anything happen to him. Not now.

"I really just want to get home, Doctor."

"I understand, but I promise it will just be tonight."

"And I'll feel so much better if you're here, Daddy. It'll give me a chance to go home, and get some of my things, because I want to spend the next few days with you."

The thought of that must've pleased him; it calmed him enough to finally agree.

"Okay, then," Dr. Benjamin began, "I'll check on you in the morning and we'll get you out of here as fast as we can." Then he stepped outside of the room and Pastor Ford, Sheridan, and Asia came back in.

The moment I told them that Dad was going to stay overnight, Pastor Ford went right into her action mode. Within seconds, she'd made the first call, then the second and third and fourth. She talked fast, she got straight to the point, and she moved on. Not even ten minutes passed before she clicked off her cell and stuffed it into her purse.

"All right, I got everything handled," she said. "We've got a team and someone will be with you till morning."

I could see the protest rising up in my father, but then he looked at Pastor and remembered who he was talking to.

She kept on like she was in charge—and she was. "There'll be five shifts, and I have the first." She looked up at me. "So you get going."

I hadn't planned to leave so early. I was bone-weary, but there was a part of me that didn't want to leave my father at all.

As if she could read my mind, Pastor Ford said, "You'll be no good to him if you're not strong." Turning to Sheridan, she commanded, "Take her home."

That was it. Pastor Ford had spoken. And maybe this was really a good thing. Because at home, maybe I'd find a way to start this Sunday all over again. Maybe I'd get into my bed, go to sleep, and wake up from this nightmare.

Leaning over, I held my father and hugged him tight. And I pressed back tears as he whispered, "I love you so much, baby girl, and we're gonna make it through this."

I held my father until Pastor Ford gently pulled me off of him. Then she held me, kissed my cheek, and sent me on my way.

Asia and Sheridan said their own good-byes to my father and our pastor. And Sheridan assured my dad, "We're going to take good care of her, I promise."

"Thank you."

I pressed my fingers against my lips and blew a kiss to my father. He raised his hand in the air, then curled his fingers as if he caught my kiss. Then he held his still-clutched hand to his chest, and his lips curved into a small smile.

And together, we remembered.

I'd taught Sabrina to blow kisses when she was just three

years old. And Dad used to catch them. It tickled Sabrina so much that she walked around the house blowing kisses, and all day long, my dad, my mom, and I would catch them.

I'd blown that kiss to make my father smile. I'd blown that kiss and it cracked my heart.

It wasn't until Sheridan took my hand that I was able to shift my immobile legs and walk out of the room.

"Whew!" I exhaled once I was in the hall. I felt like I was just coming up from being held underwater. Leaning against the wall, I tried to steady my breathing.

From behind the nurses' station, Harmony rushed over to me. "Are you okay?"

"Yes. I just need to get home."

"You're taking her?" Harmony asked Sheridan.

"I am. And thanks for everything. Thanks for taking care of my friend."

"No problem. I'll be here tomorrow."

When Harmony moved to the left, we walked to the right. And Asia whispered, "I can't believe Quentin's Harmony was taking care of your dad!"

"I know," I said, glad to have something else to talk about for a moment. "I would've warned you," I said to Sheridan. "But . . ."

"Well, I asked her how was Quentin and she told me she didn't know," Sheridan said. "I didn't probe, but I don't think they're together anymore."

I tilted my head. Sheridan sounded just a little too happy about that, and if this was any other time, any other place, I'd be all over her about it. But this was now, and we were here. And remembering all the moments of today made me sigh.

"I know, it's tough, huh?" Sheridan said as she put her arms around my shoulders.

I nodded.

"Well, I'm going to take you to your house, you can pack a bag, and then you can stay with me."

Asia jumped in: "I think it would be better if you stayed with me since I don't have a husband and we can just do girl time."

"But I think it would be better if she stayed with me," Sheridan told Asia. "She'll have me, my mom, and Brock."

In the elevator, the two of them debated, as if I wasn't there. In a way, I wasn't. So I didn't need to be part of this discussion. Especially since I wasn't going home with either of them. If I wasn't going to be with my dad, then I needed to be alone.

The two were still wrangling over me when we stepped out of the hospital.

Sheridan said, "Well, since I'm the one driving, I'm making a decision. I'm taking her."

I was just about to shut down all of this back-and-forth when we heard, "I got her."

The three of us looked up and there he was. D'Angelo. With his arms crossed, he leaned against his Lamborghini, which was blocking the entryway, of course.

He pushed himself off the car, nodded at Sheridan, then Asia, then turned his eyes to me.

Softly, he said, "I got you."

I nodded and then watched as Sheridan hugged him. "Thank you," she said. And she whispered in his ear, "Please take care of her."

"I will," he said. Then he took my hand and led me to his car. He helped me inside and strapped me in, before he sprinted to the driver's side. He jumped in and cranked up the engine.

And then he took me home.

·  ·  ·

Before he took me home, though, D'Angelo drove. Just drove and drove, staying close to the coast so that I could see the view as the sun made its westward journey. And as he drove, D'Angelo just let me be.

He let me lean back and think.

No music. No conversation.

We were surrounded by silence and the magnificent artistry of the day giving way to night over the Pacific. It made me sigh. If D'Angelo was trying to remind me of God, this did it.

But neither God nor the beauty of His creation could stave off my thoughts. Or maybe, I should say thought. It was singular: Sabrina was dead. My sister was dead. I would never see her alive again.

That thought played over and over.

Another sigh, and D'Angelo rested his hand on top of mine. At that moment that was all I needed.

When the car finally stopped in front of my cottage and D'Angelo turned off the engine, I sat still for a couple of minutes, staring into the ocean. After a while I twisted so that I faced him. "Thank you."

He nodded. "But you know you don't have to thank me, right? I'm here for you."

I reached for the door, but in a second D'Angelo was on my side, with his hand held out to help me up. He walked me to the front door, but before I put the key into the lock, I faced him.

"Thank you." I was hoping that he'd catch my hint. That this was as far as he was going.

He said, "Don't worry. I just wanna walk you in." He took the key from me, unlocked the door, then stepped aside so that I entered first.

I walked in, and gasped. All around were votive candles, dozens of them, perhaps even one hundred, if I took the time to count them. They were everywhere, on the tables, on the mantel, on the kitchen counter, even on the deck outside. I saw light from my bedroom and I was sure there were candles in there, too.

The room glowed as the lights flickered. This was serenity.

"You did this?" I faced D'Angelo.

He nodded.

There were so many questions—like how had he gotten into my house? But interestingly enough, I didn't feel like I really needed to know. Maybe if this were someone else . . . but this was D'Angelo. And though there was little that I was sure of at this moment, one thing I knew was that this man would make sure that I was safe.

"So, is this cool?"

"It's amazing." But then I turned to him. Because a house full of candles meant only one thing.

As if he knew my thoughts, he held up his hands. "I know my purpose, and I play my role. This is not about anything else except making sure you came home to some kind of peace. This is all about you, not us."

I nodded.

"Now, I will stay if you want me to; I'd like to stay." Again, he held up his hands. "But this is up to you, pretty lady."

I gave myself a moment, even though I already knew the answer. "Thanks, but I think I really need to be by myself." I paused. "You understand, don't you?"

"I know you, so I do." He kissed my cheek, turned around, and then walked out the door.

I leaned against the closed door and took in the light that glowed in the middle of the darkness. It was so peaceful, but I felt no peace.

Emotions burned deep inside of me, and I fought to squelch that flame. I didn't want to cry, didn't want to feel. I was so afraid of what that might look like if I were to just let myself go.

I had to stay strong. Be the Kendall Stewart that I always was, the woman that everyone expected me to be.

With a deep breath, I took two steps toward my bedroom. But then I stopped.

And my legs began to tremble. I spun around and ran to the door. Surely, D'Angelo was gone, but maybe, just maybe, he'd been held back by a phone call or something. Maybe he wasn't yet on Pacific Coast Highway, and he would see me running up the road chasing him.

I swung the door open. And there he stood. As if he knew I'd come back. He was just waiting for me.

Without saying a word, I wrapped my arms around his waist and he held me, too. Once again, he lifted me into his arms, this time, carrying me into my bedroom. He tossed back the duvet, and gently laid me down. Then he climbed onto the bed and held me. Just held me.

D'Angelo had been wrong. He'd set up my house so that I'd have nothing but peace. But as he held me now, what I felt was better than that. What I felt was what I needed the most. What I felt was love.

# Chapter
# Forty-One

I shot straight up in bed!
    Panting and trying to catch my breath. My eyes focused through the darkness.

Where was I? I scanned the room, then reached across my bed to turn on the lamp. But the lamp was not where it was supposed to be.

That was when I remembered. I wasn't in my home. For three nights now, I'd been here, in my father's house. I'd have to get out of my childhood bed to turn on the light in this bedroom.

I jumped out of the twin bed, and even though I hadn't lived in this house for way more than twenty years, I knew my way in the dark.

The switch was right at the door and I clicked on the light, then stood back and studied the room that I'd slept in until I left home for college. Even when Sabrina left home seven years later, my father never changed the room. Our twin beds, the dresser, and the rocking chair that was between our beds were still in place. As if my father hoped that one or both of us would return home one day and just resume our lives.

Slowly, I moved back to my bed and then sat on the edge. It took a moment for me to raise my head, but when I did, I stared at the bed across the room. Sabrina's bed.

I wondered when was the last time she'd stayed in this room. Had she ever come back and stayed here the way I did?

Not that I did this too often. I'd stayed in this room on the night before Christmas. And now here I was again. And it was the night before the funeral.

The funeral.

Maybe it was because of the funeral tomorrow that I couldn't sleep for more than ten minutes tonight . . . or last night . . . or the night before that. Maybe it was because of the funeral that every time I closed my eyes, I was besieged by those loud voices in my head.

The voices were as familiar as the words . . .

"You have a cancer within you that is eating you up inside . . . you have to find a way to deal with your unforgiveness."

"This thing about your own time . . . you don't own any time. All time belongs to God . . . He wants forgiveness that He tells you to give to others to be just like the forgiveness He gives to you. Instant."

"'Cause when God teaches you the lesson finally . . . I've just learned that hard hearts get the harshest lessons."

My dad, my pastor, D'Angelo . . . all of them were shouting at me. Even now, though I was fully awake, I could still hear them, though at the moment they weren't shouting. Now their words were soft whispers, telling me over and over what I already knew.

This didn't happen during the day. Those hours had been filled with the planning of the services and I'd taken on that responsibility like I was opening a new spa. I took on every detail—from the flowers, to the music, to the scriptures, to the programs. I spoke to the police myself about the escorts, I spoke to the soloists about what key they would sing each of the three songs in, I selected the font for the program and decided that it should be filled with pictures.

The only thing that I didn't handle was Sabrina. I left everything that had to do with my sister to Anthony and my father. I didn't even go to the funeral home or the wake last night because there was still so much to do. So many people to greet, so many calls to make . . . Anthony had even asked me to speak with the insurance company and I had gotten on top of that right away.

Every day, I worked myself until I was ready to just drop. Each night, I was overcome by exhaustion.

But I guess exhaustion had nothing to do with sleeping. Especially not when your heart was being haunted.

I scooted all the way onto the bed and leaned against the wall. All I wanted to do was sleep, but I wondered if sleep would ever come again. Maybe this was my punishment. A lifetime of waking hours so that I would be conscious 24/7. So that every hour of every day for the rest of my life, I'd be aware of what I'd done.

With a sigh, I moved to stand up and do what I'd done the past couple of nights. Go check on my father, then walk through this house and remember Sabrina.

Every night, I'd had my own memorial. Of the Christmas when I'd used my own money to buy Sabrina a tricycle. Of the Christmas when she'd used her own money to buy me a lipstick holder. Of the days when she was a teenager and I'd take her on shopping sprees. And of the nights when I was preparing to leave for college and she cried and told me how much she was going to miss me.

While I cherished those memories, I was being tormented by them, too. So, I didn't want to do that tonight. I didn't want to walk through this house and remember. I just wanted to sleep and forget.

Maybe I needed to call D'Angelo since I was with him the last time I slept. But I hadn't seen him since Monday morning when he'd awakened me to a bagel and tea in bed. He'd left me with just a kiss on my forehead and told me he'd be in touch.

My father told me that he'd come by the morning that Anthony and I had gone to sign some papers at the funeral home. But he was gone by the time I came back. So, D'Angelo was not an option. I was going to have to find a way to rest my bone-tired body on my own.

Leaning over, I laid my head on my pillow. But my eyes never closed and I just stared across the room. At Sabrina's bed.

My eyes stayed on that side of the room, and I could see her sitting there when she was just four and was so determined to tie her own shoes. Or when she was six and she brushed out her pigtails, because now she wanted to wear her hair in a ponytail the way I wore mine.

I sat up, swung my legs onto the floor, and moved to turn off the light. But this time I didn't go to my bed.

It took a moment for me to sit down on Sabrina's bed, and then another moment before I pulled back the blanket and slid down beneath it. I lay on my back with my eyes wide open staring at the ceiling.

My eyes didn't close, but on this side of the room, the voices had quieted. Maybe I wouldn't sleep, but in Sabrina's bed, maybe I could pretend to have a little peace.

The ringing startled me out of my sleep.

That was my first thought. And my second: I'd been asleep.

I slipped out of the bed, then grabbed my phone from the

other side of the room, hoping that it hadn't awakened my father.

"Hello," I said, sounding like a frog.

"Kendall, this is Pastor. I'm really sorry to call this early and wake you, but I really need to see you. Can you meet me at church?"

"When?"

"Right now."

I pulled my cell away from my ear so that I could check out the time. It was just a little after six. "Is everything okay?" I figured she needed to speak to me regarding the services today.

"I need to see you."

"Okay . . ." Then I paused. "But I don't really like leaving my dad alone."

"Oh, I know that. I called Blanche, and she'll probably be there before you hang up from me. She'll stay with your dad while you come over here."

It had to be serious if Pastor had already taken care of that. "All right. I'll take a quick shower and I'll be right there."

As I clicked off my phone, the doorbell rang and I tightened my robe as I rushed to the front of the house. Just like Pastor said, Sister Henderson was standing there with a shopping bag filled with groceries, as if we needed any more food. The refrigerator was already overstuffed with dishes and pans that would make a fabulous feast for a family of five.

"Good morning." Mrs. Henderson stepped into the house with the kind of cheer that came from already being awake for hours.

"Good morning and thank you for coming over so early."

"That's okay, baby. You know I was going to be here anyway to whip up breakfast for you and your dad." She paused and took her smile away for just a moment. "You're gonna need all your strength today."

I just smiled because I didn't want to tell her that like sleep, my appetite had failed me. Even the sight of food made me feel just a little bit sick.

But while Mrs. Henderson made her way to the kitchen, I dashed to the bathroom, showered, and slipped back into the sweatsuit that I'd worn yesterday. The entire time my head was filled with thoughts of the funeral. I scanned through the checklist in my mind and the only reason I could think of for Pastor to be calling had to be the programs. Something had gone wrong with the programs.

Before I left, I peeked in on my father, and then asked Mrs. Henderson to let him sleep as long as possible.

"Okay, baby," she said.

But she already had the skillet sizzling on the stove and I knew by the time she dropped strips of bacon in there, my dad would be up and on his feet. He had to watch his diet while he was on chemotherapy, but I figured I wouldn't talk to him about diet. Not today.

Even for a Thursday, this was early, and so with the before-seven traffic, I made it to the church in just a little over fifteen minutes. It was easy to park right across from Hope Chapel, something that I was never able to do since Kelso Street was always filled with cars.

I turned off the engine, then stared at my home church. It wasn't hard for me to imagine the scene that would unfold here in just a few hours. I could see the hearse and the two limousines that would be following Sabrina to her resting place.

And I wondered . . . was there any way for me to get out of attending the funeral? I'd been able to work it with the wake last night—I'd told everyone that I was waiting for an important call from the insurance company. Of course, that wasn't true, but no one knew it. Would anyone believe that lie today?

I'd have to think about that some more, but I couldn't handle it right now. I had to get in to see Pastor Ford.

The door to my pastor's outer office was open, and when she heard my footsteps, she called out, "Kendall?"

"Yes, Pastor."

I had barely stepped into her office before she rushed around her desk and squeezed me in a tight embrace.

"How are you?" she asked as she held my hand and led me to her sofa.

"I'm good. I was just worried that something had happened with Sabrina's services. I was thinking the programs?"

Pastor shook her head. "Everything is fine. I wanted to talk to you."

"Okay."

"Would you like some coffee?" Pastor Ford said as she stood and walked toward the brewer that she had in the corner of her office.

I shook my head. Really, I would never be rude to my pastor, but I hoped that she didn't call me over here to have a little chat. I mean, didn't she know all that I had to do? My plan this morning was to do all the follow-up, call the florist, call the police escorts, check in with the cemetery. I had to make sure that everything went as smoothly as any other event that I was responsible for.

But either my pastor didn't know my schedule or she didn't care. She took her time pouring her coffee, took her time coming back to the sofa, and took her time sitting down.

I was just about to scream when she said, "Have you been to the funeral home?"

"What?" I blinked. I was so tired I couldn't even hear what my pastor was saying. It sounded like she'd asked if I'd been to the funeral home. What did that have to do with anything?

And then she repeated her question and I was shocked that

I had heard her right. "To the funeral home?" I asked, because I needed some kind of explanation to understand this question.

She took a sip of her coffee and nodded. "To the funeral home to see Sabrina."

Why in the world would she ask me this? "No," I said. "I've been busy handling other things."

"Too busy to see your sister?"

*What is the point?* I wanted to ask her. Was seeing her going to bring Sabrina back? Was seeing her going to give me a chance to make it all right? But I reeled in my attitude and said, "There's been a lot for me to do, Pastor."

Pastor Ford sipped more coffee, then placed the cup and saucer on the table beside us.

Turning back to me, she took my hands inside of hers. "I love you, Kendall."

And the burning began in my stomach.

"I love you and I know you. I know that you spent six years in a very dark place."

The burning began to rise inside of me.

"And I'm not going to let you do that again."

Now she lost me. If she were to just ask me whether or not I'd forgiven Sabrina, I would've told her that I had. Death fixed all of that. Her death had punished me.

Pastor said, "You went through something awful, and I know that you were beginning to move forward, and so there is no way that I'm going to let you go back." She let go of my hands and then held my face, forcing me to look straight at her. "No more unforgiveness in your heart. Now you must forgive yourself."

"Forgive myself for what, Pastor?" I asked, snatching myself away from Pastor Ford. I stood and looked down at her. "For never forgiving Sabrina?"

"No," she said calmly, staying on the sofa. "That's not what I'm talking about, because you *have* forgiven Sabrina, haven't you?"

"Yes!" I cried. "But only because she died and now it's too late. Because I never got to tell her that. She doesn't know that I've forgiven her."

"But that forgiveness was never for Sabrina." Pastor Ford moved her hands, punctuating each word. "That forgiveness was always for you. That was something that I was trying so hard to get you to understand. That a heart that was hardened with unforgiveness only hurt you. It never hurt Sabrina."

I covered my face with my hands, hoping that I could hold back the burning emotions that swelled inside of me.

Pastor Ford said, "Yes, she loved you and wanted a relationship with you. But in spite of how you felt about her, in spite of how you treated her, Sabrina moved on with her life. With joy and happiness. You were the one who suffered. You were the one who was left with that bitter pill you swallowed every day. You are the one who hasn't experienced complete joy in your life. And that's why I'm not going to let you go down this road again.

"I want you to have the life you deserve and you will *never* have that as long as there is any unforgiveness in your heart. Learn from this, Kendall. Live now with an open heart. An open heart that can give love fully—to your father, to your niece, to Anthony and all of your friends. And I want you to have an open heart so that you can receive love, because I know that God's not through with you yet. You were born to be a wife and He has someone for you, but your heart has to be able to receive love. You will never live the life you deserve with a hardened heart." She paused. "So forgive yourself, Kendall. Forgive."

That burning rumbled up through me, pausing first to

leave a fiery lump in my throat and then escaping through my lips in wrenching sobs. I crumbled down onto the sofa and into my pastor's arms.

"I'm just so sorry," I cried.

"I know you are. God's forgiven you, your sister is smiling down on you. So go ahead and forgive yourself."

And I cried. And I cried as my pastor held me. I cried until for the first time in years, I truly felt relief.

# Chapter
## Forty-Two

I hadn't been sure that I would be able to do this, but after that talk with my pastor, I knew that I could.

I held my father's hand as we marched into the church after Pastor Ford. Behind us, Anthony walked side by side with his brother. I'd been so glad to see D'Angelo this morning. Not for me, but for Anthony.

It was Anthony who wanted my father to walk into the church first, and that gesture reminded me just how generous of a man he'd always been. As we stepped slowly down the aisle while Pastor Ford read from the fourteenth chapter of John, I glanced at the solemn faces that stared at us. So many I knew, so many I didn't. There were church members, of course, and a few people from my business. Closer to the front were the people I loved the most: Sheridan and Brock, Christopher and his new wife, and Asia, and even Angel had come with her.

Then we took the seat of honor, next to Anthony and D'Angelo in the front row.

As the service began, I kept my eyes on the golden casket and tried to imagine my sister inside of that coffin. I just couldn't do it. But in my mind's eye, I could see her so clearly. And, I could hear her, too . . .

"Kendall!"

It was just a whisper, but even at the kitchen table, I could hear Sabrina calling from our bedroom.

"Kendall!"

I pushed my seventh-grade math book aside and rushed to my sister.

"Kendall!" Sabrina reached her arms up to me.

"What's wrong?" I asked as I sat on the edge of her bed and held her.

"I had a bad dream."

"Oh, I'm sorry. But you know it was just a dream, right?"

She nodded.

"Do you want me to turn on the light?"

She shook her head. "No, 'cause Mama said we have to save lectressity."

"Do you mean 'electricity'?"

She nodded.

"Okay. Then we won't turn on the light, but you know what I'm gonna do?" She shook her head. "I'm gonna lie in the bed with you until you go back to sleep, okay?"

She nodded.

I climbed into the twin bed and pushed my body against the wall so that Sabrina would have enough room. Then I wrapped my arms around her and said, "Is that better?"

"Uh-huh. I'm not scared anymore. I'm never scared with you, Kendall."

"That's good."

"I love you."

"I love you, too . . ."

The memories kept coming, like a video stream of the greatest hits, the best of times with my sister. I remembered it all. Her first day at kindergarten and how she was so proud that she had homework. She'd sat at the table with me, and while I tackled algebra, she'd colored a picture of a princess and tried to stay inside the lines.

And then, as the years went by and her homework became more challenging, we'd sit together every night, Sabrina just as determined as I was to get straight A's.

"I'm going to UCLA just like you!" she'd exclaimed when I'd received my acceptance letter and scholarship. "And then we can be roomies again."

"No, golden girl," my father had said. "Kendall will be long gone by the time you go to college."

Sabrina had been so disappointed by that news, but I'd promised her on that day that no matter what, in a way we'd always be roomies because we had each other's heart.

The service continued through the scripture readings and song selections and acknowledgments, but I barely heard any of it. I didn't even want to hear, not really. All I wanted to do was think about Sabrina.

And so, I just let the memories go on. Until it was time to say good-bye.

When they opened the casket, I turned away and instead focused on the well-wishers who streamed by. Who said their good-byes to Sabrina, then turned to us with more words of condolence. I greeted everyone with a hug, even people I did not know. I had to because it gave me something to do.

It came to the point where I couldn't delay this anymore. Anthony whispered to his brother, who reached for my father, and together they went up to say their good-byes. I breathed, relieved. No one expected me to go up to the casket, and for that, I was grateful.

As my father's body convulsed with his cries, I was so glad that he was with D'Angelo, who stood next to him and held him, even as he leaned over to kiss his golden girl. Then D'Angelo brought my father back to the pew.

But before I could take my father's hand, Anthony reached for me. "Come on," he whispered.

I wanted to protest, but before I could, I had already taken the five steps to the casket. And as Anthony held me, I looked down at my sister and sobbed. Even in death, she was just gorgeous. Sleeping Beauty.

And, she was smiling. A smile meant for me, I had a feeling.

I stood there for a moment, then leaned over and gently kissed her forehead. "I'm so sorry, Sabrina. I will always love you."

And this with a final gasp, I turned around. My father was standing right behind me. And we hugged. And we sobbed. Together.


I was a teenager when my mom passed away, so I should've remembered. But I didn't remember this many people being in our house. There was hardly room to move around, but that didn't seem to bother any of the almost one hundred people who were eating and drinking and chatting. It felt festive, a celebration of life, exactly the way my father wanted it.

But about four hours had passed now since we all said good-bye to Sabrina and left her to the hands of the Inglewood Park Cemetery workers. And it had been about three hours since my friends had taken one look inside my father's home and told me that they would catch me later. Even D'Angelo had stayed for only a couple of minutes.

"I have to make a quick trip out of the city," he told me as he gave me a hug. "I'll call you when I get back."

I'd watched every one of my friends drive off and I'd

almost wanted to run after each car, begging them to take me, too. But I had to stay. I had to be here for my father.

The kitchen was as packed as the living room, but at least by being in the kitchen, I was closer to the place where I knew I could go to get some air. I eased my way through the crowd, twisting and turning, making my own path until I got to the hallway. Then I rushed to my bedroom and closed the door behind me.

The chatter, though muted, made its way through the door, but it was so much better in here. Compared to what was out there, it was almost silent.

I sat on my bed and allowed my mind to wander through the events of the day. But no matter what I tried to focus on, I kept going back to one thing. Seeing Sabrina sleeping. That's how she looked to me. Like she was just asleep. She looked like she'd seen the face of God and had nothing but joy.

The expression on her face wasn't much different today than it had been the first time I saw her, the first time I had the chance to look down onto her face . . .

I'd been standing behind my mother when she opened the door for my father and he'd rushed in with a baby doll.

For me? The excitement of this made me tremble. My birthday was still a week away, but I guessed my father remembered that I wanted one of those new talking dolls. I clapped my hands. "Yay, a new baby doll."

"Not a doll, baby girl. This is a real baby." And then my father had glanced at my mother. She looked like she had tears in her eyes and I was just about to ask her why when my dad said, "Do you want to hold her, baby girl?"

"Can I? Please?"

My dad nodded and pointed to the sofa. I couldn't sit down fast enough. Then I held out my arms and my father placed the pink-bundled baby into my arms. She was so beautiful with hair that looked like it was gold, long curvy eyelashes, and lips that had so much pink on them I thought she was wearing lipstick. The only thing was, her skin was a little yellow. And I wished that it was more brown, like mine.

"This is your little sister," my dad said.

I looked up at him, not quite understanding. "My sister?"

My dad nodded, and when I looked at my mom, she nodded, too. But after that, she ran into her bedroom.

"Daddy, what's wrong with Mommy?"

For a moment he looked as sad as my mother. Then he shook his head. "I think she's not feeling very well, but I'll take care of your mom. I'll make sure that she's happy. You just help me take care of your sister, okay?"

"Okay!" That sounded like a fantastic deal to me. I loved this wiggling, gurgling baby already . . .

I sighed. For many years, I'd kept that promise and I'd done all I could to take care of Sabrina. Until . . . I shook my head. I didn't want to go back there. There was no need to go back to what had happened. It was over. All of it was over.

I'd wanted to be alone, but when I heard the knock on the door, I felt a little bit of relief. Just about anyone would make good company right now. "Come in."

The door opened and the best company possible walked in. I smiled the way I used to when I saw Anthony. But now I smiled because of what he held in his hands. A pink-bundled baby.

"Mind if we come in?"

I shook my head. "No, come on. Just close the door."

He chuckled. "I know what you mean. There're a lot of folks out there." But though I'd invited him in, he took tentative steps toward me. As if he wasn't quite sure.

I helped him out. I reached up and held my arms open. Exactly the way I'd done all those years before when Sabrina was a baby. He lowered Ciara into my arms and I held my niece for the first time.

As I cradled her in my arms, I studied her the way I didn't the day Sabrina had brought her into my office. And I could see that Ciara was definitely her mother's child. Yes, she was the same gorgeous chocolate as Anthony. But the rest was all Sabrina. Ciara's golden hair, her long lashes, and lips with so much color she looked like she was wearing lipstick.

"My goodness!" I said.

"Yup," Anthony agreed, already knowing what I was thinking. "She looks just like Sabrina."

I rocked her in my arms and felt Anthony sit next to me, but I didn't take my eyes from the baby.

"I hope I wrapped her up good. I was worried about bringing her out finally, but I wanted you and Dad to see her, since I kept her home all week."

"I'm actually glad you kept her home. I wouldn't have wanted her around all this sadness. But today, it's fine. Today is a celebration of a life well lived."

He sighed. "A young life."

I looked up and squeezed his hand. He nodded and blinked hard as if he'd made the same commitment that I did—no more tears!

For minutes we sat in the silence as I rocked and stared at this baby. She was still sleeping as I lifted her to my chest, and when I held her against my heart, I couldn't help it—I cried. I sobbed and held Ciara tighter. And as I held Ciara, Anthony held me.

When she cooed, I lowered her just a bit so that I could see her face. "Hi, baby," I said. "Was I holding you too tight?"

"No," Anthony answered for his daughter. "Tell her, Ciara, an auntie can never hold you too tight."

I smiled and then, "But what about a godmother?" I said to

Ciara at first, and then turned to Anthony. "Sabrina had asked me . . ."

He nodded before I could finish. "Yes! That's what we both wanted. Yes, Kendall. Thank you." Then he stood up. "I'm going to get her diaper bag and then grab something to eat. Do you want anything?"

I shook my head. "I'm fine. I have everything that I want right here."

Anthony stepped out of the room, leaving me and Ciara alone. And I said, "Let me tell you about your mommy. She was such a special lady . . ."

# Chapter
## Forty-Three

The first of May.

As I leaned back on the lounger and peered into the ocean, I couldn't believe how time had moved so quickly. It had already been two weeks since Sabrina had passed away and it didn't seem like that much time could have possibly gone by.

But then, in some ways, it seemed like I'd lived through an eternity. Because in two weeks, I felt like a different person.

The tables had turned for real. I was mellow now. Not angry, not bitter. And like Pastor Ford had asked, my heart was open. The only thing about an open heart was that it made me mushy. Before Sabrina passed away, I never cried. But now . . . those Mother's Day commercials that had just hit the TV were getting to me. And sometimes, just looking out at this ocean and beauty of God's majesty . . . it was too much. I shook my head and wiped my eyes. See? I was turning into a crying fool. And that thought made me laugh.

I took another sip of my tea and noticed a lone figure far away walking on the edge of the beach. This stretch of the coast was private, so there were hardly any people on it. The weather was just breaking, so I expected my neighbors to be setting up on the sand pretty regularly soon.

But in the two months that I'd lived here, I never saw anyone just strolling the way this person was. I watched as the figure came closer, closer, closer. And then close enough for me to make out all parts of him. It was his swagger that was most distinctive. And then there was what I called his uniform: today, a black T-shirt, black jeans, and his Tims that were now covered with sand.

By the time he trotted up the steps to my deck, the tips of my lips had connected to each ear.

"D'Angelo Stewart," I said. With my hand, I shielded my eyes from the glare of the sun. I wanted to get a good look at this man.

He leaned over and kissed my forehead. Then he sat at the end of the lounger. "What's up?"

"Just you. Did you just get back?"

He nodded. "Yeah, just the morning. And I wanted to make sure that I came and saw you. So, you're good?"

"I am. I have my days. I have to try hard not to think about all the things that I wish I'd done differently."

He shrugged. "We all wish for a do-over at some time or another."

I took a deep breath. "Well, tragedy brings clarity."

"At least you got clarity. At least you learned the lesson. And now you need to stand up in front of the world and shout out that message. 'Cause there are people out there who profess to know the Lord, but they pray, they send their petitions to God, and they have such hard hearts. I just don't get it. Don't they know that God can't honor that?" He shook his head. "I was worried about you. I never wanted that to be you. I never wanted you to be one of those people that God wasn't able to hear."

I tilted my head. "Sometimes you sound just like a preacher."

He laughed. "Maybe that'll be my next vocation. Who knows?"

"Who knows?" I agreed. "One of the lessons I've learned over the last few weeks is that none of us knows what the future holds."

"The future," he said with a side glance at me that sent my heart a-thumping. After a silent moment he said, "I made a tough decision; I'm heading back to Iraq."

I nodded. "I'm not surprised."

"Really? You should be. Because I gave it some serious thought. I thought about staying here."

"But you're not that kind of man," I said. "Remember, you told me that you couldn't imagine settling down."

"I couldn't. Before. But now . . ."

He spoke in incomplete sentences that I completely understood. "Me, too," I said. "I couldn't. Before. But now."

He chuckled. "Pretty lady, you made this hard for me. But I think you need some time. And, I need some time, too."

I nodded.

"And who knows?" he said.

"Who knows?" I agreed, thinking that the tables had turned for real. Was I really considering this? Was I really having this talk-nontalk about the possibility of a maybe relationship someday?

"We can always stay in touch," he said. "We can Skype or do that FaceTime thing."

I shuddered at that thought. After what had happened to Asia? But I said, "Maybe." Then I asked, "So, when do you leave?"

"Tomorrow," he said. "That's why I had to make that run down to San Diego. Just got our new orders."

He didn't say anything else and I didn't want to know.

But neither one of us got to say another word, because Ciara's cries came through the baby monitor. He looked at the machine on the table and his eyes widened. "Ciara's here, with you?"

I nodded and then giggled. "She spent the night with me last night," I said as I jumped up from the lounger and rushed into my bedroom.

"And she's still alive?"

I slapped D'Angelo's arm playfully before I peeped into the bassinet that I'd sent to Sabrina and Anthony when Ciara was born. But just days after Sabrina's funeral, Anthony had brought the bassinet over here for visits such as this. "Oh, what's wrong with the baby?" I said as I lifted her up.

As if she could feel all of my love, right away, her cries stopped.

"The magic touch," D'Angelo said. "And I should know."

If I were a few shades lighter, he would've seen the heat rise beneath my skin. I said, "A godmommy's touch."

He paused for a moment. "Well, can her godfather get some love?"

I looked at him and he nodded as he held out his hands to hold Ciara. As he took her from me, he said, "Anthony asked me the day of Sabrina's funeral."

"That's great. I guess this means that you and Anthony are cool again."

"I told you that we would be. But what this really means is that if you're the godmother and I'm the godfather, we're going to have to do some duties together."

Then, while he still held Ciara in his arms, he leaned forward and kissed me. A soulful kiss that made me glad that I wasn't the one holding the baby. When he backed away, he handed Ciara to me, then strutted from my bedroom.

Still holding Ciara, I followed and stopped at the deck

door. He trotted down the steps then went back the same way he came—along the beach. I watched him and rocked Ciara. I watched him until I couldn't see him anymore.

But even though he was gone, he'd left me with a smile on my face. And a tear rolling down my cheek.

Pastor Beverly Ford

*Lessons Learned*

# Chapter
## Forty-Four

This wasn't the first time that I'd done this.

I'd summoned the ladies to the church before, most of the time, though they were by themselves. But today, I'd called them to the sanctuary together, just like I'd done a few days after Christmas.

But today was so different from that time almost five months before. Today, I had something special for them.

I stepped into the sanctuary and marveled at just how different it was. The last time I'd been here with them, I'd walked in and it was so silent. They were spread across the sanctuary as if they didn't even know each other.

But today, it didn't seem like they were waiting for a death sentence. Today, the three of them—Sheridan, Kendall, and Asia—sat in the front pew right in front of the altar, chatting like the friends that I'd always known they'd become.

It almost brought tears to my eyes just thinking about the way they'd grown in God. When I brought them together all those years ago in a prayer support group, I knew I was doing the right thing. And today, seven years later, this was proof of it.

Even with the tragedy that was still fresh in our lives, these ladies were smiling. Kendall was not wallowing and that was what I was most proud of. Each of these ladies knew that they would get through Sabrina's death, and anything else with the Lord. And with love. And with friendship.

It wasn't until I was almost in front of them that the ladies noticed me.

"Hey, Pastor," they said in unison. Then, as if it was choreographed, they each jumped up to hug me.

I saved Kendall for last because I wanted to give her a little extra.

When they sat back down, Sheridan said, "So, you wanted to see us?"

I nodded and looked at each of them. What amazing lessons they had all learned.

"Do you know how proud I am of each of you?"

The beamed as if they knew exactly how far they'd come.

"It's been a long journey," I said.

"Hold up, Aunt Beverly," Asia said. "You're talking like our journey is over." She laughed.

"Well, in a way, it is."

That wiped the smiles off of their faces.

I said, "Don't worry, your friendship will go on forever. There's nothing that anyone can do to stop that. But did you realize that we're coming up on the seventh year of the Ex Files?"

Their stares told me that meant nothing to them—at least not yet.

"Well, I know you know that seven is God's number of completion. And though He is a long way from being finished with you, or me, I think this is a good time for us to think about where do we go with the Ex Files in the eighth year. The number eight—God's number for new beginnings."

"Okay," Sheridan said. "What do you have in mind?"

"I'm glad you asked." I chuckled. "I think each of you has learned some amazing lessons over the past few months that need to be shared. For example, Sheridan, what do you think you've gotten out of this journey?"

I could see her measuring the words in her head, not sure at all how much she wanted to say.

"I guess the biggest lesson I've learned, Pastor, is that I'm not anybody's savior. And it seems like a simple lesson, but I think sometimes, as women, we take on everybody's issues. Our children's, our husband's, even our friends' . . . when they have issues, we think we can solve everything. When most of the time, the best thing we can do for anybody is just take them and their issues to the altar."

I smiled. That sounded like a sermon to me.

Normally, I would go to Kendall next, but I glanced instead at my niece. I still had to shake my head at the hard lessons she'd learned. Even now I wanted to strangle her, ask her what she'd been thinking. But she had a powerful message for so many women . . . and girls.

I didn't even have to ask Asia what she'd learned; she began, "Well, I know what I'd want to tell some people, especially these young girls out here." Her finger swayed in the air with each word she spoke. "We need to educate these girls on tablets, social media, and how all of it is the devil's playground!"

Sheridan, Kendall, and I laughed out loud. But Asia didn't crack a smile. She was serious.

"I'm not playin'," she said. "I think Satan created all of that. Look at how people are getting in trouble. That ain't nothin' but the devil!"

"Or maybe not," Kendall said before I could say anything. "Maybe there's nothing wrong with tablets and social media and the Internet. Maybe it's just how we use it."

"Whatever! Somebody needs to be teaching these girls something. I don't want people to have to go through what I went through."

I nodded.

"Oh." Asia raised her hand again. "And, my biggest lesson is that I can't even tell if someone loves me until I learn how to love myself first. I think it was because I wasn't sure of myself that I didn't recognize Bobby's game. But now that I am, nobody will be able to step to me like that again."

Lesson learned! Can I tell you how proud I was to hear my niece finally talk this way? I knew that the seeds she'd sown with Bobby Johnson had not been good. He was always another woman's man. But he'd gotten to my niece when she was young, nurtured her to be the woman he wanted her to be, then almost destroyed her.

It had to be difficult—Bobby had been part of her world for half of her life. And with the good things that he'd done for her, he was a hard man to get over.

But Asia seemed to be doing it. And what I loved best was how her focus was now on Angel.

Now I turned to Kendall.

Without me saying a word, she took a deep breath. "I learned that we don't get many chances to have do-overs in life. So, when you know better, you should do better. I was stubborn for so long. I just wanted the world to know how much I'd been hurt. And I wanted everyone to understand and agree with me and hate Sabrina, too. But really, while people listened to me, the only person who cared about that mess was me. And what good did that do?"

Kendall sighed and glanced down at her hands. "Love has to trump everything; no one in this world is as bad as the worst thing they've ever done. Sabrina was amazing in my life for over thirty years, until . . . and I never gave her a chance to make a comeback. I wiped thirty years out like it was nothing.

"After a few years, I should've done something. Counseling, something, especially since she'd always tried to make an effort with me. And I'm really sorry that I didn't. But I'm determined to not have any more regrets like this. Never again."

I wanted to raise my hands in victory, do a Holy Ghost dance, and shout *Hallelujah!* But what I said was, "Excellent. You've learned lessons that no man could ever teach. Only experience could be this kind of teacher. And I'm hoping that you're willing to use your experiences to teach."

"What do you mean?" Asia asked.

Before I could answer, Kendall said, "You want us to stand up in front of the world and shout out this message," as if she already knew what I was talking about.

"Well, you can put it that way . . . just leave out the shouting." I laughed. "Seriously, though, I think you ladies have a show that needs to go on the road. The three of you are dealing with issues that women need to hear, and learn from."

The three of them looked at me, and then, when they glanced at each other, they shrugged and nodded.

"So, what do you think?" I asked. "You think we have something here?"

"Yeah," Sheridan said. And then Kendall and Asia agreed.

"Okay. Well, you ladies get together and let me know what you come up with. And we'll make it happen."

"Okay," they said together, seeming like they liked the idea.

They may have only liked it, but I loved it. Because I knew that their lessons were going to touch so many.

Standing up straight, I reached for their hands and they stood, too. And just like we always did when the four of us got together in this way, in this sanctuary, we formed a circle of four and held hands.

I never had to say a word, the ladies all bowed their heads. And then in the quietness of God's house, we sent our prayers to the Lord.

# A Note from the Author

I think many people would be surprised to know that I'm not crazy about sequels. That's hard to believe, huh? Especially since I have a series of six Jasmine books (not counting the ones I've done with ReShonda) and now this "Exes" group (which really began with *Grown Folks Business*—Sheridan's story). So for a person who doesn't like to write sequels, why do I do so many? Because I listen to my readers and to the marketplace. And when I can, I respond to them. But what I love as a writer is taking new journeys, meeting new people, and listening to new voices in my head. If I had my way, I would have more than twenty books out there filled with people you would never see again. But I look at this career as a partnership—me, my publisher, and you, the readers. So in this partnership, as in any great partnership, we've all compromised. And I've written books that will satisfy a little for a lot of people.

Now, while I'm not crazy about sequels, every time I finish a novel, I'm glad I went back to revisit these folks. I love to see characters grow so I've never regretted a single sequel that I've written, and I was really happy with the way *Forever an Ex* turned out. The story lines shocked me, especially Kendall's. I was so sorry when that tragedy hit her. I argued with the writing voice in my head that told me I had to do it. I. Did. Not. Want. To. Do. It. But after complaining and being a little pissed about it, I went with that tragedy because that story had to be told. People have to see the possible consequences of nonforgiveness in their lives. So I hope a heart or two will be changed by what went down between Kendall and Sabrina. And if one heart is, then writing *Forever an Ex* in that way was worth it.

*The Ex Files* (and by default, *Forever an Ex*) has been optioned to become a movie. That is another reason why I'm happy I did revisit these characters. While the author has little to say about the movie script, writing this story gives the producers and the other powers that be more to work with . . . so we'll see what happens. (The Hollywood process is a long, long, long, long journey. So no, I have no idea when the movie will be finished or when it will come out.)

Well that explains why I wrote this novel, and really, I'd love to end this author's note right here because the next part gives me such anxiety that sometimes I break out in hives. It is hard to write acknowledgments because I will inevitably leave out someone by accident. Like the time I acknowledged my nieces who'd helped me spread the word about my novel. My mother called me and said, "You forgot Ciara! Why did you leave out Ciara?" I tried to explain that yes, Ciara is my niece, and yes, I didn't include her, but that was because she didn't help me spread the word about my novel, being that she was only four years old at the time. I've been traumatized since. So all I say about the people I love is that I'm acknowledging all of you. And that I love you. And that you know that already and don't need validation in a book. That goes for all of my friends and family!

Whew! Now that that's over with, I can get on to my professional acknowledgments. I've been published by a major publisher since 2000, and I've spent most of those years with Simon and Schuster. I just celebrated my tenth anniversary with Touchstone Books, an imprint of S&S, and ten years is like one hundred years in publishing. Seriously, very few authors are blessed with such longevity, let alone as a writer with one publisher, so this is a special time for me. This hasn't been an easy journey. Right in the middle of my career, the digital market exploded, making bookstores close and taking away the opportunity for people to buy print books with ease. Honestly, for the past several years, it's felt like my career has been touch and go—some years more touch than go. But the thing is, Touchstone has stayed with me and I am grateful to the entire team. I'm very excited to be working with two new people at Touchstone: Susan Moldow, my publisher, and my new editor, Lauren Spiegel. I am thrilled about Lauren—she's a writer's editor, the kind who will get down in the ditches with you and help you figure out your whole crazy story. Thank you, Lauren, for helping me make *Forever an Ex* a better, tighter novel. (And as much as I love this book, I cannot wait for the next!) And then there's Shida Carr, my publicist for the past ten years. There are no words to completely say what I think about Shida so I'll keep it simple: Shida, you're the best in the business . . . period! It's because of you that I've been able to hang on during these tough times and I have a feeling that it's all about to pay off. So a major thank-you! And to everyone else at Touchstone: Sally, Meredith, and those in the editorial, publicity, and marketing departments: the fact that you believe in me means the world. I'm blessed to be rolling with Team Touchstone.

That's what I call the inside team but there's also the outside team, who are equally important. Just as I've only had two publishers, I've only had two agents. And I must be living right because how can one person possibly end up with the best publisher and the best agent? Not possible, right? Wrong. Liza, I don't think there's anyone who believes in me more than you do, with the exception of my mother. But mothers have to believe; agents don't. It could be all about business. Not with you, though. Every time I speak with you, I hang up and feel like I can conquer the writing world. Thank you for all that you do, but most important, thank you for how much you believe! And to everyone else at Liza Dawson Associates, from Jamie to Monica and Havis, thank you all for never getting tired of me and my calls and emails.

Thank you to Courtney Parker for the hookup and for believing in this project. And thank you, Malik Yoba, for the same.

My sorors of Delta Sigma Theta Sorority, Inc.: What can I say about the world's greatest sorority? Of course I love my other Greek sisters, but there is nothing like the love I've been shown by my sorors. To all the Deltas who've been supporting my work from the beginning to the ones who had never heard of me but are supporting me now: my gratitude goes from here to infinity. I thank you, thank you, thank you! (I do have to give one special soror shout-out. Well, maybe not one, more like three: Essie Jeffries, who has supported me since I was self-published; Stephanie Perry Moore, whose first words to me—"I've been praying for you for a year"—still touch my heart; and Suzzanne Douglas Cobb, for just believing in me. Thank you, sorors!)

Finally to all the readers out there: I wish I could list each and every name, but the good news is that that list is growing once again so there are not enough pages. :-) For years you've been there and I am so grateful. I wouldn't have a career without you and I am well aware of that. So thank you for supporting me and for getting into these crazy characters as much as I do. And to one of my special readers who just happens to be a soror, Denise Dowdy: What would my life be like if I hadn't sat next to you that day at the Los Angeles Times Festival of Books! You know you rock, right?

So now that I've finished this note, I can begin work on my 2015 novel. Wait until you hear about this one . . .

# TOUCHSTONE READING GROUP GUIDE

## *Forever an Ex*

### FOR DISCUSSION

1. How does Asia reconcile her faith and her relationship with Bobby? Does her faith seem sincere to you?

2. Asia keeps her friend Noon separate from Kendall and Sheridan, yet all three seem equally important to her. How would Asia be different without Noon, or without Kendall and Sheridan?

3. Caroline admits to Asia that she planted the idea of moving to New York in Angel's mind, yet Asia keeps that information to herself. What would you have done in her situation? Would you have moved to New York or allowed Angel to go?

4. After Angel catches Asia and Bobby together, Asia has trouble understanding why her daughter is upset, asking, "How had I become the villain?" How might she have handled the situation better? Do you think she becomes a better parent by the end of the novel?

5. While Angel, Tori, and Christopher seem to have made it through their parents' drama without too many problems, how can Bobby, Caroline, and Asia work together better in the future? What about Quentin, Brock, and Sheridan?

6. Sheridan sees her ex-husband, Quentin, with his former lover Jett and informs Harmony, Quentin's fiancée. What would you have done in her position? Do you agree with Brock that it was none of her business?

7. How would Sheridan and Quentin's relationship be different if he had left her for another woman?

8. Pastor Ford gives a sermon on keeping secrets and declares that not all secrets are bad. Have you ever kept or told a secret and wished you hadn't? If you could go back and change the situation, how would you handle it differently?

9. Do you agree with Pastor Ford that Kendall needs to forgive herself, not Sabrina, in order to live a full life? Would Kendall have built a relationship with Sabrina and her daughter, Ciara, had Sabrina lived? Why or why not?

10. How do you feel about Kendall's relationship with D'Angelo when they first get together? Do you think she would be better off with someone who is not so connected to Anthony and Sabrina? Or does his knowledge of her past help her overcome it?

11. D'Angelo says all of the roads in his life have led him to God, especially when he has had "a gun in [his] hand." What do you think he means? As with Asia, consider how his lifestyle conflicts with his faith.

12. Each woman learns her own lesson and moves on from her ex by the end of the novel. What about the men in the novel? What would it take for Quentin, Anthony, and Bobby to learn their own lessons?

13. Each chapter of *The Ex Files*, which features Sheridan, Kendall, and Asia seven years earlier, shifts between the main characters' points of view while this novel tells each character's story before moving on to the next. Why do you think Victoria Christopher Murray changed the format for this novel? Which style do you prefer and why?

# A CONVERSATION WITH
# VICTORIA CHRISTOPHER MURRAY

**Why did you wait so long to revisit Sheridan, Kendall, and Asia? Is this a story you had planned to tell from the beginning?**
I never planned on writing this sequel. In fact, I'm not that crazy about sequels. I know that's hard to believe given all the sequels I've written, but my sequels are usually a response to the marketplace rather than what's in my heart. I wrote *Forever an Ex* because *The Ex Files* was optioned to become a movie and I was asked to submit more "material." So, compared to my other novels, it was tougher for me to write *Forever an Ex*. In the end, I was really happy that I went back to see what was going on with these ladies—and the men in their lives. And I'm really anxious to see what they're going to do with the movie.

**Do you have any plans to continue writing about these characters? Are the ladies finally over their exes?**
I hope this is the end. I want to discover new people, new characters, and take my readers on new journeys.

**If you were to write *The Ex Files* today, would you change anything?**
No. Absolutely not. Once I've written a novel, I put that story to bed. That was the story at that time; that was the best that I could do at that time.

**What is the message you want your readers to take away from *Forever an Ex*? Has that message changed at all from *The Ex Files*?**
You know, I never write to a message . . . I just write stories. That's it. I feel so great that readers take away messages, but the messages come at the end. The messages are not part of my writing at the beginning.

**The scene when Angel walks in on her parents having "tech sex" was uncomfortable on many levels. Are scenes like this difficult to write? Why did you feel it was important to have the relationship come to a head in that manner?**

That scene wasn't uncomfortable for me to write at all. I'm just taking dictation for the characters when I write, so that was Asia's drama, not mine. LOL. Asia lived her life recklessly without regard for other people and I wanted her to have to face her own demons. There is one thing that's true about Asia: she loves her daughter. I wanted her to contend with losing the true love of her life. Also, in this world that we live in now, all of this technology lends itself to these kinds of situations. While I made up that scene with Asia, I bet it's happened in real life. More than once. More than a hundred times. I have friends who have sent pictures to their husbands only for their children to find those pictures on their iPads. I hope that scene will encourage adults to be more careful.

**Are any of these characters more difficult to write than others? Why?**
No, no characters are more difficult than others for me. I've written about terrible people. But those people are not a part of me. They're the characters I create; they're not me. So I don't have the kind of connection that would make it difficult for me to write them. All characters—good and bad—make up a good story.

**How does your faith influence your writing? Is Pastor Ford based on any of your spiritual advisers?**
Pastor Ford is completely based on my pastor, Dr. Beverly "Bam" Crawford. From the beginning, she's been in my novels and she's there as the voice of reason, the voice of God. When I joined Dr. Crawford's church in 1995, my relationship with God flourished and it was because of her teachings and her preaching that I wanted to write. She released my gift. My faith will always be part of my writing because my faith is a part of me. I always tell people that regardless of what career I had chosen, everyone would not only know about but they would also see my faith. So the fact that it shows up in my writing is no big deal to me. It's just who I am. My faith is my center.

**You also write novels with ReShonda Tate Billingsley. How is the process of collaboration different from writing alone? Do you prefer one more than the other?**

At this point in my career, I prefer writing with ReShonda. With more than twenty books on the shelves, it's hard to come up with new, stimulating plotlines. But when I write with ReShonda, though we have to come up with stories together, I am challenged to keep up with her. The way we work is that I write a chapter, then she responds to it, then I respond, and so on. We never know what the other is going to do, so it's a refreshing way to work. Every chapter is exciting. I love writing with her.

**What are you currently reading? Does what you're reading ever influence your writing? Have any books in particular made an impact?**

I just finished reading what is probably one of the most important fiction books that's been written in years: *Anybody's Daughter* by Pamela Samuels Young. That book is amazing and every woman needs to read it with a young girl. Google it! As far as what I'm reading influencing my writing, I have my own voice so I can read and write at the same time and I do. I don't have a lot of time to sit down and read, so I read daily on the elliptical machine. (That keeps me exercising!) But reading motivates me, challenges me to get better. I read for entertainment, but I learn from everyone. If I want to be a great writer, then reading is my job.

**What is the best part of being on tour and getting to meet your readers?**

I love touring, especially when I tour with ReShonda. Meeting readers inspires me! Readers are always so grateful that we've come out to visit them, but they have no idea how happy I am to meet them. Readers have no idea how they encourage us. Touring keeps me on top of my game and I love it. Many publishers and authors say touring doesn't work, but I don't know why—it works for me and ReShonda.

**You have written both adult and young adult novels. How are they different? Which do you prefer?**

I actually enjoyed writing young adult more than I thought I would and I wish I had the chance to continue. With my YA books, I knew that I was doing something important, something that was more than just entertainment. I did want my YA books to deliver a message. I did want the young girls to see characters who looked like them so that they could learn lessons. But while I love writing YA, my heart will always be with my adult novels.

## ENHANCE YOUR BOOK CLUB

1. Read *The Ex Files* to see how Asia, Kendall, Sheridan, and Vanessa first became friends. Discuss how each of the characters has—or hasn't—changed.

2. Take some time at the beginning or at the end of your book club meeting to check in with your fellow readers. Lend an ear and support your friends; you may be surprised to find out what else you have in common.

3. Pastor Ford wants Kendall, Sheridan, and Asia to share their lessons with the world. Think of what you have learned through your relationships and experiences with love and share with the group.

4. In honor of Kendall's passion for her work, have a spa day! Find a local spa and enjoy some relaxation time with your friends.

## Praise for *Sinners & Saints*

"Murray and Billingsley keep things lively and fun."

—*Juicy* magazine

"Double the fun, with a message of faith, *Sinners & Saints* will delight readers with two of their favorite characters from two of their favorite authors. It's a match made in heaven!"

—*Grace Magazine*

## Praise for *The Deal, the Dance, and the Devil*

"Murray's story has the kind of momentum that prompts you to elbow disbelief aside and flip the pages in horrified enjoyment."

—*The Washington Post*

## Praise for *Sins of the Mother*

"*Sins of the Mother* shows that when the going gets tough, it's best to make an effort and rely on God's strength. It gives the message that there is hope no matter what, and that people must have faith."

—FictionAddict.com

"Final word: Christian fiction with a powerful kick."

—Afro.com

## Praise for *Lady Jasmine*

"She's back! Jasmine has wreaked havoc in three VCM novels, including last year's *Too Little, Too Late*. In *Lady Jasmine* the schemer everyone loves to loathe breaks several commandments by the third chapter."

—*Essence*

"Jasmine is the kind of character who doesn't sit comfortably on a page. She's the kind who jumps inside a reader's head, runs around and stirs up trouble—the kind who stays with the reader long after the last page is turned."

—*The Huntsville (AL) Times*

Praise for *Fortune & Fame*

novel demonstrate why she is the grande dame of urban Christian fiction."

FreshFiction.com